Dedication:

Dedicated to my husband and best friend, Paul – without him I wouldn't be where I am today.

How to Have an Affair

"O curse of marriage,
That we can call these delicate creatures ours,
And not their appetites!
I had rather be a toad,
And live upon the vapour of a dungeon,
Than keep a corner in the thing I love for others'
uses."

Othello- ACT III Scene 3.

William Shakespeare

Contents

Prologue

'Where on earth is your bloody father?' Robyn muttered as she stood with her hands on her hips looking out of the lounge window.

Molly tutted. 'Daddy says you shouldn't say bloody.'

'I'm sorry, sweetheart, but Mummy has a train to catch and Daddy's late *again*.'

'We could go to Grandma's,' suggested Molly.

'That's a really good idea, sweet-pea, but I haven't time to take you. I'll just try Daddy again.'

Robyn delved in her handbag for her mobile. *Bloody typical, I arrange one weekend away and the sodding man can't even make an effort to come home on time.*

'He's here,' Molly shouted as she saw her Daddy quickly get out of his car and run up the drive.

'About bloody time. Oops! Sorry Molly.'

Dave burst into the lounge, 'Sorry I'm late. I had some letters to sign that needed to be off today.'

'Oh, that's alright then. Far more important than my plans,' Robyn answered, glaring at her husband. 'And that took you two hours? You were supposed to be home at one.'

'Look, I've said I'm sorry. I'm here now.' Dave rolled his eyes.

'But I'm sick of it. Last week you left me sitting here all dressed up and you didn't even bother to ring.'

'Why are you bringing that up again? I told you I had an important meeting that ran over.'

'It's always something with you.'

'Hadn't you better get off? You've got a train to catch.'

'Oh really! You noticed.'

God that man! One day he'll put me and the children before his bloody work.

'Dinner's in the oven, all you need to do is turn it on,' she reminded him as she picked up her bags from the hallway. 'If you can remember how,' she added under her breath. 'And don't forget it's bath-time tonight, and Jake needs his medicine.'

'I thought you said you'd leave me a list.'

'I have, but you'll probably be too busy to read it ... Jake, come and give Mummy a kiss,' she said to her two and a half year old son, who was sitting on the sofa watching Fireman Sam.

'Where are you going, Mummy?' asked Jake as he ran to give her a hug.

'I've already told you, pumpkin, I'm going on a course.'

'Can I come?'

'No sweetie, we've talked about this, remember? Daddy and Grandma are looking after you until Mummy comes back.'

Jake's bottom lip started to quiver and tears welled up in his eyes.

'Don't cry, darling. I'll see you soon.' She hugged him close. 'I'm sure Daddy's going to do some fun things tomorrow.' She looked at Dave. 'Come and take care of your son. I've got to go.'

Robyn bent down and kissed Molly. 'Take care of Jakey for me.' Molly, at six, loved the responsibility of looking after her younger brother.

'I will, Mummy, I promise.'

'Don't I get a kiss?' Dave asked.

'No. I'm still mad. I'll ring you later.'

She hadn't meant to leave it on a sour note, but he was so frustrating!

Chapter 1

April

By the time she arrived at her destination, Robyn had calmed down. *Maybe this seminar weekend isn't such a bad idea*, thought Robyn, in the lift going up to her room at the luxurious four-star Theroux in Leeds. She felt excited, free even – two whole days on her own, without husband or children. She loved the buzz here, so vibrant and cosmopolitan compared to her provincial home town of Hull. *Who knows? I might even enjoy myself.* Alone in the lift, she stretched luxuriously and took off her suit jacket. The little silk vest top underneath clung to her breasts – it was certainly warm for April.

The lift juddered to a halt on the floor below hers and a man entered. Conscious of her exposed cleavage, Robyn moved to the side and pretended to search her holdall. As she glanced up, her gaze locked with a pair of the bluest eyes she'd ever seen – and they were openly admiring. Blushing, she looked away at once, aware of something electric in the stuffy, confined space – and her own heart racing.

The man – tall, slim with golden blonde hair curling unfashionably long over the collar of his expensive, perfectly tailored suit – gave her a slight smile and turned to face the lift doors as it reached the third floor. As Robyn stepped forward, her companion moved also, brushing her bare arm with the sleeve of his jacket.

'Sorry,' he grinned, white, even teeth gleaming in the tanned features. 'After you. These lifts are far too small, don't you think?'

Robyn picked up her holdall, muttered something inaudible and rushed away out of the lift and down the corridor. Fumbling with the key-card, she entered the room, shut the door, and drew breath. *What on earth's wrong with me! I'm behaving like a silly schoolgirl! This is ridiculous. Come on Robyn, pull yourself together.* She was sure it was just the feeling of being on her own in unfamiliar surroundings. What else could it be?

The introductory session of the seminar was scheduled to take place before dinner, and it made it clear in the itinerary, you needed to be sitting in your seat by six thirty. Robyn dropped her bag and threw herself onto the enormous bed, still thinking about the man in the lift. *I wonder what he's doing here? Probably not what I'm doing if he's got any sense. I'm sure he doesn't need an Effective Communication seminar – whereas I on the other hand, couldn't string two words together.*

Just in case she bumped into 'Mr. Hunk' at the reception, she slipped on skinny jeans and another silk vest top, this time in russet, a colour that complemented her deep auburn, shoulder-length hair and brown eyes. Squeezing herself into the new size 10 jeans, she looked in the full-length mirror and realised that eating Crunchy Nutz for two meals a day had really paid off.

Glancing at her watch, she saw it was already six thirty. *Shit! I'd better not be late.* She pulled flat ballet pumps out of her bag, quickly brushed her hair, applied deep copper lipstick, and hurried to the stairs. The conference room was already filling up.

'Excuse me … Is this seat free?' she asked the neighbouring occupant.

'Er … yes, I think so.'

'Hello. My name's Robyn by the way,' she said, sitting down.

'Oh er, hello…Mine's Julie.'

'I'm surprised we haven't been given name badges. At similar events I've been to we were given a badge on registration.'

'Right … It's my first experience of anything like this, so I didn't know what to expect.'

'What made you come?' Robyn asked.

'I read this article in *Bella.*' Julie showed Robyn the page. 'I really like what he has to say. He seems to know everything there is to know about relationships and I think I got one of the last places. How about you?'

'My boss saw it advertised and thought it would be good for my continuing professional development. He must think my communication skills need improving or something…. Watch out, it's starting.'

The lights in the unusually bright room dimmed, and a stern voice from a loud speaker asked people to hurry up and take their seats.

Devoted fans at the back of the room got to their feet and began the slow hand clap, increasing in intensity and speed as Dr. Max Hammond made his grand entrance. Robyn looked over her shoulder and smiled as the rousing music built to a crescendo.

'He definitely knows how to play to his audience,' she whispered to Julie.

Max Hammond was smiling and waving as he made his way up the central aisle. He stopped to shake a few hands *en route* before leaping, with the grace of a gazelle, onto the stage.

'Apparently he always does that. Isn't he great?' Julie whispered.

'I can see why he has so many devoted fans. I didn't know he was so popular.' Robyn replied.

'I think I'm in love,' Julie said, looking longingly at the tall, slightly greying, Adonis of a man on the stage.

The music stopped and the man on the stage addressed the crowd. 'Thank you very much, everyone, for coming here today. I'm so grateful you've chosen to spend your well-earned weekend with me and, more importantly, with yourselves.

'We've a lot to get through, so let's make a start. Unlike most seminars, I don't like name badges. I want you to learn people's names by talking to each other. So, please stand up and move to the back of the room.'

Robyn groaned. All she wanted was to be fed information without having to make an effort, but sadly, she could see that wasn't going to happen. Dutifully, she pulled herself to her feet and followed the rest of the participants.

Max continued. 'I want you to introduce yourselves to as many people as you can in ten minutes. You'll say your name and a bit about yourselves. The aim of the exercise is to pair up with someone you have something in common with. Be creative in finding a link.'

He smiled and added, 'I'm also giving you an incentive. The couple with the most original connection will win a weekend at *any* of The Theroux hotels in mainland Britain.' He paused. An excited whisper passed through the crowd, as people realised the crowning glory of the hotel chain was located on Park Lane in London.

'After ten minutes of quick introductions, I want you to be thinking about the most interesting connection you've made. Go and seek out that person and see if they agree … Are you ready?'

His devoted fans answered with a resounding "Yes".

Soothing music began playing in the background as people looked around, not knowing where to start.

'I – I can't do this,' stammered Julie.

'Of course you can … just practice making eye contact and take it from there.'

Julie sighed deeply and reluctantly walked off as though heading for the gallows, leaving Robyn on her own, wondering who to talk to. She didn't have to wonder for long, as a confident young man, about mid-twenties with an athletic build approached her.

'Hello, I'm Matt. I like windsurfing and rock climbing, how about you?'

'Hi, I'm Robyn. Sadly we don't have that in common. I'm petrified of heights and don't like getting my hair wet. I speak Spanish and love cooking.' Robyn laughed.

'Okay! It was nice talking to you.' Matt smiled and moved on.

Robyn was scanning the room for her next contact when she spotted him, the man from the lift. *Oh my God! He's here,* she thought, moving quickly behind a large pillar. She peeped her head round and watched him. He was in complete contrast to her husband who had hair the colour of dark Belgian chocolate and olive skin. *Just look at that smile!*

Eventually he turned away from the woman he was talking to and caught Robyn staring at him from her hideout. Smiling, he started walking across the room towards her. She remembered back to the lift and her stomach dropped three floors. Before she could compose herself, he was standing right in front of her.

'Hello again, remember me? I'm Jay Trethedick.' He held out his hand and just the touch of him sent a tingle the full length of her arm.

It seemed an age before Robyn could form the words, 'Er … I'm Robyn Fisher.'

'Yes!' Jay punched the air. 'We've probably just secured our weekend away.' He leant across and kissed her cheek.

Robyn took a step back and touched the imprint of his lips.

'Oh, I'm so sorry … It's just our names!'

'What?'

'We're both named after birds, how cool is that? I never thought my name would ever be a bonus. I usually have to explain that Jay isn't my initial.'

'And I usually get jokes about being batman's sidekick. Surely it won't be good enough to win?'

'Let's put money on it. I bet you a fiver.'

'I don't usually gamble,' Robyn laughed.

'I also bet you don't go to London for a weekend away with a man you've only just met.'

'We couldn't go away together …I'm…I'm married.'

'I'm not, but if I was, a weekend in The Theroux Hotel on Park Lane would be worth cheating on my wife for! I'm only kidding,' he quickly added when he saw the look of horror on Robyn's face.

'That's ten minutes, folks. You need to be finding your most creative connection,' shouted Max Hammond from the stage.

'Have you found anyone better?' Jay asked.

I doubt that's possible.

'No. You're only the second person I've talked to.'

'Then I guess you're stuck with me.' Jay grinned. 'We should maybe tell each other a bit about ourselves. As I take it, the purpose of the exercise wasn't just to win the prize. Do you want to go first?'

'Okay…' Robyn paused, trying to think of something to say that would make her sound interesting to this hunk standing in front of her – but nothing sprang to mind.

'As I said, I'm married to Dave. I'm thirty three. I have two children: Molly, six, and Jake, two and a half. I'm a Human Resource Officer for the NHS which *I hate,* and I'm here because my boss thought it'd be a good idea.'

'What do you do for fun?'

'Fun … what's that?' Robyn sighed, 'I don't have much time, what with working, looking after the children and a husband, who, more or less, lives for his work. I force myself to go to the gym. Oh… and I suppose I enjoy cooking. Sorry, it sounds quite boring.'

'Aren't most people's lives?'

'I suppose so, but I bet yours isn't?'

'Trust me, it is. So, I'm Jay and I'm not as old as you. I'm thirty.'

'Oy, watch it,' she nudged his shoulder and he laughed.

'I live with my partner, Maria. We don't have children and I'm a psychologist specialising in marriage guidance … and I don't do much for fun either.'

'So you're as boring as me then?'

'Told you I was … And I'm here because I've just read Max Hammond's latest bestseller and want to challenge him on a few of his concepts and steal some ideas for my own book. If he can make so much money out of his relationship advice then maybe I can. '

'Ah! So you're a trouble maker?' suggested Robyn.

'Not really, but there are some things he says I don't agree with.'

'Such as?'

'He believes we're meant to be monogamous and looking for the ideal person to mate with for life.'

'And you don't agree?'

'It's a lovely thought, but it's a bit too idealistic for my analytical brain.'

'How does your partner feel about that? ... I wouldn't be very impressed.'

'I love Maria for now, and we'll be together as long as it suits us both.'

'You make it sound so romantic!' Robyn quipped.

'Just realistic.'

'So don't you believe in marriage?'

'Not really ... No, that's not true, when it works, it's great. But trust me, in my job I've seen what marriage can do to couples – some people should never have got together in the first place. And then, when it's not working, they stay together making each other unhappy. Don't you agree?'

'Er ... I don't know. I haven't really thought about it like that.'

Maybe that's what's wrong with my marriage. Robyn stared into the distance.

'Sorry, are you okay?'

'Yes, I'm fine. I'm just not used to speaking to someone as blunt as you. It's a bit unnerving when someone asks you a question you haven't considered before.'

'Another product of my job, I'm afraid. My clients need to feel they're getting good value for their money, so every minute of their hour has to contain something worthwhile. I'm sorry I didn't mean to make you uncomfortable.' Jay gently touched Robyn's arm.

'It's okay. It's actually quite refreshing. You could, perhaps, give me a few pointers. I tend to skirt around issues at work. What do you...'

Just then, a loud taped voice came over the public address system, '... three, two, one. Please stop talking now and find a seat with your partner.'

Robyn looked around the room in surprise – the chairs had been moved to a more casual layout. She followed Jay to the two closest seats.

He leaned over and whispered, 'We could carry on this conversation later, perhaps over dinner, if you'd like?'

The hair on the back of Robyn's neck stood on end as she felt his warm breath on her ear.

'Er … I suppose there'd be no harm … okay then.'

Jay started to laugh as he saw the uncertainty on Robyn's face. 'Are you sure? I promise I won't bite.' He nudged her arm playfully. 'I think we'll really like each other. And, seriously, I'd like to get to know you better. I'll book us a table … say an hour after we finish here?'

The background music started again and Max Hammond called the room to order. Everyone went silent.

'I hope you enjoyed our first of many exercises this weekend.' He smiled at his audience. 'Just before you go for dinner we have a couple more things to do.

So, please stand up again and face your partner … This person is your "buddy" and they'll know you inside out before you go home on Sunday. They'll be your first point of contact at every session, and you'll check out with them before you have your breaks.'

Robyn slowly turned towards Jay, who stared deep into her eyes and winked. She swallowed hard hoping she didn't look too awkward, and he smiled reassuringly.

God! He's so utterly stunning. She could feel her face turning a rich shade of puce.

Max Hammond was full of surprises tonight as he flicked a switch from the stage, plunging the room into total darkness.

'I hope no one's afraid of the dark,' Max said, as people gasped with surprise. 'The next part is optional, and I do appreciate it'll be harder for some than for others. But I want you to make physical contact with your partner to see that effective communication isn't just about speech. This might be something as simple as shaking hands. Just be in each other's presence. Enjoy the experience.'

The room was silent.

Jay reached his hand across in the pitch-dark and, fumbling, found the top of Robyn's leg.

What is happening to me? She felt the hairs on her arms standing to attention and her whole body switch to red alert.

He gently circled his fingers with the lightest of touches. Robyn fumbled for his other hand and gave it a gentle squeeze. They both took a step closer, their bodies not quite touching, but so near, she could feel his breath on her lips.

Robyn gasped. Being as aroused as this seemed like a distant memory.

'The lights are about to come back on,' Max Hammond warned the audience.

Robyn reluctantly took a step back, still holding onto his hands.

The bright lights of earlier illuminated the room. Robyn let go of Jay and shaded her eyes with her hand.

Max added, 'and finally for this evening, your homework is to get together with your buddy and write down your connection in less than two hundred words, then hand it to reception tonight before midnight. The winning couple will be announced tomorrow in the first session. So, you all have a good evening, keep on talking, and I'll see you bright and early at nine o'clock. Goodnight.'

Max Hammond left the stage to another standing ovation.

'Well, that was different,' Robyn gave Jay a shy smile, but was saved further embarrassment as Julie ran up to her.

'Wow, what did you make of that, Robyn?' she asked excitedly.

'Better than I anticipated,' Robyn said – grinning inwardly as she remembered exactly where Jay had stroked her.

'Who's your partner?' Julie asked.

Robyn turned and said proudly, 'This is Jay, my "buddy". We both have birds' names, which Jay is convinced will win us the prize.'

'Pleased to meet you, Julie,' said Jay as they shook hands. 'And who did you partner up with?'

'A man called Steve. It's a real coincidence; we actually live on the same road. How strange is that? But we've never seen each other until tonight.'

Robyn couldn't take her eyes off Jay and was starting to have second thoughts about having dinner with him alone.

'Would you both like to join us for dinner?' Robyn offered, checking with Jay to make sure he didn't mind. He nodded, but she was sure she could see the disappointment in his eyes.

'I'll just ask Steve, but I'm sure that'd be lovely, thank you.'

'I'm booking a table for eight thirty. Will that give you enough time?' Jay asked.

Robyn looked up and saw a man in his mid-forties walking over to Julie, whose face lit up as she spotted him. Julie introduced everyone, and they all agreed to meet in the dining room at eight twenty-five, plenty of time for Robyn to regain her composure.

Robyn felt a gentle touch on her arm.

'Have you time for a drink in the bar before dinner?' Jay asked.

Robyn froze, 'Er … It'll have to be quick,' she said looking at her watch. 'I need to get changed, and we're meeting Julie and Steve in three quarters of an hour.'

'Are you sure you've time? I don't want to rush you.'

'Sorry, that sounded rude,' she said. 'Yes, that would be lovely, thank you.'

In the bar, Jay handed Robyn a glass of warming Shiraz and sat down opposite. 'Cheers! Here's to the weekend.' He lifted his glass and smiled.

'Cheers! I think it could actually be fun.' said Robyn. 'I wasn't really looking forward to this weekend. It's so much hassle going anywhere without the children. There's so much organising to do and then it's back to work on Monday. It felt like such a waste of a weekend.'

But looking at the lovely man in front of her, Robyn realised it wasn't going to be wasted at all. In fact, she was totally shocked by his effect on her. Usually she had no interest in other men – she hadn't the time or the energy. So what made Jay so different?

'I quite like weekends away. I feel it breaks the monotony,' Jay said, relaxing into his chair.

'That's true. And it's nice having some time to myself. I can actually be me for once.'

'And that's always a good thing.'

Robyn sipped her wine and smiled.

'So you didn't have a choice about coming here?' Jay asked.

'No. My boss volunteered me. Well actually, once I read about it, I thought it might help me. I always tend to take things personally, and I'm not good at putting my point across without losing my cool... Was your only motivation for coming to challenge Max Hammond?'

'Not solely. I like to keep up with new ideas and most of the seminars are in London. When I saw this advertised, I thought I'd make the most of its proximity, and I'm really glad I did.'

'So am I ...' Robyn took a long gulp of wine.

'What do you think of the buddy system?' she asked.

'I think we've been very lucky! Did you see some of the pairings?' Jay laughed.

'I did! They'll probably end up killing each other before the weekends over.'

'I'm more than happy with my buddy.'

'I don't think I could've picked anybody nicer for a fellow bird friend.' She paused. 'Unless Jack Sparrow turned up, and I'm afraid if it was a contest between you and Johnny Depp, he might win.' *But only just!*

'I don't blame you,' Jay laughed. 'If I was a woman I'd fancy him myself.'

'Do you really think we'll win?' she said, wondering what would happen if they did.

'I think there has to be some reason why we've been put together.'

'Do you believe in all that fate stuff then?'

'The logical part of me would answer no, but I do have a feeling there's something in it. Max Hammond certainly does.'

'I haven't read his book yet and don't know much about him.'

'Hopefully, he'll rectify that for you this weekend. Who knows he might even convert me!'

Neither of them spoke for a few moments. Robyn swirled the wine round in her glass, avoiding direct eye contact – trying desperately to blank out the thought of his hand caressing her thigh.

Jay broke the silence first. 'Who's looking after your children, your husband?'

Robyn landed back in the room. 'Yes,' she sighed. 'He finished work early, well, early for him. He should've been home for one o'clock, but dashed into the house at three with another one of his great excuses. I was absolutely livid. I only just caught my train.'

'It must be hard having a family and working. I don't know how you do it.'

'Tell me about it! Just sitting down and having a glass of wine at this time is unheard of at our house. I'm still making tea and putting the children to bed until at least eight o'clock. We don't eat until nine … Sorry, listen to me going on.' She looked at her watch. 'I really must go and get changed.'

'Okay, I suppose it is getting late,' Jay added reluctantly. 'But thanks for coming for a drink. I wanted us to have a bit more of a chat before we met the others … so, I'll see you in the dining room in a while,' Jay said, touching her arm as she got up to leave.

'I'm looking forward to it.' *I know I shouldn't, but I am.*

Robyn was glad she'd packed her little black dress as she reached down her back struggling to pull up the zip. Black eyeliner and deep red lip-gloss were dug out from the bottom of the make-up bag and applied carefully, despite the shaking hand.

She still hadn't fully recovered from the exercise of earlier. *Who knows what would've happened if the lights hadn't come back on!* Her mind started to wander to her hand on Jay's thigh. Only a few inches separated her hand and his ... *Stop it! I can't go there.* Robyn threw open the door to the mini-bar and screwed the top off a small bottle of red wine – she gulped directly from the bottle.

Looking at the clock, she was torn between wanting to make sure the children were fine and enjoying their time with Daddy and putting her family completely out of her mind. The life she shared with them in Hull seemed a million miles away, and she didn't want to be brought back to reality just yet. In fact, as she thought about Jay, she didn't want to be brought back to reality ever!

She sighed as she picked up the phone, the dutiful mother getting the better of her.

'Hello, Molly speaking, how can I help you?'

'Hi, sweetheart, it's Mummy. Are you and your brother having a good time?'

'Hi, Mummy. Yes, we are thank you. We went to the park and Jake fell off a swing, but he's fine. He scratched his leg and cried for ages just like a baby. Then Daddy took us to... oh no, he told me to keep it a secret. Then we came home and played some games. I won more times than Jake, but he sulked so Daddy told me I had to let him win. He's in the bath now, and I'm getting ready for bed,' Molly said without drawing breath, then added as an afterthought, 'Do you want to talk to Daddy?'

Robyn hesitated, 'If he's bathing Jake I won't disturb him. Just tell him I phoned, darling, and I'll see you soon. Love you.'

'Okay, Mummy, love you too, bye.'

Her children were obviously fine.

Robyn finished off the last of the wine. After one last look in the mirror, she took a deep breath and went down to face the music.

The dining room resembled a can of sardines, as it seemed everyone from the course had shared the same idea. Strewn all over the tables were pads of paper and pens instead of menus, as couples tried to write the wittiest piece of prose to win the coveted prize. She spotted a solitary Jay waving frantically at her from a table at the far end of the dining room.

Edging her way through the organised chaos and the melee of waiting staff taking orders and serving food, she finally reached their table.

'Hello, Robyn. You look very nice tonight,' Jay said, openly staring at Robyn's figure and long legs.

'Thank you,' Robyn replied, desperately trying to pull down the hem of her short dress.

'You look worried, is everything okay?' he asked.

'Sorry, I just didn't expect it to be this busy,' she said, claiming the chair opposite his.

'Me neither. We could try somewhere else if you like?'

'No, it'll be fine. We're here now.'

'Maybe we could eat somewhere else tomorrow?' he suggested.

'That's rather presumptuous of you,' Robyn laughed.

'I'm only following orders from Boss Hammond. He said we have to spend as much time together as we can this weekend, and I always do as I'm told.'

'I'm sure that's not true. You don't strike me as a man who likes being told what to do at all.'

'I do under the right circumstances.' Jay winked.

Robyn's stomach had already completed more flips than an Olympic gymnast. 'I wonder what's holding Julie and Steve up?'

'I can guess. Did you see the look on their faces? I've seen enough couples in my work to know when sex is on the cards. It was so obvious.'

Oh no, not the dreaded 'S' word so early in the evening.

'No, it won't be anything like that. They'll be just doing their homework and have got carried away.'

'It won't be the homework that carried them away. It'll be sheer ecstasy!'

Robyn was trying really hard not to blush.

'Talking of homework, when are we going to do ours?'

'You weren't one of those goody-two-shoes who always did their homework as soon as they got home from school, were you?'

'Yes, as a matter of fact I was. It was the best thing to do, then the rest of the evening was mine to do with as I pleased.'

Jay feigned a yawn. 'You sound just like my mother. I always left things to the last minute; it was more exciting that way. I like living life on the edge.'

'Oh no! I like to be organised.'

'But that's boring,'

'Anyway, you haven't answered my question.'

'We could always have a sleepover and write our two hundred words during a midnight feast.'

'Now I know you're teasing me. It has to be in before midnight.'

What perfect timing, Robyn thought as she saw Steve and Julie approaching the table looking flustered.

'I'm sorry we're late. We were doing our homework and forgot the time,' Julie said looking down at the table.

Robyn noticed Julie's blouse. The bottom two buttons were in the wrong holes. She hated to admit it, but it looked as though Jay was right.

'No problem,' smiled Jay. 'We were just deciding when to do ours. Did you manage to keep to two hundred words?'

'Er, I think so,' Steve said as he shuffled from one foot to another.

'Can you give us any tips?'

'I don't think you need them. You seem to have enough of an advantage. I don't want to help you even more by giving away our secrets.' Steve squeezed Julie's hand affectionately.

'Do you want to have a drink first or order the food?' Robyn couldn't risk the conversation returning to the 'S' word.

'A drink, I think! Ooh, listen to me, I'm a poet,' Julie giggled. 'I fancy some champagne, anyone care to join me?'

'What are we celebrating?' Jay asked, looking knowingly at Robyn.

'Nothing really, just meeting new friends.' Julie smiled tenderly at Steve.

'In that case we'll have a bottle of the Dom Pérignon. Is that okay for you, buddy?'

As she saw the price of the most expensive bottle on the menu, Robyn spluttered,

'Have we got that much to celebrate?'

'What the hell! Let's treat ourselves.' Jay said sitting back on his chair.

The waiter returned with the Dom Pérignon and poured four glasses before taking their food order.

It might be half the cost of my grocery bill, but a nice bottle of champagne slips down so easily. In fact, too easily – I could feel tipsy already. These bubbles are going right up my nose.

'I've an idea,' said Jay. 'I guess tomorrow we'll be asked to introduce our buddies to the full group, so why don't we practise now in front of our smaller group? It'll be less daunting.'

'That's a great idea. I know I'll go to pieces. I hate speaking in front of people,' Julie said enthusiastically.

'I'll go first then,' offered Jay, gesturing across the table. 'So, this is Robyn with a *y*. She's married to Dave and has two children, Molly and Jake. She's a Human Resource Officer working for the NHS, although she doesn't enjoy it.'

And so he continued, all the time staring deep into Robyn's eyes. He'd paid so much attention to what she'd told him it was as if he was reading an internal autocue.

'... she's funny and witty, even though she doesn't realise it sometimes. When she speaks you get her soul, no frills attached, and that's a real quality.'

Shit! How's he remembered all this? His job probably helps ... but what can I say? I can't even remember his partner's name. Think Robyn, think!

Finally he drew to a close. 'I'd just like to finish by saying I'm so glad I came on this weekend. You know when you meet someone you just click with? That's what I feel like with my buddy, Robyn. Shall we have a toast?'

Robyn's brain was still whirring as she picked up her champagne flute.

'To us all and this weekend!' Jay reached across to clink his glass with Robyn's giving her the most tantalising smile.

'Here, here,' toasted Steve as they all clinked glasses.

'I'll go next,' offered Julie.

Finally, it was her turn and Robyn still hadn't decided what to say. She took a long swig of champagne.

'I'm really sorry; my mind's gone blank... Er ...this is Jay, he lives with his partner ... Erm, oh yes, Maria. He hasn't got any children and he's a marriage guidance counsellor, hence the insight into people's characters.' Robyn paused and then seemed to come alive.

'I only met Jay a few hours ago, but I feel as though I've known him for years. He's easy to talk to and he makes me laugh ...' Robyn's eyes glazed over. 'I love his long hair and that beautiful face! The way he wrinkles his nose when he speaks and, oh my God, the wink ...'

Robyn suddenly went quiet.

'Sorry ... Did I just say that out loud? ...'

Robyn ran her fingers through her hair. *Talk about opening my mouth before putting my brain in gear. Oh my God, I'm such an idiot!*

Even Jay looked bemused by Robyn's spontaneous outburst.

'It really is a mutual appreciation society,' laughed Steve. 'Who could dream you could learn so much about each other in the ten minutes you had to speak? I hope you're going to keep it shorter tomorrow, both of you, otherwise there won't be time for anyone else to have their say.'

Just then the waiter brought the starters and Robyn kept her head down, eating her Thai salmon fishcakes in silence. Luckily for her, the conversation through the rest of the meal was about the hotel, the course, and the horrendous journey there. Everyone managed to stay clear of human emotions.

Although the champagne went down very well and served its purpose in loosening tongues, it was a unanimous decision to order a bottle of Chardonnay instead of another Dom Pérignon. It was better for everyone's sanity and bank balance.

'I don't know about you all, but I couldn't eat a dessert. I think I'll just order coffee,' said Jay, placing his knife and fork onto his empty plate.

'I'm not bothered about a coffee, are you, Julie?' Steve asked.

'No, I think it's about time I turned in,' she said, yawning. 'It's been a lovely evening; thanks so much for inviting us to join you, but I need my sleep, otherwise I won't be fit for our early start.'

Steve took out his wallet. 'The meal for Julie and me comes to 123 pounds and 56 pence. If I leave you 130 that should cover the tip.'

'How did you work that out so quickly?' Jay laughed.

'Probably because I'm a sad loser. I keep a running total in my head. I can't help it; it's just force of habit.'

'I don't think you're a sad loser.' Julie reached over and touched his arm. 'Gosh! Is that the time?' she said looking at her watch. 'I'm glad we did our homework first.'

Looking at Robyn with a concerned expression she added, 'You haven't even started yours yet. You've only got three quarters of an hour before it has to be in.'

'In that case, shall we have our coffee in the lounge? It'll be easier to concentrate,' Jay asked Robyn.

Despite the late hour, the dining room was still full and the noise level hadn't yet lowered to thinking pitch.

'Okay. Do you want me to nip to the room and get a pad and pen?'

'If you're sure you don't mind. I'll meet you in the lounge after I've settled the bill,' Jay said.

Robyn reached for her purse.

'Put it away,' he gestured. 'It's my treat.'

'I can't let you spend so much on a meal.'

'Yes, you can. Trust me, it was worth every penny. If you want to, you can pay tomorrow.'

'In that case, do you like burgers or kebabs?'

Jay gave her a playful nudge.

'Very funny! …but we can decide tomorrow. Now you'd better hurry up, the clock's ticking and we don't want to be late. You'd never forgive me.'

As she was opening the door to her room, her mobile phone sounded in her bag. She looked and saw five missed calls from home.

'Hello, sorry I didn't hear my phone; it was very noisy in the restaurant.'

'I'm surprised you're still up. I can never get you to stay up past eleven,' Dave replied curtly.

Here we go!

'Actually, I was having dinner with a nice girl I've met.' She purposely didn't mention Jay. He was her guilty secret and she intended to keep it that way.

'I thought you said you'd ring.'

'I rang earlier. Didn't Molly tell you?'

'Obviously not. Well, I won't keep you. I thought I'd just see how you were. But, I needn't have bothered.'

'Oh! Dave, give it a rest. You've been away on courses. You know you're expected to be sociable. Don't you think I deserve a night out?'

'Of course I do.'

'Anyway, I've just arrived at my room now.'

'Well, enjoy tomorrow, and don't worry about us – we're all fine here. I read three stories tonight as a special treat.'

'You're such a soft touch. They'll be expecting that every night now.'

'No, I told them it was only because Mummy's away.'

'Give them a kiss from me, won't you? I'll speak to you tomorrow.'

'Don't I get a kiss?' Dave asked in a much softer tone than earlier. She half-heartedly blew a kiss down the phone.

'You're not still mad at me are you?' Dave asked giving his best puppy dog impersonation.

'I suppose a bit.'

'I said I was sorry.'

'You always do – but then you let me down again.'

'I'll try harder.'

'Okay. I'll hold you to that.'

'Good night, Mrs. Fisher.'

'Good night, Dave.'

Why does he always call me that when he wants to get round me? He's done it again – spoilt my mood… I don't think I'll bother going back downstairs. I'll just go to bed.

But I can't just leave Jay sitting there.

Armed with paper, pen and a resolute expression, Robyn made her way back to the lounge area where she spotted Jay sitting on a comfortable sofa drinking a cup of coffee.

As she sat down beside him, her arm brushed his – she moved discreetly away. No way could she concentrate on the matter in hand while making physical contact with this intoxicating man.

'Are you okay, you seem a bit stressed?'

'It's nothing. Dave rang. That's all.'

'Can I pour you a coffee?' Jay offered.

'Please, black with one sugar. So, where do we start?'

Very soon, two hundred words appeared on the page.

'That wasn't as hard as I thought,' Robyn said as she put down the pen.

'It could be!' Jay gave her a wicked grin and she blushed. 'Sorry,' he said 'I must stop embarrassing you – but you do make it so easy.'

'I know. I really wish I didn't blush. It's such a give-away.'

'I think it's really sweet.' Jay reached out and squeezed Robyn's hand tenderly.

Robyn started to pull away but changed her mind and gently curled her fingers round his.

'Are you looking forward to tomorrow?' Jay asked as he held on tightly to Robyn's hand.

Robyn took a long deep breath. 'I am. I wonder what he'll have us doing. Something shocking if tonight is anything to go by.'

'As long as it involves more touching, I'll be a happy man,' he said as he circled his index finger on Robyn's palm.

'It was a good way to get to know someone, but a bit challenging don't you think?' she said trying to stop thinking about Jay's lips on hers.

'I suppose so, but for me, it felt perfect.'

Robyn looked into his eyes. The silence was heavy with anticipation.

'Do you want a top up?' Jay asked.

'Don't you think we'd better go and give our homework to reception? It's ten past midnight and we've already missed the deadline,' Robyn said averting her eyes.

'I suppose so. We don't want to jeopardise our chance of winning.'

Robyn reluctantly moved her hand from his.

Max Hammond was leaning over the desk as they walked closely to reception.

'I hope we're not too late,' Robyn said, as she handed Max their sheet of paper.

'Strictly speaking the deadline was ten minutes ago but I think I can make an exception for you two.'

Max grinned.

'What makes you say that?' Robyn asked.

'I can't divulge any information until tomorrow, but suffice it to say, you two are the very reason I do this job and hold weekend seminars like this one. On that note, I'll bid you goodnight.' Max took his pieces of paper and was gone before either of them had chance to comment.

'What do you think he meant by that?' Robyn asked curiously.

'Who knows? Perhaps he'll enlighten us tomorrow.' Jay shrugged.

'So ... I think I'll turn in.' Robyn stretched.'

'I suppose we better had. I need my beauty sleep.'

Without speaking, they walked across to the lift. Robyn pressed the button for floor three, Jay pressed floor four. *God, could this lift go any slower?* Robyn looked down at the floor.

The door eventually slid open for her to exit. Jay held it open with his arm.

'I've had a wonderful evening and everything I said at the dinner table was true. In fact, that's not even the half of it. So, until tomorrow then ...'

He took his hand away from the door, which slowly closed, leaving Robyn to ponder over his words.

Chapter 3

Jay smiled warmly as Robyn approached his chair in the conference room for the first session of Saturday morning.

'Did you sleep well, buddy?' he asked, standing up to give her a hug and kissing her cheek.

'I slept fine, thank you.' Robyn moulded herself into his embrace. 'How about you?'

'Not too bad. It was nice to have a double bed to myself, but a bit lonely.'

'I'm not going to blush today, I'm determined.'

'Spoilsport.' Jay nudged her arm.

Robyn had lied – she hadn't slept well at all. Her night consisted of waking up in a hot sweat, her legs tangled round the duvet. She'd been dreaming about making love to Jay on the stage of the conference room. All the audience members were jeering and clapping as Jay rhythmically pulsed up and down on top of her. Max Hammond was giving a running commentary about how they were his star couple.

Every square inch of Jay's body came to mind and, from what she could recall, there were a lot of inches to imagine! At five o'clock this morning she was in a hot bath, deep in bubbles, and at six o'clock, was wandering round Millennium Square soaking up the atmosphere of a city just waking up and coming to life.

Max Hammond's entrance was more low-key this morning, but he still leapt onto the stage.

'Good morning, everyone. I trust you all slept well in this fabulous hotel. Let's put our hands together and thank the Manager and his staff for making us so welcome.' The Manager at the back of the room took a little bow and left them to it.

'Now it's the moment you've all been waiting for. I'm going to announce the winners, and then we can get on with some serious work.'

Max paused, building up the tension. 'There were some really original entries. I liked the couple who both bungee jumped off Sugar Loaf Mountain, but I couldn't let you win because you'd met before. So, for finding each other and the link of both being named after garden birds, the winners of a luxury weekend away are Robyn Fisher and Jay Trethedick.'

'See, I told you it was good enough to win,' Jay whispered to Robyn as they rose to their feet.

'Looks like you were right.' She followed him onto the stage, cringing inwardly as she recalled her dream.

Max handed the envelope to Jay and quietly said to them, 'Let me know how it goes!' Everyone applauded as they made their way back to their seats.

Robyn's mind began to wander as Jay squeezed her hand. *I can't go to London with him, but I can dream ...*

Max soon brought her out of her reverie. 'Now the excitement's over; we can get on with the real reason we've come on this seminar – to learn how to communicate with each other in all areas of our life.'

It was after the morning break when Robyn got to work with Jay again.

'Hope you all enjoyed your refreshments, and now I want you to find your buddy and come and collect a blindfold from the stage.' Max gave the audience a few minutes to pair up and collect the prop.

'Now decide who's going to go first. One of you needs to blindfold the other.'

'Do you want me to go first?' Robyn offered. Jay carefully placed the blindfold over Robyn's eyes.

Max continued, 'I want you to take hold of your blindfolded partner as soon as the music starts, and lead them round the room. Try not to go round in a circle, keep changing direction, so your partner has to build up total trust in you. The partner that's blindfolded, try to walk as normally as you can, don't shuffle or put your hand out. Your job is to trust completely... and no talking.'

Jay placed his arm round Robyn's shoulder and pulled her close. 'Are you ready?' he whispered in her ear.

'As I'll ever be. It feels so weird.'

'I promise you'll be fine,' said Jay as he set off slowly, gently guiding Robyn along.

'Can I hold your hand?' Robyn asked, feeling vulnerable with both hands loose by her sides.

Jay gently took her hand and her apprehension vanished. When he turned her round she didn't flinch, keeping tightly by his side.

Max shouted from the stage, 'Please, would you all stop walking and find a space where your partner can walk a few paces on their own. I want those of you who are blindfolded to tune in to your partner's voice and, once you clearly recognise it, listen for their instructions. You're going to walk towards the sound of their voice.'

Jay led Robyn to a space at the back of the room and let go, leaving Robyn standing on her own.

'Can you hear me?' he asked.

Robyn instantly recognised his smooth, velvety tone and nodded.

'Robyn, I want you to come towards me.'

She set off walking and, at that moment, would've followed him to the ends of the earth.

'That's it, you're nearly here.'

After three long strides, she fell into his outstretched arms, and he held her close. She breathed in the scent of his newly washed hair as he gently caressed the fine hairs on the back of her neck.

'Well done, everybody.' Reluctantly, Robyn removed her blindfold and took a step back.

Wow! That was amazing. The most exciting thing I've ever done.

'Now I want you to swap partners,' Max instructed from the stage.

Robyn carefully tied the blindfold round Jay's eyes, scrutinising every detail of his face. She held tightly onto his arm and started leading him round the room, oblivious to the rest of the crowded room. In her mind they were the only two souls that existed.

It was lunchtime before the whole exercise finished.

'Would you like to go for a walk before we eat?' suggested Robyn. 'I could do with the fresh air.'

'That'd be great. I'm not actually hungry, but I'll need to change. Come have coffee while I do? You can keep your eyes closed ...'

All the time Robyn was getting changed in her room she kept reciting *The Night before Christmas*. It was the only poem she could remember– anything to keep her mind away from Jay.

She ran up the flight of stairs and knocked on Jay's door.

'Come in,' he whispered opening the door. 'I'm just on the phone to Maria,' he mouthed as he tried to button up a casual shirt with one hand. Her eyes widened as she caught a sneaky glimpse of his body with its sparse covering of blonde hair. *Maybe coming to his room was a bad idea.* She shuffled uncomfortably.

'I'll have to go, love; a few of us are going to lunch. I'll see you tomorrow. You too, bye.'

I don't think Maria would be as understanding if she saw him now. Robyn smiled to herself. *I know Dave wouldn't!*

'Sit down, make yourself at home,' he said pointing to a large armchair. 'I've made a coffee, do you want one?' He moved to pour her a cup.

'I'll get it, you finish getting ready.'

'If you're sure?' Jay picked up his denim jeans and walked into the bathroom, leaving the door slightly ajar. Robyn could see his reflection in the mirror and watched as he unzipped his trousers, letting them fall to the floor. She should've politely averted her eyes, but they were glued to his half naked body. *Get a grip, Robyn, you're a married woman for God's sake.*

'Have you rung home today?' Jay shouted from the bathroom.

Robyn abruptly fell back to earth. 'Not yet. They had a busy day organised. I'll try tonight,' she shouted back.

'I don't blame you. I feel these weekends are a bit like being in a cocoon, any disturbance from the outside world feels like a real intrusion.' Jay appeared from the bathroom doing up his buttons, 'I just need my shoes and then I'm ready. Did you get that coffee?'

'I did, thanks,' she said, taking a sip. 'I hope it's not too cold outside. I haven't brought any gloves.'

'You can always hold my hand if you get too cold.'

'Or I could put my hands in my pockets.'

'That's just mean.'

'We'd better be getting off.' Robyn yawned. 'If I sit here any longer, I'll fall asleep.'

'Let's see if the fresh air can wake you up.'

They both stood up at the same time, bumping into each other as they tried to negotiate round the bed.

Only a few inches separated their faces. Jay looked intently into Robyn's eyes, 'Oh, Robyn, If only you knew what I was thinking ...' he whispered stroking the side of her face.

Robyn froze. 'But we can't ... '

'I know we *shouldn't* ... but this is driving me crazy ... '

'Me too... Believe me, I want to ... so much,' she moved a stray lock of hair away from his eye.

'But I just couldn't live with myself – or Dave – if I did.' A lone tear sneaked out of Robyn's eye and ran down her cheek.

'But no-one would know,' Jay reached out for Robyn's hand.

'But *I'd* know,' she said, still not moving away from him.

Jay pulled her close, enveloping her in his arms. He lifted her chin and wiped away another tear with his finger.

'It's okay. I understand.'

She held onto him tightly, burying her face in his neck. When she finally released her grip, she gently kissed his lips.

'Thank-you,' she whispered.

'What for?'

'I don't know,' she replied sadly.

The walk along the river Aire was a subdued affair. The atmosphere between them had changed. Robyn linked Jay's arm as they walked. Despite being in the heart of the city, the world felt still and calm, the only sounds were distant traffic and the meandering of running water.

'Tell me about having children?' Jay said.

'Surely you don't mean the actual birth process?'

'No, I want to know what it's like for you to be a mother.'

Robyn thought for a second before answering, 'Mostly it's wonderful, but I'd be lying if I said it was always fantastic. I felt I lost a part of myself when I had children, and I was never going to be number one in my own life again. I love my children more than life itself … I don't know how else to describe it. They drive me insane and I can't wait for them to grow up, but then I want them to stay this age. Motherhood drives you nuts.' She looked directly at Jay. 'Sorry, I'm rambling. Does that make sense?'

'Yes, I think so.' He smiled, warmly. 'I feel a bit like that about marriage.'

'What do you mean?'

'To me, marriage is giving a part of yourself to another person and what if you make a mistake and give it to the wrong one? Obviously plenty of people do, hence the high divorce rate.'

'But surely there are other pieces of you to give away. What about the love you have for your parents and your sister? I love my mum and dad and brothers as well as loving my husband and children. Do you not love any of your friends?'

'I can honestly say no to that. I don't know if it's because I'm male. I love my mum and sister and I'm fond of my niece but loving a husband or wife should be all encompassing to me, and I don't think it is.'

'Is this what you want to write a book about?'

'Yes, but I've yet to find a way to phrase it that doesn't make me sound like a bitter, twisted misogynist.'

'No-one would ever accuse you of that,' she squeezed his hand tenderly. 'Maybe you just haven't found the right woman. How long have you been together?'

'We met five years ago. She was one of my clients.'

Robyn raised her eyebrows.

'Before you accuse me of professional misconduct, let me explain. I studied hypnosis at night school. A friend of mine knew Maria and I agreed to help her stop smoking. It didn't work, but she kept asking me out. In the end, I said yes. That was five years ago.'

'That doesn't sound very romantic.'

'It wasn't. We sort of fell in love, moved in after a year and we've been together ever since.' Jay paused. 'I'm probably not being fair. I think I love Maria and most of the time it's good, but this feels better.'

'What does?'

'The way I feel now… I don't know.' Jay paused and turned to face Robyn. 'I can't help it. I love spending time with you and … I just can't explain it. I know I shouldn't say it, but I fancy you like crazy and you've just taken over my head.'

'Jay, please.' Robyn turned away. This was in danger of turning into something much more than the erotic fantasy she'd experienced since first setting eyes on him in the lift.

'Let me finish,' he said as he carried on walking, linking her arm. 'I think this is why people stray, because how they feel at the beginning of a relationship far outweighs the mundane day-to-day feelings they have for their partner.'

'But …' Robyn protested and had already prepared her indignant face. 'But you can't spend your whole life chasing after new experiences with new people. Surely there's a certain satisfaction about coming home to the same person, sharing your day and your bed?'

'Absolutely. I'm not saying it can't be good. Plenty of people have very happy marriages. I see golden weddings in the paper every week, but in my daily practice I see more unhappy couples than happy ones.'

'But in that case, it's your job that's coloured your view on relationships, surely?'

'Possibly, but tell me honestly, and I might not like the answer, but where would you prefer to be right this minute, with me or sitting down to Saturday lunch with your family?'

'That's not fair. I'd rather be with you right now; in fact, I wish we'd never left the bloody hotel,' she said under her breath, recalling Jay's half naked body. 'But I can't risk hurting my family just to satisfy my desires,' she paused, then added quietly, 'No matter how much I'm tempted.'

'See, that's my point. You stay with someone while they make you happy, and then you should move on when they don't. But as a society we don't do that. We make these out-dated vows and then, come hell or high water, we spend our lives trying to uphold them.'

'But if marriage is such an out-dated institution, why is it still as popular as it used to be?'

'Because people want to believe in it. It's like Santa Claus. Everything was less complicated when you were a child and believed in fairies and Santa. But my reality is different. I'd love Max Hammond to be right and there was one person you could spend your life with.'

Without thinking Robyn blurted out, 'What if that one person for you was me? Would that make a difference?'

Shit! Where did that come from?

Jay spun Robyn round and kissed her with hurricane force that threatened to knock her off both feet. She felt the passion rising from the tips of her toes and exploding from the top of her head. They were both gasping for breath when they finally pulled apart.

'Yes, it probably would, but I can't have you,' he said. 'You're someone else's and even if we were to go back to the hotel and make mad, passionate love for the rest of the day, you'd still be going home to someone else. Proving my point that marriage sucks!'

Robyn just stared at him. *What on earth have I just done?*

Jay put his arm round Robyn's shoulder, pulling her close, and she melted into his touch. They turned round and retraced their steps along the tow path walking in complete silence. When they were only a stone's throw from the hotel, Jay stopped. Lifting her chin, he moved his lips onto hers. This kiss was warm and tender and, despite the conflict in her head, Robyn responded.

'This will be the last time I try anything again. I know we can't be together, but nothing has changed my opinion so far. In fact, it feels worse now because I have to go home to Maria knowing I want someone else.'

'It's going to be hard for me too,' Robyn admitted. 'I love what we've had these past hours and yes, there is an amazing connection. But don't you think it's something to do with the cocoon you talked about? We've been away from our normal lives and our day-to-day routines, but it would be different if we saw each other every day. We'd have to watch each other being ill and washing dishes and first thing in the morning. Trust me; you wouldn't fancy me with my hair standing on end.'

'I don't know how I'd feel about you if I saw you every day, but all I know is that I'd like to give it a chance. But we'll never know.' Jay let go of Robyn. 'I don't think I'm going to stay until tomorrow.'

Robyn's heart thumped in her chest. 'Don't go Jay, especially on my account. You haven't even had chance to talk to Max Hammond on your own.'

He sighed. 'I'll see how it goes.' Jay walked off to the conference room.

Robyn had managed to fend off tears up to now, but without warning, they started flowing and wouldn't stop. She ran to the lift. It was only half an hour to the next break. Hopefully by then she'd have composed herself.

Robyn woke to the sound of her mobile phone ringing. She sat up with a start, forgetting for a second where she was. It was beginning to get dark outside and the room had that dusky feel about it. Looking down at her tear stained pillow and her clothes, she realised she was still wearing her walking gear. She blinked – her eyes felt like she'd bathed them in acid. *Where's the bloody phone?* She followed the ring tone.

'Hello, Dave,' she said flatly.

'Hello, love. I'm just ringing to see how your day's been.'

What on earth am I going to tell him? 'Erm … quite good.'

'Are you okay, your voice sounds croaky?'

'I'm fine … I must have fallen asleep.'

'At this time? It's alright for some.'

'What do you mean? What time is it?'

'It's seven o'clock.'

Shit! Where did this afternoon go?

'Robyn? … Are you sure you're okay?'

'Dave stop fussing! I've said I'm fine.'

'Don't snap. I was only asking.'

'I know … I'm sorry. I don't think I've properly woken up yet.'

Just then there was a loud knock on the door. A rush of adrenalin surged through her body as she imagined Jay standing outside the door. 'I'd better go, there's someone at the door.'

'The children are missing you. Molly sends you a kiss.'

There was a second louder knock this time.

'I really must go. I'll see you all tomorrow.'

Robyn threw the phone onto the bed.

'Hold on, I'm coming,' Robyn shouted and reached for the lamp on the bedside cabinet, catching a glimpse of herself in the mirror. The black rings round her eyes did nothing to enhance her appearance. Whatever would Jay think of her looking like this?

She looked through the privacy hole and her heart sank when she saw Julie standing there just about to knock again. Robyn opened the door a fraction.

'Thank God you're alright. Can I come in?' Julie said, as she caught sight of her new friend.

'Sorry, yes of course.' Robyn fully opened the door and Julie walked in. Turning, she put on the main light. 'Where have you been? You missed all this afternoon session. Jay looks like he's been hit by a bus and his favourite puppy got run over at the same time. I couldn't get him to string two words together … You look dreadful by the way.'

'Not nearly as bad as I feel,' Robyn sobbed as she smeared black mascara further down her cheek.

'Do you want to talk about it?' Julie asked, sitting herself down in the big arm chair.

'I don't think you have to be Einstein to guess what's the matter. It's me and Jay.'

'I guessed as much. I only had to look at his face. Unrequited love written all over it.'

'But that's just it, Julie! I don't think it *is* unrequited. You don't know how close I came to sleeping with him today.'

'But you didn't, that says something about your integrity, surely. So why are you crying?' Julie asked.

'Because I feel like I've let myself down. For God's sake, I've got a husband and two children at home. I know we haven't been getting on too well recently but I never expected to feel like this about another man, but with Jay, it was so easy. I just wanted him,' she said reaching for a tissue.

'I envy you,' Robyn continued. 'You can fall in love with Steve and there's nothing to stop you.'

'It's strange how the tables have turned. I spent all last night envying you. I thought you were so confident and together. It was obvious you fancied each other, but I assumed it was just harmless flirting.'

'That's exactly what I thought too, at first, but now I feel like a love sick teenager. When he told me he was thinking of going home early, I could've been physically sick. How stupid is that? I've only known him since seven o'clock yesterday, exactly twelve hours.'

Julie shook her head. 'It isn't stupid at all. I knew as soon as I set eyes on Steve that he was the one for me. It wouldn't have mattered whether he found me attractive or even liked me, I knew how I felt. Do you not believe in love at first sight?'

'I've never given it much thought. I'd only been seeing Dave for a few weeks when I thought he was the one. We've been together since we were twenty one and married for seven years.'

'In chapter two of his book, Max Hammond, talks about the reality of the seven year itch. Maybe it's just that?'

'Does he give advice about how to get rid of it? Is there some cream to rub on or something?'

'That's better, a smile!' said Julie reassuringly. 'Come on, get changed and let's go have some dinner. I'm sure Steve won't mind. I told him I was coming to see you, and we can always get together later. Although I am having trouble walking!' Julie grinned.

'You hussy!' Robyn gave a watery laugh. 'I'm only jealous. It's been at least seven years since I felt like that, and then it wasn't even on my honeymoon. Dave got pissed and slept with his head down the toilet on our wedding night.'

Jay had a change of heart and decided not to go home. As soon as the seminar finished on Saturday evening he went straight to the bar and ordered a double of his favourite single malt. His intention was to have a couple of drinks then order room service. Being sociable was the furthest thing from his mind tonight. Robyn hadn't shown her face at the rest of the afternoon session, so he didn't know how she was coping. Better than he was, probably. He just wanted the weekend over with so he could resume his life, pretending the past two days had never happened.

He was just downing the last gulp of his first double when he heard a voice behind him,

'Can I get you another?' It was Max Hammond.

'Oh, hello! That's very kind, it's a Lochaber,' replied Jay.

'Double or single?'

Jay hesitated. 'Double, if you're feeling generous.'

'Make that two,' Max Hammond said to the bartender.

'What brings you in here? Aren't you frightened of being mobbed by your loyal fans?' Jay asked.

'If you notice, this is the quietest time. Everyone has gone to make themselves look beautiful for the courtship rituals of tonight. I like to sneak in a couple, then I order room service and prepare for tomorrow.'

'Can I ask you a personal question?'

'You might as well because I intend to ask you a few,' Max replied.

'Are you married?'

'Yes, and have been for twenty years, to my lovely Barbara. You look surprised.'

'I am. People in our profession have often been married and divorced a couple of times.'

'That answers one of my questions. I guessed you had a psychology background from some of the answers you gave today. I actually have been married before,' revealed Max. 'I married at twenty to a lovely girl who just wasn't the one for me. We had a daughter and stayed together for four years until we'd both had enough of making each other miserable. I see my daughter every week and my ex-wife about twice a year. We all get together to catch up.'

'How does Barbara cope with that?'

'She's fine. She knew about that part of my life and totally accepts it. We respect each other, and I'm still in love with her after twenty years.' Max paused for a moment. 'So what has turned you into such a cynic at, what are you, twenty eight … thirty?'

'Ouch! And I thought I was hiding it so well. I'm actually thirty and as for the cynic –I don't know. I've been trying to figure that out since I got here.'

'Haven't you done all the psycho-babble on yourself?' Max joked.

'Yes, I have to go for supervision as part of my practice. I'm a private marriage guidance counsellor,' Jay said.

'That explains part of it, being surrounded by the misery of others all day can't help your own.'

'Who says I'm miserable?' Jay enquired.

'Your soul. – and your face this afternoon.'

'That's a bit deep!' Jay downed his drink. 'I need another double if I've got to go there. Same again, Max? Is it okay if I call you Max?'

'Yes and yes.' The bartender poured another round of drinks.

'So what's wrong?' Max asked.

'It's this seminar. Everyone seems to be looking for that perfect person to marry.'

'And you're not?'

'No, I'm not. I'm afraid I don't believe in marriage,' Jay continued.

'Oh, you're one of those that believe marriage is an institution, and it's like living in one.'

'Something like that.'

'I felt like that for a while but I love being married now.'

'Well, it's not for me. I've lived with girlfriends. In fact, I've been with my current partner for five years.' Jay paused to gulp down more whisky. 'But as for marriage …'

'Are you sure? I see the way you look at your buddy, Robyn.'

'Don't go there … this …' Jay pointed to his glass, 'is meant to take my mind off that particular dilemma.'

'Where was she this afternoon?'

'Who knows? We had this … sort of … a moment… but she's married and, basically, she turned me down.'

'Oh dear! Do you remember what I said to you last night? You two were the reason I do this job. Weren't you a bit intrigued as to what I meant?'

'Yes, but I guessed you sensed the chemistry between us.'

'I think you'd have to be blind not to.'

Jay sighed. 'Do you know I came here to de-bunk your theories?'

Max raised his eyebrows. 'No! And I thought you agreed with everything I said.' He added, 'Believe me, I understand your dilemma. I had an affair with Barbara whilst I was married to Celia. I knew it was wrong, but I fell in love. I met her at work. We started with the playful banter and the flirting. Then we'd have a drink at lunchtime.

'I found excuses to work late and we finally had sex in the back of my car when I offered her a lift home. Sordid, I know. Everyone said it wouldn't last and it was just a fling, but we proved them wrong. I'd met the right woman. If things had gone differently I might be in your cynical shoes today.'

'In that case, have you any tips to save me from myself?' Jay asked hopefully.

Max reached down and picked up a copy of his book from his briefcase.

'Chapter ten.'

'Will you sign it for me?'

'Are you serious?' Max was surprised.

'I've never been more so. Thanks for the chat and the drink. I owe you one.'

Max signed the copy and gave it back to Jay.

'It's been a pleasure talking to you, Jay. See you tomorrow, don't have too many more of these,' he added, downing his own drink. 'Sunday is a good day.'

Jay opened the book to see what Max had written,

To Jay and Robyn – my favourite love birds!
Yours in monogamy
Max.

'Bastard,' Jay mouthed smiling and downed the rest of his drink.

Robyn couldn't believe she'd slept for ten hours, especially after spending so much of Saturday afternoon asleep. Dinner had been one course in the dining room and a glass of red wine. She ended up picking at her food and finally retired at nine o'clock with the excuse of a headache.

Only another seven hours and she could be on a train home. She was even looking forward to going to work – anything to take her mind off Jay. She felt like a spoilt child who'd had their favourite teddy taken from them. Hopefully, talking to Molly and Jake could distract her.

'Hi, it's Mummy,' she said as Dave handed the phone to Jake.

'Hi, Mummy, when are you coming home?' he asked in a soulful tone.

'I'll be there to make your tea today.'

'Can we have sausages? Daddy doesn't make them like you do.' Robyn smiled. That boy would eat his own body weight in sausages if he had the chance.

'I've missed you. How many sleeps before I see you?'

'No more sleeps, sweetheart. I'll see you after your nap this afternoon.'

'I love you, Mummy.'

How could I consider for one second risking all this?

'Are you still there?' asked Dave.

'I am.'

'What time's your train? I can pick you up if you'd like.'

'It gets in at 5.10. Are you sure you don't mind?'

'No, we'll all be there.' Dave replied. 'What do you want to do for tea? Have we to have a take-away?'

'We could have Indian and open a bottle of wine?'

'What's got into you? You normally don't like to drink on a Sunday. What are we celebrating?'

Me, saving our marriage.

'Nothing … Dave?'

'Yes'

'I love you.'

'And I love you. Are you okay, you sound a bit down?'

'It's just been a long weekend. I'll have to go. The session starts in ten minutes, and I'm still not ready. So, I'll see you later then.'

Not waiting for his response she threw the phone onto the bed.

How am I going to go back home and act normally?

Maybe Max Hammond will have an answer for me today. I hope so, because right at this moment I certainly don't have one.

Robyn paused before walking into the full conference room. Quickly scanning the room, she spotted Julie who waved. Robyn made her way up the centre aisle feeling as though all eyes were on the cheating woman. What was it they used to draw on adulterous wives, a red letter? Maybe she should paint one on her forehead.

'I saved you a seat,' Julie said, removing the cardigan for Robyn to sit down. 'I didn't think you'd want to sit next to Jay.'

'Thanks, but I'm going to have to face him sooner or later. He *is* my buddy and we might have to do some exercises together.'

'Apparently this morning is quite different, Max warned us yesterday … Oh look, he's here.'

More people than ever gave him a standing ovation. The applause died down as Max jumped onto the stage. 'Welcome to your penultimate session of Effective Communication. As I warned you yesterday, this morning is taking a different format.

'We saw yesterday how honesty is vital in good relationships and is actually the foundation for long lasting partnerships. But I have a proviso. Before you rush home and bare your souls to colleagues or partners, let's have a look at why you're *being* honest. Is it to make *you* feel better?' He paused, giving time for people to think, 'Because if so, then that's not the correct motive ... So, here comes the fun part ...

'If there's a burning issue you want to get off your chest, now's the time and the forum to do it. What I want you to do is stand at the front of the room and tell your peers three secrets about you. It could be anything from stealing a bubble gum when you were five to having sex on the back row of the cinema.

'You'll queue down this side of the room and when it's your turn you'll stand up and say, "Three secrets about me are..."'

Robyn looked around and saw sheer panic on at least half the faces. She eventually spotted Jay sitting at the front with his head down. *Hopefully, he's as miserable as me.*

'Do you know what you're going to say?' Julie asked.

'I've got no idea. I might just slip away for this one.'

'You'll be lucky; he's got guards on the doors.'

Much to Robyn's amazement hordes of people stood up to join the queue – Jay was one of the first. She couldn't believe what people were admitting to. What people had done with root vegetables left nothing to the imagination! Some confessions were serious and a sobbing lady admitted to being too busy to visit her dying mother in hospital, who died that afternoon, and she never got to see her again. Robyn wondered if Kleenex sponsored this part of the weekend, as there wasn't a dry eye in the house.

Jay's hands were shaking as he took his place on the rostrum. He quickly scanned the room and took a deep breath.

'Three secrets about me are.... I encouraged my first serious girlfriend to have an abortion.' He paused before continuing.

'I've cheated on my partner this weekend, and thirdly, I want her more than I want my partner.'

Jay didn't say another word and exited to the right of the stage, catching Robyn's eye as he passed her row. He didn't return to his seat but kept on walking out of the double doors at the back of the room. Depositing a letter at reception for room 301, he picked up his overnight bag and left.

Chapter 5

It wasn't until three days, two hours, and thirty six minutes later that Robyn finally admitted she was really missing Jay. Not that she was counting! She knew the lovemaking she and Dave were uncharacteristically enjoying every night was because of Jay. He had definitely awoken something inside that had been dormant since the heady days of first love. She was also finding it hard to concentrate on anything, which made work especially challenging.

Robyn was expected to give a presentation of the weekend to her departmental colleagues. It had been hell trying to condense Max's words of wisdom into an hour's power point presentation, when every time she thought about the seminar she saw Jay's face. She breathed a sigh of relief when one by one, her colleagues left the room leaving Robyn to clear away.

As she opened her brief case she saw the note addressed to Robyn Fisher, Room 301, staring back at her. It hadn't left her since reading it on Sunday afternoon and she'd lost count of how many times she'd read it since. *Just another peek*!

"Dear Robyn,

I'm so sorry to walk out on you like this but I just needed to get away. I couldn't bear the goodbyes and the thought of not seeing you again. I won't ever forget our time together and that kiss is imprinted on my lips for the rest of my natural life. Just in case you have a change of heart, my mobile number is: 07820 457851. You could just text me sometime, no strings attached.

Goodbye, have a good life without me.

All my love,

Jay xx"

It was only now she could read it without tears sneaking out of her eyes – but had a lump in her throat, trying to hold it together. Every time she saw his phone number she was tempted to send him a text – *one text wouldn't harm. Surely, that's not cheating!* So far she'd been strong, but her resolve was diminishing with every passing day. She gave a deep sigh and carefully folded the note back in its envelope, placing it in the side compartment of her briefcase, inside a work file.

The walls of the conference room felt like they were closing in around her.

I need to get out of here.

The city centre was only a twenty-minute walk away, and it was perfect weather for a gentle stroll. There was nothing she really wanted to buy for herself or for her children, but she could always treat herself to a hot chocolate and some sort of high calorie indulgence as a reward for not texting Jay.

As she was on her way to town, she felt her mobile phone vibrating in her pocket but, as she hurriedly got it out, it stopped. *Damn! What if it was him?* Since Sunday her heart skipped a beat every time her phone rang, just on the off-chance Jay had managed to track down her number and was ringing to say he couldn't live without her.

She didn't have a clue how she'd respond if he was doing just that, but she liked to fantasise. In fact, she'd already imagined a scenario where their eyes would lock across a crowded room and she'd run into his arms. The dream she had on the Friday night still replayed in her mind. But now she imagined them making love without disturbance from the rest of the audience or Max Hammond.

What had she spent her time thinking about before meeting Jay? She certainly didn't fantasise about Dave. Their sex life was like she read about in women's magazines. Most weeks they managed it once, moderately satisfying, but it didn't raise the roof any more. But since meeting Jay, five minutes didn't go past without her mind wandering back to sex.

Her phone vibrated again.

'Did you just try and phone me a minute ago?' Robyn asked Denizon, her sister-in-law and best friend.

'Yes, from my mobile but the signal's crap. What time's your lunch hour?'

'I'm on it now, why?'

'Can we meet? I really need to talk to someone.'

'Yes, of course. Is everything okay? You sound really stressed.'

'No, it's not and yes, I am. That's what I need to talk about before I burst. I'll see you at Costa Coffee in fifteen minutes.'

Denizon had been Robyn's best friend since school, even after her friend fell in love with Robyn's older brother, Chris. The couple had married three years ago and despite trying for over a year, they had yet to conceive. Robyn hoped she wasn't going to impart any bad news on the child bearing front.

Chris was two years older than Robyn. As an older brother he was everything she could wish for. He'd defended her against school bullies and made sure her boyfriends knew exactly where they stood. But it was a shame she couldn't say the same about his husband potential. To say he was a bit of a Jack-the-lad was an understatement. His bed post could've collapsed with all the notches carved in it. He was a tall, muscular, good looking fireman with a head of deep brown hair and still improving with age.

Robyn knew all about her brother's past and the many conquests and tried to put Denizon off him, but to no avail. She'd become besotted with him at age sixteen and waited for him to reciprocate, which he eventually did.

Denizon was the antithesis of the kind of girl Chris usually found attractive. He liked his women to be larger than life – yet her friend was petite, had beautiful long blonde hair and delicate features. Robyn had never seen what her friend saw in Chris because, although she loved him as a brother, she would've hated him as a husband.

But her friend seemed happy, that is, until Robyn caught sight of Denizon's face as she sat outside Costa Coffee in Hull's marina. It didn't bode well.

'Hi, that was quick! I'll just get myself a drink and a bun,' Robyn said. 'Do you want anything else?'

'No, I can't eat a thing.' Denizon replied, examining her cup of coffee.

Robyn went inside and ordered a hot chocolate and a blueberry muffin.

'Why are we sitting out here?' Robyn shivered as she sat down on the cold metal chair. 'I know it's a nice day but its bloody freezing.'

'Because they won't let me smoke inside.'

'But you don't smoke; you gave up ten years ago when I did.' Robyn said concerned as her friend got out another cigarette.

'How would you know if someone was being unfaithful?' Denizon said as she took a long drag.

Robyn's face was a picture. 'Er … what do you mean?' *How does Denizon know? Surely it's not that obvious?*

'Would you know if Dave was having an affair?'

'I've no idea,' Robyn breathed a sigh of relief. 'What made you ask that?'

'I think Chris is seeing someone else.'

'Are you sure? You've thought that before.'

'This is different. I found the other phone he uses to call her.'

'What were you doing looking for another phone?' asked Robyn. 'Surely that's asking for trouble.'

'I've had my suspicions for a while but I checked his main mobile and there was nothing suspicious on it, but he kept disappearing upstairs and then making some excuse to go out. So I searched his stuff and found the other one hidden in one of his work boots.'

'Have you asked him outright?'

'No, you're the first person I've told. I wanted to run it past you first. Do you think I'm being paranoid?'

There must be something in the air! Was everyone thinking about cheating on their partner? I wonder if infidelity can run in families?

'Robyn … say something.'

'Sorry … I think you need a bit more proof.'

'More than "I can't wait until Saturday to see you and rub that oil all over your body." Is that not proof enough?'

'Who wrote that?'

'She did, and the silly thing is, I know which oil she's talking about. Chris came home with a bottle of Body Rubbing Oil from Sanctuary for me last week. He told me it was a gift for being special. That in itself is strange because one, he never buys me gifts. Secondly, I'm allergic to most perfumed products so I tend to buy my own.'

'Did you ask him why he bought it?'

'He looked so disappointed when I wasn't pleased that I didn't have the heart to say anything.'

That's so typical of my brother, she thought angrily. It was always about him. 'Do you want me to have a word?' Robyn offered.

'No thanks, he'll go mad if he knows I've even discussed it with you.'

'What are you going to do?'

'I haven't figured that out yet. I suppose I'll have to confront him. But it's not that he can deny it, I've seen the phone. I have to face facts; it might be the end of us.'

'Surely he wouldn't be that stupid. He loves you, Denizon.'

'I know that, but he loves himself more, and he's never been able to resist praise and flattery.'

Robyn thought back to her walk with Jay and knew perfectly well how she'd responded to the praise and flattery herself.

'You'll have to ask him, but it might be nothing.'

'He's bound to deny it.'

'You'd know if he was lying.'

'I doubt it. I can't tell when you're lying.'

Robyn gulped. 'But I've nothing to lie about.' *Do I look guilty or something?*

'You're a bit jumpy today, Robyn. Is everything alright with you?'

'Yes, why shouldn't it be?'

'You're just acting a bit strange, that's all.'

'I'm just annoyed at Chris. I hate to think of him hurting you. I know he's my brother, but he's still an idiot.

'I love him so much, Rob.'

'I know you do, love.' Robyn stroked her friend's arm.

'It's all right for you – the perfect happy couple. Dave would never cheat. He worships the ground you walk on.'

If only she knew!

Chapter 6

Over in Leeds, Jay wasn't fairing much better. He thought he was doing a good job of trying to convince himself that his increasing infatuation with Robyn resulted from a lack of direction. What he needed was something to fill his time and stimulate his atrophying brain. Looking for another relationship was not the answer to his problems.

Robyn was probably a sexual attraction and nothing more. He would use the passion she'd excited in him to create a masterpiece. It was time to write his book, and he'd already thought of a great title,

"How to Have an Affair"

His plan was to divide the book into five sections. Temptation, Consummation, Suspicion, Discovery and Decisions. It was going to give tips about navigating through an affair, using his many years of experience in listening to the stories of struggling couples. A fresh idea, but he couldn't seem to get started.

But he was just deluding himself – all he could think about was Robyn. Since walking out of the seminar on Sunday, she'd occupied his every waking thought. He'd tried everything to put her out of his mind, but the more he tried, the worse it became. It was like someone telling you not to imagine a pink elephant.

If only he could talk to her she might reconsider her decision. He knew they'd be good together – she just had to see that for herself.

While he was sitting in front of his computer waiting for inspiration to strike and thinking of Robyn … again, he clicked onto Facebook to see if any of his thirty five friends had anything of interest to say about the world.

A girl he went to university with had just bought a tabby kitten that was apparently the cutest thing on the planet, but there was nothing more earth shattering than that. He hovered over the button, 'Find Friends' and typed in the name Robyn Fisher. Two names appeared. Jay's heart did a little dance as he saw Robyn's smiling face looking back at him.

He hesitated before pressing the button – but to hell with it. He had to know whether she would see him again.

Dave arrived home at five o'clock Friday evening just as Robyn was preparing the children's tea. He dashed in to the spaciously planned kitchen and diner.

'Do you think we could get a baby sitter for tonight?' he asked Robyn, who was peeling potatoes for the mash. 'I know its short notice, but Alex has spare tickets for the Fireman's ball. His sister's children have chicken pox and he's offered them to us.'

'I suppose I could see if Mum's doing anything. What about your Mum?'

'She's on her way to Tenerife.'

'You never said…'

'It's a last minute thing. Malcolm surprised her.'

Dave's mum had recently got herself a new man and was living life to the fullest since Dave's father decided he'd had enough of being married to her and moved on. 'I'm only sorry it took him thirty five years to decide,' she'd confided in Robyn.

'Lucky her,' Robyn sighed. 'Why don't you ever surprise me?'

'What do you think I'm doing? I'm offering you a free night out. The tickets are usually sixty five pounds.'

'You're too good to me! I'll go and ring Mum now, watch the sausages under the grill.'

The phone was in the lounge, and as she picked it up, she noticed one unread message on her laptop – she loved new messages. It was a "New friend request" from Facebook. She collapsed onto the sofa when she saw who it was from. The option came up to accept or decline the request and without a second's hesitation, she pressed accept.

The carefully simmering feelings from the week bubbled to the surface. *Yes, he still cares. Thank you God!*

'Have you finished? The sausages are burning,' Dave shouted from the kitchen.

Oops!

'The line's engaged. I'll just try again,' she lied – but she didn't care. Jay had contacted her again and that was all that mattered.

After her shower, Robyn checked her in-box. After she applied her make-up, Robyn checked her in-box and so it went on – checking every five minutes to see if Jay had replied. But nothing. As she closed the bedroom door, she sighed. She'd have to go a whole night not knowing.

Dave collected Doreen, Robyn's mum, at seven o'clock. She was more than happy to babysit as Robyn had a forty-two inch LCD television and the soaps looked so much better on a big screen. Molly and Jake were happy to see their 'gamma,' as Jake called her. It meant they'd get double ice cream and could stay up until late.

'You will see they are in bed by eight, won't you Mum?'

'Of course I will,' Doreen gave a surreptitious wink to her grandchildren.

'They only have one story each; don't let them tell you they have two.'

'Yes, dear. I have looked after children before. You go and have a good time. Don't worry about us, we'll be fine. Don't forget, if you want to have a taxi I can always sleep in the spare room. Just let me know so I can tell your Dad.'

'Bye you two, be good for Grandma.'

Neither child turned to look at Robyn and Dave as they bade them farewell, Fireman Sam was far more interesting than either parent.

The Fireman's ball was the highlight of the Fire Service's social calendar. Dave was wearing his evening suite and Robyn, a long black and red dress she purchased last year to go to her own Christmas party at work. It was low cut both front and back and had turned a few heads that night as it was doing tonight.

They were sitting at the same table as their friends, Alex and his wife, Sue, and adjacent to Chris and Denizon.

'Hello, Dave, Robyn.' Alex stood up to shake his friend's hand and kiss Robyn's cheek. 'Can I just say, you look stunning tonight, Robyn.'

'Thanks, Alex.' Robyn beamed.

'She does, doesn't she? We nearly didn't leave the house!' Dave ran his hand all the way down Robyn's back and squeezed her buttock.

'Dave, stop it.' She pushed his hand away.

'Yes, stop it; you'll be making me jealous.' Alex looked at Robyn lustfully.

Robyn thought back to Dave's erection as she was sliding into her dress. He'd made it obvious he was up for it, but all Robyn could see was Jay's face with his tussled, long hair and dazzling blue eyes …

Since Denizon's outpouring of emotion on Wednesday, they hadn't talked since, and Robyn signalled for her friend to accompany her to the toilet.

'You're looking lovely tonight. I hope my stupid brother appreciates the effort you've made.'

'He does.' Denizon smiled. 'I challenged him about the phone. I was going to ring you, but he's been so attentive since then I really haven't had any spare time. There's a perfectly simple explanation.'

Robyn couldn't wait to hear. She'd heard her brother's perfectly simple explanations before.

'I'm all ears.'

'Don't be like that Rob, I have to believe him.'

'Sorry, go on – oh, just a minute.' Robyn bent down to check the toilet cubicles – all clear.

'Apparently, Chris doesn't get a very good deal on his mobile phone contract, but he has to keep the same number for work. He bought himself another phone with Orange which gives him more minutes and free unlimited texts. One of his colleagues, who has a bit of a crush on him, got hold of the number and started texting him. She found the present he bought me and thought she'd have a bit of a laugh. I took it out of context; she was only teasing him.'

Even Robyn had to admit her brother had excelled himself with this story. He should write a book – fiction came so easily to him.

'As long as you're happy with his explanation, that's all that matters.'

'You don't sound convinced, Rob.'

'It doesn't matter what I think. I just want to see you happy.'

'He also said we can go for tests to see why we haven't conceived. I've asked him so many times before but he's always said there was no rush.'

'I'm really pleased for you, Den.' She hugged her best friend, knowing how desperate she was for a baby.

The cynical side of Robyn thought her brother was making this gesture out of guilt, but she could have read him all wrong. There was always a first time!

'Let's go and get a drink to celebrate,' Denizon said as she linked arms with Robyn.

Anything to stop her thinking about Jay and the e-mail that was probably sitting on her computer at home.

By ten o'clock, Robyn had resorted to water as she was feeling slightly nauseous.

She whispered to Dave, 'I'm just nipping outside for a short while.' He was engrossed in a football conversation and didn't look up.

'Dave, did you hear what I said?'

'Sorry, love … yes I'll see you later.'

Robyn walked into the large manicured gardens of *The Oaks Country House* and found a wooden bench to sit on. The darkness in the countryside had its own special quality with only the stars and an imitation gas lantern to illuminate her chosen seat. She reached into her evening bag and pulled out her ancient mobile phone.

Note to self, really must join the twenty first century and get an android version.

One text wouldn't hurt and she was desperate to know if Jay had replied to her acknowledgement. Looking round to make sure she was alone she pressed 'Messaging.'

Jay's number was already programmed into her phone so it was just a matter of going to 'Compose new message.'

What should I put?

"Hi Jay, thanks for requesting me as a friend. I hope you've had a good week."

Far too boring! She deleted the last sentence. Whether it was the drink talking, who knows, but she added,

"I've really missed you, and I'm sorry we didn't get to say goodbye."

She paused. *Have I to? … What the hell!*

"Lots of love Robyn xx."

Yes, that'll do!

She went to her sent file and deleted the incriminating evidence.

As she got up to join the party, she noticed a dark shadow over to her left behind a pillar and realised it was a couple entwined in an embrace. Creeping quietly past, she got the shock of her life when she saw who it was. Chris had his tongue down the throat of a dark haired girl, his hands wandering inside the bodice of her silver gown, totally oblivious to any audience.

Robyn didn't know what to do. She'd just sent a text to a man she'd kissed last weekend, and here she was just about to take the moral high ground with her brother. Her fake cough stopped Chris in his tracks and he looked behind him.

'Oh fuck! What are you doing here?' he asked, doing up his fly.

'Shouldn't I be asking you the same question?'

His friend looked suitably embarrassed. She adjusted her dress and skulked away back to the party.

'Please don't tell Denizon,' he begged.

'Give me one good reason why I shouldn't? She is my best friend after all.'

'Because I do love her and don't want to lose her.'

'You've got a funny way of showing it. I thought the simple explanation was a bit too simple.'

'What do you mean?' He looked puzzled.

'She told me about finding your phone and gave me an update tonight about how there was a reasonable explanation. I didn't believe it then, and I certainly don't believe it now.'

Chris held up his hands, 'What can I say?'

'You can tell me why you keep cheating on one of the sweetest, kindest women in the world.'

'Probably because she is so kind and sweet I can get away with it.'

'Bollocks! You've always been the same. What I can't understand is why you got married in the first place.'

'I wanted children. But a fat lot of use she is in that department.'

Robyn swung back her hand and slapped him hard across the face, 'Don't ever let me hear you speak like that about my best friend again.'

'Christ Rob! That hurt. Look, you've drawn blood.' He wiped away a small speck from the side of his mouth.

'It bloody well serves you right. I won't say anything this time but sort your act out. If you don't want to be with her, let her down gently so she can find someone else. I always knew it was doomed from the start.' She saw Chris's lip start to swell.

'Er... I'm sorry about your face ...You know I love you, but I love her as well. You've put me in an impossible situation. If she finds out I've seen you tonight, she'll never forgive me.'

'I promise I'll sort it. Thanks Rob. I owe you one.'

'You owe me an awful lot more than one, now get back to your wife and give her the attention she deserves or you'll get another one of these.' Robyn held up her open palm.

'Not again, please or I'll tell my mum!' Robyn tried not to smile – no-one could stay mad at Chris for long.

Chapter 7

Jay had just stepped out of the shower in the en suite when he heard his phone bleep from the pocket in his jeans. Drying his hands on a towel he opened the message.

'Yes!' he said with clenched fist when he saw Robyn's name followed by two kisses. He sat on the closed toilet lid reading the text over and over again.

Should he reply straight away? What the hell! He'd waited all week for this text and wasn't going to wait another night.

All his resolve to forget her left him in an instant as he planned ways for them to meet. He could fake a meeting in Hull and drive to see her. But for what reason would he ever be in Hull? It wasn't exactly a place you passed through, so she'd have to come to Leeds. But wasn't he jumping the gun? She'd only sent him one text.

"Thanks for text it was great to hear from you. I've waited all week but thought you'd forgotten about me." He paused before continuing, should he go for it?

"Do you fancy meeting for coffee one day soon? Let me know, anytime is good for me." He pressed send and, like his co-conspirator, deleted any trace.

As he continued drying himself, he watched his phone and didn't have to wait long before it bleeped. The message read,

"Yes. I'll text you tomorrow with time and place." Jay smiled and his hand reached down to his growing erection.

'This is for you, Robyn,' he groaned quietly as his hand started working up and down, increasing in speed as he fantasized.

Despite drinking far too much Robyn hardly slept a wink with the excitement that had taken over every inch of her body. Dave was snoring beside her, but she ignored the noise and kept reading the text Jay had sent.

He wants to see me. He wants to see me again! Do you think he just means coffee? ... But what if I bottle out like last time? An angel kept telling her to be sensible and knock it on the head before it even started – but a devil was tempting her to be satisfied in a way that she knew her husband couldn't.

It was five thirty before she finally gave up on sleep and stumbled downstairs to the kitchen. Fruit and muesli just weren't going to do it for her today and as she ate chocolate spread on toast and drank a large mug of coffee. She decided on Wednesday next week for her illicit rendezvous – that is, if Jay was free. She would drop the children off at school and nursery and head over to Leeds, giving herself the whole day and drive back in time to pick the children up. She reached for her phone.

"Sorry it's so early, but I couldn't sleep. Would you be free to meet Wed? I'll book the day off and come to Leeds. We could meet at the coffee bar in the Theroux. Love Robyn x x."

She'd hardly had time for another sip of coffee before her phone bleeped.

"I couldn't sleep either. Wed would be great. Can you be there by ten? We can have breakfast together and then decide what to do. You don't know how much I'm looking forward to seeing you. All my love, J."

So there it was – her duplicitous life had started.

Robyn yawned. Too late to go back to bed, she'd just have to keep herself awake with caffeine. The kitchen door opened and her mother's head popped round.

'What are you doing up so early? I didn't think we'd see you until at least nine,' Doreen asked. 'Haven't you got a hangover?'

'It's swimming lessons at nine thirty so I'd be up anyway, but I couldn't sleep and no my head feels fine.'

'Is there any more coffee? Dad's picking me up at seven; we've arranged to go to the caravan.'

'Sorry, Mum. I didn't know you'd anything planned. I didn't mean to spoil your weekend.'

'You didn't. Dave said he'd get up with the kids so I could get off early. He's a good one, your husband.'

'Yes, he is Mum.' Doreen worshipped Dave and took every opportunity to remind her ungrateful daughter how lucky she was.

'I'm very lucky; I know which is more than can be said for Denizon.'

'You're not going to have a go at your brother again are you?'

Robyn knew she shouldn't say anything, but her mother was always having a dig at her and it did get rather wearing.

'I caught him kissing another woman last night ... and it wasn't a kiss between friends.'

'Robyn, don't you be saying such things about your brother.'

'Did you hear what I just said? He was kissing another woman.'

'Boys will be boys at that age. Your father was just the same, it'll be harmless fun.'

'Mother, when will you wake up and smell the roses? He's been cheating on Denizon for years and what do you mean that age? For God's sake he's thirty five.'

'Now there's no need to take that tone,' Doreen tutted.

'I'm just trying to get you to see your perfect little boy isn't that perfect. What if I kissed another man?'

'Then it'd be wrong. It's just sex for men but it has to mean something for us.'

'But that's double standards ... Have you forgotten we've got the vote, Mother?'

'Don't be clever with me. I know exactly what Denizon is going through. I had to put up with exactly the same behaviour from your Dad. But look at us now? We're as happy as Larry. He grew out of it, and I'm sure Chris will. He's a chip off the old block.'

'Are you trying to see how many clichés you can fit into one sentence?' Her mother did exasperate her. 'I didn't know Dad cheated on you,' she added with surprise.

'It's not something I like to admit. Dad married me in the early 1970's when I was twenty two and he was twenty four. We shouldn't have got married when we did; your dad just wasn't ready, but there was still pressure on a woman to find a steady husband. He was a good catch and the first boy I'd known who'd been to University. Your Gran and Granddad didn't want me to let him get away, so I didn't. I kept on at him to get engaged, and when he got his first teaching job he finally gave in.'

'But surely he wouldn't have married you if he hadn't have wanted to?'

Doreen looked sheepish, 'I sort of gave him the impression I was pregnant.'

'How can you sort of give someone that impression?'

'I'd missed a period and really believed I was the one percent that fell pregnant on the pill. So when I started my period I forgot to mention it.'

'So you conned Dad into marrying you? I can't believe you did that to the poor man.'

'He did love me and we planned to get married eventually but I just brought it forward.'

'So, it's not surprising he cheated on you. I bet he was livid when you told him the truth.'

Doreen blushed, 'That's just it … I told him I'd had a miscarriage.'

'I take it he knows now?' Robyn was incredulous. Their whole family was founded on lies. *It's hardly surprising me and Chris are like we are.*

'Of course he does. That's what I'm telling you for. Me and your dad grew into each other. By the time he was about Chris's age he'd stopped looking at other women. I was finally enough for him.'

Robyn quickly did the sums in her head.

'But you had two children by the time Dad was thirty five.'

'I know and that's all I cared about. I didn't show him any attention and you know what it's like when your children are babies, you go off sex.'

Robyn was about to disagree but found she couldn't, she'd gone off sex for nearly a year when she had Molly.

'But it doesn't give a man *carte blanche* to sleep with every woman he meets just because he can't get his end away for a while.'

'Yes, in theory I agree, and feminists would have a field day with what I've just told you, but life is more complicated than all the grand theories. I never thought I'd tolerate a husband being unfaithful, but Dad kept it discreet. He didn't flaunt it in my face and I never asked. We still had a good sex life. In fact it was better when he was seeing someone.'

That's true! Robyn felt her face and neck glow a deep shade of red.

'So you've told me all this just to justify Chris's behaviour. I'm sorry I still can't, Denizon is my friend.'

'… And she's my daughter in law. You're not the only person she confides in. She's very much like I was. You're different; you're so much more confident and sure of yourself. Where would Denizon be without Chris?'

'A damned sight better off. She could make a new life for herself.' Robyn was indignant on her friend's behalf.

'But that's just it, she doesn't want to. Trust me, Chris loves her and he'll come to realise she's all he needs, particularly if they have a family.'

'So you've become a relationship expert all of a sudden?'

'These things happen, and knowing they're wrong won't stop human nature. Anyway, enough of baring my soul I need to go and get ready. The love of my life is picking me up in half an hour.'

'I just hope you're as understanding when I have an affair,' Robyn said boldly.

Doreen laughed, 'Don't be stupid. Why would you want an affair when you're married to someone as wonderful as Dave?' She put her coffee cup in the dishwasher and chuckled all the way up the stairs.

Chapter 8

Only two more nights and Robyn would see Jay again. The thought was both terrifying and exciting. She'd taken to texting him two or three times a day and, when she felt the desperate need to speak to him, she'd make up an excuse to go out.

'I'm just nipping to Sainsbury's, Dave. I forgot the ham for tomorrow's sandwiches.'

'Its okay, give us cheese,' Dave shouted from the office.

'No, it's okay, the children prefer ham. Just listen out for them; they're playing in Molly's room. I won't be long.'

Robyn picked up her purse and car keys.

'Hi, it's me can you talk?' she asked Jay as she parked on a patch of waste ground.

'Just a second. I'll go to my car,' he said quietly. The phone went silent as Jay put her on hold.

'Hello love, I'm here.'

'I just wanted to hear your voice.'

'That's sweet. I love it when you ring unexpectedly.'

'Being in the house is driving me mad.'

'I know. Just try and keep yourself busy, I do. I spend all my time on my computer.'

'My house has never been as clean! Anyway, I can't be too long. I'm supposed to be shopping. Are you still looking forward to Wednesday?'

'I can't tell you how much.'

Robyn gave a deep sigh.

'Are you okay, love? Not having second thoughts?'

'No… It's just that … No, it'll be fine.'

'It's just coffee.'

Robyn paused. She wanted it to be much more, but the thought of it was weighing heavy on her mind.

'I know. I'm sorry.'

'Cheer up love. Wednesday will be great.'

'I know it will.' Robyn thought back to the glimpse of Jay in his boxers and grinned.

'I'll text you before bed.'

'I'll be waiting.'

Tuesday evening was almost unbearable for Jay. His temper was getting shorter and his mood darker, which he blamed on pressure of work and the fact his book wasn't going as well as he expected. Maria had offered to make a special meal to see if that could cheer him up.

'Jay, come and sit down at the table, the starter's ready.' A large crayfish and prawn ravioli with red pesto sauce was set in front of him.

'Can I get you another drink?' she offered.

'No thanks, I'd better slow down that's my second already. Aren't you opening a bottle of wine?'

'No, I'm going to stick with the coke … But I'm glad you noticed I'm not drinking because I might as well tell you now the reason for the meal.' Maria paused and with the biggest grin on her face said, 'I did a test today and it was positive. I'm pregnant.'

'Fuck!' Jay whispered. 'God, that's a shock,' he said a bit louder.

This will spoil everything, he thought. *Robyn certainly won't sleep with me if she knows Maria's pregnant. Shit!*

'Is that all you've got to say?' Maria asked, disappointed by his reaction.

'We hadn't really talked all that seriously about children.'

'No, I know, but it appears that baby,' she rubbed her stomach fondly, 'had other plans.'

'But we've been so careful,' Jay said.

'I take it from your reaction it's not good news?' Maria said her eyes moist with tears.

'I'm sorry, love.' He knelt down by her side. 'You've had a few hours to come to terms with it. I'm sure once it sinks in I'll be as happy as you are.' Although he knew that'd never be true because he didn't want children. There'd been so many times he'd wanted to broach the subject with Maria, but hadn't and now it was too late. What an idiot!

He was only thirty, far too young, in his opinion, to consider being a father. He felt totally cornered and it wasn't just about Robyn. Without her in his life he doubted he'd be any happier with the news.

Jay hardly spoke a word through the rest of the meal. Maria talked endlessly about babies' names and how they would decorate the nursery, which was now his office. Jay feigned interest until he couldn't bear it any longer. If he smiled anymore his face would be permanently caught in that position.

'The meal was lovely, Maria, thank you so much for cooking it. Would you mind if I went to bed? I've got an early start tomorrow.'

Maria reached across the table and took his hand. 'I know it's a shock, but I'm sure we can make it work. We love each other so much and a baby will be the icing on cake. I promise.'

If only he could be so sure.

Dave had come home from 5-a side football and was feeling particularly chatty. Robyn had done bath time and settled the children, and was now running a hot bath for herself. A luxurious pamper session was just what she needed in preparation for tomorrow.

'I'm having a beer, can I get you anything?' Dave shouted from the kitchen.

'I think there's just one glass of wine left in the fridge, you can pour me that. I'm in the bathroom.'

He handed her a rather large glass of Cool Zinfandel. 'I can come and talk to you in the bath.'

Great! That's all I need.

'Why don't you watch television? I won't be too long.'

'But I could wash your back,' Dave nuzzled and kissed her neck.

Robyn flinched and moved away.

'Come on, where's my new sexy wife gone?'

'It's not always about sex, Dave. I'm tired. I just want to treat myself to a long soak.'

'Be like that then … I'll go and have a shower in the en suite. They were freezing in the sports centre.'

Thank God for that! All Robyn wanted to do was go over in her head what could possibly happen tomorrow. In just over twelve hours she would be seeing Jay again and the anticipation was eating away at her.

'I was talking to Alex tonight,' added Dave, still standing in the bathroom watching Robyn undress. 'Is everything okay between your Chris and Denizon?'

'I think so. Why do you ask?'

'Don't say anything to anyone, Alex told me in confidence, but Chris has become very friendly with one of the female fire-fighters at the station. Alex has been watching them and wondered if anything was going on.'

'Denizon hasn't said anything, but she probably has no idea.'

'I know he's your brother, but he's an idiot. Fancy jeopardizing a perfectly good marriage for a fling with someone at work.'

Robyn gulped, 'It might be perfectly innocent.'

'Yes and I'm going to win Euro-millions this week,' Dave retorted.

'Alex shouldn't really be saying anything until he has proof. That's how rumours start. I know Chris isn't a saint, but I hope Alex hasn't spread this malicious gossip to anyone else.'

'Calm down, Rob, I'm sorry I said anything. You usually don't defend Chris. I thought you might like to have a chat with Denizon to see if everything's okay.'

'Sorry. I didn't mean to snap. You're right I'll see if they seem happy the next time I talk to her. But it really is no concern of ours or Alex's for that matter.'

'Wouldn't you want to know if I was playing away? I'd want to be told if you were, so I could plan ways to kill the bastard,' Dave joked.

Robyn swallowed nervously, 'Well, that's not going to happen is it? Who'd put up with me and my mood swings?'

'You've got a point. But I'd still like to know, so I could warn him about what he's getting himself into.'

'Go and have your shower, you cheeky sod. Lots of men would have me, given half a chance.' She playfully hit Dave on his bottom. As she stepped into the delicious bubbles, she hoped one particular man would have her tomorrow...

Chapter 9

It was the day of reckoning, Wednesday was finally here. Robyn jumped out of bed earlier than usual after a restless night and stared at her double wardrobe bursting at the seams with clothes. *What do you wear to see a potential lover?* She knew she couldn't be too casual, as to all intents and purposes, she was going to work. Finally she decided on a low-cut teal and brown cashmere short tunic, which highlighted her breasts, and teamed it with long dark brown leggings, which showed off her shapely legs. It was a bit too warm for boots, but she put them on anyway as the high heels accentuated her figure.

Dave commented on her appearance as she walked into the kitchen. 'Wow! You look a bit dressed up, what's the occasion?'

'What? … In this old thing,' she said casually looking down at her outfit. 'I'm interviewing. We've got a few nursing vacancies to fill and I'm on the panel.' Robyn was glad the story of Pinocchio was fictional, as her nose would have rivalled his.

'Well, you'll do for me.'

Robyn shrugged. 'Thank you.'

'Does that mean you'll be late home?'

'No, I shouldn't be. I'm picking the children up from school.'

Dave reached across to kiss her lips, but she turned her face and he clipped her cheek.

'Have a good day, love. I'll see you later.'

Robyn looked at her watch. What was taking Molly so long today?

'Are you nearly ready, Molly? We're going to be late.'

'I can't find my pencil case,' Molly shouted from her bedroom.

'You've got plenty, get another one from your desk,' Robyn shouted back.

Jake already had his coat on and was waiting patiently by the door.

'I need my Princess Petunia one. I had it last night.'

'For God sake, Molly. Get another one and hurry up.

Molly finally appeared from her bedroom sobbing, holding a plain pink pencil case.

'What's the matter now?'

'You're shouting at me, and I only wanted Princess Petunia because I told Miss Dodds all about it and she told me to bring it in today to show and tell.'

Robyn felt the first pang of guilt deep in the pit of her stomach.

'I'm sorry love, I didn't mean to shout. What's so special about Princess Petunia?'

'Don't you remember?' Molly's eyes were still moist with tears. 'Daddy bought it for me when he went away with work. He called me his little princess.'

'Yes, I do remember, pumpkin. If it means that much to you we'll look for it. Do you want to come and help, Jakey?'

Robyn kept looking at her watch as the minutes ticked by.

'Found it,' said a muffled voice from under the bed.

'Clever boy,' Robyn sighed with relief. 'Now can we get to school?'

Robyn dropped Jake off first and drove quickly round the corner to Molly's school.

'I'm glad I've caught you,' said Debra, the mother of Molly's best friend, as Robyn got out of the car.

Could anything else hold me up today? Robyn took another look at her watch.

'Taylor wants Molly to come and play after school today. Is that alright by you? I'll pick them up from school and you can come for Molly later.'

This could actually work in my favour, I'll just have to ring Jake's nursery to say I'm going to be late. Yes! I'll have even longer.

'Robyn?'

'Sorry, I was just thinking. Yes, that'd be great. I'm interviewing today and it might drag on so that would be really helpful.'

'Did you hear that girls? … Molly can come for tea.'

'Could you take Molly into the classroom for me?' Robyn asked aware of the time. 'I'm a bit behind schedule.'

'Of course.'

'Come and give Mummy a kiss, Molly.' Her daughter ignored her.

'Molly, hurry up.'

Finally Robyn closed the car door, breathing deeply to compose herself. She put her foot down and headed to see Jay at ten o'clock.

The M62 heading towards Leeds was relatively quiet and Robyn didn't hit standing traffic until she came into Leeds City Centre, and then it was gridlocked. *Damn! Is there some force at work preventing me from meeting Jay today? Maybe I should just turn round and go home.*

Robyn tapped her fingers on the steering wheel. It was already ten thirty and there was no sign of the traffic moving. As she was crawling along, she spotted a car park a few yards on the left and pulled into the nearest available space. She looked in her purse, damn, no change! Luckily, there was a machine that took cards.

'Robyn!' She looked round as someone called out her name.

Shit! What's she doing here?

'Hi, Robyn, what a coincidence seeing you here. I've just got off the train,' said Belle one of the mums from school. 'Are you shopping as well?'

'Er … yes. Hull just doesn't have the same choice does it? I love Harvey Nicks.'

'So do I. Do you want to walk up together?'

'I'm … er … meeting someone first, you know …a work thing.'

'Okay, I'll catch you later. You can show me what you bought at school.'

'Will do, bye.'

Robyn set off running. Breathlessly, she fell through the double doors into the foyer of the Theroux hotel and marched directly into the restaurant where they were serving breakfast. She spotted Jay before he saw her. He was engrossed on his laptop.

She sneaked up behind him and whispered in his ear, 'Sorry I'm late.'

'Hello you… come round here and let me look at you,' he gently took her hand and led her round to the front of his seat. 'You look fantastic,' he added.

Even with the bright red face?

Robyn shifted from one foot to the other feeling slightly uncomfortable. *Shit! What do I do now?*

'Are you alright?' Jay asked as Robyn still hadn't spoken.

'Sorry, yes, I think so,' she said sighing deeply. 'I've been imagining this moment since we agreed to meet, but now I'm here … I don't know …it … feels … Oh! I don't know.'

'It's okay … I'm so happy to see you.' Jay held tightly onto Robyn's hand. 'Are you going to sit down?'

'Sorry, yes.' Robyn perched at the edge of the opposite seat.

'You don't need to keep apologising,' he said squeezing her clammy hand. 'Can I pour you a coffee?'

'Please, that would be lovely.' Robyn said fiddling with her wedding ring.

'Do you want anything to eat?' Jay asked as he poured a cup of black coffee.

Robyn shook her head. 'I couldn't eat a thing.' She looked at Jay and he laughed.

'I didn't think we'd be stuck for things to say.'

'Me neither.'

'Have you decided what you'd like to do after this?' Jay asked taking a sip of his coffee.

I know what I want to do, but I don't know if I dare! The anticipation of seeing him had aroused her, the sight and touch of him was almost more than she could bear, but she just shook her head.

'Shall er ... Shall I see if they've got a room free? No pressure, but it'd just give us a bit more privacy than here.' Jay asked.

'Yes,' she sighed. 'I think so.'

'You don't have to say yes. It's okay we can just go for a walk.'

'Sorry. It's all I've been thinking about, but it's just ...'

'I do understand ... but we can just talk.'

'I don't want to talk.' *What the hell!* Robyn leaned across and kissed him.

Without speaking, Jay put away his laptop and pulled Robyn to her feet. He held her hand as they walked to reception. The receptionist was discretion itself, but Robyn looked toward the floor, knowing it was all too obvious what the room was for.

'Do you remember the first time I saw you in this lift?' Jay asked as the door closed behind them.

'I do,' she said leaning against him. 'I couldn't string two words together.'

Jay took Robyn in his arms and pulled her close. Running his fingers through her hair, his lips lightly touched hers, and his tongue gently caressed her bottom lip. The lift ground to a halt and, as the door opened, they moved apart. She held onto his hand as they walked along the corridor. He fumbled with the key card and finally let them into room 314. Slamming the door shut, he kissed her again.

'Are you sure you want to do this?' Jay asked, stopping for a second.

'Ssh! just kiss me,' she said thrusting her tongue deep into his waiting mouth.

They stumbled across the room. Jay lay down on the bed next to Robyn. He looked at her longingly as he removed first her boots, then her leggings. Robyn reached across and slowly unzipped his trousers. His finger slid gently up the inside of her thigh.

'Oh God, Jay. You've no idea what you do to me.' Robyn gasped.

'I think I have.' Pulling her pants to one side he slipped the tip of his finger between her waiting lips.

'Don't stop there,' she groaned, reaching her hand inside his boxers. She held on to his hardness. He thrust the rest of his finger inside her.

'Oh, please …I want you inside me,'

Jay pulled his erection free and positioned himself above Robyn.

He hesitated, 'Are you sure?'

She took hold of him and forced it inside her. Her wetness engulfed him.

He moved up and down slowly, with Robyn responding to his every thrust. She lifted up her legs pushing him in deeper.

'Oh Jay!' she closed her eyes and surrendered.

He held back until he could feel she was ready to climax and then let go with all the force of a tidal wave.

Robyn held onto him tightly, burying her face into his shoulder. *My God, what have I just done?* It had been over ten years since she'd made love to another man and now she'd crossed the line.

Jay lifted her chin. 'Are you alright?'

'I think so.' She paused, smiling, 'Yes, I'm great.' She lifted her head and kissed him.

Jay smiled back as he lifted the tunic over her head. Sitting back, admiring her body he whispered, 'You really are gorgeous! I've been trying to imagine every inch of you, but even in my wildest dreams, I didn't imagine you being this beautiful.'

Robyn smiled. 'I'll let you into a secret. I had a dream the Friday night of the course that we made love on the stage in front of Max and the audience. I imagined you in all your glory and, let me tell you, I'm not disappointed.'

'Thank you, I do my best,' he grinned.

'How about we take these off?' she said, pulling his boxers off, leaving him completely naked.

She was feeling much braver now and slid down the bed. Jay groaned as she nearly swallowed him whole.

'Watch out you'll have me coming,' he gasped as he moved her head away.

'That's the general idea.'

'I want to come inside you.' He pushed Robyn onto her back and gently entered her.

'I never thought it would be that good with anyone,' admitted Jay after they climaxed for a second time. 'Words can't describe what that felt like.'

Robyn smiled as she fingered his blonde pubic hair. *That was just the best feeling ever!*

It was lunchtime before they surfaced after a record breaking three more sessions.

'I'm hungry,' Robyn said, hearing her stomach rumble.

'Do you want to go out and get something to eat or shall we order room service?' Jay asked.

'Let's go out together.'

It took them another half an hour to get dressed and had to kiss every time they donned an item of clothing. The bed covers looked like a war zone, but it didn't matter – they'd be using it again later. Jay took hold of Robyn's hand as they walked out of the hotel. Every few steps he'd lean across and kiss her lips.

Cafe Rouge was busy with lunchtime trade and they took the only spare table at the back of the restaurant.

The waiter gave them menus and took their drinks order.

Robyn sat back in her chair soaking up the atmosphere, feeling totally at peace with the world. *How much better could life get?*

'What are you smiling at?' Jay asked.

'This!' she sighed contentedly. 'It's good isn't it?'

'It is now, but don't you think it's been hell these past few days?'

'Absolutely.' Robyn agreed. 'I didn't want to talk to anyone apart from you, and Dave wouldn't leave me alone last night.'

'Tell me about it! I had to sit through a boring meal Maria cooked.' Jay paused, thinking back to the previous evening and shuddered. 'What time do you have to leave?'

'Not until about four. Molly's at a friend's house and as long as I get Jake before six it's okay.'

'When you've gone I'm going to do some writing before heading off back. Did I tell you I've started my book? I've decided to call it, "How to Have an Affair!"'

'How apt! It's not about us is it?'

'Obviously, I'm not going to mention any names, do you think I've got a death wish or something?' Jay laughed. 'But I am going to write about the turmoil and the ecstasy of being involved with two people at the same time. I've asked some of my clients if I can use their stories, and quite a few have agreed to be interviewed.'

'Sounds good! It seems that everyone's at it. I found out on Sunday that my dad slept around for years.'

'Snap. Mine was the same,' Jay admitted.

'And my brother has never been faithful to a woman in his life. I'm beginning to think it runs in families. Do you think there's an infidelity gene?' Robyn asked seriously.

'I never thought of that, but I think it's more likely to be learned behaviour. Nurture not nature.'

'Did your Mum and Dad split up?' Robyn asked. 'Mine didn't and seem really happy now.'

'No, she stayed with him, but he died six years ago of a heart attack.'

'Oh, I'm sorry, you never said.'

'Don't worry. I'm more or less over it.'

'Did you get on with your dad?'

'Not really, he was a bit of a bully. He wanted me to be a doctor like him, and when I refused he didn't like it.'

'My dad wanted me to be a teacher like him, but I couldn't think of anything worse, apart from maybe, Human Resources.' Robyn laughed.

The waiter came back and took their order. Jay reached across the table and held Robyn's hand.

'This is just so great, being here with you,' he said grinning.

'That's my phone,' Robyn said reaching into her bag. It was Dave.

'I'd better get this, excuse me a second,' she said, getting up to go outside so Dave wouldn't hear the sound of a busy restaurant. She took a deep breath,

'Hello, Dave. What can I do for you?'

'Sorry to bother you, love, when you're interviewing, but the school has just rung. Molly has fallen in the playground and cut her knee quite badly. They're on the way to hospital with her. It's going to need stitches.'

'Oh no! The poor love. I'll 'erm ...' She suddenly realised she couldn't say she'd go straight to the hospital as she was at least forty five minutes away.

'Don't worry, I'll go and pick her up,' Dave offered.

'I'll be there as soon as I can. I'll just stay for the next interview.'

'That's fine, don't you rush back. If we finish at the hospital I'll take her to work with me.'

'Thanks for that, love. I'll see you soon. Give her a kiss from me.'

Robyn returned to the table just as the soup arrived.

'Is everything okay?' Jay asked, looking at Robyn's furrowed brow.

'Not really. That was Dave. Molly's fallen and cut her knee at school.'

'Oh dear. I hope she'll be okay. Does that mean you'll be getting straight off?'

'Yes, I'll just eat this and then I'll go. I don't think I left anything in the hotel. I'm so sorry for running out on you.'

'Don't worry. These things happen. Look, I know its early days yet but do you know when we can get together again?' he asked. 'I take it you want to?'

'Of course I do, but I wished we lived closer.' Robyn sighed.

'I can formulate another conference if you like. I'm always dashing about here and there. I can come over to you next time.' Jay offered.

'But I don't know where we'd meet. Hull's not like Leeds, it's so much smaller. I'm much more likely to be seen.'

'I could pick you up somewhere discreet and we could find a secluded spot.'

Robyn thought for a second. 'I suppose we could go across the Humber Bridge. It's quieter on the other side and I don't know anyone there.'

'Can you do next week? Jay asked.

'Yes,' she said emphatically. 'I'm still owed a lot of flexitime.'

'See what you can arrange and I'll come over next week, Wednesday again?' he said.

'Yes, perfect, but we can still speak and text can't we?'

'Of course, I couldn't go until next Wednesday without speaking to you.' He squeezed her hand.

The waiter brought out the huge baguette.

'You'll have to eat that I'm afraid, I've got to go.'

'Here take some to eat in the car,' Jay said as he cut it in half. 'You've got to keep your strength up!' He winked.

'Never stop winking at me, will you?' She laughed, feeling her insides go all wobbly. 'It's so sexy.'

Jay winked again. 'I remember you commenting at the meal.'

'Don't remind me. I still cringe when I think of it.'

Jay reached under the table and taking Robyn's hand guided it toward his crotch.

'Just to give you a reminder what you'll be missing.' She gently rubbed, feeling him hardening with her touch.

He groaned in frustration, 'That's enough!' Reluctantly she removed her hand.

'Do you want me to walk you back to your car?' Jay offered.

'Damn right I do! I want a proper kiss and we can't do that here.'

Jay slid into the passenger side of Robyn's car and leaned across to kiss her. She reached behind for the car blanket and threw it over his knee, heading down south for his erection.

'You're doing it again, you'll have me coming,' Jay groaned.

Thrusting her tongue deep into his mouth, she stopped short of bringing him to climax, 'That's to remember me by.'

'There's no fear I'll ever forget you,' he said as he pulled down her leggings, thrusting two fingers inside her. 'I want to make you come,' he whispered as he ran his fingers across her clitoris. He found her exact spot and her whole body shivered.

Driving back to Hull and her life there, Robyn replayed every second of her morning with Jay. He was such a good lover! Better than she'd ever imagined. A thought suddenly struck her. She'd expected to be hit by an overwhelming feeling of guilt by now – but whether it was the adrenalin coursing through her body or something else entirely, the only thing she could feel at this moment was sheer, unadulterated lust, and she loved it.

Robyn slumped down on the leather reclining sofa,

'What a day! I never thought we'd get out of the hospital.'

'I know, six hours just to get a few stitches in a knee,' Dave agreed.

'But wasn't Molly brave? I'd have cried more than that.'

'She was, bless her... Can I get you a glass of wine?' Dave offered.

'Yes, please, a large one.' Robyn unzipped her high boots and rubbed her feet.

'Red or white?'

'Surprise me!'

Dave returned with two large glasses of red wine, handing one to Robyn, he sat down next to her. As he accidently touched her arm, she flinched.

'You're a bit jumpy' Dave said.

'Sorry. You startled me.'

Since coming home from Leeds, every time Dave made any attempt to touch her she was immediately catapulted back to being in bed with Jay. The only way she could come to terms with her indiscretion was to keep her poor husband at arm's length.

'Do you want me to rub your feet?' he offered, taking her left foot in his hands. Her automatic reflex took over; she kicked out and sent her glass of wine flying all over the sofa and her cashmere tunic.

'Now look what you've done,' she snapped as she tried damage limitation by holding her tunic so wine didn't go on the carpet. 'Go and get me a cloth.'

'Sorry, I didn't mean to make you jump, but I hardly think it was my fault.'

'You know my feet are sensitive. It's a stupid thing to do when I'm holding a glass of wine.'

'Hey, it's no big deal. Take your tunic off and I'll rinse it out for you,' Dave offered.

Robyn felt self-conscious as she sat on the sofa in her bra and leggings, so different from the feeling of earlier.

'Do you want me to put it in the wash?' Dave shouted from the kitchen.

'If you want to totally ruin it! It's hand wash only. Leave it, I'll do it later.'

'For God's sake, Robyn. It was an accident,' Dave said as he returned to the lounge.

'I know, I think I must be tired. I might have an early night.'

'Probably best. It might improve your mood.'

Over the next week Robyn tried hard to avoid social contact with too many people, especially those who knew her well, in case they could read her mind. But when Denizon asked if she'd accompany her on a hospital visit she felt she couldn't let her best friend down. As it turned out the appointment was first thing Wednesday morning and Robyn had already booked the whole day off work, in readiness for meeting Jay at midday at the Humber Bridge.

'Why have you got the day off again?' Dave asked on Wednesday morning as he was dashing round getting ready for work.

'I told you that Denizon wants me to go to the hospital with her and I've still got quite a bit of flexi-time owing, so I thought I'd book the whole day and we can go girly shopping. In fact I seem to remember it was your suggestion.'

'Oh yes! I remember. I thought you might want to get some clothes for our holiday. Where do you want to go this year?' Dave asked.

'Oh, I don't know … Maybe a Greek island, I suppose.' But she couldn't actually imagine two weeks without contacting Jay.

'Don't you think we'd better start looking? We've normally booked by now.'

'I don't think there's any need to panic. There's still plenty of time.'

'Or we could go further afield like Mexico,' Dave suggested.

'The flights are a bit long for the children. I can't imagine Jake sitting in one place for twelve hours.'

In any case, she didn't feel inclined to take a once in a lifetime holiday with how she was feeling at the moment.

'Maybe not, but I'd like to book somewhere with lots to do. You know I can't sit on a lounger for two weeks.'

'Maybe we'll have a look at the weekend. You'd better get off; otherwise you'll hit the traffic.' Robyn didn't want to carry on this conversation; it detracted from her thoughts of Jay and what they were going to do today. She would deal with the problem of a holiday later.

Dave kissed her. 'I'll see you later, have a good day skiving!'

Denizon offered to pick Robyn up, but she declined, wanting her own car in case they were delayed. She pulled into the hospital car park at exactly the same moment as her friend.

'That was good timing,' Denizon said, getting out of her car.

'Do you know where you're going?' Robyn asked, looking at the big sign outside the building.

'Obstetrics and Gynaecology, through the double doors on the left and down the long corridor it says here.' Denizon waved her letter of appointment.

'Couldn't Chris make it today?'

'No, he's got a shift. I think he's just on call but needs to be at the station. He said he'd cancel it and come with me, but I'd rather go with you anyway.'

'Have things been alright between you two recently? We haven't had much time to talk.' Robyn asked.

'Much better thank you. He hasn't used his other phone once or nipped out at all. I think he's seen sense.'

Robyn doubted that very much. He'd just been more careful. 'Good, let's hope so.' She let out a long sigh.

It was the first time since being children Robyn had kept anything from her best friend – and it was killing her.

'Are you alright, Rob?' asked Denizon, looking at Robyn's vacant expression. 'You've started to do that funny thing with your lip. You can tell me anything, you know.'

'Er… No, everything's fine.'

'You've been there for me so much over the years and I've never had to sort out the cool, calm and collected Robyn Fisher. Is it work? Because it's surely not Dave.'

'Why can't it be Dave?' retorted Robyn. 'You sound just like my mother. Yes, he is lovely, and I know I should be so grateful that I'm married to him. But I'm sick of everyone assuming our marriage is perfect. It's not surprising I keep stuff to myself because no-one understands what it's like to be me. He works at least twelve hours a day and when we are together he's distracted, thinking about his next project. You've all set me up as being so happy with no problems. But let me tell you...' Robyn stopped mid-sentence.

'Robyn, I'm sorry. Whatever's the matter? I was only joking. I know Dave isn't perfect. I also know he takes you for granted, and I've told him that before.'

'You have?' Robyn was surprised.

'Yes. If you have words, he rings me to ask how he can make it right. I don't tell you because he asks me not to. If I thought he didn't take my advice, of course I'd mention it to you.'

They arrived at the Gynaecology-Obstetrics reception desk. Denizon registered and they both sat down in the waiting room.

Robyn was intrigued about the conversations between her friend and husband.

'When did you last speak?' she enquired.

'Funnily enough, he rang me on Saturday when you were food shopping. He asked if you'd said anything to me because you were acting a bit strange, you know, distant.'

Robyn gulped. And she thought she was hiding everything so well and acting perfectly normally.

'I don't actually like the idea of you two speaking behind my back. Why can't he just come out and ask me?' Robyn said sharply.

'I guess he doesn't want to start an argument. I think it's really considerate. He obviously adores you and wants to make sure you're happy, that's all.'

'Or he's checking up on me. I can't believe you haven't told me before.'

'It's no big deal! It's not as if he rings me every week. The last time we spoke was about three months ago and I can't even remember why.'

'Well, I'm fine! You can report that back to him,' Robyn snapped.

Just then a nurse appeared and called, 'Mrs. Cartwright.' Denizon and Robyn followed her to a doctor's office.

All the tests performed at the clinic showed no physical reason why Denizon hadn't conceived. Her tubes were clear and she didn't have an alien environment in which to receive sperm. Now she was just waiting for the blood tests to come back, which would take forty-eight hours. The two of them had sniggered like naughty schoolgirls when the doctor started talking about alien environments. The next step was to test Chris's sperm, and she was given a list of times when he could go in and leave a sample.

'I think this is why Chris didn't want to look into why we haven't fallen pregnant. He was fine when he thought it was my fault, but I don't think he's too keen to find out it could be him.' Denizon said as they walked back down the corridor.

Robyn thought it was some sort of divine retribution for all the times her brother had put it about, with no thought of the consequences, but she didn't say anything.

'Do you think he'll come? So to speak,' Robyn asked. They both burst out laughing again.

'He said he would. I wouldn't imagine he'll be in a rush though. Do you want a coffee before we get off?'

Robyn looked at her watch. It was only ten thirty and she wasn't meeting Jay until twelve.

'Yes, that's fine.'

'We could go shopping after, if you like.'

'No, I can't, sorry. I've said I'll go round to mums and help her with some decorating.' Robyn could have kicked herself. It wasn't a very good lie. But Robyn had to think on her feet and it was all that sprung to mind.

'Sorry, when was that arranged?' queried her sister-in-law.

'Why?' snapped Robyn.

'Don't jump down my throat, I'm only asking. Your mum never mentioned she was thinking about decorating.'

'She doesn't have to tell you everything, does she?' Robyn was digging herself an even deeper hole and was in danger of disappearing into it. 'Actually I think I'll skip the coffee and go straight round there.'

'Robyn, I'm sorry. This isn't like you at all. I know something's bothering you, so I assume you'll tell me when you're good and ready. If you don't want a coffee, that's fine, but let's not leave on this note.'

Robyn knew she was totally out of order, 'No, I'm the one who should be apologising. I don't know what's wrong with me recently. I just feel anxious and on edge all the time. I might go see the doctor.'

'Could it be hormonal?'

'Yes, more than likely. I might need my pill changing.' Robyn saw a way out of her earlier lie and grasped the opportunity. She looked sheepish,

'I'm not actually going to my mum's. I just wanted to be by myself today. I'm sorry, it's nothing personal. I just want to try and sort my head out.'

'Then why didn't you say? You don't have to lie to me. Come and give me a hug.'

Denizon held her arms out and an awkward, tense Robyn returned the embrace. Denizon knew guilt in her friend immediately. Robyn had only acted like this once before in all the years she'd known her. When they were both nineteen, Robyn slept with Denizon's boyfriend. She had apologised profusely, blaming the alcohol and Denizon had forgiven her, knowing how bad she felt. Robyn obviously wasn't sleeping with Chris, but there was definitely something going on. The guilty hug had just given it all away.

Jay had to listen to Maria's insecurities again as he'd been getting ready this morning. Since finding out she was pregnant, she'd become exceptionally clingy, wanting to know where he was at all times of the day – yesterday she rang him three times at the office. She was also crying a lot more. It was probably the hormones, but it was starting to get on Jay's nerves. He couldn't make himself want a baby, nor could he make himself love Maria.

All he wanted was Robyn and lived for the texts and phone calls and for days like today when he would see her again. He couldn't wait to leave the house and, by nine o'clock, he was sitting at his computer in the office typing chapter three of his book. Robyn must be his muse, because since sex with her last week, the words had really started to flow. He needed to write twenty thousand words to send off to the publishing house who'd previously published one of his papers. They'd shown an interest in the title and Jay was hopeful.

But words eluded him, so he set off to Hull far too early and arrived at the Humber Bridge viewing area with plenty of time to spare. He wandered round the car park a few times biting his thumb nail and, as he spotted Robyn's car approaching from a distance, his heart lifted. Robyn opened her door and flung herself into his arms. They kissed before they even spoke.

'It seems like forever,' Robyn said, nuzzling into his neck.

'I know, tell me about it! I've had a hell of a week.' Jay still wasn't inclined to divulge Maria's condition. He knew he would have to own up sooner or later, but he didn't want anything to spoil the time they had together.

'Where do you want to go?' He asked after they finally stopped kissing.

'Over the other side of the bridge where no-one knows me, or there's a small car park up the road. It might be emptier than here,' she gasped. 'We'll take my car, you leave yours here.'

She sped up the road to the smaller parking area and pulled up away from the other two empty cars. Robyn looked to make sure no-one was around as she hoisted up her skirt to reveal a skimpy thong.

'You want to go for it here?' Jay said, unzipping his fly.

'I've wanted you every day since last week. I'm not waiting a second longer,' Robyn whispered.

'Climb on here then!' He offered. Robyn moved across and sat on Jay. He thrust himself deep inside her, fondling her breasts through her silk blouse.

'God! Robyn. I'm ready to come,' he said pulling her toward him for a kiss.

'Just a second!' Robyn moved her right index finger onto her clitoris to climax at the same time. They both groaned as Jay let himself go.

From a distance Robyn spotted a couple walking along the road. She climbed off Jay and returned to her seat, re-arranging her clothing as she sat down.

'Well, that's a first for me,' Jay admitted still breathless.

'Me too, and it won't be the last. It felt amazing.'

'I'm thinking of staying in a hotel tonight, do you think you could get away for a couple of hours later on?' Jay asked.

'I sometimes go to the gym on a Wednesday night, but it would only be for about an hour and a half.'

'Any extra time would be a bonus. If I come into town you could sneak away and we'd have longer together.'

'There's a Premier Inn next door to the gym. You could book in there?' Robyn suggested.

'Do you want me to do that now? We could always go and spend a few hours in my hotel room.'

'It'd be good … but what if I'm seen?'

'I don't know, but isn't it a risk worth taking?' Jay kissed her and stroked her nipple, 'Please.'

'Isn't Maria suspicious that you're staying out?'

'Upset, yes, but I don't think she's suspicious. Anyway I don't care if it all comes out into the open.'

'No, but I do. I've told you right from the start I'm not ready to leave my husband. I've a lot more to lose than you.'

'But this tells me you want me.' Jay sneaked his finger inside Robyn's thong.

She groaned. 'I know I want you, that's not the issue.'

In a few seconds she was on the verge of coming and that made up her mind.

'Okay, let's go to the Premier Inn. You set off first, and I'll follow you in fifteen minutes. Text me the room number.'

Jay booked a double room and was lying on the bed gently stroking himself, ready for a repeat performance. God! She turned him on.

Robyn left her car at the far end of the gym car park, close to the hotel. She had a careful look around to make sure she didn't recognise any cars and made her way to the hotel entrance. Room 19 was on the first floor and Robyn knocked quietly on the room door. Jay jumped off the bed and let her in, standing to attention!

'You didn't waste much time!' she joked, watching him grow before her eyes.

Without speaking, Jay held onto her shoulders and guided her towards an empty wall, hoisting up her skirt and pulling down her thong as he kissed her. He lifted up her leg and found his target. Robyn had only read about multiple orgasms in magazines, but they came thick and fast as he thrust as hard as he could.

'God! You're so wet, Robyn.'

'And you're so hard,' she moaned, digging her fingers into his naked flesh.

She cried out loudly as Jay finally let himself go. Robyn's knees buckled and she staggered across to the bed to sit down.

'What are you doing to me?' she said breathlessly.

Jay followed, forcing Robyn to lie down. 'I'm doing this,' he whispered as he started stroking her again. She moaned.

'Surely, you can't get hard so quickly?' she gasped.

'Just watch me!' He moved her hand on to his growing erection.

'Then it's my turn to be on top,' she said climbing astride Jay. 'Keep going with that finger…that's it, just there. Oh, that's the spot.'

Jay manoeuvred himself inside her and, even though it took slightly longer, he still managed to climax.

'God! Is that the time? I'll have to go,' Robyn said catching a glimpse of Jay's watch. 'I'll be late picking the kids up if I'm not careful.'

'Are you sure?'

'Yes, I'm sure. I don't know where the time's gone.'

'I do.' Jay winked. 'But I'll see you in four hours. Will you have eaten? Or shall we get something in the hotel?' Jay asked as Robyn collected her belongings from the floor.

'I'll have to eat as usual when I get home, otherwise Dave will think it odd.'

'In that case I'll have a take-away before you get here.'

He kissed her again, 'I'll miss you.' He tried to pull Robyn back onto the bed.

'Get off,' she said playfully. 'What are you going to do when I'm gone?'

'My book, I've got some good material from this afternoon,' he joked.

'Is that all I am to you, material for your book?'

'Come here and I'll show you what you are to me.' He grabbed her tightly round the waist and pulled her close.

She eventually pulled away. 'I really am going now.'

Robyn let herself out of the room and looked along the corridor. She walked with her head down, passing two conference rooms. One was empty, but unknown to Robyn the other was filled with Chief Fire Officers on a training day and as it happened they were taking a break... Alex was sure the lady walking past the Gent's toilet as he was coming out was Robyn Fisher. He nearly called out but decided he must be mistaken. Why would Robyn be in a Premier Inn at one o'clock on a Wednesday afternoon?

Chapter 11

June

Jay and Robyn soon became a regular occurrence. They spoke every day on the phone during her lunch time, shared texts later in the day, and tried to meet every week. But instead of the whole affair getting easier, the double life was starting to have a negative effect on Robyn, and she'd started to get an ache in the pit of her stomach when she went too long without physical contact. It was two weeks since she'd seen Jay and her temper was fraying round the edges.

'Will you two stop making so much noise, come and sit down for your tea.'

'Someone's had a bad day at work!' Dave said, winking at Molly.

'Don't you belittle my authority in front of the children.'

'I wasn't. I just think you're being a bit harsh. They were only playing.'

'It's okay for you, coming home from work, your dinner on the table. I work full time as well you know.'

'And whose fault's that? I've suggested you go part-time. The business can afford it. We've just got a new contract in, which is set to be very lucrative.'

'Great, that means I'll see less of you than ever. And don't patronise me, I have a career as well.'

'Which you tell me you hate,' Dave interrupted.

'That's for me to decide, I don't need you to organise my life for me.'

'Can we talk about this later? I don't want to have another argument in front of the children.' Dave noticed Jake had his fingers in his ears and was humming a tune.

'No! I've said all I've got to say on the subject. Here, have your tea. I hope you choke.' Robyn threw the plate down on the table and stormed upstairs into the bedroom.

When did I become such a complete bitch? Dave didn't deserve that.

She lay on her bed crying. All she wanted was to see Jay and feel him inside her.

'What's got into you recently, Robyn?' Dave said as he put his head round the bedroom door. She shrugged her shoulders.

'You've managed to upset both children and ruined perfectly good family time.'

Robyn's anger had dissipated. 'I really don't know,' she said, biting her lip, 'I'm just feeling out of sorts. It's probably work, but before you say anything, I'm not going to be a kept woman.'

'Is that what you think you'd be? I see us as a partnership and if I can help you out at this time, I will.'

'But you're never here as it is. I thought when you took on more staff, it'd free your time to spend with us, but the opposite's happened. You've got busier and busier.'

'I'm not apologising for the success of the company, but I am sorry if you feel neglected. It is for our future, after all.'

But Robyn wondered just what the future held. What she did know, is that she couldn't carry on like this for much longer without having some sort of a breakdown.

She looked at Dave. 'I just feel like being by myself, is that okay? Would you bath the children tonight? I'll come and read them a bed time story.'

'Of course. Don't jump down my throat, but can you not take your frustration with me out on the children. It's not fair.'

'You're right. I'll say I'm sorry.'

Dave closed the door, leaving Robyn to her thoughts. She reached for her phone, if she couldn't talk to Jay, a text would have to do.

"Wot u doing? Missing you. I need to see you soon."

A reply came straight back. "I've got my cock in my hand thinking of you."

"You naughty boy! I thought you were saving that for me!"

"But a man's got needs. When can I feel your hand round my cock?"

"Don't worry, I'll work something out."

"Good girl. I'm just about to come, bye for now xxx."

"Bye, my darling xxx"

While Dave was bathing the children, a thought came to her. Dave's mum was always offering to have Molly and Jake for a weekend. *And there's no time like the present. This weekend would be perfect. I'll say I'm staying at Julie's.* Robyn reached for her laptop,

"Hi Julie, are you free Friday evening? I'd like to come and see you in Leeds. I'm taking advantage of my mother-in-law's kind offer to have the children." She pressed send.

Within five minutes she'd had a reply, "That would be great. Steve will be here but we can go out on our own if you like."

Should Robyn risk writing about Jay? She'd have to – Julie would need an explanation as to why she had to leave early.

"I'm meeting Jay later on in the evening. I know I'm all things wrong but I'll explain when I see you. Shall I come straight to your house for, say, six thirty?"

"Yes that'd be good, I'm intrigued. Look forward to seeing you then. My postcode is LS25 1KL. Number 36."

"Great, see you Friday."

Robyn did a little dance. *Yes! A whole night with Jay!*

She went into the bathroom where Dave was playing *Octonauts* with Molly and Jake.

'I've just had a message from Julie, you know the girl I met on the course. She and Steve have decided to get engaged and they're having a party this Friday night. Would you mind if I went for the weekend? Your mum's always offering to have the children,' she paused. 'Do you think we could ask her?'

'I don't see why not. You look a bit happier anyway.' Dave said the look of relief evident on his face. 'If you get back in time we could go out for a meal on Saturday night. We haven't had a night out on our own for ages.'

'You're sure you don't mind? '

'No, if it cheers you up, you go.'

That was easy.

'Do you want to ring your mum or do you want me to?'

'I will. I haven't spoken to her since last week. I'll ring her while you read a story.'

Robyn couldn't concentrate on *"The Twits"* and kept making mistakes.

'Mummy, it doesn't say that,' Molly said, indignantly. She'd learned her favourite Roald Dahl book by rote and knew every word.

'Well?' Robyn said to Dave, after kissing the children goodnight and closing the bedroom door.

'Yes, no problem. She's offered to have them from Friday afternoon. I said you'd drop them off after school. I might ring Alex up to see if he's allowed out for a drink.'

'Good idea. That way we'll both get a break. I hope Jake won't be upset with me going away again.' Robyn felt a quick pang of guilt when she thought how upset her little boy got whenever she left him.

'I'm sure he'll be fine. Mum spoils them rotten, and she's got Malcolm to help out this time. Apparently he's got five grandchildren of varying ages, from one to eighteen.'

Robyn's guilt didn't last until Dave finished his sentence. All she could think about was telling Jay the good news. She couldn't wait until tomorrow dinnertime and went into the bathroom to text,

"Great news! If you can get away, I can see you from 4.30pm Friday. I'll have to go to Julie's for a bit but we can meet again later. A whole night together, how fantastic is that? So get that hand off your cock! Xxx"

The text came straight back, "It's off! You're a genius I can't wait to reward you. All my love J xxx."

Robyn usually spoke to Jay for half of her allotted lunch hour, but he was in meetings all day today – so she was feeling at a loose end. Sarah, her assistant, was always asking to have lunch together. Today she'd make the suggestion instead.

'I wondered if you wanted to grab a sandwich, Sarah.'

'Yes, that'd be good, here or in town?'

'Its years since I've eaten in the canteen, what's it like?'

'Cheap and cheerful! But you can't make too much of a mess of a tuna mayonnaise sandwich can you?'

'In that case you've sold it to me. Do you want to go now? I'll put the answer phone on. We shouldn't be too long.'

'Are you not ringing your friend today?'

'What … do you mean?' Robyn stammered.

'Hey, it's no biggie. I can't say anything. I never see just one bloke at a time. I get bored too easily.'

How the hell does she know about Jay? It's not exactly tattooed on my forehead.

'You didn't think I knew, did you?'

'Know what? There's nothing to know.'

'Are you serious? Everyone in here's talking about it.'

'Shit!' blurted out Robyn. 'Is it that obvious?'

'Only to those who know you. At exactly twelve thirty every day for the past couple of months you start to fidget and constantly look at your watch. You jump every time the phone rings and when it nears one o'clock, you can be positively rude to anyone who might hold you up for a millisecond. You take your bag, with phone already in hand and go outside. If it's nice you sit on that bench,' Sarah pointed to the bench in the side garden. 'Or if it's raining you sit in the smoker's shelter, which in itself is unusual, for someone who doesn't smoke.'

Robyn flopped down in the nearest chair, listening to this exact rendition of her lunch hour.

'We watch you. You smile and laugh and talk for half an hour. You can almost see the flirting from here! When you come back in, you're a different person. You're more pleasant and laid back and fun. Not that you're never fun other times, but it's different. You're not telling me your husband has that effect on you because I won't believe you. We've thought of having a sweep stake on what your other man looks like.'

'Well, it seems I've been caught red handed.' Robyn started to panic. *Maybe Dave and Denizon do suspect something but just haven't said.*

'Don't worry. I've wanted to say something for a while, but I've never found the chance. Today seemed like the perfect opportunity. Let's go and get that tuna sandwich, you look like you need it.'

Sarah led the way to the canteen and went to order the food. Robyn chose a seat which looked out onto her bench. Maybe the whole building was talking about her.

'I don't think I'm actually hungry,' Robyn said, as Sarah deposited a tuna mayo on brown and a latte in front of her.

'Do you want to tell me your side of the story? It'll save us having to make it up,' Sarah laughed.

Robyn's face was burning. *What have I to say?* Sarah was waiting.

'I'm sort of seeing someone,' she said eventually.

'Sort of?' laughed Sarah.

'Listen,' Robyn said. 'Please don't say anything…'

Sarah leaned across the table.

'I met him at that seminar thing.' Robyn cleared her throat. 'He's just… I have to talk to him every day, it's the only … oh, God.' She buried her face in her hands.

'I bet all the flexitime you suddenly started taking was to see him. I think it's great, it's so romantic.'

'You mean, you don't think I'm the worst whore you've ever met?'

'No, that'd be me, but I'm proud of it. I'm seeing three men at the moment and one of them is married. I only hope it's not your husband … Only joking, his wife is a nurse in paediatrics.'

'Don't you feel ashamed of yourself?' Robyn asked.

'Not really. I'm not the one who's married. I don't lead them on, and I'm not serious with anyone. We go out with each other while we want to and then we move on.'

'You sound as though you've been talking to Jay. He thinks the same.'

'Is that his name?'

'Yes,' Robyn smiled as she thought of him.

'Sounds like my kind of man. When you've finished with him pass him in my direction.'

'I can't imagine not having him in my life, but I also don't want to leave Dave.' Robyn sighed.

'It's so exhausting.' Robyn went quiet for a minute. 'I don't know why I'm telling you this, I've not told anyone before.'

'That's why then. Doesn't it feel good to get it off your chest?"

'I suppose it does a bit … Have you ever been in love?' Robyn added.

'Love … Infatuation. What's the difference? I've been infatuated with a man before, but he broke my heart, so I decided to stay casual for a while and I'm enjoying it.'

'I'm finding it really hard. In fact, the longer it goes on the harder it is,' Robyn admitted.

'It is hard at first, but I've got used to it. Just don't get too involved, that's my motto.' Sarah smiled. 'Have you ever got the wrong name in the heat of the moment? I have, and it wasn't pretty. I had a lot of explaining to do, but you get used to lying, don't you find?'

'That's true. I reckon I've had so much practice I could pass a lie detector test.'

'That's better! Don't look so serious.' Sarah said as Robyn gave her a half hearted smile. 'Have you been hit with the guilt bug yet?'

'Not as much as I thought I'd be. I imagined I'd be racked with guilt. Of course, I don't want Dave to find out.'

'I bet he already suspects.'

'Surely not, I've been so careful.'

'That's exactly what serial killers say just before they leave trace evidence on their last victim.'

'Well, that's a new one! I never thought having an affair could be compared to serial killing.'

'It was just an allergy,' Sarah said.

'I think you mean analogy.' Robyn tried not to laugh. She was seeing a completely new side to her assistant.

'Whatever! You know what I mean. Are you sure he doesn't suspect? You thought no-one at work suspected either.'

'Shut up! You'll have me paranoid. I thought I was handling it so well.'

'You probably are. It's just a tip from someone who's been burned before.'

Robyn found her appetite had returned and tucked heartily into her sandwich. 'I do feel a lot better, thank you, Sarah.'

'No problem. If you need to tell me anything else please do, otherwise I'll ask. I'm the nosiest person in the world.'

'I'm really pleased we've had lunch today; we should've done it sooner.' Robyn smiled.

'Who knows, you might even get invited on the girlie nights out. I feel you're one of us now.'

'What, you have a club for cheats and liars? Count me in. I can be a full member.'

PART 3 – Suspicion

Chapter 12

Whilst driving over to Leeds, Robyn received a text from Julie offering Steve's house as a place for her and Jay to meet. Robyn was surprised, not expecting her friend to approve of extra-marital relations – but then Julie had seen her and Jay together. Maybe she thought she was helping the course of true love. What she was helping was more sex with no noise restrictions. It also gave her and Jay more time together. She sent Jay the postcode and told him to meet her there.

Julie was waiting at Steve's house and gave her friend a key and guided tour. The house was immaculate just as Robyn would have expected from Her Majesty's Tax Inspectorate. Nothing out of place and there was a distinct lack of clothes in the wardrobes.

'It looks like he's already moved in with you,' commented Robyn, when she saw the empty wardrobes.

'He stays at mine most nights. Although I don't know why, his house is much nicer and it's bigger.'

'Why don't you move in here then?'

'I actually think he's a closet scruff; he likes the homely feel of my place, for homely read messy.'

'You could sell them both and have a whole new start.'

'We've talked about it, but its early days yet. We've only been together less than two months.'

'I know, but you said he was the one. Do you still think he is?' Robyn asked.

'Definitely, we're just trying to be sensible.'

'Sod sensible! I spent years doing that, yet look at me now. I'm having the best time and the best sex I've ever had,' Robyn said with a glint in her eye.

'Do you want to tell me all about it or wait 'til later? Me and Steve would like you both to come for a meal this evening.'

'Are you sure? I don't want to put you in an uncomfortable position.'

'You forget I don't know your husband. I've only ever known you and Jay together and I saw the effect he had on you. It was only a matter of time. Do you think you'll leave your husband?'

'Christ, no! I've no intention of getting divorced to be with Jay. He keeps hinting about leaving his partner, but I keep putting him off. I don't want to be responsible for his break-up.'

'You don't think sleeping with him constitutes a good reason to break up then?'

'We're just having fun and lots of sex. I've got two small children; he's not going to want to take them on.'

'Have you asked him?'

'No, we haven't got that far, but I know he never wants to get married, so I take it from that, he doesn't want children.

'But you never know.'

'That's right, you don't and neither do I. We're just enjoying each other for now and not thinking about the future. Well at least I'm not.'

'Okay I get the hint, mind your own business,' Julie shrugged.

'I'm sorry. I can't give you any more answers... Isn't that a car? Robyn looked out of the window and saw Jay's Black Mazda MX-5 pulling into the drive.

'I'll leave you two lovebirds to it. Do you want to come round at eight? Will that give you plenty of time to get reacquainted?' Julie nudged Robyn's arm.

'We'll have been reacquainted a few times before eight o'clock,' Robyn laughed.

Jay was delighted to be invited to eat with Julie and Steve later in the evening.

'It's like we're a real couple,' said Jay, when Julie had left.

'This is like we're a real couple,' she replied, unzipping his trousers. 'It's been so long I can hardly remember what you look or feel like.'

'Here, let me remind you.' Jay pulled Robyn's hand onto his erection.

'Oh yes, it's all coming back to me now.'

'If you give me a minute I'll be coming back to you now.' He grabbed hold of Robyn, pushed her onto the black leather couch, pulling down her thong as he positioned himself on top of her. He thrust himself deep.

'God, I've missed this and I've missed you,' Jay muttered. 'Let's go upstairs. We don't want the postman getting the shock of his life.'

'That was so good,' Robyn said, lounging on the bed after making love a second time. She leaned across and kissed him, 'It's just been too long without seeing each other.' She snuggled onto Jay's chest.

'I know. I'd see you every day if it was up to me.'

'Dave is pushing me to book a holiday. Why don't you go at the same time so we don't have to be apart for two lots of holidays?'

'What, you want me to book the same place? Won't that be risking it?'

Robyn hadn't actually meant that but the more she thought about it, the more the idea appealed to her. 'We wouldn't have to stay in the same hotel; we could just go to the same resort. It'd be fun. We could go jogging in the early morning and find a secluded beach.'

'But we don't jog, and I thought you said you never wanted to be found out.'

'We could start and why would we be found out? No-one would know us. I'd find us somewhere to make love that couldn't be discovered. It'd be so exciting.'

Jay had to admit it would be exciting – but it would mean telling Robyn about Maria. She'd already started to show and by the height of summer her pregnancy would be really prominent.

'Let me think about it, you reckless woman. We'd better start getting ready if we've to be at that meal for eight.'

'Let's have a bath together,' Robyn suggested going into the bathroom.

Jay found it hard to resist anything Robyn suggested. 'God! You make me so horny.'

Dave couldn't remember the last time he'd had the house to himself. He let himself in through the front door and was deafened by the silence. No children saying, "It's my turn" or "Daddy, he's just hit me." Peace! He reached for a cold lager from the fridge and switched on the television, flicking through the channels – utter garbage.

He'd just got time to browse through a few holiday sites before Alex and his fire-fighter mates picked him up at seven. He was gate crashing a works "do" which had been arranged before Dave rang, but he was up for it, despite being a light weight compared to the serious drinkers in the Fire department.

Dave took his second cold lager into the fourth bedroom which doubled up as their office and sat down at the desk.

Maybe if he found a decent holiday, he might get Robyn to agree to booking. The family always had a two week break in August, but it was already June and he hadn't been able to pin Robyn down. It was as if she didn't want to go. In fact, she didn't seem to want to do anything with him recently. Her face couldn't have looked more uninterested when he suggested they go out for a meal tomorrow night.

He opened the computer and saw Robyn was already signed into Facebook. *Just for a change!*

There were twenty six friends listed and he recognised most of the names with a couple of exceptions – Jay and Steve. Recent notifications made for a pretty uninteresting read and it made him realise why he didn't have a personal account. He clicked onto Robyn's photos. A group of work mates at last years' Christmas party, a picture of him and the children on holiday and a beautiful one of Robyn she'd had taken professionally last year. The most recent photo was of a man with blonde hair.

'Who the bloody hell's this?' Dave said out loud as he stared at the man. It could be someone from work but it was a strange photograph to have of a colleague – wearing nothing but trunks. Dave glanced at the clock and realised if he didn't have a shower now he'd be late. He closed the computer down and went to get ready.

At seven fifteen he heard a horn sound outside. He gulped back the dregs of his third lager and felt drunk before he even set foot outside the front door. The first port of call was *Wetherspoons,* where the beer was cheap and potentially full of young girls ready to fall in love with a fireman.

While Dave ordered the drinks, Alex had his arm draped round a girl, young enough to be his daughter. As Dave handed his friend a pint, Alex said slurring a little,

'Dave come and meet Stacey, she's a student, this is my friend Dave.'

'Hi, Stacey,' Dave said.

She giggled, 'Are you a fireman as well?'

'No, nothing as exciting. I run my own Design company.'

'Are you rich?' she asked, detaching herself from Alex's grasp and sidling over to Dave.

'Not a footballer rich, but I get by,' he admitted modestly.

'What car do you drive?'

'A Mercedes. But it's not brand new, more of a classic.' At the mention of Mercedes, Stacey totally ignored Alex and latched onto Dave's arm.

'You're in there mate! Do you want me to leave you to it, you jammy bastard?' Alex whispered to Dave.

'Don't you dare,' Dave said through gritted teeth.

Stacey soon moved on when it was obvious Dave wasn't interested.

'I thought you'd have gone for it there, what with Robyn being away. Where is it she's gone anyway?'

'To Leeds. It's her friend's engagement party.'

'That's what she told you! She could be out in Leeds City Centre picking up young students, a male Stacey.'

'You know we don't have that kind of relationship and neither do you. I don't know why you pretend otherwise.'

'I like to keep my options open, if you know what I mean. I bet Robyn does.' Alex nudged his friend.

'Give it a rest, mate, you're all talk.'

'I didn't mention it before, but I thought I saw Robyn a bit back when I was at a course at the Premier Inn. She walked straight past me. Has she had her hair cut?' Alex asked, suddenly not sounding as drunk.

'Yes, she's had a few inches taken off, it's more of a bob, I think they call it.'

'I don't think she saw me. I meant to ask you at the time but it slipped my mind. At first I thought she was ignoring me, but she had her head down and was hurrying past.'

Dave tried to think what Robyn would be doing at the Premier Inn, but nothing sprang to mind.

'I'll mention it to her if I remember. She'll have been in a world of her own. When did you say it was?' Dave said.

'Oh, I don't know... Wait a minute, yes I do. It was sometime in April. I remember it being a Wednesday as England was playing the same night. But forget I said anything mate, do you want another?' Alex said holding up his empty glass.

Chris had finally plucked up enough courage to go the hospital to deposit a sample. Denizon had been on at him every day since her tests had come back with the all clear. Since being caught by Robyn at the Fireman's Ball, he'd been more careful in his illicit relationships. That said, his colleague was still game for sex whenever he could get away with it. And he'd met an attractive girl at a bar a couple of weeks ago, and they had sex standing up outside the back door of a club.

He felt bad for cheating on Denizon, but not bad enough to curtail his activities. One day no-one else would want him and then he'd settle down, but until that time why deprive himself when he was still in such demand.

Apparently he didn't need an appointment for the clinic; he just needed to turn up. He arrived at the hospital as soon as the department opened. The nurse gave him a jar and a bottle asking him if he could also provide a urine sample, preferably before he ejaculated. He was shown to a room with a video machine and Men's magazines. He smiled as he gave the nurse both samples.

'Please take a seat in the waiting room until we quickly check your samples. The results will be sent to your GP next week.'

The same nurse came back after five minutes, 'Mr Cartwright, the doctor would like a quick word. Would you please follow me? Take a seat in there, the doctor will be with you shortly.'

'Sorry to keep you, Mr. Cartwright,' the young male doctor said as he entered the room.

'I've had a quick look at your sperm sample and it looks like you might have an infection. Have you been having any unusual symptoms?'

'How do you mean?'

'Any discharge from the penis or a burning sensation passing urine?'

'No, nothing.'

'Can I just take a quick look? If you take everything off from the waist down and lie on the couch.'

The doctor pointed out the thick, yellow creamy substance under Chris's foreskin. 'How long have you had this discharge?'

'Ow! Careful.'

'Sorry ... I thought you said you didn't have any unusual symptoms.'

'Oh that,' Chris said dismissively. 'About two weeks I think. I don't pay much attention.'

'It looks to me like you've contracted gonorrhoea, but I'll have to wait for the urine test to confirm it,' the doctor said, removing his surgical gloves.

'No, there must be some mistake.' Chris started to panic.

'Have you had unprotected sex in the last four weeks?'
The doctor asked.

'My wife is off the pill, we're trying for a baby.'

'Have you had any other sexual partners without using protection?'

Chris thought – he'd used a condom with Jen at work, but it had been a spur of the moment thing with that girl … he couldn't even remember her name.

'Yes,' Chris admitted quietly.

'You realise you've got to tell everyone you've had sex with so they can be tested?'

'You've got to be kidding. My wife will kill me.'

'But if you're wife was to conceive it would be dangerous if left untreated … What about your other partners?'

Chris felt embarrassed as he admitted, 'I don't know how to find one of them.' The doctor sighed and added, 'Oh dear.'

'Is there any treatment?' Chris asked.

'Of course, once we've confirmed the diagnosis, you'll be given a strong course of antibiotics and an anti-viral. I'll give you some cream today, but you need to make an appointment with your GP for early next week. The surgery should have the results by then … But I do urge you to tell your wife and try and find your other partners. Reception will give you a leaflet explaining what to do next.… Have you any more questions?'

'Do you know a good divorce lawyer?'

The doctor smiled. 'The nurse will sort out your medication and the results of your sperm sample will be sent to your GP probably a few days after the urine test.'

Chris felt like a pariah as he waited for his medication. Never in his wildest dreams did he expect this to happen to him, despite his chequered past. He needed to talk to someone, but who? He couldn't tell his mother, it was too embarrassing and any mate would just laugh. The only other person was Robyn. He'd probably get another slap across the face, but he had to risk it. This was serious and he needed help. She was always good with advice, but this time he was going to take it.

The meal Julie cooked was delicious, and they all had just as much fun as the Saturday night of the seminar. At the end of a very pleasant evening, Jay shook Steve by the hand, 'Thanks mate, for the use of your house.'

'No problem. Just keep hold of the key. I take it there'll be a next time.'

'Too right.' Jay squeezed Robyn's hand and she smiled.

The hosts stood at the front door and waved as Jay and Robyn walked down the street. Jay put his arm round Robyn's waist.

'What a brilliant couple,' Jay said.

'They do seem happy,' Robyn admitted.

'I wonder if they say the same about us,' Jay asked.

'Probably.' Robyn turned and kissed his cheek.

The evening had gone really well and, even she had to admit, they felt like a couple. Tonight had reaffirmed it in her mind. She couldn't live without Jay and didn't want to even try. They didn't make love again when they got into bed but lay talking until after midnight. When it was time for lights out, Jay snuggled into Robyn, and they fell asleep in each other's arms.

It was nine o'clock before they finally surfaced. Jay loved morning sex and wasn't going anywhere until he'd experienced it with Robyn. He reached over and fondled her nipple until it hardened.

'Morning, gorgeous,' he said as he edged his way over to Robyn's side of the bed.

She lifted up the covers, 'I take it you want to put that to good use?'

'Damn right! Are you up for it?'

'I'm sure I can be persuaded.'

'What time do you have to be off?' he asked, after the long love making session.

'No particular time. I'll go about twelve.'

'So soon. I thought we could spend the day together.'

'I'll go this afternoon then. What do you fancy doing?' Robyn asked.

'How about a walk? We could head up to Ilkley Moor and have lunch at the Cow and Calf.'

'That's a great idea. It's a place I've never been, Robyn said enthusiastically.'

'Okay then, let's get ready and be a couple doing perfectly normal things together.' They both swung their legs out of bed at the same time.

'You think taking a leisurely stroll and having dinner at a pub is a normal occurrence for me on a Saturday? Laughed Robyn. 'By now I've been swimming and I'm on my way to horse riding.'

'I forget our lives are so different,' Jay said as he reached for his trousers. 'I usually read the papers until eleven. Maria cooks a breakfast and then we either go shopping or somewhere for the rest of the day.' Jay felt the knot tighten in his stomach. Once the baby arrived, they wouldn't have this life and it was scaring the shit out of him.

'When do you do the cleaning?'

'I'm ashamed to admit, Maria does it. She works part time and there are only two of us. We don't make much mess.'

'I'd love a cleaner, we have four bedrooms and I have to clean one a night so I can keep up to it. Working full time is a real pain.'

'Why do it then?'

'Why do you think? So I can pay for the swimming and horse riding lessons.' Robyn realised the absurdity of her own answer.

'I could call you mad, but you'd only hit me.'

'I told you my life was very different to yours. Don't you want children then?'

Here it was – the opening he'd been waiting for. Should he tell her? He paused.

'There is actually something I've been meaning to tell you.' Jay looked sheepish and Robyn's heart sank.

'Don't tell me – Maria's pregnant?'

Jay nodded.

'Really? …How far?'

Jay looked down. 'I don't exactly know. She found out the day before you and I met at The Theroux.'

'And you still slept with me? What, were you frightened I wouldn't fuck a man with a pregnant girlfriend?' Robyn said, throwing her side of the duvet across the bed.

'Please don't be like this. I knew how you'd react and that's why I haven't told you before.'

'Don't you dare turn it round so it's my fault. You'd just got her pregnant and you thought, hey ho, I'll just shag someone else because I'm such a spineless coward and can't face up to my responsibilities, is that how it went?'

'No, it didn't. I'd already laid my cards on the table at the weekend. You knew how I felt about you. The news was as much of a shock to me as it is to you now.'

'I doubt that. You must have known there was a chance if you were fucking her.'

'I'm not supposed to make love to her now, is that it?' retorted Jay.

'Not if it means her getting pregnant.'

'I seem to remember you were the one who confessed undying love for your husband and told me we could never be together. Of course I'm going to want sex, because no matter what I feel about you, I'm not ready to sign up to the nearest Convent yet.'

'Monks live in Abbeys not Convents – unless you were planning on a sex change as well.' Robyn gave Jay a weak smile. 'You're not off the hook yet, mister,' she added.

'I know, and I'm sorry. But I was so excited we were going to meet I didn't want anything to spoil it.'

'But it will spoil it. You're having a baby and trust me, everything will change.'

'But I don't want it to … I don't want a baby. I never did and nothing has changed my mind.'

'Maybe if you go with her for a scan and see the life you've created, you'll feel differently.'

Robyn thought back to when she and Dave had seen Molly moving for the first time. It was overwhelming, and she doubted even the hardest heart would fail to melt at such a sight.

'It's such a mess.' Jay banged his fist against the wall. 'Don't you think I feel like a bastard cheating on a pregnant woman? But I don't love her. I love you.'

'You love me?'

'Of course I bloody do. Isn't it obvious?'

'I …I've not thought about it.'

'I've wanted to tell you for ages. I think I've loved you from the first kiss.'

Robyn sat at the foot of the bed with her head in her hands.

'Say something, Robyn, please.'

'Maybe we shouldn't see each other for a while and see if you change your mind.' Sheer panic ripped through Robyn's body as she realised the implication of what she'd just spoken out loud.

'No, I'm begging you, please don't finish it. I promise I'll work something out. I've never felt like this before. I need you, Robyn.'

'On my last inspection, magic wands didn't really work, and that would be the only way of working this thing out.'

'I've hated myself for this, but I keep praying she has a miscarriage.'

'You can't be serious!'

'Probably not… I don't know.'

' … I think I'd better go home.'

Jay held on tightly to her hands, 'Please don't go! We've had such a fantastic time. And I do love you, Robyn.'

She stood quite still, her stomach churning, 'I know you think you love me, Jay. But it's probably because of the sex. And I haven't told you, because I'm not sure I do.'

Still holding her hands, Jay looked gutted as she continued, 'Don't get me wrong, I feel intensely towards you … When you just told me about Maria it pierced my heart … But it's not real life. I have two children and you've just told me you never want children.'

'But...' Jay interrupted.

'Let me finish. Molly and Jake are mine and Dave's, they'll never be yours. Half the mum's at school are single parents and the dads see their children possibly twice a week. I don't want that for my family.'

'But you can't love Dave that much if you're having an affair with me.'

'That's not true. It's not about Dave; it's about me. Before I met you, I'd never even looked at another man … But … I can't explain my attraction to you as anything other than physical,' she sighed. 'You turn me on more than anyone has ever done. I love the sex, but it's as if it's not me… It's like I get taken over by someone else when I'm with you, and I leave that persona behind when I leave.'

'Please spare me the psychoanalysis. It's my job remember,' he said scathingly, letting go of her hands at last.

'I'm only trying to explain how I feel!' she responded, stepping back from him. 'What I'm trying to say is, you're an escape route from my regular life.'

'Thanks for that. I'm glad I serve some purpose, even if it's just to relieve the boredom.'

Robyn looked aghast. 'I didn't mean it that way… Oh shit! I'm obviously not explaining myself very well.'

'Damn right, you're not!' he said, furious now. 'In two short sentences you've debased the totality of our relationship.'

'I didn't mean to. I've loved these past couple of months. You make me feel alive.'

'What, until you go back home and get on with real life?'

'Yes. Harsh as it sounds, that's the reality. Do you know since April we've spent a total of forty eight hours together? The rest has been anticipation and excitement at the thought of seeing you again.'

'In that case it might be the best thing to finish now like you said. I don't want to put you to any more trouble. You can go back to your horse riding and swimming and whatever else constitutes real life but you've got it all wrong, you know. I think what we have *is* real and the rest is playing at life. Do you think we came to earth to have swimming lessons, and run around after our children?'

Robyn shrugged.

'Well I don't. I believe we came here to find love and happiness, and I think that's what we give each other. But I bow to your greater wisdom. After all you have *got* children, which somehow makes your argument stronger than mine.'

Robyn was speechless. She'd never seen this side of Jay.

'Have I silenced the all-knowing Robyn Fisher?' Jay felt smug until he saw the tears welling up in Robyn's eyes.

'I'm going to pack my things and go home before we say anything else we regret,' Robyn said. She threw the rest of her clothes in the holdall, collected her shower bag and hurried downstairs.

Jay ran to the top of the stairs, 'Robyn, please let's not leave it like this. I'm sorry.'

Robyn turned to look at him. 'But what you said is probably right … I just need some time to think. How about I ring you on Monday as usual?'

'Can I at least have a kiss?' Jay came down the stairs.

Robyn stopped and gave him a quick kiss on the lips.

'I'm sorry it's ended like this today,' he said, as he let her go.

'So am I,' she replied quietly as she closed the door behind her.

Chapter 13

Robyn arrived back to the outskirts of Hull far earlier than she intended on Saturday morning. She spent most of the journey wiping away tears from her eyes. How could she have been so stupid to think it could end happily? Someone was bound to get hurt, and at this moment, it was her. The same sentence kept replaying over and over in her head, Jay was having a baby. She didn't want to care, but she did – desperately.

She had until Monday lunchtime to decide what to do. As she saw it, there were two choices either put the baby news behind her and carry on the affair until Jay fell in love with his family again, or finish it now before she got more deeply involved. She'd never understood the phrase, "between a rock and a hard place," but now understood only too well.

Home and Dave wasn't an option yet, so she decided to park in the Humber Bridge facility. Maybe looking at such a huge feat of engineering would put her trivial dilemma into perspective. Getting out of the car, she walked to the viewing area. All that was going through her mind was the last time she'd been here with Jay. The tears started to flow again.

She was so tempted to text him and ask he forget the earlier conversation, but that wouldn't solve anything. She really did need to think long and hard before making a decision.

Her phone rang. She quickly got it out of her bag hoping it was Jay, but it was only her brother, Chris.

'Where are you? I've been ringing your house all day yesterday and today,' he said urgently.

'Hello, darling brother. I'm fine, thanks for asking. I've been to Leeds to an engagement party. Didn't you get hold of Dave?'

'No, he wasn't in either.'

'What is it you want?'

'That's nice! Do I have to want something to speak to my sister?'

'Usually, yes.'

'Do you think you could spare me half an hour? There's something I need to run by you.'

'Yes, I'll come round now.' It was just what she needed to take her mind off her own problems.

'No, not here, can we meet somewhere? Where are you now?'

'I'm at the Humber Bridge car park.'

'What on earth are you doing there?'

'It's such a lovely day I wanted to stop and admire the view.'

'You're so weird.'

'Thanks a lot!'

'There's a transport cafe called the "Red Hut" near there. Do you know it?'

'Yes.'

'I'll see you there in twenty minutes.'

'Okay, in that case you can buy me a full English. I didn't have any breakfast before I set off.'

Robyn wondered what was so urgent to make her brother travel at a moment's notice. She looked in the rear view mirror and wiped her eyes. The puffiness and swelling had started to subside and hopefully by the time she arrived at her destination, she'd look relatively normal.

Chris pulled up shortly after Robyn and his hand was visibly shaking as he pressed the remote control to lock his car. Nothing usually phased the controlled, laid back Chris. *It must be serious*, Robyn thought when she saw his pallor. The "Red Hut Transport Cafe" was quiet on a Saturday morning, and Chris ordered two English breakfasts and mugs of strong Yorkshire tea.

'What on earth is the matter? You look awful,' asked Robyn.

'I've gone and done something really stupid,' Chris said quietly.

Robyn would usually come up with a quip but, looking at Chris's expression, she didn't feel it appropriate.

'I went to the hospital yesterday for my test.'

'How did it go?' Robyn asked cheerily.

'I'm trying to tell you. The doctor examined me and he thought I'd got gonorrhoea. The surgery confirmed it an hour ago.'

'Shit! Shit! Shit! You idiot!' Robyn put her head in her hands.

'Thanks for that constructive advice, Sis. I need to know what to do.'

'Wear a condom, for a start. Where have you got that from? Is it from that woman I saw you with at the ball?'

'I don't think so. I always wore a condom with her.'

'Then who? Because I'm pretty sure it couldn't have been Denizon!'

Chris looked sheepish and finally said, 'I met a girl at a club when I was out with my mates a couple of weeks ago. One thing led to another, and I found myself out the back giving her one against a wheelie bin.'

'And they say romance is dead!' she scoffed. 'Have you told Denizon?'

'What do you think?' Chris snorted. 'That's why I've been ringing you. I haven't told anyone.'

'Not even the girl?'

'I don't know her name or anything about her.'

'Oh Chris, you're such a dickhead. You know it's going to destroy Denizon. She'll forgive a lot, but I think this'll stretch even her tolerance to the limit.'

'I know. I was thinking about not telling her and waiting to see if she gets any symptoms.'

'That's a really responsible attitude. Are you sane?' enquired Robyn.

'If I tell her we'll be over.' Chris looked utterly dejected.

'I'm sorry to have to say it, but it serves you right. I've been warning you for years that nothing good would come from your messing around.'

Chris wasn't getting the sympathy and advice he was looking for, so he thought he'd try a different approach,

'Don't come the high and mighty with me, "Miss Self-righteous". Alex mentioned he'd seen you walking with your head down looking cagey in the Premier Inn a bit back. What were you doing there on a Wednesday afternoon? Have you taken a job as a part time chamber maid or something?'

'What …what are you talking about?' Robyn tried to hide her shock. 'Anyway, this is about you.'

'Yes, but we all make mistakes. Alex thought you were up to something, but I defended you and said you'd never cheat on Dave, but tell me what you were doing.'

'I don't have to listen to this. You wanted my help and now you're accusing me of having an affair.'

'Am I?'

Chris took her silence as admittance of guilt. 'So you *were* messing about? … Now what have you got to say?'

'I haven't given my husband gonorrhoea.'

'I didn't think I'd given it to my wife, but these things happen. We're obviously tarred with the same brush, you and me.'

'I'm nothing like you. I just did it the once, you've made it into a full time hobby.'

'Does Dave know?'

'Of course not, and you'd better not say anything.'

'I don't like to use the word blackmail because you're my sister, but you won't say anything to Denizon until I've decided what to do, will you?'

'Is that why you wanted to see me? To get me to agree to keep your sordid secret?'

'No, it wasn't, but I'm using your silent confession to my advantage. You can't blame me for trying.'

'I can blame you for lots of things, most of all, upsetting and ruining the life of my best friend. I've finished with you Chris! From today I only have one brother. You can rot in Hell for all I care. I won't say anything to Denizon, not because I'm frightened you'll tell Dave, but because I couldn't bear to see her face if I did.' She got up and started towards the door, shaking with anger.

'Robyn, come back. You haven't eaten your breakfast.'

Walking past a cold unfinished plate, she picked up a greasy fried egg and turning round, slipped it down the back of Chris's shirt. As he felt the slimy food slide against his skin, he knew he'd pushed Robyn too far. All he was looking for was advice, and now she would probably never speak to him again. He tried to dislodge the soggy egg, reflecting what a balls up he'd made of his life.

Dave screwed up both his eyes.

'Robyn, what's with all the banging?'

'I'm not banging.'

'I think you are,' he said holding onto his head.

'God, you look rough!' Robyn said coming into the bedroom.

'You've some room to talk, your eyes look as red as mine.'

'I think mine's lack of sleep,' she said unpacking her holdall. 'Did you have a good time?'

'I'm not cut out for a night on the tiles. All I've got to show for it is a lighter wallet and a sore head ... You're home earlier than you said. Was your party good?'

'I know, there wasn't much going on so I thought I'd come home and get this holiday booked.' *Maybe a holiday to look forward to would help.*

By lunchtime they'd decided on Cyprus, at an all inclusive resort with plenty of activities for them all. It had three pools, so Robyn could take her pick which one to lie beside each day. Half an hour later it was all booked.

'Thank goodness.' Dave said, as he keyed in the number of his credit card to pay the balance.

'Do you realise it's only eight weeks until we go?' He said, relieved to have finally got it sorted.

'I know, it'll fly by,' Robyn sighed.

'You didn't answer my question, was the party good? How's the happy couple?'

'It was nice. They seem very much in love.'

'When's the big day then?'

'Oh, not for a couple of years. I think they want to buy a house together first.'

'That's sweet …So, what do you want to do with the rest of the day?' He winked, 'We could take advantage of having no children around.'

Sex was the farthest thing from Robyn's mind, but if it was good, it might make her decision easier.

'Move over then,' she said unzipping her trousers.

'You'll have to be on top, my head is killing me,' he said, pulling back the duvet.

Chapter 14

The rest of Saturday turned into a 'duvet day,' with Robyn and Dave only getting out of bed to eat a snack at lunchtime. Unlike her time in bed with Jay, she spent most of it asleep – exhaustion of the past few weeks finally catching up with her. Dave seized the rare opportunity to read one of the autobiographies he'd been bought last Christmas. They did make love before Robyn fell asleep, but all she could see was Jay's face, closing her eyes and wishing it was him inside her. When she finally roused it was getting toward tea time.

'Where do you want to eat tonight, I'd better book a table somewhere?' Dave asked a sleepy Robyn.

'How about La Scala?' she yawned. 'We haven't been there for ages.'

'Good idea. Is seven o'clock too early?'

'No, I'll get up now and have a bath. I can't believe I've slept for so long.'

'You must've needed it. It's probably all the extra gym sessions, they've worn you out.'

'It must be something. I haven't felt as tired as that in a long time.' Robyn welcomed sleep. It was the only time she could put Jay out of her mind.

'It's all booked for seven,' he said as he ran back upstairs.

'Well, I'd better get a move on.' Robyn pulled back the duvet and dragged herself out of the warm, comfortable bed.

Dave looked uncomfortable, 'Can I ask you something?'

'Er … yes.'

'If we could go back in time, would you marry me again?'

'What kind of a question is that?' she said.

'Well, would you?'

'Of course I would. Whatever made you ask that?'

'I don't know. Sometimes you look at me as though you really despise me, like I'm an intruder almost.'

'Don't be ridiculous.' Robyn was horrified.

'So you still love me?'

Robyn had never seen him like this. He'd always been emotional in a masculine way. But this was entirely different. He seemed insecure and vulnerable.

Still reeling from the shock of Dave's last statements, she said softly, 'Yes, I still love you. I've never stopped loving you, and I'm sorry if I give you that impression.'

'That's alright then,' he said, giving her a quick hug. 'Because you know I still love you.'

'I didn't doubt it for a second,' she said, smiling.

Where on earth has this come from? Does he suspect something?

She'd been with Jay for two months without discovery – but maybe it was time to put an end to it before Dave did find out. She leant across and kissed him.

'Come here and I'll show you how much.' Robyn climbed back under the covers pulling Dave with her.

The food at La Scala was as good as they remembered. They had three courses of wonderful gastronomic cuisine and shared a bottle of crisp Chardonnay. It was only nine o'clock when Dave was paying the bill.

He said, 'Do you want to call at the Fox and Grapes for a drink with Alex and Sue? We might as well as we're passing.'

'I don't really like that pub, it's too noisy.' Robyn had no desire to see Alex after hearing what Chris had said earlier.

'We don't have to stay for long. We haven't been out with them for ages.'

Robyn couldn't really think of another excuse without seeming awkward. 'Just one drink then, it's supposed to be our night.'

The Fox and Grapes was as busy and noisy as Robyn said, so hopefully it would be too noisy to indulge in much conversation. Karaoke was due to start at nine thirty and Alex liked to get up and sing any Oasis song, believing he sounded like Noel Gallagher. Sadly, it was only Alex himself who thought so.

'What a surprise.' Alex said, standing up to shake Dave's hand and kiss Robyn's cheek.

'Can I get everyone a drink?' Dave asked.

'I'll have a glass of wine,' said Robyn, as Dave had volunteered to drive home.

'We'll have our usual,' Alex said and went to help Dave at the bar.

'Come and sit here,' Sue patted the seat next to her. 'I haven't seen you for a while. What have you been up to?'

'Oh, you know this and that. I've been busy at work and going to the gym a lot, trying to lose some weight.'

'You lose some weight? You're already like a stick,' Sue mocked.

'No, I'm not … but I do put weight on if I don't exercise.'

'I keep meaning to join a gym, but I hate exercise.' Sue had been on a permanent diet since being at school.

'Well, I don't love it,' conceded Robyn, 'but it has to be done.'

At that moment the men returned with the drinks. Alex sat opposite Robyn and Dave slid in next to Sue.

'What has to be done?' asked Alex.

'Exercise, Sue said she doesn't enjoy it, and I was just saying I don't love it but it has to be done.' She picked up her drink, contriving not to look directly at Alex.

'That explains why Sue's the size of a house and Robyn has the figure of a page three girl,' Alex said, looking at his wife as he spoke.

'That's really mean, Alex,' said Robyn, shocked at Alex's cruel words.

'Take no notice,' Sue said, half laughing, 'I don't. He's always telling me I'm fat.' Sue seemed totally unaffected by her husband's cutting remark.

'Well, he shouldn't say that!' Robyn said, defending her friend.

'Ah, but we all do things we shouldn't now and then, don't we?' Alex said looking directly into Robyn's eyes this time.

She gulped but quickly responded, 'Yes, I suppose we do, but being mean to your wife shouldn't be one of them.' Her voice had a challenging ring as she looked right back at Alex.

'Let's change the subject,' Dave said diplomatically. He had witnessed arguments between Alex and Robyn before, and it wasn't a pretty sight. The gloves came off and no punches were spared.

Robyn could feel Alex's glare was in danger of burning a hole in her skin.

'What have you been doing at work?' he asked her suddenly.

She dropped her gaze, 'Er, the usual. Interviewing and stuff. It's as boring as ever. Why do you ask?'

'I just wondered if you'd been on any courses recently. I'm always being sent on courses,' he added, 'it's the downside of management, don't you find?'

Robyn knew exactly where this conversation was heading and she was prepared. 'Yes, since that seminar in April I've been out and about a few times. Bill, my boss, is always sending me on errands. We've got an award ceremony coming up and I've had to check out a few hotels for a suitable venue.' *That's a good one, beat that, mate!*

Alex looked disappointed. But she could tell he didn't believe her.

Robyn couldn't drink her wine quickly enough and suggested to Dave they get an early night. It could mean a repeat performance of sex, but anything was better than being subjected to the third degree by her, so called friend Alex.

'Didn't you think Alex was acting a bit strange tonight?' Dave queried as he drove them home.

'Yes, I'll say! He's so horrible to Sue. I don't know why she puts up with him.'

'I think it's just the way they are.'

'Well I'm glad you're not like him.' Robyn made a mental note to stay well clear of Alex in the future. He was a loose cannon and secrets were definitely not safe with him.

Dave's mum brought the children back on Sunday morning. They decided to have a family day and Robyn realised, as she put the children to bed, she'd hardly thought about Jay at all. When she couldn't see him or hear his voice she could easily be persuaded to call the whole thing off. But all that changed when she rang him as promised on Monday, during her lunch time as usual. As soon as he said, 'Hello, gorgeous!' she could feel herself melting at the sound of his voice.

'Hi, did you have good weekend?' she asked politely.

'Hello! It's me you're talking to! And no, as a matter of fact I didn't. I've been desperate to speak to you. You don't realise how close I came to sending you an e-mail.'

'I'm glad you didn't. A friend of the family spotted me at the Premier Inn when I was on my way to your room. He tried to drop me in it on Saturday night.'

'What did you say?'

'Not much, but I think enough to head him off at the pass.'

'Good ... Well, come on then, put me out of my misery. Have you made any decisions?' Jay asked.

'Sort of ... I don't want to stop seeing you, but I do think we should go back to seeing each other for a few hours in the daytime. I can't risk another night away.'

'Thank God for that! I've been imagining all sorts of scenarios and none of them great. We've got too much going for us to throw it all away. I've made a decision as well. I'm going to move out, regardless as to whether you're in my life or not. I might be many things, but a hypocrite I'm not. When you're not happy you should move on. Maria knew that when we got together.'

'But you've only just bought that flat. Isn't it a bit soon to quit? And she's pregnant.'

Jay was quiet.

'What do you think she'll say?'

'She'll hate me, and I'll no doubt get a beating from either her father or brother. But I've made my decision. If I don't answer my phone one day, it's because I've become the latest target for the mafia.'

'Don't joke about stuff like that … But I do think you're rushing into it.'

'Trust me, I'm not. Anyway, I don't want to talk about it now, when can we see each other again?'

'I think we should leave it for a bit?' Robyn said, thinking back to Dave's emotional outburst.

'I suppose so,' he said sounding disappointed. 'I could come over to you.'

'I don't think that's a good idea. We've still got the key to Steve's house. I'll come over to Leeds next Friday. How's that?'

'I suppose it'll have to do.'

The conversation wasn't as loving as usual, but Robyn was relieved as she put the phone back in her handbag. They weren't going to finish, she would still get to see his gorgeous body and feel his hardness inside her again.

Even though they hadn't seen each other, the daily phone calls resumed and Robyn had been trying to persuade Jay not to leave Maria, but thus far she hadn't been very successful and wondered what else she could say to change his mind. She admitted it was for purely selfish reasons. She didn't want him to put any more pressure on her to leave her family.

Then she had an idea. She knew how much Jay liked talking to Max Hammond and had come to see the older man as a bit of a mentor. Maybe Max could have a word with Jay. She didn't have a phone number, just the e-mail address that he'd given out at the seminar. She clicked on "compose" and typed,

"Hi Max, I hope you remember me, Robyn Fisher. We won your prize for the most original connection (we still haven't used it!). I could do with your help. I don't really want to e-mail with the gory details, suffice it to say, it's regarding me and Jay. If you could spare a few minutes out of your busy schedule, I'd be ever in your debt. My telephone number is 07620 233455. Look forward to hearing from you."

She typed in the address, pressed send and minimised the internet window, before returning to her previous task, yet another risk assessment. What did Human Resources do before the advent of the risk assessment? An hour later she saw she had one unread message. It was from Max,

"Hello Robyn, it's lovely to hear from you. Of course I can spare the time for a chat. I've always got time for my ex-students especially two as intriguing as you and Jay. I take it you don't want me to ring you in the evening because I'd have to be stupid not to guess what it's about. We can speak at five o'clock this evening if that's convenient? Send me a yes or a no."

Robyn replied with "Yes." At five o'clock she was sitting in her car, waiting for the phone to ring.

'Hello, Robyn. Max here,' he said as Robyn answered. 'How are you?'

'To be honest, I'm struggling.'

'Fire away and I'll see if I can help.'

'I feel really embarrassed talking about it… Er … I've been seeing Jay since the seminar in April. Because of the distance, we don't see each other very often. He's been here a few times and we've met in Leeds. We actually spent last Friday night together.'

'As yet I don't see a problem.' Max said.

'But I'm married and you believe in monogamy.'

'Didn't you listen to anything I said that weekend? I believe in monogamy with the right person. Maybe Jay *is* the right person. Have you thought of that?'

'Of course I have. But I think I still love my husband. Dave's a lovely man and doesn't deserve what I'm doing to him. Max, the thing is, Jay's partner is pregnant and he's going to leave.'

'So? Oh!… Let me guess, you want me to have a word with him.'

'Yes, please,' Robyn let out a sigh of relief. He did understand.

'No, I can't do that,' Max said.

'What? …What do you mean no?'

'Exactly what I said. It's neither my, nor your concern what Jay does. Do you think anyone can persuade another against their will in this kind of situation? I would've thought even you'd learned that by now.'

'But I don't want him to leave. It puts too much pressure on me.'

'Oh, *you* don't want him to leave … that's different of course! And I thought Jay was responsible for himself,' he added sarcastically.

'I know it doesn't sound like it, but I do have his best interests at heart.'

Max was unmoved. 'Have you heard how you sound?' he said, making Robyn feel extremely uncomfortable. 'What Jay does, is absolutely nothing to do with you and the sooner you realise that the better.'

'But he's in a relationship with *me*. Surely I have some say?'

'The only person you're responsible for is yourself and your *own* feelings. Jay will do as he pleases whether you like it or not. I admire the man. He has the courage of his convictions and, from what I know of him, I'm sure he didn't take a decision lightly.'

Robyn was quiet.

'Did you read chapter 7 of my book?' Max asked.

'I read it all.' Robyn felt like she'd just had a telling off from the headmaster at school.

'Then I suggest you go back and read it again. It repeats what I've just said but in more depth.'

'Then you won't help me?' Robyn pleaded.

'I think I already have.'

'But I don't know what to do.' She was close to tears by now and hoped there were no nosey passers-by.

'And there's the crux of it! …You think by trying to sort Jay out you won't have to look at your own situation. You have some decisions to make yourself, Robyn. I've known some affairs go on for years but most are short lived because it's too stressful to live with the fear of discovery for any length of time. I know you'll find this hard to believe but most people secretly wish they *could* be found out. It brings matters to a head and couples can move forward, either separate or stay together. Do I take it Jay doesn't know you've contacted me?'

'You take it correctly. I'm sorry if I've put you on the spot.' She sighed and added, 'But you're right as usual.'

'I really wish you luck, Robyn,' he said quietly, 'and believe me, I know what you're going through. But remember; only you can go through it. We can talk again if you like, but leave Jay out of it. *If* he needs to, he'll contact me.'

Robyn saw little point in extending the call and said, 'Thanks so much for listening anyway, Max. I appreciate how busy you are.'

'That's no problem. If I have any advice, it's spend some time on your own without either man and decide what you really want and what's best for you.' As Max rang off, Robyn realised that though he'd been hard on her, he was only trying to help.

Chapter 15

The end of July

Denizon didn't dare hope. Her period was four days late, and she was always exactly to the day. She'd already purchased three home pregnancy testing kits and was deciding which one to use first. No doubt she would try all three. She wanted to ring Robyn and tell her the news, but the atmosphere had been a bit icy recently between the two families and neither her husband nor her best friend wanted to talk about it. They had apparently fallen out, with Robyn disowning Chris. As if that would last, Denizon thought, but Robyn did seem determined to stick to her guns this time.

She hadn't pushed because she really didn't want to know. It was bound to be something to do with her, and ignorance was bliss, especially at this nail biting time. If she was pregnant it was probably because she'd stopped worrying about it. They always said that once you stop worrying, nature can take over and hopefully for her, it had. Chris had been to the hospital and the GP said his results were normal, so full steam ahead.

Without forcing the issue, she suggested they make love at the most optimum time in her cycle. Chris was game and they made love on five consecutive nights just to make sure. It was now the moment of truth and she'd just drunk two pints of water to have enough pee for three sticks.

She unwrapped the first kit with a conception indicator, which as well as giving a positive or negative result, indicated how far you were along. Well here goes!

The three minutes wait was interminable. She had her eyes closed while her kitchen timer ticked away the seconds. Then, opening her eyes, she picked up the stick. It read "Pregnant, 3-4" She started to do a little dance.

'I'm pregnant, I'm pregnant. It's finally happened,' she chanted along with the dance.

She went to look at herself in the full length mirror, turning sideways to see if there was the smallest hint of a bump. A completely flat stomach looked back at her. *Well, it's only early days*, she thought.

Was one test enough she wondered? It was supposed to be ninety nine percent accurate... Yes, she would trust it for now.

Chris was due home at half past two, after his early shift finished. It was going to be so hard to keep it to herself until then. She looked at her watch. Time to go into the studio, her art always took her mind off things, and she did have a deadline to get next year's calendar finished and to the printers.

July was a busy time at work and Robyn was preparing adverts, job descriptions and application forms for the new batch of school leavers applying for positions to commence in September. Bill, her boss, had surprised her last month by offering her a three day management course in London. It was this coming weekend, and she would be returning home the day before the family flew to Cyprus next Tuesday. But she'd jumped at the chance and wasted no time in telling Jay, so he could book the time off and create a conference for himself.

Robyn wasn't going into the office today, but working from home to prepare for the course at the weekend. She intended to spend time packing for the family holiday and then driving down the M62 to see Jay for a couple of hours in Leeds. She was up earlier than usual and at seven thirty, was reading through the course content. There was some preparation to do and a short essay to complete, but nothing too taxing. By ten o'clock she'd broken the back of the work and was ready for a break.

She hadn't seen her parents much recently. Not since the row with Chris. She'd never let a grudge last so long, and it was slowly gnawing at her conscience. Backing down wasn't an option because what he'd done was intolerable. Blackmailing her was bad enough, but what he was doing to Denizon was unforgivable. Maybe she ought to discuss it with her mother – she'd probably take Chris's side but she did make nice cakes!

'Not working today, love?' Doreen switched on the kettle and then cut two large pieces of homemade Victoria sponge, oozing with butter icing and jam.

'Not today,' said Robyn, biting into her cake. 'I'm on a course at the weekend so I'm working from home and packing for the holidays.'

'You said you wanted a chat,' said her mother. 'I'm hoping it's about Chris. I know you've had your differences in the past but you've always resolved them. It's never gone on as long as this. You know I don't like to interfere, you're both adults, but I really think you're acting like children. Chris has given me his side of the story. I was just waiting for yours. Coffee or tea?'

'Tea please…What has Chris said then?'

'He said he went to you for help about a delicate matter and you laid into him, calling him names and throwing food at his new shirt.'

Robyn burst out laughing. 'And you believe that's all there is to it?'

'Probably not. I know you think I'm always on his side, but I do see him for what he is. He's the oldest in years, but Tiggs has a far more grown up head on him at twenty-three than Chris will ever have. That's why I'd like to hear your version.'

'What does Dad say about it all?' Robyn could never understand how her father managed to stay clear of family dramas.

'Not much, as usual. He may come out with a pearl of wisdom now and then, but he hasn't commented this time. He *has* asked why you haven't been round recently. He's in the greenhouse, go and say hello before you go.'

'I can't really tell you what Chris and I talked about because it'd be breaking his confidence. He's done something really stupid though and I think he's putting Denizon at risk.'

'Have you seen Denizon recently?

'Not for a couple of weeks, why? Is she okay?'

'Between you and me, I think she's pregnant.'

'She can't be! She'd have said something to me. Does it show, then?'

Doreen shook her head. 'I could be wrong, it's just a feeling. They came up on Saturday for their tea and she looked different. Her hair seemed more greasy than usual and her ankles looked a bit puffy. They left after an hour as she couldn't stay awake.'

'Poor Denizon, I hope she's not coming down with a virus. I spoke to her on Sunday and she never said anything. I suppose she'll tell me when she's good and ready.' Robyn felt slightly anxious in case these symptoms were the gonorrhoea manifesting itself; she made a mental note to check them on the net.

'If she doesn't tell me soon I'll have to ask her outright.'

'Some people don't like to tell everybody until it's confirmed, in case they tempt fate,' Doreen said.

'But I'm not everybody, I'm her closest friend.' Robyn sighed. She'd been so wrapped up in her own stuff she hadn't bothered much with anyone else. She knew it was all because of Jay – she'd tried to keep her two lives separate but it came with a cost.

'So are you and your brother going to make up?' asked Doreen, her voice sharp. 'I think he's waiting for an apology for your ruining his shirt. He showed me; the grease mark won't come out and it was an expensive designer label, petrol or something, he said.'

Robyn grinned, 'I think you mean "Diesel" Mum.'

'That's it, that's the one.'

'The shirt is the least of his worries. I really think you need to ask him exactly why I laid into him and threw a fried egg down his back. Trust me, he deserved it.'

Her mother snorted. 'That's just childish. Is it to do with other women?' We've talked about that before and you know my view. It's none of our business.'

'It is if he gives his wife an illness...' Robyn stopped short. 'Sorry, I've said more than I intended. Whatever he's done I'll still keep my word. If he wants to tell you he will.

Do you want me to take dad a drink and a piece of this yummy cake?'

She grabbed a slice of sponge and a cup of tea, put them on a tray and headed out of the kitchen door. At the bottom of the garden, her father was sweltering inside the greenhouse, examining his courgettes. He straightened up and stretched as he turned to greet her.

'Hi, Dad!' She set the tray down on a handy shelf. 'Thought you could do with a break. I can't stop long though. Bit of a flying visit, just popped in to see you and Mum.'

'You're always dashing somewhere, Robyn! You'll get to the end of your life and realise you've missed it.'

Robyn smiled. This was one of the "pearls of wisdom" Mum mentioned earlier.

'But I'm always so busy.'

'In my experience, people who're always busy tend to be running away from something they don't want to face.'

'Have you been reading the amateur psychology magazine again, Dad?' Robyn laughed.

'Look here.' Peter pointed down. 'These little plants get to exactly where they want to be at just the right time, but do you ever see them rushing? In fact the slower they grow the better. We're just the same. Nothing worthwhile was ever accomplished by rushing.'

'Here, eat your cake, its lovely.' She knew she couldn't reason with him when he was in this mood.

'Robyn, I've known you for thirty-three years, and I know when you're hiding something. You were like it as a tot and the same as a teenager. When you'd done something you shouldn't, you'd dash around from one thing to the next, keeping busy so you didn't have to feel guilty. Do you remember when you broke the next-door neighbour's best gnome? You came in and cleaned the house, including your messy bedroom; you did your homework on time and took the dog out. All so you didn't have to own up. I take it you haven't broke anyone's gnome this time? Your Mother thinks it's because of our Chris, but I don't. I think you've got another man.'

'Dad, what are you saying?'

'You know jolly well what I'm saying. Don't forget you're talking to a past master. Mum told me she confessed all.' He paused and looked at Robyn, 'You're not so clever now are you, young lady?'

Robyn swallowed hard, 'What makes you think I'm seeing someone else?'

'People think I'm not interested in what goes on, but I see everything from a distance. I've noticed the way you've been acting in front of Dave, fawning over him, being extra attentive so he wouldn't get suspicious. I used to do the same with your mother.'

'But Dave's never accused me of anything.'

'And why would he? He loves you and while there's nothing definite, he can ignore it.'

'Have you said anything to Mum?'

'You've got to be kidding. She can't even hold her own water! And I know how much she thinks of Dave. I take it from your lack of denial, it's true.'

Robyn sighed. There was no point in lying. Her Dad knew her too well.

'Yes, it's true and I'm not proud of myself. I love Dave, and I hate to think he may be suffering in silence.'

'You can't hate it that much, otherwise you'd put a stop to it,' her father said sharply.

'It's not as easy as that, Dad … I've thought about ending it so many times, but I can't seem to find the strength. We're so good together.'

'I know exactly how you feel,' said Peter, 'and believe me, there's no easy way to say this, but you *have* to finish it now.'

'How did you do it?'

'In the end I made a list of what I wanted in my life and, it was a close thing, but you're mother won. I know making a list sounds cold-blooded now, but I was in love with two women.'

'But you already had me and Chris.'

'Well, you've got Molly and Jake – but do you think about them when you're in the throes of passion? I can remember the intense excitement I felt every time I saw my lover like it was only yesterday. It's like a drug habit – very hard to break.'

Robyn nodded. 'You're right. I keep hoping I'll go off him and not find him attractive anymore. But it hasn't happened yet and now I think I might be in love with him.' She sighed. 'How long did your affair last?'

'Two years. And I was in love with her too. We talked about leaving our families and nearly did. She worked with me at the school so I saw her every day. We had a week's holiday together when I told your Mum we were on a school trip.'

'Father, you're incorrigible.'

'Oh! Believe me. I was an awful lot worse than that.'

'But you're happy now aren't you?'

'I am… Well, if I'm honest, it's more contentment than actual happiness, but do I regret the decision I made? Sometimes. I often wondered what my life would've been like had I taken the other route. I still see her round town occasionally. I keep hoping she'll put on ten stone and lose her teeth but she hasn't,' Peter joked. 'She's still an attractive woman.'

'Does Mum know her?'

'They met a few times when it all came out, but obviously never became bosom buddies. They say hello if they meet in town. She lost her husband last year, and I was tempted to send my condolences, but thought better of it. It took me years to get over her; why open up old wounds when they've well and truly healed?'

Suddenly, Peter looked sad and pensive and Robyn wondered if the wounds were as healed as he said. She went to hug him. 'I can't believe we've had this conversation, Dad. You're such a dark horse,' she added.

'As are you, Robyn. I thought only Chris was a chip off the old block, but it appears I was wrong. I hate to think of you suffering as much as I did. I wouldn't wish that feeling on anyone. Just be careful and make a decision before one is made for you.'

'I will Dad, I promise.' She kissed his cheek, picked up the tea-tray and left him to tend to his vegetables.

Chapter 16

Jay was impressed with how his book was going. He'd already written thirty thousand words and was awaiting a decision from the publisher. Every time he sat down to write, inspiration flowed through his fingertips. He'd already finished Parts One and Two and was well underway with "Part Three: Suspicion."

He was using the experience of his clients, as well as emotions he was currently experiencing. It was going to be an invaluable guide to anyone in his position because, as much as he was enjoying his affair with Robyn, it wasn't easy being deceitful.

He hadn't changed his mind about leaving Maria and was waiting for the right moment to tell her. But when he'd attempted to have a conversation about his needs being very different than hers, she didn't want to talk about anything but the baby. On her insistence, he'd accompanied her to the scan. Whereas she was so excited and tried to spot an arm, all Jay could see was an amorphous blob that moved. He certainly couldn't see the heart or the sex of the child. Maria was convinced it was a girl and had decided on Felicity Cordelia as her name.

Jay knew leaving Maria while she was pregnant was unimaginable in some people's eyes, but he would do right by them both. He'd already decided to sign the flat over to her and would provide adequately for his offspring.

He'd only another hour to wait before setting off to see Robyn at their second home in Garforth. It did feel like going home, and they'd made themselves very comfortable in Steve's house. Robyn had cooked a few meals and also left a change of clothing in the double wardrobe. All in all, it made Jay feel like they were living together. He hoped it was having the same effect on Robyn and slowly permeating her psyche.

What wasn't working at the moment was his relationship with his assistant. In the past she'd always been so supportive, but recently a dramatic change was apparent.

She was sullen, snappy and increasingly interested in where he was going. Now she wanted to know where, for how long and what time he'd be back. There was also an annoying habit of ringing his mobile every hour as if checking up on him.

In addition, Simone had become very pally with Maria, which was worrying in itself. Apparently, they'd been to lunch a couple of times and Simone was always dropping Maria's name into the conversation, much to Jay's annoyance. Some days were so bad he thought about sacking her, but despite the problems, she still did an excellent job.

As a result of Simone's extra interest in his life, Jay had to be a lot more inventive in his lies. He had created a fellow Psychologist at the University who was collaborating with him on his book. The fictitious man had written something similar and was a great fount of knowledge. Jay and Mr. Dalton got together on a regular basis for coffee and to share ideas.

Simone knocked on Jay's door, 'Your twelve o'clock appointment is here, shall I show them in?'

'What appointment?' he snapped. 'I haven't booked anyone in. I've already told you I'm meeting Mr. Dalton at one o'clock.'

'Oh, I'm sorry I forgot. The lady sounded so desperate this morning I thought you wouldn't mind. It won't matter if you're a bit late, surely? He'll understand, being in the same line.'

Jay was furious. 'Come in and close the door, Simone,' he said, glaring at her. 'How dare you take it upon yourself to arrange my diary without permission? I shouldn't have to remind you that I'm the boss, although you seem to have forgotten that recently.'

'I'm sorry, I just thought…'

'That's just it, you didn't think. Now it's too late to cancel.'

'Do you want me to ring your colleague and tell him you'll be late?' Simone offered.

'No, thank you. You've done enough damage for today. Why don't you take an early lunch or something?'

Simone looked as if she was going to burst into tears.

'It's a Mr. and Mrs. Hobbs,' she said, her voice shaking. 'Here's their profile.' She handed Jay the sheet of A4 paper used to introduce clients.

Jay realised he'd been a bit harsh.

'I'm sorry I spoke to you in that way, Simone, but you know I hate being late. In future, please run anything by me before you book last minute appointments.'

'I'm sorry, Jay,' she said, looking happier. 'So – Mr. and Mrs. Hobbs. Shall I send them in?'

'Give me a few minutes. I need to make a couple of calls. I'll come and get them when I'm ready.'

He wouldn't get to Garforth until at least half past one. Only half an hour late, but every minute spent with Robyn was precious and worth more than an hour spent with anyone else. He suspected Simone might listen in on her extension or eavesdrop at his door. So using his mobile and a loud voice he pretended to speak with his colleague, explaining he'd been delayed.

Ringing Robyn from his office was just too risky so he sent a quick text.

"Sorry, going to be a bit late 1.30, don't start without me! Love you x."

After a shortened session, he made a further appointment with Mr. and Mrs. Hobbs for the following week. He sincerely hoped there were no speed cameras in place today as he headed down the road at eighty miles per hour.

Simone was standing at the window with the mobile phone in her hand as she watched Jay's car pull out of the car park, 'He's set off.'

Denizon was waiting patiently for Chris. His shift finished at two thirty and it was a twenty minute drive door to door, so he should be home for three. It got to four o'clock and he still wasn't home. The pregnancy kit was on

the table and she'd bought a quarter bottle of champagne to
celebrate. She tried his mobile, but it went straight to
voicemail. Maybe there was a last minute emergency and
he'd been called away. Denizon had learnt not to check up
on her husband, but she was so desperate to tell him the
news she phoned the fire station's number.

'Hello, could I speak to Chris Cartwright, please.'

'Could I ask who's calling?'

'It's his wife.' Denizon was put on hold and listened to
Re-light my Fire by Take That.

'I'm sorry; he's not been in today.'

'Are you sure? There must be some mistake; he was on
a 6.30-2.30pm shift.'

'Er – he swapped with a colleague,' said the speaker.

'I see. Thank you.' Denizon slammed the phone back in
its cradle.

How stupid could she be? She'd kept hoping and
praying he'd change, but obviously not. A leopard couldn't
change its spots. He was such an accomplished liar, and
even she hadn't been suspicious recently, not since the
incident with the phone in the work boot. Why hadn't she
listened to Robyn? All these years she'd waited to get
pregnant and, now it looked like she was, she might end up
being a single parent. But she was bursting to tell someone
her news, Robyn would want to know; she was certain of
that. She rang Robyn's number. Blast! What was it about
today? Why were all phones going to voicemail?

'Hi, Robyn. Ring me when you've a minute, got some
news, bye.'

Denizon felt totally deflated. It was at times like this she
missed her own mother. She was only thirteen when her
mother died of breast cancer. Her dad did his best for a few
months, but he was so wracked with grief, he deposited
Denizon with a great aunt and drove the wrong way down
the M1, killing himself and the other driver instantly. Aunt
Maud looked after her young charge as best she could, but
she was already sixty five when she took Denizon on, and
her own failing health meant that Denizon spent most of
her time at her best friend's parents, Mr. and Mrs.

Cartwright. She loved them as if they were her own, and of course they did in fact become her in-laws, but Chris was their son and they owed him their loyalty above hers.

It was five o'clock before Chris finally walked into the house and, with each passing minute, Denizon's patience was disintegrating as her hurt and anger grew.

'Sorry I'm late,' Chris said breezily. 'There was an emergency shout just as my shift finished; a car had driven into the Humber. We had divers and everything.'

'Oh I'm sorry to hear that,' Denizon said, outwardly calm. 'Was the driver killed?' She looked directly at him. 'But I suppose it'll be in the local paper on Friday. I can read about it then.'

'Are you alright, Den? You seem a bit edgy?'

'Do I? I wonder why that could be.'

'I don't know. Are you going to share it with me or what?'

'Where did you say you've been again, the Humber? Did you go in your own car? Because you certainly didn't go in the fire engine,' she said, keeping her voice level.

'What are you talking about?'

'I rang the station today and guess what? You weren't there.'

'Oh, so you're checking up on me now?' he answered.

'And it's a good job I did! Where have you been? And the real truth, please, not the truth according to Chris.'

'Den, I can explain.'

'Go on then. I'm listening.'

Chris shifted from one foot to the other awkwardly.

Denizon sighed, her face set with unhappiness. 'You've always been crap at lying, Chris. I never really believed you before. I just didn't want to face facts.' She shrugged and sat down at the kitchen table.

'It – it was her who chased me!' Chris protested. 'She's been after me for months and she wore me down. What could I do? I'm just a weak man, after all.'

'And you think that's a defence?' Denizon mocked. 'I don't think a divorce lawyer would agree.'

'What! Come on Den, you don't mean it. You'll calm down tomorrow – it was only a one off. It didn't mean anything.' As he went to put his arm round her, Chris spotted the Clearblue test on the table. 'What's that?'

'That's the reason I was ringing you.' She pushed him away and stood up. 'I'm leaving you now, Chris. Don't try and follow me. It's over.'

Denizon picked up the bag she'd already packed and walked out of her house.

There was only one place to go and she headed straight for Robyn's. She felt almost shocked that she wasn't crying and in pieces without Chris. She stood on the doorstep and rang the bell.

Dave opened the door, 'Hello, Denizon. Lovely to see you, come in.'

'Is Robyn around?

'She's not back from work yet? Can I help at all?'

'I've left Chris.'

'Oh my God! What's happened?' Dave said looking at Denizon's pale face. 'Go and sit down. I'll make a coffee. Then you can tell me all about it – only if you want to,' he added, seeing her expression.

Over their hot drinks, Denizon gave Dave a potted history of the story to date, leaving out the pregnancy.

'Do you think that's why Robyn's fallen out with Chris then? Maybe she found out.' Dave queried.

'I – don't know,' said Denizon slowly. 'We haven't talked about it. I haven't seen much of her recently.'

'Hmm – you and me both. She's always so busy at work.'

'Where are the children? It seems awfully quiet.' Denizon had expected to see her god-children running round the house.

'Still at the childminders. I thought Robyn would be home by now.'

'Well, don't make the mistake of ringing her at work, that's how this all started.'

'What do you mean?'

'Sorry, I didn't mean anything. I'm just a bitter and twisted soon-to be-divorced mum-to-be.'

'Are you pregnant?' Dave said picking up on the slip.

'I found out today. That's why I was ringing Chris, not because I wanted to check up on him. I wanted to tell someone and now you happen to be the first person I've told.'

'Haven't you even told Robyn?'

'I rang but it went straight to voice mail. Do you think I could stay, just until I sort myself out? I've nowhere else to go?'

'Of course. Stay as long as you like, Robyn is away on a management course this weekend and we go to Cyprus on Tuesday. You'll have the house to yourself.'

'I don't intend to stay that long. I'm going to see a solicitor tomorrow. I want my house back. It's where I work. Surely I've got a good case? My husband *has* cheated on his pregnant wife.'

'I don't know why anyone would want to cheat,' Dave said heavily. 'Why can't they just have the balls to leave if they're not happy?'

'You're asking the wrong person. I've never cheated on anyone.'

'Me neither…Er … Do you think Robyn has?'

'The only time I know about is when we were nineteen. She didn't actually cheat, but she did sleep with my boyfriend.'

'She's never told me that before,' Dave paused before continuing, 'Can I ask you something? Do you recognise the names Steve or Jay?' Dave asked.

'Isn't Steve the name of Julie's fiancé in Leeds? You know the couple who've just got engaged.'

'Oh yes, that's right.' He just hadn't made the connection.

'Why do you ask?' Denizon asked, unsure where this was going.

'Don't say anything, but I looked on her Facebook page and those two names were ones I didn't recognise.'

Denizon tutted, 'That's how it all starts, Dave. Believe me.'

'I know, I came away from her page after that – well, after I looked at the photograph of this other guy called Jay.'

'There's a picture of him?' Denizon was surprised.

'Yes and the bastard's too good looking for my liking.' He laughed.

'Robyn has mentioned Jay a few times to me. I think she said he's Julie's buddy she met at the seminar in April.'

'She's never told me about him, that's all.'

'Maybe it's because you don't know them. She didn't want you to feel left out.' Denizon felt she had to defend Robyn. She just hoped her friend was worth defending.

Chapter 17

Jay was driving so fast, Maria could hardly keep up. His sporty Mazda left her Ford Focus standing when it came to moving off at traffic lights. But luckily for her, the traffic was busy so he couldn't speed away. She made sure she stayed at least two cars behind.

It was soon apparent Jay wasn't going to the University as he headed out of town towards the M1. Maria didn't know this particular area of Leeds. Jay signalled from the main road into a housing estate and took a left turn, followed by a right, pulling up outside a well-kept semi-detached house. She pulled up a couple of cars behind his. Jay got out of his car, locked the door and ran up the drive, hammering on the front door. It only took a matter of seconds before the door flung open and a tall, slim auburn haired woman threw herself into Jay's arms. Their kiss seemed to go forever.

She sat staring as Jay followed the woman into the house.

'Oh my God!' Maria said as she buried her head in her hands. Maria hadn't known what she was going to find when she made the decision to follow Jay, but she hadn't expected this. The embrace and kiss hadn't been between casual acquaintances, for sure. It was from lovers who couldn't bear to be apart.

She hated to admit it, but it looked as though her father was probably right about Jay. He'd never trusted the blonde English man with long hair and thought his only daughter would be much better off marrying a fellow countryman – a young butcher named Luigi, the son of his best friend back in Naples. But Maria was adamant it was Jay she wanted. Had she made a big mistake?

She picked up her phone and punched in a number.

'I've found him,' she sobbed. 'You were right' she sniffed. 'He hasn't g …gone to an office near the University. I think we're in Garforth. Oh Simone, he kissed her. Why would he do that to me?'

'I don't know, love. I'm so sorry,' Simone said.

'What should I do now?'

'Well, let's be practical. If it was me, I'd get more proof. Call on the neighbours and see who lives at that house and what their situation is. I certainly wouldn't stay there. You'll only get depressed. Come back here and we'll go for tea somewhere.'

'Okay. I'll try and pull myself together. See you in a bit.' Maria wiped away the tears and removed the black trails of mascara from under her eyes.

As discreetly as she could manage, Maria looked through the downstairs windows of the house for any movement. The front room was empty, but looking upstairs she saw the woman close the curtains. Quickly she turned away. No need to see any more.

She knocked at the adjoining semi and a young woman holding a tiny baby answered the door.

'Hello!' Maria said as brightly as she could. 'I'm sorry to bother you but I'm looking for the man next door.'

'Oh, he'll be at work,' said the young mother, rocking her baby. 'He doesn't get home until about six, if he comes home at all. He mainly lives with his girlfriend down the street.'

'I've just knocked on the door thinking I saw movement but no-one answered,' Maria said.

'Oh, they won't answer the door; they'll be at it all day now.'

'Sorry?'

'The couple. They're friends of Steve's. They use the house for you-know-what. They're a bit late today.'

'You mean they've been here before?'

'Yes, regularly. Nearly every week. They're a lovely couple actually. They always speak, but between you and me, I think they're married to other people.'

Maria caught her breath and leaned against the door.

'Would you like a coffee or something?' the girl offered looking at Maria's pale face.

'No thanks… I'll be okay. I must be getting back.'

The woman smiled. 'If you're sure. I'll tell Steve you called, who shall I say?'

'It's not important, I'll catch up with him later … Sorry, could I ask your name?'

'I'm Cheryl and this is Zachary.'

Maria hadn't paid much attention to the new born infant before now.

'What a lovely name, and he's very handsome.' She stroked the baby's tiny hand. 'I'm four months pregnant,' she said as a wave of nausea swept over her. *What will I do about the baby?* she wondered in sudden panic.

'That's great! Your first is it?'

Maria nodded.

'Are you sure you're okay? Let me get you a glass of water,' Cheryl offered.

'That's kind. I am feeling a bit faint.'

Cheryl returned with a full glass. 'Drink this. I got really bad sickness. It lasted all day.'

Maria took a few deep breaths and sipped the water.

'That's better, thank you. I'm sorry to put you to so much trouble.'

'No problem, we have to stick together.'

Maria took a few more sips and handed the glass back to Cheryl.

'I really must be going; thanks again.'

'Anytime. If you're passing, call in again. I'm always here.'

Maria smiled. *That's never going to happen*, she thought. She took one last look up at the window next door and walked back to her car.

Why is this happening to me, she thought as the tears started to flow again. She loved Jay so much. It had been a dream come true when they bought their beautiful two bedroom flat in the new Brewery Wharf complex last year and the magic had just continued – she was pregnant with his child. So what had gone so horribly wrong?

She knew Jay wasn't as happy about the pregnancy as she was, but it was all part of her plan to get him to marry her. Maybe she had been a bit self-centred and neglected his feelings… Yes, it must be that. This woman was only a fling. They could be happy again; she'd see to it.

Robyn intended to be on the road by four at the latest, but Jay was insatiable today.

'I've really got to go now; otherwise I'll hit all the traffic. You'll see me again on Friday night.' Robyn slithered her way from under Jay's armpit.

'I know, but it's getting harder to leave as the weeks go by. I want to squeeze in as much of you as I can before you leave me on Tuesday.'

'Why don't you see if you can book a last minute deal? It doesn't have to be the same complex. Anywhere in Paphos would be good. We wouldn't be able to see each other very often, but I'm sure we could sneak away for a couple of sessions.'

'Did you ever start jogging?' Jay asked.

'I've been a few times, but I used to jog regularly when we first met, so Dave wouldn't think it strange if I wanted to jog on holiday.'

'I'd have to clear my diary.'

'How hard would that be? Just come for a week, please,' she said running her finger across his chest.

'I'd also have to bring Maria. Even I couldn't get away with spending a week in Cyprus on the pretext of interviewing clients.'

Robyn got a pen and a piece of notepaper from her handbag, 'Here, I've written down where we're staying. We fly Tuesday 2nd August to the 16th. Go on the Internet and see if there are any last minute deals. Anything's better than two weeks apart.'

Jay took the paper and thought. 'It's really tempting …I'll let you know on Friday. What time am I seeing you?'

'The course finishes at 4.30. I'll ring you when I've finished.'

'I'll come and wave you off.' Jay stood at the bottom of the stairs in his boxer shorts.

'I love you,' he said as Robyn opened the door.

'I love you too,' she replied.

Jay held on to the handrail in total shock.

Robyn didn't intend to tell Jay she loved him – It just slipped out. She'd admitted to herself that she loved him weeks ago but planned to keep it to herself. The conversation she'd had with her father this morning had thrown up another complication. What if everyone suspected she was having an affair? *Shit! Why can't I keep my big mouth shut?*

The traffic was horrendous as soon as she pulled out onto the main road. It was five o'clock and she hadn't even got onto the motorway. The local radio station reported that an accident on the slip road coupled with extensive road works meant a tail back that was going to take an hour to clear. That would make her late collecting the children.

She couldn't phone home, where could she say she was?

'Shit!' She shouted as she banged her hand on the steering wheel.

She used her hands free kit to ring her childminder, 'I'm sorry Pauline. I'm stuck in traffic and might be a bit late. Would you mind keeping them a bit longer? I'll pay you for your time.'

'Don't worry about that. They're just having tea and watching television. You get here when you can.'

It was six thirty when Robyn finally collected the children. It had taken her the whole journey to come up with a plausible story, but she decided to tell Dave the traffic was really heavy coming back from Bill's house. It was a spur of the minute thing to drive over to see him, but she wanted his opinion on the work she'd done today, just to make sure she was on the right lines before the course at the weekend. He lived in the opposite direction to Leeds, but Dave needn't know that. It should be foolproof as Dave and Bill never saw each other. The children would hopefully detract from too many questions. She sent Molly and Jake in first to put Dave in a good mood.

'Only me, sorry we're late,' she shouted from the kitchen.

'Mummy, Auntie Den is here,' Molly shouted back.

'Hello, what are you doing here?' Robyn asked her friend who was sitting in the armchair watching television.

'She's waiting for you,' answered Dave sharply.

'I've been to Bill's and the traffic was horrendous on the Hessle Road.'

'Then why go at this time?'

'Less of the questions please, we've got a visitor.'

'No, we haven't, we've got a house guest,' Dave corrected her.

'I've left him, Rob,' Denizon said sadly.

Molly was trying to attract Denizon's attention by pulling at her sleeve.

Robyn sank onto the settee, 'Auntie Den will play with you in a minute, can you please go get into your pyjamas,' she said to Molly.

'But Mummy…'

'No but's, you can come down again. I just need to talk to Auntie Den for a few minutes. Help Jake won't you?' She dismissed both children upstairs and returned to Denizon.

'So, what's happened?' Robyn asked.

'I rang Chris at work and he wasn't there. He swapped shifts, but told me he was still going to work. He finally came home at five with an elaborate cock-and-bull story about how he saved a motorist who'd driven into the Humber. I don't know how he thought of that one.'

Robyn felt a stab of guilt as strong as if it'd been made with a knife. How could she criticise her brother when she was doing just the same?

'Did he try and explain?'

'I didn't give him the chance. He more or less admitted he was seeing someone and blamed the fact that he was a man on not being able to resist.'

'I don't know what to say.' All Robyn could think about was her situation. If Dave found out, he would do exactly the same as Denizon and leave as quickly as he could.

'That's unusual! You're not usually reticent about giving an opinion on your brother's philandering,' Denizon said.

'Do you think you can work it out?' Robyn asked, resisting the urge to look at Dave who was keeping out of the conversation, as Denizon added abruptly,

'I thought you'd be happy I've left him.'

'No, I'm not. It's sad when anybody splits up.'

'It's even sadder when the woman is pregnant.'

Robyn froze. *Had Denizon somehow found out about Maria?*

'Don't look so shocked, Robyn. You know we've been trying.'

'You mean *you're* pregnant?' Robyn let out a huge sigh of relief.

'Yes, who did you think I meant?'

'No-one, I'm just surprised that's all.'

'Aren't you going to congratulate me?' Denizon smiled. 'At least something wonderful happened.' She shot a puzzled look at Robyn, who said hastily,

'Erm… yes, of course. It's great news. Any more surprises while we're at it?'

'No, that's it for one day.'

'Oh, come here you,' Robyn went to hug her friend. 'I'm really pleased for you, love. What did Chris say?' She knew how much her brother wanted children.

'I didn't give him chance. I showed him the pregnancy test and walked out of the house.'

All the time Robyn and Denizon were talking, Dave was observing his wife. He hardly recognized the woman in front of him. She looked strange, vacant even, like the lights were on but no-body was at home. Even the tone of her voice sounded different. There'd been a few more nagging doubts creeping into his mind of late, but he tried to bury them deep and get on with family life. It wasn't working anymore, and he was feeling increasingly uneasy. Her behaviour tonight only compounded his thoughts. Robyn had never been to Bill's house before regarding work. If anything, she avoided taking work home at all costs. Why would she set off anywhere in the rush hour? He hated himself for thinking it, but he believed she was lying. But why lie about something like that?

There was one obvious explanation – she was seeing somebody else. The words hit him hard in the stomach and he felt himself retching.

'Excuse me. I'll just go check on the children.' Dave ran upstairs and threw himself onto their bed. Where had he gone wrong? Was it because he was working too hard? Or hadn't he been showing Robyn enough attention? He couldn't think of another valid reason why Robyn would do this to him. They were going on holiday next week – should he confront her before or after? If he chose before and she decided to leave, the children would be distraught. For Christ's sake! The children would be distraught anyway.

In the past he'd thought about what he'd do faced with such a situation, and it involved being a rational, forgiving adult. Fuck that! He wanted to kill the pair of them. What a sodding mess!

Chapter 18

Three days had passed since Robyn had come home late and Dave felt he may have over-reacted. Robyn's behaviour could be perfectly innocent. He certainly didn't want to go rocking the boat and accuse her of being unfaithful on a hunch and, at the moment, she was the epitome of a perfect wife. She was attentive, loving, and horny – all indications that he'd got it wrong and there was some other reason for her strange behaviour. Maybe the upset with Chris was affecting her more than she cared to admit.

Robyn was travelling down to London today for the Management course. She was telling the truth about that as he'd seen the paper work and hotel reservation. He'd booked today off work to have the children and both sets of grandparents were helping at the weekend.

The cases were already packed for Tuesday, as Robyn wouldn't be back until late Monday night and they were flying from Robin Hood Airport at nine o'clock Tuesday morning. A holiday was just what they needed to get their marriage back on track. He would make it as special as he could. The children were booked into the "Koala Club" during the day, giving him and Robyn plenty of quality time together.

'I seem to be away a lot at the moment,' Robyn said as she brought her small case down stairs, 'I wish you were coming with me.'

That's exactly what Dave wanted to hear. He would forgive her anything as long as she still wanted him.

'I wish I was too, but you'll be too busy learning to do nothing and getting paid a lot of money for doing it.'

'How do you know so much about the NHS?' she laughed.

Robyn had seen the look on Dave's face when she came home late the other night and had done everything in her power to make him feel secure since then.

'I do love you, you know,' she said as she went to give him a hug and kiss goodbye.

'And I love you. I'm sorry if I don't always show it, but I never stop feeling it.' Dave hugged her close.

'I'll ring you every night, and I'll see you for our holiday. I'm so much more excited about that, than this silly course.'

'Are you sure you don't want a lift to the station?'

'No, I'll be fine, go see to the children. I've already given them a kiss.'

As Robyn waited on the platform, she was hit with a real sense of déjà vu. Only four months had passed since she last caught a train and met Jay for the first time, and now she was on her way to spend the longest time she'd ever spent with him. Wasn't life strange?

Jay was pacing up and down the hotel room floor in anticipation of Robyn returning. He couldn't wait to tell her about his day. He'd queued for Saturday evening tickets for *Wicked*, the show he knew she really wanted to see. Then he booked a pre-theatre meal at The Theroux hotel. Although Robyn didn't want to stay at The Theroux, their voucher covered them for an evening meal and the management was more than happy for them to take it tonight.

Robyn probably hadn't brought a dress suitable for such a grand hotel, so he took one of her dresses from the wardrobe, and went in search of a designer boutique. The assistant in *Opulence* was delighted to show him some of her exclusive designs. They finally opted for a gold and black dress in stretchy fabric with a large cowl-neck and plunging back. Just jewellery to choose and the perfect outfit for a perfect evening would be complete.

Jay was just perusing the engagement rings in an up-market jeweller when the assistant asked him to describe what he was looking for. But sanity prevailed, and he chose a gold half hoop eternity ring and a diamond bracelet. Later, as he laid out all his purchases on the bed, he hoped Robyn would appreciate the gesture and not think he'd taken leave of his senses. He loved her so much and just wanted to spoil her.

Robyn walked into the room at four thirty after a day practicing interviewing techniques. She stopped short when she saw the bed.

'What's all this?' she asked, looking at the dress and the tickets strategically placed on top.

'It's your surprise,' Jay said beaming.

'You've bought me a dress,' Robyn said, taken aback. 'How did you know my size?'

'I took your black one to the shop with me. Do you like it?'

'It's amazing, but what's the occasion?'

'Our first trip to London and celebrating three whole nights together.'

Robyn picked up the tickets and saw they were for *Wicked,* tonight at seven thirty.

'Wow! You managed to get some. I assumed it'd be fully booked.'

'I had to queue.' Jay knew it was worth it just to see Robyn's face.

She walked across to kiss him. 'Thank you so much, no-one ever buys me gifts. It's such a surprise. I suppose you want me to try this lovely garment on?'

'After the bath I've run you.' Jay said, opening the en suite door to reveal a bubble filled bathtub.

'You're certainly spoiling me tonight.'

'I just want you to know how much I love you.'

'You don't have to buy me gifts to prove you love me.' She kissed him again.

'But it's nice to spoil you occasionally. I'm afraid you'll have to get a move on though. We've a table booked at six fifteen at The Theroux and the taxi will be here at six.'

'The Theroux! Have you won the lottery or something?'

'No, we're using the meal part of the voucher.'

'What a great idea… Well, I'd better get in that bath then, care to join me?' She started to undress.

'I thought you'd never ask.'

The bathroom looked like a war zone by the time they finished making love in the bath and then on the floor on top of the fluffy towels. Water had splashed the mirrors, the toilet and was soaking the mats.

'We're going to be late if we don't get dressed soon.' Robyn walked out of the bathroom and carefully picked up her new dress. The stretchy fabric felt perfect to the touch. She slithered it over her head and asked Jay to zip it up. It could have been made for her.

'Well?' she said, doing a twirl.

Jay was speechless for a moment. Then he laughed and said, 'Magnificent… Now to finish it off.' He walked over to the drawer where he'd hidden the jewellery boxes.

'Close your eyes,' he said as he took the bracelet out of the box and fastened it round her wrist.

'You can open them now.'

'Oh Jay!' Robyn was almost speechless herself. 'It's absolutely beautiful, but you shouldn't have.' Jay put his finger to her lips.

'Ssh! You're worth it and finally…' He handed her the ring box.

'What's this?' Robyn started to panic, hoping it wasn't what she thought. That would be taking things a bit far.

'A token of my eternal love. I know you can't wear it all the time, but I hope you'll wear it when we're together.'

Robyn stared at the eighteen carat gold band inlaid with four square diamonds. It made her actual engagement ring look like a gift from a Christmas cracker.

'It must have cost you a fortune. I can't accept this, Jay.'

'Yes you can! The thing is – do you like it?'

'I love it,' she said. 'It's the most beautiful ring I've ever seen.'

'Try it on then,' he encouraged.

For a few seconds, Robyn was unsure which finger to put it on. Then she slipped off her engagement ring, putting it on the dresser, and placed the diamond eternity ring over her plain gold wedding band. She held out her hand for Jay to admire.

'You can practice being Mrs. Jay Trethedick tonight.'

Robyn gulped. *Mrs. Trethedick? How had that even become an option?* Nothing had ever been discussed about such future plans. She'd promised her Dad she would try and end it, but how, when Jay was so obviously besotted with her?

'Hello! Did you hear what I said?' Jay was impatient for her response. 'You seem miles away! Aren't you happy?'

'Of course, I'm just a bit overwhelmed that's all,' said Robyn, touching his cheek lightly. 'I've never been showered with such gifts before. It takes a bit of getting used to for a simple girl like me.'

'There's nothing simple about you, my love. I just want you to know you're the most precious thing to me, and one day I'd love to marry you.'

There it was again, the talk of marriage. Robyn hadn't even considered leaving her present husband, never mind marrying a second. 'I thought you didn't believe in marriage?'

'For you, I'd change my mind.'

As much as she loved Jay, this was all getting a bit too much. She'd always maintained she wasn't ready to leave Dave and didn't think she ever would be. She still loved him and despite the marriage sometimes being monotonous and his long working hours, Dave was still a good husband. Maybe she should take a leaf out of her father's book and make a list. But where to start!

On Sunday morning during a boring lecture on the Management role in accountancy, she tore off a sheet of A4 paper and divided it down the middle, heading one column "Dave", the other "Jay". What criteria should she use in comparing her run-of-the-mill husband with such prominent shows of affection from a second man who loved her so deeply? On Dave's side she put the children, the house, mutual friends, friendship, routine, security. She thought about putting "sex" but decided against it and wrote it in capital letters on Jay's side, then added excitement, fun nights out, long talks, gifts.

This isn't helping! She sighed as she examined the beautiful ring on her wedding finger. It *looked* fantastic but, somehow, it just didn't feel right. Dave had taken an extra bar job just to supplement his meagre salary, so he could buy her small solitaire engagement ring. He'd been so proud when he got down on bended knee to propose in *Salvatori's*. Jay's ring was much bigger and bolder, but bigger isn't always best, she decided and slipped the ring off her finger into her purse.

She looked at Jay's side of the paper. If they didn't have sex – what did they have? Robyn let the thought wash over her as she listened to a man drone on about spread sheets in a monotonous voice. *God, what am I doing here?*

So, by her dad's reckoning, Dave won hands down apart from the sex, but was she ready to give that up? She thought back to her multiple orgasms last night. No, she'd play the game a bit longer! She'd got away with it thus far, why rock the boat? She opened her purse and put the stunning ring back on her finger. She couldn't throw Jay's adoration back in his face just yet.

This list is a bad idea! She scrunched up the piece of paper and dropped it into her handbag.

PART 4 – Discovery

Chapter 19

August

The Oasis Springs was a four-star luxury resort with every facility a family of four could need. Every day was scorching hot and most of the time was spent playing in the pool or lazing beside. It was the third day of their holiday and Jay was arriving tomorrow. Robyn was on edge and wished she had a magic wand to make a week pass in a flash. She was torn between yearning to see him and regretting the decision to invite him at all.

Dave was being extra affectionate and attentive. Usually on holiday, he was restless moving between one activity and another, but so far he'd spent every minute by her side – fetching drinks from the all inclusive bar and on hand to rub suntan lotion on her slowly tanning body. They played cards, read at the same time and messed about in the pool while the children were at the Koala club. Sex was always more frequent on holiday, when the pressure of work was off, but this holiday Dave couldn't get enough of her and more often than not, in the afternoon they found themselves in bed.

'Are you having a good time? You seem more relaxed,' Dave asked, on Robyn's return to their room after dropping Molly and Jake off at the Koala club.

'It's fantastic! … I'm so glad you pushed. If it'd been left to me, we probably wouldn't have got further than Southsea.'

Dave grinned. 'So – what do you want to do this morning? We've got three hours before the children need picking up again. We could hire a scooter and go snorkelling in a quiet cove somewhere,' he said winking suggestively.

It was ages since Dave had flirted with her, and she realised that's what she was missing. If they could get the romance back in their marriage she might not need Jay. But there was still an ache in her heart whenever she thought of him.

'I'm just going for a jog before it gets too hot. You don't mind do you?'

'You've not jogged for ages,' said Dave, a bit puzzled. 'I thought you'd given it up.'

'I've been thinking about doing it again for a while now. It'll be good to get into a routine while I'm here, then I'll be able to continue when I get home. I won't be too long. Why don't you go to the gym or have a swim?'

Robyn donned her shorts and running vest. Armed with a towel and a bottle of water she kissed Dave's cheek, 'Enjoy yourself. I'll be about an hour.'

'Okay! I'll go and have a work-out in the gym, meet you back here all hot and sweaty.'

The jog nearly killed her. Robyn hadn't realised how unfit she'd become. She thought her twice-weekly visits to the gym were enough to maintain her stamina but, after today's performance, she would have to reassess her training regime. When she got back, Dave was already in the room, naked on the bed,

'I've been waiting! Do you want to take a shower together or – wow?

Robyn was pulling off her clothes. 'I forgot how these exercise endorphins make you feel,' she said as she threw herself onto the bed reaching for Dave's growing erection. Within seconds he was driving deep inside her.

'Oh my God,' Dave shouted as he let himself go. Robyn held onto him for as long as she could as tears flowed down her cheeks.

'What's wrong?' Dave exclaimed in alarm. 'I wasn't that bad was I?'

'Far from it, that was wonderful,' said Robyn. She was in turmoil. Loving two men was crippling her. How could she ever decide between them?

'I thought you'd gone off me,' Dave said as she lay in the crook of his arm.

'Whatever gave you that idea?'

'I don't know… Please don't be mad,' his voice was hesitant. 'A bit ago, I looked at your Facebook page and I saw two names I didn't recognise, Jay and Steve … It's been playing on my mind …. Denizon told me Steve is Julie's fiancé in Leeds, but you've never mentioned Jay.'

Shit! He's been spying on me.

Calmly Robyn said, 'He's Julie's buddy. I met him at that seminar in April and we all got on really well. Why do you ask?'

'That's okay then.'

Right! Let's head this thing off at the pass, 'Surely you don't think I'm having an affair or anything, do you?' She laughed.

'No … It was just strange you hadn't mentioned him, and yet you have his photograph.'

God! What else has he been prying into?

'I have his photo because he sent it to me. I'll delete it if it makes you feel better.' Robyn could no longer disguise the anger she was feeling.

'No, I'm sorry, I shouldn't have looked. It was unforgivable.'

'Don't you trust me?'

'Of course I do, I don't know why but I've been feeling a bit insecure lately. Forget I said anything.'

But Robyn couldn't forget. She would have to be a lot more careful from now on.

Jay and Maria followed the map and located their apartment easily. It was in a block of four overlooking the sea. The Oasis Springs was visible from their balcony, and he wondered which room was Robyn's. He was longing to send her a text to say he'd arrived.

Maria looked tired from the travelling.

'Why don't you have a lie down?' he suggested. 'I'll go and find my way around so we don't get lost later.'

'If you're sure you don't mind, I'm so hot.' Pregnancy and the sweltering August sun didn't go well together.

'I'll close the curtains and put the air conditioning on for you.'

'Thanks, you're so good to me.' Maria smiled.

'You deserve it.' Jay kissed her forehead.

Picking up the room key, he let himself out of the room quietly. Maria always slept for at least an hour in an afternoon so he had that long to locate Robyn. He retraced his steps back to reception and wandered about the grounds familiarising himself with the restaurant and bar. Once he had a vague knowledge of his own complex, he walked past security and into the Oasis Springs next door. It didn't take him long to spot Robyn by the main pool wearing a high cut gold bikini, God! She looked stunning. He felt himself stirring as he caught a glimpse of her long tanned legs.

Jay took off his shirt and made himself comfortable on a sun lounger, hoping Robyn would look in his direction. It took five minutes, but she finally turned her head and gave him a sly smile. Her husband seemed to be dozing by her side as she leaned over and whispered something in his ear. There was no sign of the children.

Robyn stood up, grabbed her sarong and room key and marched off. Jay waited as she walked past without acknowledging his existence, and then followed her. She looked around as she opened the apartment door and signalled Jay to come in. He pushed her gently against the closed door, 'God, you look fantastic!'

Jay thrust his tongue in Robyn's waiting mouth. All her resolve to finish with him vanished as she tasted him and felt his hardness pressing against her leg. As she pulled the crotch of her bikini to one side, Jay released himself from his shorts and pushed himself inside her. They climaxed together in less than a minute.

Breathless, Robyn said, 'You'll have to go now. I'll meet you at the entrance to your complex at seven thirty tomorrow morning. We'll have longer I promise. I went for a jog this morning and found us a quiet stretch of beach.'

'I love you,' Jay whispered as he kissed her.

'I love you too, but this really is risking life and limb.'

Robyn wiped herself with a tissue, adjusted her bikini and went out first to check the coast was clear. Jay slipped away via the extensive grounds back to his own apartment.

It was unusual for Robyn to be up so early on holiday, keeping her voice casual, she said to Dave,
'I thought I'd jog early today if we're going to go sightseeing. It was a bit warm yesterday.' Dave stretched as he lounged in the king sized bed.
'How long will you be?'
'About an hour, probably.'
'Ok, I'll get the children ready. Do I get a kiss?'
She bent down and gave him a quick peck.
'You can have the rest later.'
Robyn walked quickly to the entrance of the Oasis Springs and, spotting Jay, she started to jog. He left it for a few metres and followed behind her. Once they were out of sight of the hotels he caught her up.
'How long have we got?' Jay asked, holding her hand as they jogged.
'An hour. The cove is about a twenty minute jog.'
'God, I'll be knackered. I hope I'll have enough energy left!'
'So do I. I've been looking forward to this since yesterday. Has Maria said anything?'
'No, she's asleep, how about Dave?'
'No, I went jogging yesterday specially to find this cove.'
It was more like a sprint than a jog, and they arrived in less than twenty minutes. The cove was deserted, and they found a secluded spot. Robyn pulled her shorts down with some urgency and Jay had her bent over a large rock.
'Good idea of yours this holiday. Do you think we can get away with it every day?' Jay said as he kissed her.
'I don't see why not; just don't come to the hotel during the day. Dave's seen your picture on my Facebook page. He admitted to snooping.'
'Has he said anything?'

'He asked who you were, and I told him you were Julie's buddy.'

'Did he buy it?'

'I think so. He didn't ask any more questions.'

'Same time tomorrow then?' he asked eagerly.

'It's a date.' Robyn said as she kissed him.

They shared ten more minutes in the idyllic early morning sun before getting dressed and setting back, this time without the sense of urgency. They were satisfied.

Despite her reservation about Jay being at the same resort, she felt so intoxicated by the danger of what they were doing; Robyn was taking even more chances. She'd find any excuse to leave Dave by the pool and visit Jay in an afternoon while Maria took a nap. He'd sorted out the gymnasium key and they met for a 'quickie' in a quiet area of the changing rooms. And Dave didn't seem the least bit suspicious. If it carried on like this, she saw no reason to finish with Jay – she could continue having them both. The situation was turning out to be a walk in the park!

So far, Denizon wasn't all that enamoured with being pregnant. She was feeling permanently sick and experiencing a gnawing ache in her lower abdomen, which she'd read on the Internet, was likely to be the baby bedding down. And so much for having increased energy, most of the time she felt like a slug having a bad day. She was sleeping in excess of ten hours every night as well as napping in the afternoon. And should she be so warm? She knew hormones regulated her temperature, but she was feeling almost feverish.

Today was Denizon's first midwifery appointment, and she was going by herself. She had to be at the doctor's surgery by eleven thirty, but could hardly drag herself out of bed, and it was already after ten.

It was nearly a week since she last washed her hair, and there was no way she could go anywhere in public with such a greasy, dishevelled mess. She staggered to the shower, holding onto the furniture to help her balance. While the shower warmed up she sat on the closed toilet lid. God, she was feeling dizzy. The sudden sharp pain in her lower abdomen took her breath away. She looked down and saw a red stain on her pyjama bottoms. Getting down on her hands and knees, she crawled to the bedroom for her mobile phone and managed to dial the final nine and ask for help before everything went black.

Robyn was putting the final touches to her make-up when her mobile phone rang. She saw it was Chris.

'Robyn, it's me – please don't hang up. I wasn't going to bother you, but Denizon is in hospital and...' Her brother began to sob.

'Slow down, Chris! What's happened?'

'The doctor thinks she could die.' Chris sobbed again as Robyn's heart jumped into her throat and she sat down heavily on the bed.

'My God Chris! What's wrong with her? Calm down and tell me.'

'The paramedics found her collapsed on the bedroom floor. She'd lost loads of blood and needed two transfusions. She's still unconscious.'

'Where is she?'

'Hull Royal Infirmary in Intensive Care.'

'Has she had a miscarriage?'

'No, it's an ectopic pregnancy. One of her tubes ruptured. Oh God, what if she dies? It'll be all my fault.'

'You should've thought of that,' Robyn snapped.

'Please don't, Rob.' His voice was muffled and she could still hear him crying on the other end of the phone.

'Sorry, Chris, that was mean. Come on, try and pull yourself together.' Robyn paused to think. 'I'm coming home.'

He stopped snuffling. 'But you're on holiday.'

'Sod the holiday!' said Robyn at once. 'My best friend is lying in hospital. I'll catch the next available flight today, and I'll be there when I can. Is anyone with her now?'

'Mum and Dad have been here since it happened.'

'Give them all my love, and I'll see you soon. Chin up, love!'

By this time Dave was standing anxiously by the bed as Robyn put down her phone. She looked at him, her face white.

'Did you hear all that? Denizon has had an ectopic pregnancy and collapsed. She's in intensive care, critical. I'm going to fly home. Are you okay to stay here with the kids?'

'We can all come if you want.'

'No, there's no need. We've a few more days left and the kids would be too disappointed. I'll get a taxi to the airport and catch the first flight.'

'Give her my love won't you?'

'I just hope I can. Chris says she's still unconscious.'

Robyn threw a few items of clothing in a flight bag and grabbed her passport from out of the room safe.

'Oh, I haven't said good bye to the kids,' she said unhappily.

'Don't worry,' Dave said, patting her arm, 'I'll explain everything to them. Ring me as soon as you know anything.'

'Fingers crossed she'll be okay.' She gave him a kiss.

Robyn asked reception to call her a taxi to Paphos airport. Within five minutes, a large, white Mercedes pulled up outside the entrance. As she climbed into the back she didn't see Jay and Maria walking past, out for a mid-afternoon stroll, but they saw her.

Maria did a double take when she spotted the same tall, slim auburn haired woman she'd seen opening the door of the semi-detached in Garforth the day she'd followed Jay. Surely it wasn't the same woman – she must have a double. But when she looked at Jay and saw the concern on his face, the pieces started to slot into place: Jay's suggestion of the holiday, but it had to be this resort, his sudden interest in jogging, and his good mood. God, she couldn't believe the nerve of the man. Not only was he being unfaithful in England, he was seeing his lover on Cyprus, as well.

This time she couldn't give him the benefit of the doubt. She was no longer sad, she was angry. 'I'm suddenly not feeling too well, Jay,' she said, assuming a weak voice. 'I'm going back to the apartment for a lie down.'

'Do you want me to come back with you?' he offered, stroking her back.

Maria pulled away. 'No, you carry on. I'll see you by the pool later when I've had a rest.'

'If you're sure, I'll finish the walk and then go for a swim.'

Jay had noted the distressed look on Robyn's face as she got into the taxi, and as soon as Maria was out of sight, he texted Robyn.

"Saw you leave, is everything okay?"

Her text came back at once. "No, flying home. Den in hospital, will explain later. No jogging tomorrow, sorry."

"Take care, my darling," he sent back. "Love You."

"Love you too." She was so preoccupied she forgot to press delete.

Maria waited behind a pillar in reception until she saw Jay carry on walking. She made her way into the complex next door.

'My friend, the lady with the auburn hair, the one's that just got into a taxi … she's left her mobile phone in my bag. Can you remind me which apartment she's in so I can return it?'

'Mrs. Fisher is in suite A213. I can make sure she gets it, if you like.'

'No, its okay, I'll take it round now. Thanks all the same.'

Maria wandered round looking for A213. It was in a block next to the swimming pool and she could see the door from a nearby sun lounger. She positioned herself under the umbrella to wait.

Shortly a man came out of the room. He looked the right age, early thirties with the same colour hair as hers, a deep rich brown. He was a lot taller than Jay and more ruggedly handsome.

Suddenly she had second thoughts. What if she'd got it all wrong and it was pure coincidence? The man started to walk away from the apartment. In a split second she made her mind up to at least talk to him while the anger was fresh. He deserved to know her suspicions. If she was right, it'd been going on long enough, and it was her duty to put a stop to it. Maria caught him up,

'Excuse me, but do you know the woman who has just left in a taxi from outside reception?'

'Yes, my wife, Robyn. Is anything the matter?'

'Have you time for a chat?'

'Not really … I'm on my way to collect the children.'

'Please, it's important.'

'Er … I'm not sure …'

'Please.'

Dave followed Maria to a table by the pool bar and they both sat down.

'What's this all about?' Dave said, checking his watch.

'I don't know where to start. Has your wife ever mentioned the name Jay?'

'Yes, we were only talking about him yesterday. He's a friend of a friend. Why?'

'I think he's also her lover.'

'What! Why on earth would you make a wild allegation like that? You don't even know me – or my wife.'

'No, I don't, but I've seen her before. Let's just say I've had my suspicions about my partner Jay, for a while and one day I decided to follow him. He told me he was meeting a colleague at the University but he drove to a house in Garforth. Your wife Robyn, let him in. According to the next door neighbour they meet there regularly. Haven't you ever wondered where she's been disappearing to?'

'Are you sure it was Robyn?'

'I've been asking myself the same question since I saw her just now. But believe me, it is… I wanted to be wrong. I love Jay and hoped I'd fabricated the whole thing in my head. I just can't ignore the facts though. It all adds up… Where was your wife two weekends ago?'

'At a management conference in London.'

'Jay was at a conference hosted by Max Hammond also in London. What about the second weekend in June?' Maria continued with all the dates she could remember. Dave thought about all the excuses Robyn had come up with over the past few months – and realised this woman was probably telling the truth.

'I think it started in April after the seminar in Leeds, Jay's behaviour changed.' Maria continued.

'But you're pregnant.'

'You noticed! With our first child. I had my suspicions on the night I told him back in April. He was totally distracted, and I could almost see cogs whirring in his brain. It looked like he was thinking of something or somebody else and not our good news. The worst thing for me is flaunting it in our faces… How long has your wife been jogging? Jay just started since we got here.'

'Robyn used to jog before, so I thought nothing of it.' Dave felt his stomach lurch.

'And why would you?' said Maria, bitterly. 'How many couples would dare to continue an affair when their partners were present? They must've been having a good laugh! What a pair of mugs *we* are! Do you feel stupid? I certainly do.'

'I don't know what to feel.' He was in total shock. He had loved and trusted Robyn over seven years of marriage and for what? A fling with a man who was expecting his first child. Words couldn't describe what he thought of a man who'd do such a thing. And, as for Robyn, well, nothing came to mind.

'I'm sorry to be the bearer of bad news. Maybe I shouldn't have said anything.' Maria looked at the devastation written across Dave's face and regretted her bluntness. She'd had longer to get used to it, but this was a total shock to the poor man in front of her.

'No!' said Dave, his voice firm. 'I'm really glad you told me, well obviously glad isn't the right word, but you know what I mean. I saw Jay's picture on her Facebook page and

I thought it was odd. It wasn't a snap shot at a seminar – it was him looking tanned on the beach, with a sultry look in his eye.'

'Wearing black and yellow swim trunks?'

'Yes.'

'That was taken on our holiday just over a year ago … Says a lot about me, doesn't it?' Maria looked down.

'No, I think it says more about the pair of them.'

'So what are you going to do?' he asked.

'I'm going to have it out with him when he comes back to the apartment and then – who knows? We're going home tomorrow anyway. How about you?'

'Robyn's flown back to England. Her best friend is seriously ill so I'll have to let it fester for a few more days yet.'

'When do you go home?'

'Next Tuesday, but I might see if I can get an earlier flight… It's not really sunk in yet.'

'I don't know what else to say, apart from good luck.' She looked at her watch, 'Sorry if I've kept you.'

After her chat with Dave, Maria went back to the room to start packing.

The cases were nearly full when Jay walked in an hour later, still dripping from his swim.

'Did you have to swim on your own? It's such a shame she's gone home,' Maria said mockingly.

'Who?' Jay looked puzzled.

'Come on Jay, your little game's been discovered. Dave and I had a lovely little chat.'

Jay looked stunned. 'How the hell did you find out?'

'I recognised your whore getting into a taxi today.'

'Do *not* call her that… Anyway, how do you know who she is?'

'Remember when you dashed over to Leeds for a supposed meeting? I followed you, and guess what I saw?'

'Why didn't you say anything at the time?'

'Because I had the misguided impression that I still loved you. I know better now.'

'In that case, what more is there to say?' Jay held up his hands. 'Guilty as charged.'

'Is that all? No explanation?'

'Will it make you feel better to know I met her at a seminar in Leeds in April and we've been seeing each other since then…How long have you been suspicious?'

'I suspected pretty much from the outset. You changed, literally overnight. If it's any consolation I don't blame you entirely. I knew you didn't want children, yet I still went ahead and got pregnant. I know I've been a bit baby obsessed and you probably turned to her for comfort.'

'I am sorry Maria for the way I've treated you. But I just fell in love.'

The calm, cool exterior Maria was assuming left her in an instant as soon as she heard the word "love". She picked up a glass ashtray from the coffee table and hurled it at Jay's head. His reactions were lightening fast and he moved to the left so it only struck his shoulder.

'What do you know about love?' Maria spat.

'Honestly,' Jay rubbed his shoulder, which was already starting to swell, 'I don't think I ever loved you like I should, and I'm sorry for that. I shouldn't have agreed to buy the flat. It was giving you the wrong impression.'

'So that's it then? We're over?' she asked.

'I think so. I don't have a clue what will happen between me and Robyn, but it's not about her anymore.'

'But what about the baby?' She said fondling her bump.

'Obviously, I'll support you both and you can have the flat. I'll move out as soon as we get back.'

'But Jay … please.'

Jay didn't want to carry on the conversation and walked away to the spare single bedroom, staying there until the next morning when the coach collected them from reception. He emerged only to go to the bathroom and to make himself a sandwich. Maria tried her best to goad him into an argument – just to invoke any emotion in him – but he just walked back into the bedroom closing the door.

Dave was extremely thankful the Koala club had provided such a busy day and by seven o'clock the children were falling asleep on their feet. He put them straight to bed and sat on the balcony with the bottle of wine he and Robyn were planning on drinking later.

He knew he would leave her, no matter what her explanation was. He didn't want to share his life with someone who had such blatant disregard for his feelings. One lie had followed another, although grudgingly, he had to admire her, the lies were so accomplished. She certainly had him fooled.

By the time Dave sunk the whole bottle he thought it was a good job Robyn was back in England. How could the children cope without both parents when their father was in prison for culpable homicide?

Chapter 20

Luck was on her side and Robyn managed to book the last seat on the nine thirty flight to Birmingham International Airport. As soon as she was inside the terminal building at Birmingham, she switched on her phone and was grateful to see she had no missed calls or messages. She tried calling Dave's mobile, but it was switched off.

Instead of trying Chris, she rang her mother,

'Hi Mum, I've landed in Birmingham. I'll be there as soon as I can. I'm going to rent a car. Any news?'

'Just hurry up, love, the doctor's say it's touch and go. Apparently the next few hours are crucial.'

'Oh Mum, what if she dies?'

'Try not to think like that, love.'

'Do they know what caused it?'

'Not yet. They keep having a word with Chris, but he can't string two words together. He's absolutely devastated, particularly because he wasn't there for her. He feels totally responsible.'

Robyn felt like adding, 'he was', but recriminations had no place at a time like this.

'Tell her to hold on and I love her.' Robyn could hardly speak through the tears.

'You drive carefully, love. I'll see you soon.'

Not only was it Chris's, fault it was hers too. If she hadn't been so worried about her affair coming out into the open, she would've said something to Denizon ages ago and this would never have happened. Her Dad had warned her to put an end to it before someone got hurt, but she hadn't listened and now the most innocent person in the world was suffering due to her selfishness.

The only car that was available at such short notice was a one litre Corsa, and it was five o'clock in the morning before Robyn arrived at the hospital. She abandoned her car in a 'Drop Off' only space and ran into Accident and Emergency.

Chris and her parents were sitting on the blue plastic chairs outside Intensive Care. Chris had his head in his hands.

'Oh God! What's happened?' Robyn cried.

'We've had to come out. The crash cart's gone in,' Robyn's mum said as she gave her daughter a hug.

It seemed like an eternity before a doctor appeared. 'She's stable for now.'

Everyone breathed a sigh of relief.

'Can we see her yet?' Robyn asked the young registrar.

'Just for a few minutes. She won't respond to you I'm afraid, she's deep in a coma.' He held the door open for Robyn to enter.

Robyn looked at a sleeping Denizon hooked up to various drips and a ventilator. She sat down by her bedside.

'I'm so sorry, my love. You can't leave me now. What would I do without you?' Robyn reached out to touch Denizon's hand, it felt cold. The only sign she was still alive was the beep of the ventilator as it rose and fell.

Robyn couldn't bear to stay for more than a few minutes and went to join the rest of her family. The four of them kept vigil outside Intensive Care until mid-afternoon with Peter plying them with horrible, syrupy coffee from the vending machine.

'Why don't you go home for a rest?' The sister suggested to the four exhausted people. 'She's been stable for a while now. At least go get something to eat and freshen up.'

'I'm going to stay,' said Chris resolutely. 'Bring me back a sandwich.'

'We'll all stay, thanks,' Robyn said to the sister. 'I'll just go and try Dave again.'

Robyn went outside and rang Dave's number, but strangely it was turned off.

Dave had seen the holiday rep., and she was in the process of arranging their flight home. The children didn't want to stay without their Mum, and he couldn't summon up the energy to argue. He'd sat up all last night going over what Maria had told him, trying to remember every time Robyn was late home. He could recall dozens of occasions and it was torturing him. Maybe her increased interest in fitness was also a lie, as he recalled his friend Alex voicing his concern at seeing Robyn at the Premier Inn one Wednesday afternoon. The gym was next door to the hotel, God he was stupid!

But now he wanted just one thing from her – to hear her confess and then he would leave. She could have the house and all its contents. He didn't need anything to remind him of their sham of a marriage.

Denizon came off the critical list the next day. She was stable but still in a coma in Intensive care. Someone from the family was always at her bedside, but it didn't require all of them to be there together, so Robyn had come home for a long soak.

She was in the bathroom when she heard the familiar chime of the front door.

'Hello?' she shouted cautiously. She looked over the banister and saw Dave standing alone in the hall.

'What on earth are you doing here? Where are the children?' Robyn asked, as she ran down the stairs.

'I've dropped them off at Mum's overnight.'

'What's matter? Has something happened to Denizon?'

'It's not about Denizon, or is she in on it as well?'

'What do you mean?'

'Stop playing games, Robyn. I know everything.'

'What … what do you know?' she asked, swallowing nervously.

'Whatever Maria knows. She collared me just after you left in the taxi.'

'But that was yesterday. Why didn't you ring?'

'And say what? … No, I needed to see your face, and by that guilty expression I take it you're not denying it?'

'Have you spoken to Jay?'

'No, why on earth would I want to speak to a man who's been screwing my wife. You must think me a bloody fool.'

Robyn sat down on the bottom stair and scraped her hair back from her face. She sighed,

'No, I don't. I know it's no consolation, but it was never about you. I never stopped loving you, but I just couldn't help it. Jay and I have this amazing connection.'

'Oh! That's okay then. Obviously far more important than having a husband and two beautiful children.'

'Don't bring them into it, it wasn't about them either.'

Dave towered over Robyn pointing his finger in her face. 'No, it was all about you and what you want. No-one gets a look in when Robyn Fisher makes up her mind.'

Robyn cringed. 'So what now?'

'I thought that was obvious. It's over.'

'Dave … But we've been married for seven years! Surely I deserve a chance to explain.'

'You don't deserve anything. Luckily, I've seen you for what you are before I waste another minute of my time on you.'

'You don't really mean that,' Robyn said.

Dave stood firm, 'Watch me!'

'But where will you go? … Dave, please don't leave, we can work it out.' Robyn stood up and tried to hold his arm.

He pulled away, 'You lost the right to touch me when you climbed into another man's bed. I've just come back for some clothes. I'm staying at my Mum's.'

'But what about the children?'

'They're alright for now; apart from they keep asking when they can see you.'

'Poor loves.'

'Poor loves! You didn't think of them when you were shagging HIM.'

'Yes I did… I mean… I always think of the children, but … Oh! I don't know. This is such a mess.'

'Damn right it is, and it's all your fault.'

'I know.' Robyn started to sob.

'Do you realise how pathetic you sound?'

'Yes,' Robyn whispered under her breath. 'Do you want to know how Denizon is?' she asked, hoping to deflect his anger.

'I've already spoken to Peter. He told me she's out of danger. I take it from his sympathetic tone your father knows all about you.'

'He guessed and told me to put an end to it, and I swear I was going to after the holiday.'

'What, after you had your fun at the beach? I bet it was exciting fucking him, knowing your husband was back in the room.' Dave clenched his fist.

'I'm sorry… I don't know what else to say? But please don't tell me it's over. I'm sure we can get through this.'

'You really think it's that simple?' he sneered. 'From now on there is no 'we' anymore. You threw it all away. I'd have done anything for you, Robyn. You only had to say you were unhappy and I'd have tried to change. I –'

'But, I wasn't unhappy,' she insisted, cutting in. 'I'm still not, but I couldn't choose between you.'

'Now you won't have to, I've chosen for you. You can have him.'

'But I don't want him. I've already decided I want you.'

Dave started to laugh mirthlessly. 'You're so naive! What did you think would happen?' He paused, but Robyn was speechless.

'I don't think you've really thought this through have you?' he continued. 'It was only a matter of time before you were caught. And now you have been. What … Did you think I'd just forgive you?…Sorry Robyn, no, I'll never forgive you.'

'Please, Dave.' Robyn was really scared now. Just then the mobile in her pocket rang.

'That's probably the great lover,' Dave scoffed. 'I imagine he and Maria have had the same chat as we're having now.' Robyn checked and saw it was Jay. She looked uncertainly at Dave.

'You'd better answer it,' he said. 'You'll need to make plans.' He started to move past her and she grabbed his arm.

'I keep telling you … I don't want him, I want you.'

He pushed her, and she fell back onto the step.

'Dave …'

At the top of the stairs he turned and said quietly 'Sorry, conversation over. I'll get my things and my solicitor will be in touch.'

'You're surely not planning a divorce already? We could go to RELATE.'

Dave laughed. 'Yeah – Why not? Or we could go and see Jay. Maria told me he was a good marriage guidance counsellor… The irony! Anyhow, forget it. I'm not going to change my mind. By the way, I'd come up here if I were you. Your bath is just about to overflow.'

Robyn picked herself up and ran upstairs into the bathroom. Then coming back to the landing she said, 'Please Dave. Stay a bit longer. I want to explain. It was just sex.'

He glared at her, his face sullen. 'Is that supposed to make me feel any better? My wife prefers sex with another man.' He shook his head. 'I don't think that's a very good argument, do you? You think I've never looked at other women? When you were at the fictitious engagement party, I was propositioned by a beautiful young girl who was most definitely up for it. But I said no, because I'M MARRIED.'

'I'm not the only one who's been unfaithful, Sue slept with a man at the Christmas party.'

She followed Dave into the bedroom, and he started opening the drawers, 'I don't care how many other couples have been unfaithful! I never expected it from you, Robyn, especially as you saw what Chris's behaviour has done to Denizon over the years.'

'I know, and neither did I. But it was exciting – and I was flattered.'

'Absolutely, so was I. But that's all it was, flattering. You didn't have to take it further. But you did, and now there's nothing else to say. I'm going.' Dave was throwing unfolded clothes and toiletries into a large holdall.

Robyn knew when she was defeated and slumped down on the bed. There was no point in trying to reason with him whilst he was this angry.

Dave zipped the holdall shut and picked up her mobile which was lying by her side.

'Give me that back,' she said trying to reach for the phone.

'Why?' He held it aloft and scrawled through the recent texts. The last one was to Jay,

'Love you too.'

'So much for "just sex", you liar!' he shouted.

He left the room, and she heard a splash as he threw her phone in the bath. The next thing she heard was the door banging behind him. She was alone.

Robyn was stunned. After letting half the water out and pouring herself a large glass of rose wine, she climbed into the hot water. Dave was right, she hadn't thought it through. Swept along by the euphoria and the excitement, she hadn't really thought about the consequences. How could it ever end happily?

Shit! Why didn't I take Dad's advice and break it off with Jay straight away. She took a long slurp of wine. *God! I'm so stupid. If only I hadn't been so selfish. But no, it was all 'me', 'me', 'me'. Dave might've neglected me a little and he bloody well took me for granted, but hey, that's marriage. I didn't have to throw it all away for a stupid fling!*

But then she thought about Jay and all the good times they'd shared … *But he isn't just a fling. I love him… But am I ready to give up my life for him?* A feeling of nausea swept over her as she thought about the children. *What will happen to them? They're just the innocent party in all this. What a bloody mess.* Tears started to flow down her cheeks and the emptiness inside was in danger of engulfing her.

The water was cold and the bottle empty before a sombre Robyn climbed out of the bath. *How can I go on without Dave?* The tears hadn't subsided as she buried herself under the duvet and didn't surface until the next day when she heard the door bell chime. She put her head out of the bedroom window and saw her dad standing on the doorstep.

'Go away, I don't want to talk to anyone,' Robyn shouted.

'Please love. I've only come round because you won't answer your phone. We phoned Dave and he told me what happened. The children are asking for you.'

'I don't want them to see me like this.'

'Come and open the door. You need someone to talk to and, trust me; I know exactly how you're feeling.'

Robyn put on her dressing gown and stumbled down the stairs. Her stomach rumbled with hunger. She opened the door.

'Have you come to gloat? You said this would happen, and it has,' she said as she followed him into the front room.

'Do you want me to make you a drink and something to eat?' Peter asked.

'A glass of water would be good.'

'You look completely dehydrated. The white's of your eyes are all red. Have you looked in a mirror recently?'

'No, I've been in bed. How's Denizon?'

'That's one of the reasons I'm here; she's woken up.'

'Wow, that's fantastic, when?' Robyn was slightly cheered with the good news.

'This morning, she was asking for you.'

'What did you tell her?'

'I told her you'd just popped home for some rest.'

'Did Dave tell you he came round?'

'He did, told us the whole story.'

'I bet Mum loved that, didn't she?'

'Your mother isn't taking sides.'

'Well, that'll make a change. I've proved her right. I was never good enough for my wonderful husband.' She sipped some water as Peter said softly,

'Stop being so bitter, Robyn. It doesn't suit you. Everything's out into the open now, so deal with it. Have you spoken to Jay?'

'No, Dave threw my mobile phone in the bath and Jay hasn't got my home number.'

'Haven't you phoned him?'

'I don't want to speak to him.'

'I thought you said you loved him?'

'I thought I did, but I was wrong.'

'How can you be so sure?'

'I thought you'd be glad I've been found out, you warned me it would end in tears.'

'No love, I'm not glad. But I think you owe it to Jay to speak to him. Nothing can be resolved by ignoring it.'

'You sound just like me. I was always telling Denizon that.'

'Well, take your own advice and sort it.'

'Dave won't talk to me.'

'I'm sure he will in time. Now, go and tidy yourself up. I'm taking you to see Denizon; hopefully she can cheer you up.'

Peter dropped Robyn at the hospital. Chris and her mother were taking a well earned rest.

'You look as bad as I feel,' Denizon said to Robyn as she gave her a kiss. Her voice was hoarse from the ventilator. 'Do you like my raspy voice? It's sexy, don't you think?'

Robyn tried a shallow smile. 'How are you really?' she asked.

'A bit sore and bruised, as though I've been ten rounds with Mike Tyson. I'm sorry I worried everyone.'

'Just don't do it again!' Robyn chided. 'You scared us all. Have you seen Chris? You know he's been by your bedside every minute of the day?'

'Yes, just before I woke up I was aware of what was going on. He was holding my hand and talking to me. Talking of husbands, where's Dave?'

'There's something I need to tell you. But I was going to wait until you're a bit stronger.'

'That might be ages. I could do with some good news.'

'Well this isn't going to cheer you up. Dave has left me.'

'Don't make me laugh, my stitches hurt.' Denizon held her wound. 'Now where is he?'

Robyn held her head down in shame.

'I've been seeing someone and he found out.'

'Tell me you're joking.'

'Truly, I wish I was. It's been going on since April.'

'I knew it! I knew you were hiding something … Why haven't you said anything to me before? I could've told you what an idiot you were being.'

'I wanted to, so many times. But I was too ashamed.'

'Poor Dave, so how did he find out?'

'Jay's girlfriend told him.' Robyn told her the whole story and, sitting up a little, Denizon said.

'Do you and your brother have a brain cell between you? Where is this Jay now?'

'At home in Leeds, I assume. I haven't spoken to him since I came back from Cyprus.'

'What are you going to do?'

'I'm waiting for Dave to calm down so I can reason with him, but it's not happened yet.'

'Where's he gone?'

'He's staying at his mother's with the children.'

'Have you told anyone at work?'

'No, I'm not due back until Wednesday. But I think I'm going to sign myself off with stress.'

'I'm not surprised … Dave will come round you know. He loves you.'

'I'm not so sure. I've never seen such contempt on anyone's face.'

'You've hurt him terribly, Rob. It's the worst thing you could've done.'

'I know.' Robyn twisted her wedding ring, 'I wish I could take it all back.'

'You do need to talk to Dave,' urged Denizon.

'I can't make him talk to me. Anyway, you didn't want to speak to Chris.'

'But we've talked now. We're not getting back together yet, but I'm not discounting it. But you do realise the chances of my conceiving again are slim to negligible, don't you?'

Robyn nodded.

'Chris says he doesn't care about children as long as I'm alright, but this time I'm not taking his word for it. He's going to have to prove it to me.'

'Good for you. Maybe I just need to give Dave more time.'

Denizon suddenly looked pale. Robyn knew how devastated she must be about the baby. All she'd ever wanted was to marry Chris and have children. Robyn took Denizon's hand in hers.

'Anyway, enough of my misery,' she said. 'Getting you well is my priority now.'

Denizon pressed Robyn's fingers. 'Would you mind if I asked Dave to come and see me? I want to make sure he's coping. I love you both, and I need him to know I'm not taking sides.'

'Of course!' Robyn said at once 'Maybe you could get him to at least talk to me.'

Jay was frantic not being able to contact Robyn. Her number was unavailable, and she wasn't replying to his e-mails. It was as though he'd never existed for her.

On the way home from Cyprus he and Maria hadn't spoken a word to each other, and he requested separate seats on the plane. Their car was in the long term parking at the airport, so after a journey in silence, he dropped Maria off at the flat, collected a few things and drove straight to his office, where he'd been sleeping ever since.

Simone, his assistant, was anything but supportive; firmly coming down in the Maria camp, so he'd had no choice but to let her go. Any motivation to see clients was gone, and his practice was falling apart, but he didn't care.

He couldn't possibly give anyone advice in his current frame of mind. The lease on the office was up for renewal next year, so he only had eight months rent to find and then he was free. Leeds had been his home for thirty years, but it was time for a fresh start. He wanted it with Robyn, if only he could find her.

His intention was to drive over to Hull today to book into the Premier Inn. He knew the name of the street where she lived, but not the number and the location of where she worked and not the actual building.

It was eleven o'clock Friday morning when Jay pulled up at the NHS Trust Headquarters on Anlaby Road, Hull. He followed the signs for reception and approached the main desk,

'Hello. I'm sorry to bother you, but I wonder if you could help me. I'm looking for an employee called Robyn Fisher, she works in Human Resources, but I'm not sure where.'

The receptionist looked down at her list and said,

'You'll find her in the Wilberforce Building. Keep going down the drive and it's the second building on the left with a fountain outside.'

'Thanks so much for your help.' Jay's heart lifted on hearing Robyn was nearby. He left his car in the main visitors' car park and walked the short distance down the drive. It was an extremely hot August day, and he was sweltering in his suit jacket. He removed it, slung it over his shoulder to reveal a white linen shirt with the sleeves rolled up. The brilliant white of the shirt accentuated his tanned arms and chest. His long, stylishly, messy hair was bleached with the sun. Wearing his shades, he resembled an A-list celebrity strutting along some street in Los Angeles. Sarah caught sight of him from her office window.

'Come here and look at this,' she said to the other girls in the office, 'I bet that's him.'

'Do you think he's come to find her?' A girl called Becky asked.

'When I spoke to her last week she told me they've broken up. You don't look like she did every day when she spoke to him to just say goodbye and leave it at that. I'd expect him to come and find me. But fat chance of that happening... look what my knight in shining armour left me with.' Sarah pointed to the small bulge developing under her loose shirt.

'Anyhow, I'm going down to ask him.' Sarah had made up her mind.

'You can't. It might not be him! Could be someone here for a meeting,' Becky said.

'In that case I can point him in the right direction.' Sarah caught the lift to the ground floor and came face to face with the man in the white shirt.

'Is it Jay?' she asked cheekily.

'Er... yes. How did you know?'

'I'm Sarah, Robyn's assistant. Do you want to come with me away from prying eyes? This place is worse than "The News of the World" before it folded.'

Jay followed Sarah outside to the smoker's shelter.

'This is where she used to ring you,' she confided.

'I take it you two have spoken?' Jay asked uncertainly.

'Not for long. But she told me it's all out in the open and she's finished with you.'

Jay paled visibly under this tan. 'That's more than she's told me. I haven't spoken to her at all. Where is she?'

'At home on sick leave. I haven't seen her since Cyprus.'

'Neither have I, and it's killing me. She isn't answering her phone. It says the number's unavailable.'

'It will be killing her just as much. But what I've learned working for Robyn for three years is that she likes to do right by people. I bet she feels a duty to her husband, and it's stopping her from seeing you.'

'But I just want to talk. Would you please give me the number of her house?'

Sarah thought. She probably shouldn't tell him, but what the hell! She could do with a happy ending, as it didn't look like she was going to get one herself.

Jay parked across the street and stared at the spacious double fronted detached house set in a large corner plot. There was only Robyn's car in the drive, but that didn't mean Dave wasn't in. They could be one of those families who kept a car in the garage – but he hadn't driven all this way to sit in his car – he'd risk it.

'Jay! My God! What are you doing here? … How did you know where I live?' asked a dishevelled Robyn as she opened the door.

'Your assistant, Sarah, told me. Don't be mad at her, I had to beg.'

Jay hardly recognised the woman he loved. Her usually vibrant locks were lank and dull, and her old tracksuit bottoms hadn't seen an iron. She wouldn't normally be seen dead in an outfit that didn't match.

'I had to see you! You aren't answering my calls. Can I come in?' She moved aside, and he stepped over the threshold into the messiest house he'd been in since his student days. There were dirty dishes piled high in the sink, pizza boxes and take-away cartons strewn on the floor next to a bulging rubbish bin. Clothes were piled up outside the washing machine. And that was just the kitchen.

'Are you going to offer me a cup of coffee?' Jay asked.

'Yes sure, sit down.' Robyn swept the unopened mail from a kitchen chair onto the floor. 'I'll have to wash a couple of cups.'

There was no spark in her at all. Resembling the walking dead, she filled the kettle on automatic pilot.

'We need to talk,' said Jay.

'What about,' she mumbled listlessly. 'Dave won't talk to me.'

'I'm not here to talk about him!' Jay said sharply. 'I want to talk about us. We had so much going for us. What I feel for you is so much more than sex.'

'But what we did was wrong.'

'Yes, I suppose what we did hurt other people. But no-one will ever convince me that what I feel for you is wrong.'

'But I want Dave back?'

'Are you sure?' he asked. 'Because if you're really certain you want to be married to Dave for the rest of your life, I'll go now and you'll never see me again.' Jay started to head for the kitchen door.

'Don't go, please.' Robyn started to sob. 'I don't know anything anymore. I only know I can't go on like this. The indecisiveness is killing me. My children are alternating between grandparents because I can't cope, and a piece of fruit or veg hasn't passed my lips since I got home. I haven't had a bath for a week … I'm falling apart.'

'I can see that.' Jay guided her to a chair. 'But I'm here now. Would it help if *I* talked to Dave?'

'No, he'd kill you.'

'I doubt that, but I don't want to make matters worse. But ignoring you when you're in this state isn't very adult.'

'He's so angry.'

'I get that, but he's still a grown man.'

'You don't understand how much he's hurting. I'm just waiting for him to see sense.'

'Robyn, you have to decide what you want. Don't hang around waiting for others to make a decision for you. You need to take control of your own life. Have your Mum and Dad been supportive?'

'Mum's not really talking to me. It's all too close to home for her. Dad's been great. He keeps bringing me goodies to try and tempt me to eat a proper meal. He promises it will get better.'

'Then listen to him. Isn't there some part of you that's glad it's all out in the open? As much as I've hated all the arguing with Maria, I feel better. I was sick of pretending.'

'No. Blissful ignorance was far more preferable. I just wish I'd have finished it before Dave found out.'

Jay looked hurt, 'Do you really mean that?'

'I don't know, probably not.' Robyn stood up and rinsed two cups under the cold tap. 'Now you're here, I'm really glad to see you.' She turned round to face Jay, 'Would you hold me please?' Robyn whispered.

'For eternity, if you give me the chance.'

He held his arms open for Robyn, and she melted into his touch. 'Remember I love you, and I'll respect whatever you decide. If Dave loves you as much as you say, he'll forgive you in time.'

As Robyn looked deep into Jay's eyes, all her resolve slipped away. She leant forward and kissed him.

'I'm sorry if I've been ignoring you. I thought it was the best thing, but now you're here, I see it wasn't. Tell me what's been happening to you. I've been so preoccupied with myself I haven't even thought to ask.'

'Let's make a drink first, it's a long story.' Over a cup of coffee, Jay related past events to Robyn.

'… so that's my story, homeless, unemployed, living off my savings which are diminishing rapidly.'

'In that case, you must finish your book. It's such a good idea. I thought the publishers were interested.'

'They are, and I *will* get round to it. I've got nothing better to do. Now we've spoken I might be able to concentrate again. Let's tidy this house and get you bathed. I want the old Robyn Fisher back, I prefer the cleaner version.'

For the first time in ages Robyn laughed. She didn't realise just how much she'd missed Jay's company. He was such a big part of her life - she couldn't just cut him out.

'Come on you big bully, get me sorted, and then you can take me to bed. I've missed your body just as much as I've missed your mind.'

Denizon was on the verge of being discharged by the time Dave summoned the courage to visit her. He knew she'd want to talk about Robyn, but it was all too raw for him to discuss.

She was progressing nicely and was being moved from the High Dependency Unit to a normal gynaecological ward with talk of her going home in a couple of days as long as she'd someone to take care of her. Chris had volunteered and booked two weeks compassionate leave. Until Denizon made up her mind whether she wanted him back in her life as a husband, he was going to sleep in the spare room.

Dave tentatively looked round the door to Denizon's private room to ensure Robyn wasn't there.

'Do you want a visitor?' he said looking sheepish.

'Dave, come in, it's lovely to see you. I thought you'd given up on me.' Denizon beamed.

'No, of course not, I'm sorry it's taken me so long to come.'

'Never mind; you're here now. How are you?' ... you look as though you haven't slept for a year.'

'I feel like shit... did you expect anything else?'

'Not really. Have you talked to Robyn yet?'

'No, all the arrangements for the children are done through our mothers, and when I collect them I don't go in, I just hoot the horn.'

'Isn't it about time you did? You can't resolve anything without talking.'

'There's nothing to resolve,' Dave said adamantly.

'Rubbish! You've been together for too long to throw it all away.'

'She should've thought about that before screwing that bastard.'

'Dave, change the record. I know that. You know that. She knows that. But what's done is done. You'll never move forward if you keep dwelling on the past.'

'Has she said anything to you?'

Denizon couldn't tell him that Jay was back on the scene and had stayed the occasional night.

'Yes, we have talked, but if you want to know what she has to say, you're going to have to ask her yourself.'

'Okay, I can take a hint, albeit not a very subtle one… Anyway, I haven't come to talk about me. How are you doing?'

'I'm getting there, I think.'

'And what about you and Chris?'

'Chris is a changed man. I think what happened scared him. He confessed to all his affairs. He said he had nothing more to lose. I even know about the gonorrhoea.'

'And you don't mind?'

'Of course I mind, but what can I do about it?'

'Are you going to forgive him?'

'I don't think it's about forgiveness. It comes down to the fact of whether I can live with it or not.'

'And can you?'

'I'm debating that right now. I'm going to see what happens at home. I've got to learn to trust him again.'

'I don't think I could ever trust Robyn again.'

'What? You think she'd do this again?' Denizon laughed. 'I've seen her every day since I've been in here and trust me; she's suffering as much as you.'

'What do you mean?'

'Haven't you noticed how she looks? She's a nervous wreck.'

'It serves her right,' he said sharply.

'You know you don't mean that. Whatever she's done, you loved her, and I don't believe you've stopped. Believe me; I tried to stop loving Chris when I left. I tried to convince myself all day that I hated him, but you just can't switch love off. Everyone makes mistakes. Granted, some are more serious than others, but even if you decide you can't forgive her you do need to talk.'

'I knew you'd hassle me. Why do you think I haven't been to see you before? But okay, I get your point. Maybe, it is time.'

'Hallelujah! '

'Okay, enough of the sarcasm. I'll go round to the house this evening before I change my mind.'

'I'd ring and give her some advanced warning.'

'Isn't she at work?' Dave asked.

'Don't you know anything? The doctor gave her a sick note, but it runs out at the end of this week. I think she intends to go back to work on Monday. But I'm not saying another word. She'll tell you what you need to know.'

Dave stayed until the end of visiting time and then returned to work to finish off some urgent business so he could leave early. It was time to talk to Robyn.

There was one positive to come out of all this for Robyn. The time off work had given her plenty of thinking space and not just about the men in her life. She'd made one decision she was happy with and could implement on Monday – to hand in her notice at work. Human Resources wasn't where she envisaged spending the next thirty years of her working life. After everything that had transpired, fulfilment was far more important than the increase in salary for climbing the next rung of the management ladder.

She'd no idea what to do next. What she did know was that she didn't want to work in an office, doing a routine job. Looking after the children was what mattered at the moment. They'd been through so much, and she wanted to put some stability back in their lives, with or without Dave's involvement. Since Jay was back in her life and the children were living with her again, there was light at the end of the tunnel. The bleak despair that had taken hold since Dave left had started to lift.

She was standing looking at an open fridge deciding what to make the children for tea when the door bell rang.

'Dave! Gosh…this is a surprise,' she said as she opened the door.

'Can we talk?' he asked.

'Absolutely … I've been waiting such a long time for you to say that.' Robyn smoothed her hair and adjusted her top. 'Come in. Can I get you a drink?'

'Yes, a coffee would be nice.'

Robyn left Dave looking somewhat out of place while she went into the kitchen.

'Is that Daddy?' Molly shouted as she ran downstairs.

'It is sweetheart; he's in the lounge,' Robyn replied.

'Daddy, Daddy! Have you come back?'

'I don't think so. He's just come to visit.' Robyn popped her head round the lounge door and looked awkwardly at Dave.

'Daddy, come and look at my picture.'

'He will in a minute. Just go back upstairs and watch Jake for me.'

'No! Watch him yourself. I want my Daddy. It's all your fault he's gone.'

Robyn stared at Molly incredulously.

'Molly, that's enough.' Dave chastised. 'Don't speak to your Mother like that.'

Molly started to cry.

Robyn knew the children must be affected by the break up but hadn't realised to what extent. Molly looked utterly traumatised.

'Come here, angel.' Robyn held her arms out, and her daughter ran into them.

'I'm sorry, Mummy.'

'I know you are, darling, but I should be the one saying sorry. Daddy will come and look at your picture, and after that, he can talk to me.'

Robyn sat on the settee sipping her steaming mug of coffee. Eventually, Dave walked into the lounge.

'Is she alright?' Robyn asked. 'I didn't realise she had so much anger. I've never heard her speak like that before.'

'Me neither. She seems to have calmed down.'

There was an awkward silence as neither of them knew where to begin.

'I suppose one of us needs to say something.' Robyn looked at Dave.

'I need to know why,' Dave asked.

Robyn paused. 'Look Dave, please believe me, I wasn't looking for anyone else. I love you and always have. I could say I was unhappy but it wouldn't be true ... well, not really. I suppose a few things have been getting me down ... Your hours for instance. You always seem to be working, and sometimes I just feel like a slave ... but they're just excuses ... I should have said something.'

'If I'm ever going to get over this, you need to tell me what happened.'

Robyn paused. How could she explain without hurting her husband even more?

'It all started the weekend of that seminar in Leeds ... One of the tasks set was to find connections between us all. Robyn and Jay are both birds' names, so we ended up together. We just clicked. Jay did make a pass at me, but I turned him down ... because of us.'

Dave sneered, but Robyn was on a roll so chose to ignore him.

'We left on Sunday, and I thought that was the end of it, and it was. He came into my mind once or twice during the week, but it wasn't until he requested me as a friend on Facebook that I realised how much I was missing him. We arranged to meet in Leeds a week later, and I've been seeing him ever since,' she paused. 'I wish I could give you a better reason.'

'Didn't you feel guilty? I mean it'd been going on for months?

'Honestly, no!' Robyn thought for a second. 'Actually, that's not strictly true. I'd occasionally get the odd pang but not enough to stop me... In my own warped mind, I wasn't hurting anyone. You didn't know and I thought I was acting perfectly normally in front of you. Our marriage didn't seem to be suffering, and it wasn't that we didn't make love anymore. In fact, I remember you commenting that I seemed hornier than ever.'

'Yes, but I thought it was because of me, not because you were shagging another man.'

'I don't know what else I can say. I've tried to think of every reason why I slept with him, but all I can come up with is ... it was exciting whereas my life wasn't.'

'But you only had to say. We could've done more things together.'

'I know that now.'

'I did have my suspicions, you know,' Dave admitted.

'Then why didn't you say anything. It could've saved all this heartache.'

'Because I didn't want it to be true. I thought if I ignored the signs, they'd go away.'

'We should've talked about it.' Robyn sighed.

'Do you love him?'

'Seeing as we're being honest... Yes I do.'

She saw the look of hurt on Dave's face. 'I love both of you, like I love my parents and my children.'

'But you're not allowed to love two men?'

'Who made that rule? And how do you stop loving someone?' Robyn had been trying to answer that question for months.

'You decide what you want, and live with the decision.'

'You think I haven't tried? Dad told me to make a list, but every time I compared the two of you ...' she shrugged. 'So, in theory, yes, but it's not that easy. All I know is, I haven't stopped loving you even though you've left and we may not get back together.'

'But you would stop loving me eventually.'

'I suppose so, eventually.'

'So you would stop loving Jay if you stopped seeing him.'

'By that logic, yes I would.'

'Would you be prepared to stop seeing him?' Dave asked.

The thought of never seeing Jay again filled Robyn with such dread she couldn't answer, but she knew Dave wanted to hear her say yes. It had taken a lot for him to come round today, so she had to at least make an effort.

'Yes, I would,' Robyn said eventually, the words hardly leaving her lips.

Dave looked relieved, 'All right, then.'

There was a natural pause in the conversation, then Robyn spoke first,

'Do you want us to get back together?'

'I'd like to spend more time here with you, and we'll see how it goes.'

Robyn had waited so long for Dave to say those words, and now they'd been spoken, she felt sick.

'How does that sound?' Dave asked, looking disappointed by her reaction.

'I think we'd have to take it one step at a time. If we do try and make a go of it, things would have to be different. We'd have to talk more and not get complacent. I couldn't risk this happening again. My nerves wouldn't take it.' Robyn admitted.

'Mine neither.' Dave sighed with relief. 'Have you seen Jay recently?'

'Yes, I have. He found out where I lived from Sarah at work and came round.'

'And does he still want you?'

'He does.' She paused. 'But I told him I wasn't making any decisions until me and you had spoken.'

'Are you sure this is what you want?' Dave asked running his fingers through his hair. 'Because I couldn't go through all this again and you still choose him.'

'I can't pretend I don't care for him but I promise I'll give our marriage my best shot. That's all I can say for now. Will that be enough for you, though?'

'Maybe. But I need you to accept it's going to be hard for me too. It's going to take a long time for me to trust you again.' Dave sipped his coffee, deep in thought. He continued,

'How about I come round tomorrow night, and we can have a word with the children? After tonight's outburst I know they'll be thrilled to have us back under the same roof.'

'I know.' Robyn sighed remembering Molly's disparaging look.

'Do they know about Jay?' Dave asked.

'Christ! No. I've told them Mummy and Daddy are mad at each other and need some time on their own.'

Dave nodded. 'I haven't said anything. I told them I was busy at work so I had to sleep there.'

'Maybe when they see us together, it'll help. I really think we need to make an effort for their sakes, don't you?' Robyn wished she could be more enthusiastic.

'Absolutely, and I'm sorry it took me so long to come round. I've been so angry.'

'You've had every right to be angry, and I'll keep saying sorry until you finally believe me.'

Dave looked at his watch. 'I'd better be getting off.'

'If you want, I'll cook us a meal tomorrow and we can talk to the children over the dinner table.'

'If you're sure. That'd be lovely, thank you.'

Robyn looked uncertain as Dave stood up to go. He walked towards her and gave her an awkward hug. She longed to enjoy his touch as much as she had Jay's, but there was nothing – she felt flat. Maybe given time, her feelings for Jay would diminish, and Dave would be enough for her. She owed it to her family to give it a go. Didn't she?

Chapter 22

October

It was six weeks to the day since Dave moved back into the family home, and Robyn wasn't finding it any easier. They'd shared a meal on the Saturday night as arranged and told the children the good news over the dinner table. It seemed no point in delaying the inevitable, and Robyn asked Dave to move his things back in after work on the Monday. For two days the atmosphere was strained until Robyn couldn't bear it any longer.

'Dave, what *is* the matter?' Robyn's patience was wearing thin. 'You've not spoken a word since you got home tonight, and I've got a splitting headache from all the banging about.'

'It's nothing.'

'It obviously is something. Come on, we said if this was going to work we had to be honest.'

'I thought you said you'd delete Jay's number from your phone and you've still got him on Facebook.'

'Oh Dave, it's only been two days. You know I want to tell Jay my decision face to face. If it's okay with you, I'll go and see him tomorrow.' She'd been putting it off as long as possible because it was going to be the hardest thing ever.

'Anyway, what were you doing looking at my phone? I thought you were going to try and trust me again.'

'I know, and I'm sorry. That's why I've been reluctant to say anything.' He looked embarrassed and added, 'I'm finding it harder than I thought. I really want us to work, and I promise to talk to you in future.'

Robyn walked across the kitchen and hugged him. 'Let's forget it. I'll go and see Jay tomorrow and then, hopefully, we can put the whole thing behind us.'

'There's just one more thing,' he paused. 'Could I sleep in your bed tonight?

Since returning home on Monday he'd slept on the camp bed in the office. Robyn thought about it swiftly then said, 'You can, but I can't promise sex or anything. It's just taking me a bit of time to adjust.'

'That's fine. I won't put any pressure on you, but a cuddle would be nice.'

'A cuddle would be lovely,' she agreed.

It was dinner-time on Thursday before Robyn summoned up the courage to visit Jay in his room at the Premier Inn. She knocked and heard him shout, 'Come in.'

He was busy at his computer, 'Just a second love, I'm in the middle of a rather pivotal sentence.'

Robyn stood and stared at him with a blank expression. How was she going to keep her nerve when she loved him so much?

He knew her decision as soon as he saw her face. 'Why', was all Jay could find to say.

She sat down on the bed, her legs feeling wobbly.

'Because it's what I know.'

Jay gave a groan. 'But it's all you ever *will* know unless you give something else a try. What about us? Look how perfect we were together last week? You told me I made you feel like a different person – and you *were* different. By the time I left the following morning, you were the Robyn I fell in love with. Where has she gone now?'

Robyn sighed. 'She's in here somewhere. I've just buried her for a while.'

'But for how long? I know you'll regret it. By the look on your face you already do.'

'Maybe … but don't make this any harder than it already is. I don't doubt for a second I love you, but is love enough? I have a whole life with Dave, and he's willing to forgive me, so surely I owe him that?'

'You're asking the wrong person, Robyn. I really don't think you owe him the rest of your life.' Jay slammed his laptop shut. 'Yes, it's great he'll have you back, although perhaps he'll play on your guilt for a while. But what happens in a few years when what brought you to me happens again?'

'It won't!' She stood up. 'I've learnt my lesson. Anyway, it's you I fell in love with.'

'And you look as though you still are.' He looked at her searchingly.

'I know it, and you know it. We could go on like this all day, but I've made a decision, Jay. It might be the wrong one. Who knows? But I'm going to live with it. In my mind I'm giving my marriage six months.'

'Then that's doomed for a start!' Jay sneered.

Robyn ignored his comment, 'If you find someone else in the meantime, so be it. But I won't be contacting you. It hurts too much to see you, and I know if we speak, I'll end up giving in. As far as I'm concerned, this will be the last time we see each other.'

'Please don't say that! I desperately want you in my life.' Despite trying so hard to keep his emotions in check, tears pricked Jay's eyes.

'If you love me like you say, you'll have to respect my decision. I can't offer you anything else.'

'I can't stay here. You do realise that?' Jay took a handkerchief out of his pocket and blew his nose.

'I don't want you to. I'd rather not know where you are, so I can't come looking for you.'

'For the record, I think you're making the worst decision of your life. I had more faith in you than this.' He said, his voice bitter with disappointment. 'Now, if you don't mind, I'd like to get on with my book. The door's behind you.' He sat down, opened his laptop and turned away, his back to her.

Robyn walked towards him, 'Can I at least have a hug?'

He didn't turn round and said, 'No, it hurts too much. We said goodbye before, how much more do you think I can take? My heart isn't made of stone. I love you more than I've ever loved anyone or believe I ever will, but life goes on. Thanks for having the nerve to tell me to my face, I'm grateful.' He resumed typing, adding resentfully,

'If you don't mind I have a book to finish.' He never even looked up.

Robyn ran out of the room sobbing, and collapsed against the hotel corridor.

My God! What have I done?

Today was the day of Robyn's leaving party and Sarah had organised a table at *Dolce Vita* for six o'clock. Robyn had asked if she could bring Dave, Denizon and Chris along to the meal as she didn't like to go anywhere recently without the security of her family.

The anti-depressants were helping, although anxiety and panic attacks were still part of her daily routine. She'd kept her promise and hadn't contacted Jay despite being tempted every day – even deleting him from Facebook and removing his number from her phone. Although, before doing so, she copied it down on a piece of paper and hid it in her underwear drawer. There wasn't one day that passed without her wondering where he was and what he was doing.

Today was also her last at work. 'Well, that's everything cleared out of my desk,' said Robyn, closing the last drawer.

'Aren't you in the least bit sorry to go?' Sarah asked.

She shook her head. 'No, I'll miss you and the girls, but you'll be going on maternity leave soon, won't you?'

'Four weeks and counting!' Sarah gave a little grin. It had taken a while, but now she was looking forward to motherhood. Her mother was over the moon at having her first grandchild and offered to have the baby so Sarah could return to work.

'We'll keep in touch, won't we, Sarah? I know people always say that, but I mean it. I want to get to know this baby.'

'There's something I've been meaning to ask you.' Sarah said, 'Would you be my birthing partner? It was going to be my mum, but I'd rather you see my nether regions than her.'

'Are you sure?' Robyn's face lit up. Sarah nodded. 'Then I'd be honoured. When do I start?'

'The first class is next week, if you're up for it.'

'Nothing would give me more pleasure.'

'Brilliant. I'll send you the details via your e-mail. Apparently we have to take it seriously.'

'I remember it well; Dave was more nervous than I was.'

Sarah shrugged. 'I won't have that problem. I never saw the father again after that night.'

The restaurant booked for Robyn's farewell party was already busy with people having post-work-pre-weekend drinks. Their group of twenty was shown to a table at the back of the room. Robyn was placed at the head, with Sarah at one side and Dave, when he arrived, at the other. One by one, the party took their seats, dropping off cards and presents to Robyn as they walked past.

Robyn spotted Dave looking round the busy restaurant.

'Over here,' she shouted and waved. Denizon and Chris followed closely behind him. Robyn wished she had a camera to photograph the look on Sarah's face as she caught her first glimpse of Chris. Neither of them spoke, they just stared at each other and then Chris saw Sarah's swollen belly, hard to miss at her stage of pregnancy. His face was a picture.

Robyn knew in an instant what was going on, though understandably hadn't made the connection before. When Sarah had described her drunken one night stand outside a night club in Hull, Robyn's first thought hadn't been that the man was her own brother. She looked at Denizon, who at present seemed oblivious to the charged atmosphere. Robyn was appalled. Not only was her unsuspecting best friend going to have a meal with one of her husband's conquests, but she would have to look at and probably chat with the mother of his child!

However, without warning Sarah stood up, grabbed Chris by the arm and, watched by the whole party, marched him out of the restaurant.

'What's going on?' asked Denizon, 'Who's that girl? What does she want with Chris?'

'That's Sarah my assistant,' said Robyn, feeling very uncomfortable.

'Does she know Chris?' Denizon frowned.

'I think...er yes, I think so. In – in the biblical sense.' Robyn cringed inwardly as she waited for the inevitable reaction.

'WHAT?' Denizon yelled at the top of her voice. 'I'll kill him!' She dashed outside. Robyn got up and rushed after her.

'Come back inside, Denizon! You'll only get upset.' But it was too late. Denizon had caught up with them outside in the middle of a very public argument.

'Did you not think to find me?' Sarah shouted at Chris.

'How did I know you were pregnant?' he shouted back.

'You didn't, you arsehole! You said you'd call me.'

'Like that was going to happen, you mad bitch! I don't even know your name.'

'Chris what's going on?' Denizon tried to make herself heard above the shouting.

'It's Sarah,' she yelled.

'I do know that you gave me gonorrhoea though, *Sarah*,' he spat out her name.

'Chris!' Denizon shouted.

'I did not! You gave it to me. Luckily for the baby, I was treated early on in my pregnancy.'

'Why didn't you get rid of it?'

'He's not an 'it', you bastard. *We* are having a baby boy.'

'That's enough! Will someone tell me what's going on? I am, after all, his wife.' Chris and Sarah stopped short and stared at Denizon.

'You never said you were married.' Sarah looked from Chris to Denizon.

'You never asked! ... and I seem to remember you couldn't wait to get your knickers down.'

As Sarah balled her hand into a fist, Denizon said hastily,

'Do I take it you think Chris is the father of your child?'

'Yes I do! I'm sorry not to spare the sordid details but we didn't use contraception The other man I was having sex with at the time had a vasectomy.'

Chris groaned.

'So, what do you want from Chris?' asked Denizon, her voice now surprisingly calm for someone who was facing her husband's pregnant one night stand.

'Seeing as I never thought I'd see him again, I don't want anything. It was my decision to have the baby, and I'll do it by myself,' Sarah said resolutely.

'Oh, but we can't let you do that, can we Chris?' Denizon looked daggers at her husband.

Chris looked down at his feet.

'It's my husband's responsibility, and he'll do right by you, I promise. It'll be a new experience for him since he's never done right by anyone else … would you excuse us a minute while I have a word with my husband?'

Sarah shrugged. 'Be my guest! You're welcome to him. I'm going inside anyway. I need to sit down and have a drink or something.' She marched clumsily back into the restaurant.

Denizon pulled Chris to one side as he whispered defensively,

'Are you out of your mind? How do you know she's telling the truth?'

Robyn, who'd been a silent spectator to all the exchanges jumped to her assistants' defence.

'Listen Chris! I know Sarah. Besides she's already told you she's not out for anything and is prepared to have the baby on her own. Obviously, seeing you was a shock, and she wanted to see what you had to say.'

'Well then! So what are you going to do?' Denizon asked Chris.

'I -I don't know. It's all come like a bolt from the blue.' Chris looked totally bemused.

'Look, I can't believe I'm about to say this, but if you have your name on the birth certificate, it would give you rights. We could be part of the baby's life. It might be the only chance we get.'

Chris suddenly focussed on what Denizon was proposing. 'What? You'd be prepared to raise another woman's child? Don't you think we should give it slightly more consideration than thirty seconds in a car park?'

Denizon nodded. 'We will – but why don't you and Sarah have a talk without me? Tell her we're thinking about wanting to be involved if possible. I'll go and ask her to come outside again. By the way, what do you want to eat? We'd better order.'

'Just get me a Pepperoni pizza and a pint of the strongest lager they sell,' Chris muttered.

'Are you coming back in, Rob?' Denizon asked.

'Could I referee? I know both of them and they might need all the help they can get.'

'But it's your leaving party,' Denizon protested.

'But it's also the fate of my nephew which is far more important.'

Looking thoughtful for a moment, Denizon said, 'Yes, that's a good idea, Rob. I'll order something for you as well – Hawaiian okay? As Robyn nodded, she said, 'I'll get Sarah, then.'

She disappeared inside, and after a couple of minutes, Sarah emerged, looking wary. However, she and Chris managed to stay calm with Robyn's steadying influence. Now wasn't the time or the place to make life changing decisions, so a meeting was arranged on Sunday morning at Robyn's house. Once it was sorted Chris, hurried back into the restaurant to check on his wife, leaving Robyn and Sarah outside.

'Well that was a turn up for the books,' Robyn said. 'You'll have to see me now; we'll be almost family. I'm even more delighted you asked me to be your birthing partner.'

Sarah looked surprisingly contented. 'There was never any question of that, regardless who the father is. I can't believe Chris is your brother.'

'Trust me, I've thought that on plenty of occasions over the years,' Robyn laughed.

'Do you think your sister-in-law meant what she said?'

'Denizon never says anything she doesn't mean. I've known her all my life, and you couldn't have a better influence on little… Have you thought of a name yet?'

'Not definitely, but I've got a few suggestions, Buster or Rogue,' Sarah said smiling.

'Rogue? What kind of a name is that?'

'It's the name of the night club where he was conceived. If it's good enough for Posh and Beck's, it's good enough for me.'

'Maybe Chris might be able to suggest some, as well,' Robyn offered, hoping Sarah would take that name right off the table. 'Let's go and eat, I've got a leaving party to enjoy and a bottle of champagne to drink.'

'Who'd have thought tonight would turn out like it has?' Sarah said but then looked serious, 'How are you finding life without Jay?'

On hearing his name, Robyn's good mood vanished into thin air.

'I keep expecting it to get easier, but it's getting harder every day. Even drinking champagne reminds me of him. The last time I drank it was on our very first night together. Tonight, since I've been out here, has been the only time today I haven't thought about him.'

'Maybe you need something to take your mind off him.'

'I know I do.'

'You don't regret your decision do you?'

Robyn couldn't even answer. She just shrugged her shoulders and walked back into the restaurant.

Chapter 23

Robyn was preparing the coffee and cakes for the mediation meeting on Sunday morning, when Dave walked into the immaculately tidy kitchen. 'Do you *really* think we should be getting involved in other people's affairs?' he snapped.

'This isn't other people,' said Robyn at once. 'It's my best friend and my brother.'

'I should've thought you'd enough on your plate without taking on anyone else's problems.'

'What do you mean by that?' Robyn asked.

'Well, he's never going to change is he, your brother? Who knows how many more bastards he has out there? Is Denizon going to take them all on?'

'I can't believe you just said that, Dave! It's my brother you're talking about and since when did you have the right to cast the first stone?'

'I'm not the one fathering illegitimate children. I've never even been unfaithful,' Dave replied bitterly.

'You sound sorry about that! At least Chris is trying to do right by Sarah. Have you thought what this'll mean to her?'

He snorted. 'She's just as bad, putting it about all over the place. What did you say Jay's book is called? Oh yeah, *"How to Have an Affair"*. Your family ought to take over the writing of it, between you all, it should be a doddle.'

'I think we should finish this conversation now before you throw any more hurtful comments in my family's direction.'

Robyn had been trying so hard to keep on the right side of her husband, but his moods were becoming increasingly stranger. One minute he was loving and attentive and, other times, like now, he was uncharacteristically cruel. She knew he was finding it hard to come to terms with her infidelity, and a day didn't go past without him making some sort of snide comment, but she was trying to make allowances for him. This tirade was his worst yet.

'Please yourself, you normally do anyway. I'm going to take the children to the park. I can't be in the same room with your brother, it'd be too hypocritical.' Dave stormed out leaving a shell shocked Robyn to carry on with her preparations.

Chris and Denizon arrived first, half an hour early. Denizon was visibly nervous.

'Calm down, Den. I don't know why you're getting all het up.' Robyn stroked her arm, concerned for her friend. Denizon sat down and cleared her throat.

'Well, it's partly because we've got a suggestion for Sarah, but I don't think she'll go for it. We want to co-parent. We have Barney half the week while Sarah is at work, and she has him from Friday over the weekend.'

Robyn was amazed that Denizon and Chris had already come to an accommodation *and* chosen a name.

'You're calling him Barney? It certainly sounds as though you've given it a lot of thought.'

'We've talked about nothing else. Barney was Chris's idea; he's really excited at the thought of being a father.' Chris nodded and smiled as Robyn said,

'Don't build your hopes too high. I know Sarah's mother has already offered to have him when she returns to work.'

'But he'll be so much better with his father,' Denizon replied. A little uncharitably, Robyn thought and wondered who she was really thinking of, herself or the baby.

Sarah arrived at the arranged time and Robyn showed her into the dining room, where Chris and Denizon were already sitting round the oval table. Robyn felt like a high court judge in session as she sat overseeing the proceedings. At once, Denizon said,

'I know we agreed that it would be only you and Chris, but would you mind awfully if I sat in?'

Sarah looked at Robyn, feeling outnumbered.

'If you feel awkward talking in front of Denizon then I'll take her into the kitchen,' Robyn offered.

'No, it's okay. Let's just see how it goes. I don't actually know what we're going to discuss anyway,' Sarah said looking confused.

Chris had obviously been rehearsing his speech under Denizon's guidance and responded quickly,

'I want to help support our son financially, and I'd like Denizon and I to be involved in his upbringing... er... how does that sound?'

'Gosh! ...Alright I suppose,' replied Sarah, 'but it's really hard to talk about something that hasn't happened yet. I don't know how I'm even going to feel about him.'

'I know it's a lot to take in, but we really would like you to give it serious consideration.' Denizon said, looking at Sarah and then Chris.

'So what are you suggesting?' Sarah asked.

Denizon outlined her plans for the care of the baby. Robyn could see Sarah was tempted, as it meant she could still maintain the life of an independent twenty one year old and have all the benefits of motherhood.

'Obviously we wouldn't dictate to you. You'll always have the final say and your mum can have him whenever she wants,' Denizon added.

'I'll have to discuss it with my mum?'

'Of course you will. Take as long as you like.' Denizon smiled. 'We're just grateful you've taken the time to listen to what we have to say, aren't we, Chris?' Not that Chris had been allowed to say much.

'Absolutely,' he agreed.

'Er... would you mind if I get off now? Sarah said looking at her watch. 'We've got family coming for Sunday dinner?'

'No problem!'

Sarah squirmed as Denizon gave her a hug. 'You've got our number and you can always ring Robyn if you feel more comfortable talking to her.'

'Thanks for coming, Sarah.' Robyn said. 'I'll see you Tuesday evening for the first class. Seven o'clock isn't it? I'll make sure I'm on time.'

'Okay, that'll be great.' Sarah turned to Chris and Denizon, 'Bye for now.'

Robyn let a bemused Sarah out of the front door, gave her a little wave and went back to the dining room.

'Do you think I came on a bit strong?' Denizon asked.

'Maybe a bit,' Robyn said honestly.

'But she didn't laugh at our suggestion.'

'But neither did she say, "Yes."' Chris said sulkily.

'Let's just wait and see, shall we? Until last Friday she'd no idea whether she'd see the father of her child again. It's only Sunday and you've presented her with a ready-made family.'

The mediation had served at least part of Robyn's purpose and had taken her mind off Jay for an hour, which had to be an improvement.

Jay looked at his phone and his heart sank when he saw a missed call from Maria. A kind word hadn't been spoken since the holiday and Jay really wasn't in a mood for another slanging match. He couldn't think why would she be ringing? Everything had already been signed over to her – he'd no use for material possessions, living in one room in a large Edwardian terrace house in Hackney.

The room was on a short-term lease, and he'd already decided he wouldn't be renewing it. Living down South wasn't what he imagined. He couldn't get used to the fact that everyone was so busy and didn't have time to chat, and so far, he hadn't made one friend. It didn't help that he was working at a computer all day, so his chances of meeting anyone were slim to negligible.

Now that he'd secured his publishing deal and a moderate advance, he could move back up North. He never thought he'd miss Leeds, but he appreciated the familiarity of small things like walking into the same cafe and the staff making his coffee exactly as he liked it. He knew he hadn't given London a fair chance, but with his emotions so raw, he felt he'd be better in surroundings he knew.

I'd better get it over with, he thought and keyed in her number.

'Hello, Maria. You rang,' he said holding the phone slightly away from his ear in anticipation.

'Hello, Jay. Thanks for getting back to me. Don't worry, nothing's wrong. In fact, I've got good news, and it gets you off the hook as well.'

'Er …What do you mean?'

'I'm moving to Italy and getting married,' Maria paused.

'Hello, Jay. Are you still there?' Maria asked.

'You're what?

'I'm getting married.'

'Sorry… er …good … I'm just a bit shocked that's all.'

'Yes, I'll admit it's a bit sudden, but Luigi wants to get married before I have the baby. He's offered to bring her up as his own. So if you agree, I won't be needing any financial help after all. He owns six butcher's shops in Tuscany, and they're all doing rather well.'

Jay smiled to himself, guessing money would be at the root of her obvious delight.

'Good for you,' Jay said. 'I'm really pleased, although you didn't waste much time.' He laughed.

'We didn't see any point. And it's not as if I've had to get over you. You're infidelity saw to that.'

'That's true.'

'There's just one more thing … It's a massive favour actually … would you mind if Luigi puts his name on the birth certificate? His family are Catholics and we just feel it would be best,' she paused then added, 'you can keep the flat and all its contents.'

Jay laughed. 'Thanks for that! But honestly, you don't need to buy me off.'

'You can still see Sofia, if you want.'

'How is … what's his name … Luigi, going to feel about that?'

'We've talked about it, and he's fine.'

'It's not going to be very practical though, is it?'

'I suppose not.'

'Let's just see what happens, shall we? We don't have to decide now.'

'Thank you, Jay for being so reasonable. But I did mean what I said, you can have the flat. My solicitor is transferring it back into your name as we speak.'

'Wow! … I bet your Dad's pleased, isn't he?'

'Yes, he is. It was Dad's idea to go and meet Luigi. We used to play together as children, but I hadn't seen him for years. We clicked instantly, and when he suggested marriage, I thought, why not... considering my circumstances. We get on really well, and I'm sure I can learn to love him.'

'As I said, I'm really pleased, and thank you for the flat. It's not working out in London, so I'll be glad to go back home.'

'How's it going with Robyn?' Maria asked.

Jay thought she must be happy as she hadn't used Robyn and bitch in the same sentence.

'We're not together any more. She decided to go back to her husband.'

'Oh, I'm so sorry, I knew how much she meant to you. Are you sure there's no hope?'

'It's been eight weeks now, and I've heard nothing. Although, to be honest, I don't know if I want her back. There's only so much rejection a man can take.'

'I know that feeling only too well! But look at me now? I'm about to give birth to Sofia Magdelene, and I'll have a husband this time next week.'

'I doubt my ending will be as happy, but that's just life.' Jay sighed. 'I really must go now, Maria, I've got to catch the post, but it's has been lovely talking to you. I wish you all the best and hope you'll all be very happy.'

'Thank you and I hope you meet someone else soon… By-the-way, will you send me a signed copy of your book when it comes out. It can be our secret.'

Jay laughed. 'I will, if you let me have your address.'

They said their final goodbyes, and Jay returned the phone to his pocket. He was going home to Leeds! Life has a funny way of working itself out, he thought. If only all things were as straightforward.

Chapter 24

November

Never one to count time before – Robyn marked her diary, and today was day ninety one without Jay. As she opened her eyes every, morning the pain of being without him washed over her. She dragged herself out of bed at seven to make three packed lunches, eat breakfast with the family, walk the children to school, go to the gym for an exercise class, have lunch, clean the house, walk the children home from school, play in the park if the weather was nice and go home to make tea. An occasional variation was calling in on her mother or Denizon, if she was feeling up to company.

The doctor had increased her dose of anti-depressants last week because the lower dose wasn't working as intended. Life was going nowhere fast, in stark contrast to the rest of her family. Her Dad had finally owned up to his true feelings, and asked her Mum for a divorce. He was buying a villa in Spain with Marjorie, the love of his life, and her Mum was buying a one bedroom bungalow on the same street as her sister. Even younger brother, Tiggs, was deserting her, moving down to Birmingham to be with his girlfriend.

Denizon was still supportive and very sympathetic to her plight but was so excited at the imminent arrival of Barney that Robyn hated to be around her in case misery was contagious.

What Robyn needed was a job. She'd signed on with three employment agencies, and they rang nearly every day with the offer of office temp jobs, which she politely declined. There was one job she'd applied for that she still hadn't heard about. She'd seen it advertised in the local paper, and it was for an Assistant/Care worker to a tetraplegic businessman who needed someone intelligent to help him run his business. Typing was essential and knowledge of accountancy a bonus. He already had a cleaner so there would be no manual work, just the occasional meal to prepare. It was the cooking that made her mind up to apply. If she was ever going to take her vague idea of opening a café any further she'd better ensure she liked cooking for others on a daily basis.

It was two weeks since she'd sent off her letter of application and, as each day passed, she was losing hope of hearing anything. She hadn't mentioned this particular job to Dave as she knew what his opinion would be. In fact, she could almost hear him say, 'a care assistant, have you gone mad? You didn't spend four years at university to be someone else's slave.'

Dave had an opinion about everything these days, and it usually involved belittling his wife. Despite his protestations to the contrary, he still hadn't forgiven her and seemed to relish making her suffer. Of course he denied it and was constantly telling her how much he loved her and how glad he was that they were back together, but his actions didn't seem to tally with the words.

Robyn had come straight home from the school run today. She was feeling a bit run down and suspected she was coming down with a cold. Body Combat was just too daunting a task. The kettle was on for a cup of tea when the house phone rang.

'Could I please speak to Robyn Fisher,' asked an elderly gentleman, his tone refined.

'This is Robyn Fisher,' she replied.

'Hello! My name is Gerald Banfleet, I'm sorry for the tardiness of my call, but I'm ringing to see if you're still interested in the position advertised in the "Hull Daily Mail"?'

'Yes I am, Mr Banfleet, and thank you for your call. I was only thinking about my application this morning.'

'Splendid! Would you like to meet? I was very impressed with your resume. You sound just the ticket.'

Robyn smiled. A meeting would certainly be amusing if nothing else. Who said "just the ticket" nowadays?

'Yes, that would be fine. Where would be convenient?'

'My home, if you've no objections. I live on Park Avenue, near the University. Do you know it?'

'I do! I spent many a happy hour as a student in my friends flat nearby.'

'I'm at number 153. Would tomorrow at noon suit?'

'That would be perfect. And thank you again for calling.'

'It's been a pleasure, my dear. I look forward to making your acquaintance tomorrow.'

Despite her runny nose and painful ears Robyn did a little jump. She had a good feeling about this. Maybe her misery was about to come to an end. Jay wouldn't be as scathing about her choice of job as Dave and then stopped herself abruptly. She still couldn't stop thinking about him even for one second.

The children were in bed before Robyn felt like telling Dave about her interview tomorrow. He wasn't as scornful as she'd envisaged. If anything, he was a tad patronising and said a little job was just what she needed and then maybe she could get off those stupid anti-depressants.

'What do you mean stupid anti-depressants?'

'Well firstly, I don't know what you've got to be depressed about?' he said sharply. 'And secondly, once you're on them it's awfully hard to get off. I don't want you turning into an addict.'

'Don't be ridiculous! I'm not turning into an addict. They're just helping me adjust to life at the moment.'

He gave her a sour look. 'You're not still pining for your lover after all this time, surely?'

Robyn shrugged, then said, 'It's not just about him. It's everything: my job, my parents. Everything's changed and I'm finding it a bit hard to cope with that's all. I hoped for a bit more support.'

'And I hoped our relationship would go back to how it was before, but we don't always get what we wish for,' he said harshly.

'I don't know what you mean,' she protested. 'I'm doing my best, I –'

'Well, for one thing,' he interrupted, 'we never used to bicker like this. And I know our sex life didn't exactly set the world on fire, but at least we used to do it. Now look at us. You haven't wanted to have sex for over a month.'

'That could be one of the side effects of the tablets. It does say things can feel a bit numb.'

'There, I rest my case. They are stupid, and you need to get yourself off them – for both our sakes,' he said firmly.

'I'm waiting for some counselling at the doctor's. I'm sure that'll help,' she said.

'What, so you can talk about everything that's making you depressed? That'll only make it even worse. You're supposed to have forgotten about Jay by now. Come on Robyn, you really need to pull yourself together.'

'I know,' she admitted slowly. 'That's why I'm looking forward to the chance of this job. It's perhaps not exactly suited to my skill levels, but that might be quite refreshing. I'll never have to bring my work home.'

Dave grunted, 'Who is this man anyway?'

'I don't know much about him, but he sounded nice. Quite upper class, I thought. Try and be pleased for me.'

Dave thought for a moment. 'Okay, love. If it's really what you want, then go for it … Now, can we please have an early night? If you can't feel anything, fake it! I'm sure you've done it before.'

Robyn knew she hadn't been fair to her husband, but it was difficult to summon up enthusiasm to even kiss him. She couldn't blame the tablets. There was only one man she wanted to make love with, and he was out of bounds.

'You cheeky sod! I've never faked it. But you can have your wicked way. I'll just lay there and think of England.'

'I don't care what you think about as long as you're willing to open your legs.'

'Dave, that's awful,' she hit him playfully on the cheek, and he caught hold of her hand, giving it a squeeze.

'I'm sorry if I've been a bit grumpy recently.'

'I'm sorry too,' she said, squeezing his hand back. 'I will make more of an effort, I promise.'

'You don't regret us getting back together, do you?'

'No,' she lied. She'd made her bed and had to lie in it, for a bit longer at least.

Robyn didn't have to fake it after all – although she'd pictured Jay's face as she climaxed.

'That was okay for you wasn't it?' Dave enquired as Robyn lay quietly next to him.

'It was more than okay, it felt lovely,' she said, snuggling under Dave's arm.

'Do you think we'll make it, Rob?' Dave asked quietly.

'I think so,' she turned to look at him. 'I really will make more of an effort. Perhaps we should get a baby sitter once a week and go out.' Robyn suggested.

'That'd be lovely. We used to enjoy the theatre.'

'I'll have a look to see if there's anything on that we fancy.'

Dave leaned across and kissed her. 'I know I don't tell you enough, but I do love you.'

'I love you too.'

'Do you fancy another round?' Dave smiled.

'I think once is enough for tonight. Break me in gently.' She rolled over onto her front.

'In that case, would you like a hot drink?' Dave suggested. Robyn was surprised as Dave usually liked to go straight to sleep after making love. It was one of the things she missed about love making with Jay. He liked to chat afterwards.

'That would be lovely, thank you.'

Dave returned a few minutes later with tea and chocolate chip cookies.

'Don't you be making any crumbs. I've changed the bed today.'

Dave threw two biscuits at her. One hit her arm and broke in two, scattering crumbs all over her stomach.

'Too late,' he said as he jumped on the bed. 'I'll just have to lick them off.'

'Get off me, you're heavy,' Robyn laughed.

It was after one o'clock when they finally turned the light off to get some sleep.

What do you wear to an interview for a care assistant? Robyn stood looking at her extensive wardrobe next morning. One of her many suits would be exactly right for an interview in Human Resources – but this was a different matter. Gerald Banfleet didn't seem like a jeans type of man either.

Half her clothes ended up on the bed before she decided on a light wool dress in navy with high tan shoes and a matching belt. *I really must have my hair cut.* She looked in the mirror at the long inverted bob which had grown out, leaving her auburn locks in no style, hanging round her face. A couple of strategically placed clips would have to do.

She'd no idea what type of questions he would ask and carefully studied her curriculum vitae to make sure she could remember all the dates. As she set off, with plenty of time to spare, Robyn just hoped she could get through without a panic attack. She'd taken her Rescue Remedy and had stowed away a paper bag in case of emergency.

It was only eleven forty as she pulled up outside 153 Park Avenue. It was one of the larger imposing Victorian Villas on the prestigious Avenues that hadn't been divided into flats. She could see some movement in the front room through the hedge. *Is it polite to be so early or should I sit and wait until twelve o'clock?* Her decision was made for her, as the front door opened and an elderly lady wearing an apron beckoned her to come in.

'Mr. Banfleet saw you were here, Mrs. Fisher. Please follow me.' The lady, who was probably the housekeeper, showed her into the dining room.

The oak dining table had files laid out neatly in piles over its surface and a pad of paper for making notes.

'Please take a seat, Mr. Banfleet will be in shortly, can I get you a drink of anything?'

'No, thank you. I'm fine.'

'Very well, then. I'll leave you to it.'

Robyn looked keenly round the room. Its antique oak furniture was beautifully clean, chair seats and curtains in expensive fabrics of muted gold and burgundy. The focal point of the room was a stunning black marble fire place. There were two photographs on the mantelpiece, which she strained to see from her chair. One was of a young couple and, judging by the fashions, obviously taken many years ago. The woman was sitting on a swing laughing, while the man stood behind her, pushing. The second photograph looked to be the same couple many years later. This had an interior setting and was more posed. Both faces were serious this time with just the hint of a smile.

Robyn quickly turned her head at the sound of a motorised wheelchair entering the room, its occupant, a man probably in his late sixties, she decided. As the chair came to a halt in front of her own, the man smiled. He had a mass of snowy white hair with a stern, but welcoming, demeanour as she recognised him as the man in the photographs on the mantelpiece. With difficulty he held up his right hand for Robyn to shake.

'Sorry to keep you waiting, Mrs. Robyn Fisher, I presume?' She stood up, not knowing what to do.

'Yes, pleased to meet you.' She'd no idea what to expect from her potential employer's incapacitated situation and was shocked at the limited movement his disability allowed. His wrist looked so weak she felt it would break at her touch.

He could sense her discomfort, 'Please, do sit down again and we'll get started. I'll spend some time explaining about myself and what the job requires. If it doesn't put you off, you can tell me about yourself. Does that sound like a good plan?' He smiled again.

'Erm … perfect,' she replied.

'I'll start with my disability, if I may,' he began quietly. 'I'm a C6 tetraplegic which means I severed my spine at the 6th cervical vertebrae. I have no movement at all from the rib cage down and only limited movement in my arms. I can lift both my arms like this,' he added, giving a demonstration.

'Most people are interested in how I came to be paralysed, and I saw you looking at the photographs as I came into the room. And yes, they are of me.' He paused.

'Is the lady your wife?' Robyn asked. 'She's very beautiful.'

'She was,' he sighed wistfully. 'I was involved in a car accident ten years ago in which my beautiful Camille was killed. Sadly, I survived, and here I am today in this monstrosity. As I age, my movement gets less, as my hands become more arthritic.'

'I'm so sorry for mentioning her.' *Oh great, I've managed to put my foot in it already!*

'Not a problem. I only miss her for twelve hours a day, nowadays, as opposed to the twenty-four at the beginning, so things are slowly getting better. I'm an aeronautical engineer, and I've worked all over the world. I met Camille whilst I was working in Paris. She was a model but gave it all up to be with me in this Godforsaken country. If we'd have stayed in France, this may never have happened.

'I still work, but only on a consultancy basis nowadays, and I'm looking for someone who can type up all my reports and generally be my hands and legs in the working environment. The job will involve some travelling for up to four days at a time. Would that be a problem for you? I see from your resume you have two small children?'

'Would I get any notice?' Robyn asked, wondering if Dave would cope with more pressure on him regarding the children. Perhaps, her Mum might help though.

'I tend to go away once every two months, and I know plenty of time in advance. I do quite a bit of work in Switzerland. Do you speak French?'

'No, only Spanish, sorry. But I did French GCSE,' she added hopefully.

'Don't worry, it's not a requirement,' he said, his fading blue eyes twinkling. 'It would just have been a bonus, that's all. I speak fluent French, so that's fine. The other part of the job is cover when Mrs. Bennett is off. She works five days out of seven and is my cook, cleaner and general housekeeper. The two days she has off varies from week to week, so there would be weekends involved for you. How does that sound? It would only be four hours a day at the weekends and six hours a day during the week.'

'That seems very reasonable.'

He nodded. 'I wouldn't expect you to clean, but you'd have to prepare my meals, and help the carer with my other needs. I expect you'd like to know what that involves.'

Robyn decided to be absolutely straightforward. 'I apologise for my ignorance, Mr. Banfleet, but the advert doesn't give much away. I think I'm probably wasting your time as I have no experience at all in caring for someone such as yourself.'

'The advert was phrased like that on purpose because it's far more important for me to like the person, than have years in the caring profession. I already have carers who come in to do things like put me to bed and such like. It's an assistant I'm looking for, and I would rather have something in common with them. I'm sorry if that's not politically correct, but I feel very strongly about it.'

'I admire your honesty. I'm not a squeamish person, and I doubt I'd be put off by anything. But I wouldn't know if I could cope until I gave it a try.'

'Thank you for your own honesty. You'll be pleased to know my bowel functions are taken care of, but I do need help getting in and out of my wet room and dressing my lower half.'

Robyn breathed a sigh of relief. She would have no trouble doing those sorts of tasks, but more intimate toileting may have been a deal breaker.

'What would I call you, Mr. Banfleet or Gerald?'

'Mrs Bennett called me "sir" for years. She calls me Mr. Banfleet now, but I suppose I could get used to Gerald.'

'I don't think I could call you "sir",' Robyn laughed. 'I think we'd start with Mr. Banfleet. Do you want to know something about me?'

'Tell me something that isn't on your resume.'

'Well … er, I gave up my management job because I hated Human Resources. I liked the people side but disliked risk assessments and all the paper work. But, I don't dislike relevant paper work and I actually enjoy typing. But working in an office doing the same thing day in, day out was tedious.' *I'm doing it again!*

'I've always fancied opening a small cafe or bistro but, though I love to cook, I've never got round to taking it further. So apart from working in a routine job and bringing up two children, that's it really so far. I've certainly not travelled like you.'

He gave her a warm smile. 'Perhaps not – but motherhood is an admirable calling. Camille always wanted to be a mother, but nature had other plans. … Now tell me about your husband? The reason I'm asking is that he'll need to be supportive. I'm quite a demanding old misery and have been known to ring for assistance in the middle of the night if I fall or drop anything.'

Robyn didn't know what to say. In fairness to Dave she thought he would be, but she needed to talk to him first. Mr. Banfleet saw her hesitation and said,

'If you do take the job, one thing you'll have to get used to is I'm a bit of a mind-reader. Since losing the feeling in most of my body, other senses have heightened. I sense you're having difficulty with the last question so we'll move on… so how would you benefit my life?'

Robyn gathered her thoughts for a moment. 'Well, I'm organised. I've been told I'm honest and fair. I try to have a positive outlook on life; although I've been struggling with that a little recently, since I gave up work. I'm quite a perfectionist and like things done properly. Oh, and I've been told I'm fun to work with – and I think I'm …'

'That's excellent,' he said, cutting in.

'I can pay you a starting wage of fifteen pounds an hour. I appreciate it's a considerable drop in salary, but it will increase the more use you are to me.'

Robyn nodded, thinking it very fair for someone with absolutely no experience. 'Do you have other people to see?'

'Yes, I'm seeing six more people this afternoon. I will make a decision tonight and ring you at seven thirty. Would that be suitable?'

'Yes, that would be fine. Although I'll be putting the children to bed so I might take longer to answer.'

'In that case I'll make it eight,' he said, at once. 'Please consider our conversation and talk to your husband as, if I do offer you the post, I'll expect an immediate decision.'

Sensing the interview was drawing to a close, Robyn said quickly, 'Why did your last assistant leave? I hope you don't mind me asking.'

'My last assistant moved on to start his nursing qualification. I know I'm not allowed to request a female, with all this sexual discrimination nonsense, but I found dealing with a man hard work. It's only females for me from now on… Are you regretting your decision to come here today?' His eyes twinkled again and Robyn said decisively,

'On the contrary, I think I'd really enjoy working for you. It seems there's a lot of variety and you seem like a very interesting man.'

'I'm glad you came, Mrs. Fisher? Thank you. Or may I call you Robyn? You don't seem like a Mrs. Fisher.'

Robyn was tempted to add, she didn't feel like one either, but if she was offered this job, perhaps she could open up her heart to him at a later date, depending on their relationship.

She smiled and stood up. 'Robyn would be fine.'

'We'll, speak later then. Oh, just one more thing. When could you start?'

'As soon as you need me. My children are at school and nursery, so I'm free after dropping them off.'

Robyn hoped Pauline hadn't filled Molly and Jake's places as she'd want help collecting the children.

Gerald Banfleet rang the bell on his wheelchair. 'Goodbye, Robyn. Mrs. Bennett will show you out. I won't shake your hand; I saw how uncomfortable it made you.'

Is he intuitive? Or did my face give it away?

'It did at first, but it would be a pleasure to shake your hand now.' Bending down, she held out her hand, and he shook it.

'Goodbye again, my dear.'

Mrs. Bennett showed Robyn to the door beaming 'He certainly likes you. I haven't seen him so animated since losing Camille.'

'But that was ten years ago! How long have you worked for him, Mrs. Bennett?'

'I started as a housekeeper to them both fifteen years ago. I couldn't leave him after he lost her; he wouldn't have survived. I should've retired five years ago, but I'm still here. Luckily, I've got a good husband. Mr. Banfleet's a good employer though, just a bit demanding.' She smiled. 'Perhaps we'll see you again. I hope so.'

Robyn walked back to her car, confident the interview had gone well. She desperately wanted to ring Jay and tell him about it, but hopefully, if she got the job, it would help to put him to the back of her mind once and for all.

Just as she was about to pull away, her mobile phone rang, a number she didn't recognise,

'Hello.'

'Is that Robyn Fisher?

'Yes, speaking.'

'It's the doctor's surgery here. We have an opening for a course of counselling starting this Thursday at two o'clock, would that time be suitable?'

'It would for now, but I've just been for an interview for a job and, if I get it, two o'clock would be impossible.'

'If you take the slot you can always renegotiate the time with the counsellor. However if you refuse, you'll lose your place on the list.'

'In that case I'll take it. Thank you.'

'The counsellor's name is Mr. Paul Hargreaves. If you come to reception and fill out some forms at one thirty on Thursday that would be great.'

'No problem, thanks again.'

She sat for a few moments before starting her car again. Her life was really looking up, counselling and a potential job in one afternoon. Robyn needed to share her good news and what better person to share it with than Denizon. She drove past her house and saw Chris washing both cars in the drive.

'Hi, darling brother, is Denizon in?'

'She's in the studio. Why is it you never come to see me?'

'Sorry,' Robyn grinned. 'I've come to tell her some news, but I can tell you. I've been for an interview for a job, and I'm starting counselling on Thursday.'

'Good for you. What's the job?'

'Personal assistant to a disabled man.'

'Wow, that's a bit different for you.' Chris finished washing the car quickly. 'Tell me more.'

'It is different, but I saw it advertised, and I fancied it. He seemed impressed with me anyway.'

'That figures!' Chris said. 'Come in and have a coffee or something.'

Going through to their large comfortable kitchen, Robyn sat down. 'Coffee would be good, Chris, thanks.'

He put on the kettle. 'So who is this man? Anyone we know?'

'His name is Gerald Banfleet. He lives on Park Avenue.'

'Yeah, I know him. *The* Gerald Banfleet, ex-leader of the council, has his own Aeronautical Engineering Company.'

'How do you know this?' Robyn was intrigued.

'Because I keep my eyes and ears open,' said Chris. 'I was also one of the fire fighters who helped cut him out of his car on the A63 when he was involved in a head on collision. It killed his wife, did he tell you that?'

'He mentioned she'd been killed in a car accident. Did you know it left him paralysed?'

'Yes, he was lucky to be alive, the car was unrecognisable.'

'I don't think he sees himself as lucky. He's never got over it.'

'I'm not surprised, it was his fault. He'd been drinking and lost control at the wheel. The other driver was killed instantly.' Chris handed Robyn a mug of coffee and she said,

'I'm surprised he didn't get prosecuted.'

'He did. I think it was because he was such a prominent local politician, and his injuries were so bad, that he avoided prison. He was given a mammoth fine and banned for years, but he was unable to drive anyway.'

'I don't remember it at all.'

'You were only twenty-three. I assume you had more important things to think about than local news. Anyhow, what's he like?'

'He's lovely, a bit imposing, but I like him.'

'He must have mellowed then!' Chris took a sip of his drink. 'Banfleet used to terrify people.'

'I think losing his wife affected him deeply, his housekeeper said as much.'

'Do you want the job if you're offered it?'

Robyn nodded. 'I think I do. It will be a real challenge.'

'In that case, I hope you get it. Oh, if you're going round to the studio now, I'll make Denizon a cup of tea. I'll bring it through when it's ready.'

'Am I in the right house?' She could count on one hand the number of cups of tea Chris had made in his lifetime.

'Less of the sarcasm, Sis. '

She walked to the back of the house where Denizon had her studio, 'Only me,' Robyn shouted as she opened the door.

'Hi sweetie, come in. What can I do for you?'

Robyn recounted the interview story and told her friend about the counselling.

'Wow, that's great news, so why aren't you over the moon?' she said, looking at Robyn's sad expression.

Robyn looked down and said quietly,

'I miss him so much, Den.'

'Still?' She tenderly rubbed Robyn's arm. 'I'd have thought you'd have got over him by now.'

'So did I, and I don't understand why I can't? It's not as if I saw him all the time, but I suppose we talked every day. I used to tell him all about my day and my innermost thoughts, and now I don't have anyone to talk to.'

'You've got Dave and me.' Denizon offered.

'I don't want to burden you with my problems when you've got so much going on, and I have to pretend I'm fine in front of Dave or else he sulks.'

'Then contact Jay. Send him a text.'

'I promised myself I'd give it six months, though.'

'Well you shouldn't have done that! It's not as if you've promised anyone else.'

'I know that … But in any case, he might not want me to contact him. He was pretty angry when I left. He's probably got over me.'

'If he loved you as much as you said, he won't be. Besides, you won't know until you try.'

'I'll think about it,' said Robyn. 'But I'll wait to see what the counsellor says and if I get this job. Once I've got something to occupy my mind, I might be fine. How are you and Chris getting on by the way?'

Denizon blushed, 'We slept together last night, and it was wonderful.'

'So that's why he's making you a cup of tea; I thought it was strange.' Robyn laughed. 'And? What does it mean?'

'I think it means we're going to give it a try. Even if it doesn't work out with Sarah we definitely want to adopt if we can't conceive naturally. He's been a different person entirely since finding out about Barney. Your Mum was right. She always said he'd settle down when children were involved.'

'I'm so pleased. Do you want me to ring Sarah to ask if she is closer to a decision? Though I am seeing her tomorrow night at ante-natal class?'

'No, I don't feel as desperate now, I think it was filling a gap that only Chris can fill, and he filled it last night.' Denizon sniggered.

'That's way too much information,' laughed Robyn.

Just at that moment Chris walked in with a steaming hot mug of tea.

'I heard my name mentioned. What have I done now?' He asked.

'Nothing, Darling, I was just telling Robyn about last night.' Denizon squeezed his hand.

'I hope you didn't tell her everything.'

'No. Some things stay between the two of us.' she grinned at her husband.

It was lovely seeing two people so happy, but it made Robyn envious, and she wondered if she would ever feel that happy again.

Chapter 25

December

Robyn was already three weeks into her job with Gerald Banfleet, and she loved it, even the elements of personal care she took in her stride. Robyn dropped the children off at school and nursery in the morning and was at Gerald's by nine o'clock. The two of them always started the day with a coffee and a briefing.

The first overseas trip was coming up the week before Christmas. It was two nights in Brussels, and Robyn was excited – once Gerald was firmly ensconced in his meeting, she would have a few hours to shop.

Her marriage was on a much more even keel, as well. Dave had stopped the snide comments pretty much as soon as Robyn made love with him again. She couldn't say she was happy yet, but she was definitely more settled. Gerald was agreeable about letting her have the time off for the counselling without asking too many questions.

She had an appointment today and was waiting to be called into the consulting room. Robyn had never been in this situation before, and the first week had been practically silent as she kept expecting the counsellor to ask her questions, but he'd just sat there waiting for her to open up. The second session had been livelier as she'd introduced Jay and Dave into her conversation, but she was determined to be a lot more open today.

'Hi Robyn, you can come in now.' Paul Hargreaves said as he opened the door. In his late fifties, he was a smart man with stylish glasses. He wasn't easily amused, despite Robyn cracking the odd joke to break the ice, something he seemed to feel a distraction.

'Take a seat, Robyn.'

'Thank you.'

'If you remember back to last week we started to look at why you had an affair. Maybe we can start there.'

'Okay.'

'Why do you think that happened?'

'Er … Because I was attracted to Jay.'

She expected a comment from Paul but all he said was, 'And.'

Robyn paused, trying to think of something to add.

'He wanted me. I don't know … I loved the attention, and I found it all very exciting and I suppose, I thought I could get away with it,' she admitted. 'It was as if I was living a completely separate life. I was a different person with Jay. I've known Dave since I was twenty one. And we've been married for seven years. I wasn't looking for anyone else, but when I met Jay all I craved was the excitement. I lived for the times when I could see him or talk to him. Having an affair with him has been the most adventurous thing I've ever done.'

'Were you happy in your marriage?' Paul asked.

'I thought I was until I met Jay.'

'Can you explain that?'

'I'd never really questioned my marriage before. Dave's always been a good husband. He's been a good provider and takes great care of me and the children. I thought that's what I wanted, but with Jay … I don't know … I shared things. The sex was amazing, but it wasn't just about that. I felt he was my friend. I didn't see him all that often, but we talked every day which was wonderful. He was interested in everything I had to say, even little trivial things.'

'So why did you end it?'

Robyn shrugged. 'Because it was expected of me, and it was best for the children. Robyn expected another question but Paul sat there silently.

'I can't give you a better answer,' she added. 'My dad encouraged me to end it before someone got hurt, but Dave found out and I went to pieces. I just couldn't cope and, to cut a long story short, when Dave said he'd like to give our marriage another try, I agreed. I still love Dave but I haven't got over Jay. It's been four months now and I still miss him as much as ever.'

'Do you want to get over him?'

Without thinking Robyn said, 'No, I don't … and thinking about him keeps the whole thing alive for me. I've spent all this time working out ways to rid him from my mind when, if I'm honest, I don't want to at all. I thought the anti-depressants would do that but they haven't.'

'Because?'

'Because I still love him.' Robyn breathed a huge sigh of relief as she realised she'd been honest for the first time since letting Jay go from her life.

'And how does that make you feel?'

'Free,' she sighed. 'I'm tired of fighting my emotions.'

The hour finally came to an end, and Robyn walked out of the consulting room with a huge weight lifted off her shoulders.

Jay didn't bother living in the room in Hackney until his notice period ended. He packed the same day as talking to Maria and drove straight back to Leeds. The flat was exactly as he left it. He was so pleased to be home and realised how desperate he was to share it with Robyn, but there was no chance of that.

Now he was living in Leeds again, he intended getting in touch with some old clients just to tell them he was back. He wasn't going to rent any office space yet, but use the office in the flat for the time being. There were a lot of disappointed people when he left, so hopefully he could pick up a few clients to supplement his book advance and writing royalties when they came in. *"How to Have an Affair"* was nearly finished. The only thing he was having trouble with was an ending, partly because everyone's ending was different, including his own. He'd managed to take himself out of the content sticking to his original brief of using his professional cases. Even if he did say so himself, it was very good and served its original intention as a guide and work book.

There was one more section he was thinking of adding to his original five, and he hadn't yet decided on a title. It was going to be about the aftermath of an affair. He wanted to give readers a reality check – once it was all over, life would continue, but it might be a while before they come to terms with the emotional trauma – as he knew from bitter experience. A few tips and pointers would be beneficial. They certainly would be for him.

He sat at his computer and waited for inspiration. There were two unread e-mails in his inbox. One was from Max Hammond,

"Hi Jay, many thanks for sending me a copy of 'How to Have an Affair' to proof read. I'm well into it now and should be finished by the end of the week. Just a couple of constructive criticisms, you seem to still be in the book, even though you told me you've taken yourself out. I can tell you're missing Robyn and I do think you need to resolve it before you write your final draft. Secondly you seem a tad bitter. It's supposed to give your readers hope and a positive experience but some sections do exactly the opposite. If you'd like to get together I'd welcome a chance to speak to you face to face."

Jay thought carefully before starting to type.

"Thanks Max, sadly I agree with everything you're saying and I'd love to get together but I'm no longer in London. I've moved back home to Leeds."

He pressed send. And the conversation between them went as follows...

"I'm giving the same seminar you attended, in York this weekend. It'd be great if you could come along. When's your deadline?"

"The publishers suggested January but I think they're quite flexible as long as I don't go too far over. I'd like to come and see you. Shall we meet on Saturday night in a bar? Where is the seminar taking place?"

"The Rowan Court Hotel in the centre of York. That'd be great. I'll see you at 5.00pm. Looking forward to it. I'll see you have the proof read copy by the end of the week. Max."

"Cheers, see you then, kind regards, Jay."

Gerald Banfleet could tell immediately that Robyn was different as soon as she walked into his ground floor office that afternoon. Her demeanour was lighter, and the deep furrows of her brow had lessened.

'I take it the counselling went well this morning?' he asked.

'Yes, it did. How do you know?'

'Do you remember me telling you I'm a mind reader?' he teased.

'Yes,' she said, a little warily.

'It's all right! I'm not reading your mind, you just look different.'

Robyn pondered a moment. *Should I tell him? Oh, what the hell. It'll be good to talk to someone else.*

'Could I share something with you? I mean, without you judging me?'

'Of course! Put the kettle on, and we'll talk about it.'

Robyn made a cafetiére of his favourite Brazilian coffee and brought it into the sitting room. After they were settled with their drinks, she said slowly,

'I don't know if you've noticed, but I never talk about my husband.'

'I have noticed, but I've never asked about it. I thought you'd tell me at some stage, if you wanted to.'

She nodded. 'Well, the reason is … I had an affair in April of this year and broke it off four months ago. My husband found out, and we split up for a while, but we reconciled and we've been trying to make a go of it ever since.'

'But something happened today to change your mind?'

'It did. I finally admitted that I still love the man I was involved with. Is that very wrong of me?'

He shook his head. 'It could be argued there's no such thing as right and wrong when it comes to love. Both Camille and I were in other partnerships when we met. I was engaged, and she was married, but when we fell in love, nothing else mattered.'

'How did you live with the guilt?'

'I've had to get used to living with a lot more guilt than cheating on a fiancée.' Gerald paused and sighed.

Robyn had been looking for an opportunity to reveal her knowledge but had never found the right time until now.

'I know about the accident, my brother was one of the firemen who cut you out of the car.'

Placing his cup very carefully onto the small table flap attached to his wheelchair, Gerald said,

'Then I'm surprised you wanted to work for me. I was treated like a pariah for years.'

'It has absolutely nothing to do with me. Who am I to judge?' Robyn put down her own cup.

'If only more people were as understanding. But no-one knows the whole story. Do you want to hear it? ... I know we're supposed to be talking about you but this is the best opportunity for me to tell the real story since it happened.'

Robyn was intrigued, 'If you're sure you'll be okay. Go ahead.'

Gerald looked directly at Robyn and began, 'On the night of the accident Camille had been drinking. In fact every day and night for over a year she'd been drinking. It started with a few glasses of wine but soon she was hiding vodka bottles. It seems strange when we were so happy in most areas of our life but she missed France; her father had just died and it hit her hard. She missed out on so much of her family life. There were six siblings and all but Camille lived within ten miles of their parents. We tried to get her home on a regular basis, but my work kept me so busy.'

He coughed, his eyes misty with remembering. 'I tried convincing her to get help but she promised she'd stop. However, it wasn't that easy for her. I thought she'd managed to cut down but then I'd find a secret stash of bottles. Her habit was fuelled by a family friend. That was where she'd gone that evening. I got a call from Charles to say she'd passed out on his living room floor, and I should come and pick her up. I'd had a couple of glasses of wine and shouldn't have driven, but I needed to keep her safe so I set off.' His voice shook a little as he continued,

'With Charles' help, I lifted her into the car and started for home. During the journey she awoke and started screaming I'd kidnapped her and she wanted to go back to Charles' house. I knew it was only the drink speaking, but she got hold of the wheel and turned it into the oncoming traffic. We were only ten miles from home. She died instantly and so did the father of two in the other car.'

'Why didn't you tell the truth?' Robyn was amazed.

'I couldn't have everyone thinking badly of my Camille when it wasn't her fault. I just wanted to die so I could be with her, but God had other plans. I live with my punishment daily and nothing anyone could ever do to me could be as bad as losing my wife.'

'But you could put the record straight now.'

'To what purpose? I don't care what people think of me.'

'Then why are you telling me?'

'I don't know really. Er ...I assume I care what *you* think of me.'

'Did her family blame you?'

'Yes, but I think they knew about her drinking. Charles tried to put them straight, as he saw the condition he'd sent her home in.

'Are you alright?' Robyn asked, squeezing his hand.

'Yes I am. It actually feels better getting it off my chest. I've just never found anyone I could tell until today. Thank you for listening, Robyn.'

'It's been my pleasure.' She paused.

Gerald picked up his coffee cup. 'Now enough of me. You wanted to talk about your situation, so tell me.'

'Well ... I met Jay in April at a seminar that my old boss sent me on.' Robyn felt it was a whole lifetime away as she told Gerald how they met and began their affair.

'Why did you finish it when you obviously still love him?'

'Everyone asks me that, and I give them the same answer I'm about to give you. Because I thought it was the right thing to do – and mainly for the children. I could see the effect it was having on them.'

'And do you regret it now?'

'I've tried everything to get him out of my mind but nothing works. I don't know if I can stay being married to Dave while I feel like this about another man.' Robyn paused. 'I also don't know if I'm being fair, maybe I should just give it more time. If you don't mind me asking, what was your marriage like?'

'On the whole we had a wonderful marriage, but I know what it means to see through rose coloured spectacles. We had our ups and downs and my work played a large part in her unhappiness, which I refused to do anything about at the time. I only remember the good times now but, believe me, there were plenty of bad times, staying up until all hours arguing.'

Robyn was silent for a few moments, then said softly,

'I've not contacted Jay for four months, and I vowed I'd give my marriage six months.'

'Then that's doomed to failure. How can you make a go of something when it's on a time limit?'

'It felt too much at the time to say I'd never see him again.'

Gerald snorted. 'Poppycock! It sounds as if you weren't committed to your husband at all, so why don't you just contact Jay and have done with it.'

'It's not as simple as that. I have the children to consider.'

'Have they met Jay?'

'No, Dave would never let that happen.'

'If you get together he'll have no choice.'

'Jay doesn't want children.' Robyn admitted.

'Then you have an altogether different problem. As it stands now, you only remember the wonderful times, particularly the sex, but the reality would be very different. Maybe if you had some time on your own it might make things clearer.'

'I was thinking of going away for a weekend.'

'You think two nights is going to do it? I was thinking a bit longer than that.'

'When Dave moved out I went to pieces, and I'm sure that would happen again.'

'Well, if you're stuck, you could always move in here with the children,' he offered. 'It would give you some breathing space and the company would be nice.'

'Gerald, I couldn't impose on your hospitality like that.'

'Well the offer's there if you need it …' Just then the phone rang.

'I think I'd better get that. I'm expecting a call from Brussels,' Robyn said as she reached across the desk. The moment had passed and they both returned to work.

As Robyn was clearing her desk and closing down her computer ready to go home, she saw an e-mail from Max Hammond.

"Hi Robyn, Wondered if you could do me a favour. I'm giving a presentation in York on Saturday and wondered if you could spare me a couple of hours on Saturday afternoon/evening. Tell potential clients how wonderful the seminar is. I'll pay your travel expenses. Sorry it's such short notice and I'll understand if you can't. Thanks Max."

Robyn started to type.

"What time and where? It should be ok. I'll just check with Dave."

"5pm Rowan Court Hotel in the centre of York. If you wanted to stay I could book you a room on the company expenses. It'd be a nice break and you'd be really getting me out of a tight squeeze."

"Sold! It should be ok, take it as a yes and book me a room. Do I need to bring anything in particular?"

"No, just yourself. Looking forward to seeing you on Saturday. Thanks again. Max."

"I'll confirm as soon as I can. Bye for now. Robyn."

It was the third week of ante-natal classes and the focus tonight was on breathing. Back home, Robyn prepared a quick tea of spaghetti Bolognese. Afterwards, running a bath for the children, she said to Dave,

'Max Hammond sent me an e-mail today to see if I could help him out of a tight squeeze but I said I'd run it past you first.'

'What does he want?' Dave was always suspicious when he heard that name, partly blaming Max for his wife's infidelity.

Making sure the bath-water was at the right temperature; Robyn turned off the taps and straightened up.

'He's asked if I could go to York on Saturday evening, he's giving a presentation and wants help from previous participants to sell the seminar. He's offered to pay for a room, and he'll pay my expenses.'

'Is *he* going?'

'For God's sake! I doubt it. Max never mentioned him. I don't know how many times I have to tell you I haven't spoken to Jay for months. I don't even know which part of the country he's living in.'

'I don't want you to go.'

'But I more or less said it would be fine.'

'Then you're not even asking me. You've already made your mind up.'

Robyn could swear his bottom lip was pouting. She knew if she didn't placate him, he would sulk all night.

'No, I *am* asking you. I told Max I would let him know for definite later. Why don't you come with me?' As soon as the words left her lips she regretted it, but Dave brightened immediately.

'That's a good idea. It would be nice to spend a night away together. Who shall we ask to have the children? My Mum hasn't had them for a while.'

Robyn tried to hide her disappointment. She'd been looking forward to spending time with Max as she wanted to run her dilemma past him for some words of advice.

'If you come, you won't have me to yourself,' she said swiftly. 'I'm going to work, and I think Max will probably want me to have dinner with some clients.'

Still smiling, Dave said, 'I promise I'll be good. I'm sure he wouldn't mind me having dinner with you, but I'll keep out of sight during the presentation. I'll wander round York, I'll be fine.'

'Okay then! But right now I've got to get ready for the ante-natal class and I don't want to keep Sarah waiting. I'll leave it to you to ring your Mum and if she can't do it, ring mine.'

Dave gave her a hug just as Molly and Jake came charging into the bathroom.

'This time to ourselves is just what we need Robyn, thanks.'

.

Chapter 26

Robyn and Dave deposited the children at Dave's Mum's at lunchtime on Saturday. Robyn hadn't told Max that Dave was coming to York. She was going to say it was a last minute decision.

It was three o'clock as they were driving through the town centre, and the light was already fading. York looked magnificent just before Christmas; the decorations were lavish and there was an authentic "olde worlde" feel about the place. They passed costumed vendors selling roasted chestnuts and baked potatoes from stalls fitted out like the originals would've been. Robyn opened the window. The Victorian market smells of cinnamon and pine trees were so inviting, and she loved the sound of the choir singing Christmas Carols.

They quickly registered at the hotel, dropping their small case in the room and went outside to make the most of a crisp, wintery late afternoon. She was meeting Max in the lobby at five, which gave them just over an hour to sample the festive delights.

As she walked around a bustling York, holding Dave's hand, she felt totally alone. Robyn usually loved Christmas but just couldn't summon up the enthusiasm for family celebrations this year. *It'll be the first Christmas without going to Mum and Dad's … and someone else will be sleeping in my old bedroom …* Robyn felt an overwhelming sadness. *I wonder what Jay will be doing? But who knows, he may be seeing someone else by now?*

'Do you fancy a hot chocolate and a mince pie?' Dave asked as they walked past a cafe with tables outside.

'Yes, that would be lovely,' Robyn said as enthusiastically as she could muster. 'Cream and marshmallows on mine please.'

'Find a seat and I'll go and order.'

He disappeared inside the cafe as Robyn sat down at a small table for two and looked around. As she waited, her mind wandered back to the last seminar with Max and her first meeting with Jay. It seemed like another lifetime ago. Without warning, tears started to prick her eyes and she could barely swallow past the lump in her throat. Just then Dave appeared with mugs of steaming hot chocolate.

'Sorry, I've been so long.' He put the tray on the table. 'There was a queue. Are you okay? You look pale?'

'I'm just a bit cold. Perhaps the hot chocolate mug will warm my hands. Anyway, who are all these for?' She said looking at four large mince pies.

'I got one of each flavour, what we don't eat now we can take back to our room.'

Dave carried on talking but apart from nodding and giving the odd comment, Robyn was transported to her own inner world of Robyn and Jay, replaying in her head the times they'd been out for a walk and the cups of hot chocolate they'd shared. She did everything to force the tears back inside but, nevertheless, they started to flow.

'Whatever's the matter?' Dave asked.

Robyn shrugged her shoulders and looked down.

'I don't know what else I can do to make you happy,' Dave said sadly.

Robyn pulled a tissue from her handbag and blew her nose.

'I'm sorry, love. Anyway, it's not your responsibility to make me happy, it's mine.'

'But I hate seeing you like this.' He reached over and squeezed her hand. Robyn flinched.

Dave was silent for a few moments. 'If you love him so much, why don't you just go to him.'

'It's not just him,' she said, sobbing again.

'Oh, but I think it is! And you do too. I probably moved back home too quickly without giving you enough time. But I don't want to keep you if you don't belong to me. I want you to be with me because you want to, not out of duty.'

'But that's just it! I don't know what I want.' She dried her tears.

'I think you do, but you're too scared to admit it.' Dave held her hand.

'What about the children?'

'I'm sure they'll survive. They'll still see us both.'

'But it'll break their hearts,' Robyn sobbed again as she pictured Jake's face.

'But this is breaking yours. I can't believe I'm about to say this – but you need to see if what you feel for Jay is real.'

Robyn looked forlornly at Dave. 'I didn't mean for this to happen. I really tried to get him out of my mind.'

'I know you did, Rob. But maybe you were never meant to. He could be the 'one.'

Robyn let out a loud sob.

'Come on dry those tears.'

'I don't know how you put up with me?' Robyn squeezed his hand.

'I'm up for an OBE in the New Years Honours list,' he joked.

'You deserve one. I must be hell to live with.'

'Let's put it this way, it's not been easy, but neither have I. I hate who I've become. We should've taken a longer rest from each other, instead of pretending things could go straight back to normal. We've never really talked about why you had an affair in the first place. I was so angry and focussed all my attention on Jay. But surely he's a symptom, not the cause?

'I don't want to lose you, Robyn, but neither do I want you like this. I couldn't even trust you to come here by yourself – hence I'm here making you unhappy. I need to get over it as well. Let's go back to the hotel, I'll go home and come back for you tomorrow.'

'But…'

'No buts, I've made a decision, me obsessing about where you are and who you're with is not helpful to my sanity.'

'God, Dave when you're like this I love you so much.'

'But that's not good enough for me. I want you to love me the same all the time. You can't have both of us, I said that before and it's true. You need to make a decision one way or another. Come on drink up… I thought you didn't want both mince pies?'

'I didn't, but they were so nice,' she said, managing a watery smile as she wiped the crumbly pastry from around her mouth.

Jay loved York and was so glad he'd taken Max up on his offer to meet. He could even see himself living here if he couldn't settle back in Leeds. It was always so lively, especially this close to Christmas. He hadn't even thought about presents yet, not that he bought many, just for his mum, sister and niece – no trawling the shops to surprise Maria this year.

He set off from home purposefully early so he could spend some time looking round the Shambles, which were looking particularly festive. York had such a romantic feel about it, and Jay found his mind wandering back to Robyn, particularly when he saw couples holding hands and laughing, he would love to be sharing this experience with her.

He glanced at his watch – only twenty minutes to find the hotel before his meeting with Max. It was so easy to get lost in the narrow, winding streets so he turned round and retraced his steps.

Robyn linked Dave's arm as they walked silently back to the hotel. Just as they were approaching the hotel steps, a man in a brown tweed overcoat approached from the opposite direction. Robyn stopped in her tracks as she saw Jay for the first time in four months. He saw her at exactly the same time. Dave recognised him from the photograph he'd seen on Facebook.

Robyn started to shake. 'God! This is awful,' she mumbled.

'Tell me about it! I know we've just decided that you'll see him again, but I didn't expect it to happen this quickly.' Dave added suspiciously, 'Are you sure you didn't plan this?'

'I promise, Dave. I knew nothing about it. Honestly, Max never mentioned Jay would be here.'

Robyn could feel her breathing quicken as Jay approached. Any second they would be face to face. She'd dreamt about this reunion for months but didn't envisage it quite like this.

Jay was the first to regain his composure, 'Hello, Robyn….' He held out his hand, 'Dave.'

Dave ignored the gesture and put his arm territorially round Robyn's shoulder.

'Hello, Jay,' Robyn said quietly. 'Did Max Hammond invite you today?'

'He did. Not one of his better moves, I might add.' Jay said.

'Then I think we ought to see what he has to say.' Robyn moved away from Dave's grip but held his hand as the three of them went inside the hotel.

Max Hammond was sitting in a comfortable chair in reception reading a newspaper when he looked up and saw the party of three walking towards him.

'Shit! Not exactly as I planned it,' he said, as he surveyed the awkward scene.

'What were you thinking, Max?' Robyn asked.

'In my defence, I didn't know you'd bring your husband.' Max said.

'Hello, I'm Dave,' he said, holding out his hand. 'She didn't want to bring me, I insisted.'

'Pleased to meet you, Dave. I'm sorry about all this, very unprofessional of me.'

'So this weekend was all a ploy to get us together?' Jay asked Max.

'Yes and not a very good one. I'm sorry I got it so wrong.'

'So there isn't even a seminar?' Robyn asked.

'Not as such, but I am here to meet the hotel management. I'm back here in January. I've come to look at all the facilities this weekend. Would anyone like a drink? It looks like we could all do with one.'

Jay answered first, 'Mine's the usual and make it a double. I'll join you shortly.'

Dave let go of Robyn's hand, 'I'm going to get off and leave you to your happy reunion.'

'Please don't go, Dave. Not like this.' Her voice shook. 'We need to talk.'

'I think we've said all we need to say.' Dave turned and started walking towards the door.

'Don't leave me, Dave,' she begged.

'But isn't it what you've been wanting all this time? Max has just made it easy for you. You've been pining for your lover. Well here he is, enjoy!'

'Don't be like this Dave. We've had such a lovely day.'

'Robyn, I don't believe you!' Dave's voice raised a decibel. 'How do you expect me to behave? I've just come face to face with your lover. Would you like me to shake his hand and wish him luck? I feel like breaking his fucking neck.'

Robyn started to cry.

Jay was observing the scene from across the room.

'Dave, before you go could I have a quick word?' Jay shouted.

Robyn looked aghast as he spoke. 'Please Jay, leave it.'

'I've nothing to say to you,' Dave snapped.

'Please, it won't take long. I'd just like to explain.'

The whole thing was turning into a scene from a soap-opera with a live audience, so to keep the peace Dave said,

'Okay, but let's go somewhere quieter.' He pointed to the small guest lounge to the left of reception. Robyn went to follow them.

'I'd rather have a word with him on my own, if you don't mind,' Jay said gently. 'Would you mind joining Max in the bar? I'll be with you in a minute.'

Robyn stood still, unsure what to do next. Confusion had taken hold of her brain. Her body cried out for Jay, yet she didn't want to see her marriage of seven years walk out of the door. As she watched the two men disappear into the lounge, she did as requested and went to join Max.

Dave perched on the edge of a chair. Jay sat opposite.

'Explain,' said Dave curtly.

Jay shrugged. 'Now I'm here, I don't know what to say, other than I'm sorry.'

Dave looked him in the eyes and asked, 'Do you love Robyn?'

'I do,' Jay said, looking down at the floor.

'I've known her for thirteen years and loved her for twelve of them,' Dave admitted. 'And if I'm to let her go, I need to know she'll be fine.'

'I don't know if she even wants to be with me,' Jay said. 'I don't think she even came close to leaving you.'

'Maybe not, but she can't stay with me, without knowing if what you two have is real.'

'Surely, Robyn and I need to talk first. She did after all, choose you.' Jay's expression changed to one of sadness as he remembered the painful goodbye in his hotel room.

'And I think she's been regretting it ever since,' Dave responded curtly.

'But I still don't think we should be making any decisions for her without knowing how she feels.'

'I know how she feels, what I need to know is how you feel.'

'I love her, and if she'll give me a chance, I'll make her happy.' Jay looked down at his feet, embarrassed that he was admitting he loved another man's wife.

Dave got up to leave, 'That's all I've got to say. Say goodbye to Robyn for me and tell her I'll be in touch.'

Jay stood and held out his hand, 'No hard feelings, mate.'

'You've got to be kidding me!' Dave balled his fist and punched Jay squarely on the nose.

Jay fell backward onto the chair, holding his bleeding nose, 'I guess I deserved that,' he muttered, reaching for a handkerchief.

Dave walked to the lift and pressed the button. He needed to collect his belongings from the room and then he'd be on his way. Luckily the lift was empty, so no-one witnessed the tears in his eyes, knowing he'd possibly given the love of his life away to another man.

Max was contrite as he said to Robyn, 'I was only trying to help. I know you two are stubborn, but I think you need to get it sorted.'

'I don't think it was a very good idea,' she said, drying her eyes. 'I wonder what they're talking about?'

'You won't have to wonder for long, Jay's here. What's he done?' Max asked, as he saw Jay holding a handkerchief to his nose.

Robyn turned round and hurried to check on Jay. 'You poor love, what happened? Does it hurt?'

'Dave's fist is what happened, but I'll be fine.' Jay sat down on the seat next to Max, 'Is that mine?' he pointed to the drink on the table.

'It is,' said Max, and Jay downed the double whisky in one gulp.

'Where's Dave?' Robyn asked. She sat down and picked up her drink.

'He's gone. He said he'd catch you later.'

'I should go after him.' She stood up again.

Jay grabbed hold of Robyn's arm, 'I'd leave him for now, love.'

'But he doesn't deserve this! I – he – he's such a lovely man. Why? …' Tears rolled down Robyn's face again.

'Do you remember the chapter in my book called "Unconditional Love"? I think you've just seen it at its best,' Max said. 'I suggest you have to get to the place where if you love someone so much, you can still let them go if it's the right thing to do. It looks like Dave has reached that place.'

'I'm surprised,' Robyn said, 'I didn't think he'd be so understanding. He – he must really love me.'

'It's amazing what resilience people find when faced with impossible circumstances. I hope you don't waste the perfect opportunity he's given you.' Max said to Robyn and Jay.

'We'll try not to.' Robyn looked at Jay and smiled.

'If its okay, I'll have half an hour with Jay on his book and then he's all yours?' said Max.

'Fine, I'll go back to the room. I might have a sleep, I'm exhausted. I'm in room 10 when you've finished.' She squeezed Jay's shoulders as she walked past.

'I'll be with you shortly and Robyn...' Jay said.

'Yes.'

'I love you, and I've missed you so much.' He winked. Four months without the wink, how had she survived?

'I love you too.'

'That's enough – you'll be making me jealous.' Max laughed.

Robyn's emotions were torn in half as she made herself comfortable on top of the double bed. Her heart wanted Jay, but what her husband had just done was the most selfless thing she had ever witnessed. Maybe it was time to stop thinking, she told herself. And with that thought she fell into a deep sleep.

She awoke an hour later with Jay sitting in the armchair staring at her.

'How long have you been there?' she asked sleepily.

'A while. I've been watching you sleep.'

'Well, here we are,' she sighed. 'I've been dreaming of this moment for so long.'

'Can I ask you something?' Jay said in a serious voice.

'Er... Yes.'

'If Max hadn't orchestrated this meeting would you have contacted me?'

'Absolutely, Yes! I know it's going to sound contrived, but Dave and I had just agreed that I would see you again. I've been so miserable. I really tried to put you out of my mind but nothing I've tried worked.'

'I know. It's been hell for me too.'

'Come here and lie with me, please,' Robyn said as she beckoned Jay over to the bed. 'What do you want to do now?'

'I want to make love to you,' Jay paused. 'But if it's too soon we can talk or go for something to eat.'

'I've been eating and talking for all this time, but what I haven't done is this.' She leaned across and kissed him. Four months of separation came out in the one kiss.

'Maybe we could eat afterwards?' Jay said as he started to open Robyn's top.

'I'm not hungry.' She unzipped Jay's trousers and released his bulging erection.

Jay suddenly stopped, 'I love you Robyn Fisher. I need you to know.'

'And I love you, now don't just tell me, show me.' She pulled him on top of her with a passion she hadn't felt since the last time they'd made love. Having Jay inside her felt like the most natural thing in the world. Nothing she'd ever experienced before compared to the feeling as he moved up and down, thrusting himself deep inside her. The climax was electric and sent shock waves throughout her body. It was ages before either of them could find the words to speak.

'Was it as good as you remembered? Jay kissed her.

'Even better.' She hugged him tight.

'Robyn, are you happy?'

'Not yet,' she said thinking about Dave. 'But I will be now I've got you.'

Dave didn't want to be on his own tonight. The children were happy with his mother so he'd see if Alex was available to go out for a drink. He rang on his hands free kit as he was driving home,

'Hi, mate, do you fancy a drink? That's if you're not doing anything.'

'Yes, I'll make one in. You'll actually be doing me a favour. Sue and I are just about to kill each other. We're deciding where to spend Christmas day, and I said I'd rather amputate my right leg than go to her mothers. Needless to say, that didn't go down very well. Are you coming now?'

'I can do. I've just dropped Robyn in York so I'll be passing your house in about half an hour.'

'What's she doing there, shopping?'

'It's a long story, I'll tell you over a few pints.'

'You're on. We could have a curry later if you're up for it.'

'As long as I'm not intruding.'

'I think rescuing is a more apt term.'

Just under an hour later Dave pulled up outside his friend's house and could hear the row as he walked to the front door.

'Come in Dave,' said Sue, opening the door to his knock. 'Please try to talk some sense into my husband. I only ask him to see my mother once a year and he can't even do that for me,' Sue added, as she showed Dave into the battle zone.

'Once a decade would be too much, she hates me,' Alex grunted.

'She's got a point,' Sue snapped.

'How about I go and come back when it's calmed down?' Dave felt too upset to be in the middle of such a personal argument.

'Sorry mate, it's always like this at Christmas. I hate it, and I'd rather be working.'

'Well work, I'll go on my own.'

'That's the most sensible suggestion yet. It would've saved the last two hours arguing.'

'I mean it,' Sue realised too late her plan was backfiring.

'So do I. I'll rota myself in and it'll give some of the lads with young kids more time with their family.'

'I bet you wouldn't work, would you Dave?' Sue turned to him in appeal.

'Leave me out of it! Besides there's not a lot of call for graphic design on Christmas day so it's never been an option.'

'You're so diplomatic, Dave,' Sue smiled at him.

Alex mimicked his wife, 'You're so diplomatic, Dave, and you're so smarmy Sue.'

'Now, now children! Why don't we go for that drink and leave Sue to relax for a while?' Dave suggested.

'See, Dave thinks of me,' she said to her uncaring husband.

'That's because Dave's nice and I'm a bastard. But he doesn't live with you. Come on Dave, I'll get my coat. Goodbye, light of my life, don't wait up.' Alex was smiling as he gave Sue a peck on the cheek.

'Get on with you, have a good time.' She smiled back.

Dave had got used to the not-so-friendly banter between his two best friends. Sue pretended to hate Alex and he played up to her every time, but Dave thought they were really devoted or he hoped they were, at least.

They caught the bus from Cottingham into the city centre, and the bus stop where they alighted gave them the option of five pubs and bars.

'Where do you want to go first?' Alex asked.

'I'm not bothered. Anywhere they serve alcohol is fine.'

'It's like that is it?'

'That's not the half of it. I think me and Robyn have just split up.'

'Mate no!' Alex was appalled. 'If you two split up, there's no hope for the rest of us. What happened? I thought you'd sorted it all out.'

'So did I, but I was only kiddin' myself. She's never got over this Jay bloke. I thought I could win her back with my good looks and charm but it wasn't working.'

'Where is she now?'

'In York with him.'

'Are you fucking mad?'

'Probably, but what can I do? If she wants to be with him I can't stop her.'

'No, but you don't have to hand it to her on a fucking plate. Just wait 'til I see her.'

'Leave it mate, it's been hard enough to do it, let's not make it any harder.'

'She must want her head seeing to, but having said that, I never knew what she saw in you anyway.' Alex gave him a jab on the shoulder.

'Ah, Cheers mate! That's the nicest thing you've ever said to me! Now mine's a pint.'

'Bitter?'

'Yes – very!'

While they were putting the world to rights, the pub suddenly filled up.

Alex looked up, 'Where did all that skirt come from? I forget what it's like on a Saturday night… Isn't that the girl that came onto you the last time we were out? Go give her what for and show Robyn two can play at that game.'

Dave looked across just as the girl turned around and she gave him a cute wave. Alex beckoned her over.

'What do you think you're doing?' Dave asked.

'She's got a nice friend. We could do with some cheering up.'

The two girls, dressed for clubbing on a Saturday night, tottered across the room in the highest heels Dave had ever seen.

'Fancy seeing you here. Remember me? It's Stacey. I've been looking around for you but you've not been out for ages,' Stacey said, moving closer to Dave's face.

'I don't come to town very often.'

'Can I get you two ladies a drink?' Alex offered.

'Have you heard that, Gemma?' Stacey tittered. 'He called us ladies. I'll have a Smirnoff Ice thanks.'

'And I'll have a Bacardi Breezer, the red one,' Gemma added quickly.

'Are you going to come to the club with us after?' Stacey asked, almost nibbling Dave's ear as she struggled to be heard over the loud music.

'I don't know – it depends on my mate.'

'He looks up for it, go on, it'll be a laugh. Ask him when he comes back,' Stacey pleaded.

Dave was keen. He had nothing to go home for.

'I like you, you know,' Stacey whispered in Dave's ear.

Dave didn't know how to respond. Stacey was a beautiful girl, but no more than nineteen. Her long blonde hair fell around her shoulders and her burgundy lips looked so inviting. She was wearing what Robyn would call a belt. The hem of the silver lycra dress came just below her pants, that's if she was wearing any. He adjusted himself at the thought.

'Aren't I a bit too old for you?' he asked Stacey, at the same time looking over at Alex for reassurance. But he wasn't looking – he'd already got his tongue down Gemma's throat.

'No, I prefer my men mature,' Stacey said at once. 'You're married, aren't you?' she added, looking at the give-away wedding ring.

'I'm separated.' The words felt strange.

'So there's nothing stopping us then. I'm on the pill.'

He knocked back the rest of his third pint and put his empty on the table.

'Where do you want to go?' Dave asked Stacey.

'Are you going to ask your friend? He seems to be getting on with Gemma?'

'Yes, I'll see if they want to join us.' Dave took Alex to one side. He knew he shouldn't leave the bar with Stacey. But the drink and the sexy girl wearing hardly any clothes won out, and he left *Bar None* with Stacey clinging to his arm.

As soon as they were outside, the three pints of bitter took over. *Two can play at that game, Robyn*! He turned Stacey round and kissed her.

'Wow, Dave,' Stacey said squeezing him tight.

It felt wonderful to be desired, especially by a girl as stunning as Stacey. She might only want him for his money and a few drinks, but he wasn't looking for a lifelong commitment, just some fun to repair his damaged ego.

She took hold of Dave's hand and pulled him into a nearby loading bay behind the pub. He kissed her again and reached down into Stacey's dress feeling her nipple harden under his touch. She fumbled to undo Dave's trousers exposing his erection and, before long, he had her bent over a small wall, banging away as though his life depended on it.

It wasn't until they had finished and tidied themselves up that he realised the enormity of what he'd just done. He'd joined the ranks of Robyn, Jay, Chris and a multitude of others who couldn't say no to temptation. Did he feel guilty? Did he, hell!

'Wow, I didn't take you for someone who likes it a bit rough,' Stacey said, pulling her dress down.

'Sorry, was that okay? Did I hurt you?'

'No, I'm only teasing. It was great. You lasted so much longer than younger lads?'

'I take it you've done that before?'

Stacey laughed, 'Of course, me and Gemma see who can pull the fittest man. I think I've won tonight, no disrespect to your friend.'

'Thank you.' Dave beamed.

'Are you hungry?' he asked.

'No, we get a pizza or a kebab later.' She looked at her watch. 'We'd better get in the queue for the club otherwise we won't get in. Let's go and find our mates.'

The sex had been great, but Dave couldn't really see himself in a night club where the average age was under twenty one.

'You don't want to go, do you?' Stacey said, as she saw Dave's face.

'I'll buy you a few more drinks and you could go later,' he offered.

'I'll see what Gem has to say.'

The two girls settled for three more Bacardi Breezers each and then kissed Alex and Dave goodbye.

'No strings attached, just the way I like it,' Alex said as he waved them off.

'Have you done that before?' Dave was surprised.

'I've messed about a few times, but I didn't shag her, by that sick grin on your face, you sorted Stacey all right.'

'I thought I had to.'

'Good for you mate. Does it make what Robyn's done more bearable?'

'Not really, but you have to make an effort, don't you? God she's fit,' Dave commented as he watched Stacey turn the corner.

'One more drink and then we'll get a taxi before the queues get too long,' Alex said, walking into the closest pub.

One drink turned into another four and the pair of them could hardly stand upright as the fresh air hit them.

'It's ten to four,' said Dave squinting at his watch.

'Do you want to stay at mine? The spare bed's made up,' Alex offered.

'Yes … I suppose. My car's there anyway.'

The taxi queue stretched down the High Street and a Burger van tempted them to a double cheeseburger with extra onions.

It was approaching dawn as Alex fumbled to get the key in the lock, trying to be as quiet as he could, but failing miserably.

'Ssh, you'll wake Sue,' Alex said at the top of his voice as Dave stumbled over the threshold.

Dave collapsed on the large, comfortable leather sofa in the lounge and fell asleep as soon as his head hit the cushion. A couple of hours later he woke up with a crick in his neck, and a raging thirst. He stumbled to his feet and aimed for the kitchen, stepping over a sleeping Alex in the hall. He couldn't remember where the glasses were and he ended up opening every cupboard before he finally located them.

'What's all the noise?' Sue said as she walked into the kitchen.

'Sorry, I wanted a drink of water and couldn't find a glass.'

'Apart from those on the draining board.'

Dave snorted, 'Oops! I never saw them.'

'Here let me.' Sue snatched the glass from her drunken friend just as it was about to slip from his grasp. She filled it with ice-cold water and made Dave sit down to drink it.

'Why don't you go to bed?' she suggested.

'Is that an offer?' Dave slurred, eyeing Sue in her short teddy bear nightdress.

'It could be if you weren't so drunk.'

'But I'm not drunk; I still have all my fac…faculties about me. Look I can put my finger on my nose.'

'And that proves what?'

'I've no idea.' They both started laughing.

'Come on; let me help you up the stairs. Mind my pig of a husband; don't step too heavily on his head.' She held onto Dave's arm as they stepped over Alex, who was snoring away merrily.

Sue opened the door to the spare room and Dave pulled her onto the double bed.

'Stay with me, Sue. I don't want to be alone. You know Robyn's left me.'

'She must be mad,' said Sue quietly. If she had Dave she would treasure him like the crown jewels. She lay down beside him stroking his hair,

'You poor love,' she whispered.

Dave nestled into her chest and gently started fingering her right breast. She'd lost count of how many times she'd fantasised about Dave doing that and more. She kissed the top of his head, and he moved himself up the bed to kiss her lips. Sue was euphoric, even though she knew he'd probably have no recollection of it when he sobered up.

As he fumbled for his zip, he couldn't seem to co-ordinate his hand movements so she undid it for him. He slithered out of his trousers and attempted to climb on top of Sue, who moved her nightdress up to her chest to accommodate him. After years of lusting after her friend's husband she was finally going to get him. Only Dave couldn't quite manage it – the mind was willing but the body was weak.

After a few more failed attempts he gave up, 'Sorry Sue, it must be the drink.'

He rolled off and fell into a deep sleep. Sue continued stroking him, gently outlining his shape with her finger. God, he was gorgeous, his well-defined chest muscles and biceps were magnificent. Alex used to have muscles like this until his desk bound job had seen them off. Now all she had to look at was a well-defined beer gut.

She ran her fingers through Dave's thick deep brown hair, bending down to gently kiss his lips, being extra careful not to wake him. Where she was about to go was totally off-limits, but she had waited for this opportunity for most of her adult life, and wasn't going to waste it now. She bent down and took him in her mouth, sucking gently. Dave started to stir.

'What the fuck's going on?' Alex said as he stood at the door.

'I was just putting Dave to bed, he was out of it,' Sue stuttered, utterly shocked to see her husband.

'And sucking him off instead of a lullaby is it?'

'It isn't what it looks like.'

'Go on then, what does it look like? I can't wait to hear this one,' sneered Alex. But Sue was silent.

Alex moved toward the bed and nudged Dave, 'Come on, mate get up. My whore of a wife is taking advantage of you.'

Dave started to rouse, saying sleepily, 'Alex? What's going on?'

'You mean you didn't feel my wife sucking your cock?' Dave shot up in bed, covering himself with the duvet.

Shit, he thought, had Alex also witnessed his failed attempt at seducing his wife?

Alex was pacing up and down, steam almost coming out of his ears.

'Get up, you whore.' He took hold of Sue's arm and tried to drag her off the bed.

'Whoa, there mate, steady on you're hurting her.' Dave tried to free Sue from his grip as Alex continued bitterly,

'All the times I had the chance to shag other women, even tonight I said no, and I come in to find you in bed with my best friend. How did you get your clothes off, Dave? Or was I just witnessing the end of the session. Did you shag her as well?'

'It was nothing to do with Dave, I'm sorry.' Sue started to cry.

'Save your crocodile tears.' In a fit of fury Alex smacked Sue as hard as he could across the face with the back of his hand, throwing her off the bed.

'Get out of my sight!' he yelled.

Dave grabbed Alex's arm, 'That's enough! I thought you knew better than that Alex.'

'Let go of me.' Alex tried to wrestle free, but Dave's grip was too strong.

'Not until you calm down.'

Alex slowly realised what he'd done as he saw Sue's eye start to swell. Dave released his grip.

'Not only did you cheat on me last year with a total stranger you rub my face in it by making a pass at my best friend. How much more do you expect me to take?' Alex sat on the bed his head in his hands.

'I'm sorry, Alex, I don't know what else to say. But no matter what I've done I didn't deserve this.' Sue gently touched her red and bruised face.

Dave no longer felt drunk and he grabbed his clothes, 'I think it's time I got going. Who's leaving with me? Because I'm not leaving the two of you alone.'

'Can I come please?' Sue said to Dave. She turned to Alex. 'I should have left you ages ago, but it was too much effort. But this is the final straw. I can't live with a man who raises his hand to a woman.'

'Good, because I can't live with a cheating whore.'

'Let's go, Dave,' Sue walked across to hold his arm. Dave pulled away,

'Don't think I'm taking sides, Sue. What Alex did was wrong, but you provoked him. You can't cheat on him in his own house and expect him to laugh about it.'

Sue glared. 'You didn't say that when you were trying to get it up this morning.'

'What does she mean, 'trying to get it up'?' Alex asked.

'I've no idea. Come on; let's not say anything else we might regret.'

'He's naked because I undressed him, but I didn't force him on top of me. He did that all by himself, but he was too pissed to get it up. Isn't that right, Dave?' There was no answer as Dave frantically tried to get dressed and started looking for his shoes.

'You tried to fuck my wife.' Alex lunged and caught Dave's eye with his fist. As Dave fended him off, he shouted at Alex and Sue,

'You're fucking mad the pair of you. What's going on here? Do you love winding each other up? Well, I'm not getting involved in your sordid little games any longer. I'm off.' He picked up his shoes from under the bed. Running downstairs out of the front door, he slipped his shoes on as he ran and stopped in the drive to fasten his laces. His car keys were in his pocket, but he decided not to drive, knowing if he was stopped he'd never pass a breathalyser.

Could his life get even more complicated? Dave thought miserably as he started the long walk home. He'd lost his wife and best friend within the space of twenty-four hours. Sex had a lot to answer for. Maybe celibacy was the way forward from now on.

Chapter 27

Robyn woke up early Sunday morning, and the harsh reality of what she'd done made her feel nauseous. It was great to be with Jay, looking over at his sleeping form – but a few hours in a hotel room didn't constitute real life. Soon she'd have to go home and tell the children that Mummy and Daddy weren't living together anymore, again – and it would break their little hearts. But neither could she put her own life on hold any longer. And then there was the matter of them meeting Mummy's new man.

There were so many questions that needed answering.

'Jay, wake up.' She gently nudged his arm

'Good morning my love, welcome to the first day of the rest of your life.' Jay smiled.

'Enough of the clichés, I need to talk to you.' Robyn didn't feel herself in the same cheerful mood as her lover.

'Is everything okay? You seem a little stressed.'

'You could say that,' Robyn responded. 'I'm just feeling a bit overwhelmed that's all. We haven't discussed the future at all.'

'That's because there's no such thing as the future, there's only now.' Jay lay with both arms behind his head.

'What? … Is that some of your psychology mumbo-jumbo?' Robyn said.

'No! For me it's the truth and one which I live by. We can make short term plans, and I'm more than willing to do that, but how far into the future do you need to plan?'

'Like where are we going to live, if we live together? What will we do for money? But the biggest thing is – what we do about the children?'

Jay grinned and said lightly, 'In no particular order. I'll meet the children whenever you're ready. You have a good job, and I write and see clients, so money should be no object. Finally I have no idea where we can live because you haven't told me yet.'

'What do you mean? Surely it's not just my decision,' said Robyn puzzled.

'I know, but I can live anywhere,' he stated. 'And it's you who'll have to do the most adapting, so you can make all those important decisions.'

'Sorry, I'm being silly. I just woke up feeling a bit uncertain about things.'

'Come over here! Do you want something to take your mind off it?' He leaned across to kiss her.

'But Jay, we can't spend all our life in bed.' She pulled away.

'No, but we could spend the next hour in bed and then get up and have some breakfast.'

'I don't think you're taking this seriously.'

'Believe me … I've never been more serious about anything, but I deal with it differently. At the moment I'm wallowing in being able to spend every day with the woman I love. If anxiety would help, then I'll get anxious, but it never does.'

'But I can't help it.' Robyn's breath was shallow.

'Yes you can!' Jay was adamant. 'You can change your negative thoughts.'

'But how? I've been anxious for so many years I don't know any different … can you help me?'

'Of course I can.'

He beckoned her to him. 'Start by coming over here and giving me a kiss.'

Robyn did as she was told, and it was an hour later when they surfaced for breakfast.

'That wasn't too bad a distraction, was it?' Jay said as they were getting dressed.

'Not bad at all! And you're right – things didn't need to be discussed when I said. Now is a perfect time.'

He gave her a hug. 'You're learning!'

Downstairs in the dining room over a buffet breakfast and tucking into a warm pain au chocolate, Robyn said,

'Tell me what happened to Maria? Is she alright?'

Jay told the story about Maria getting married and going to live in Italy.

'So she signed the flat over to you?' Robyn asked, intrigued.

'Absolutely,' said Jay, with a certain satisfaction, 'but I don't have to live there. And I know you can't live in Leeds, your life is in Hull.'

'Gerald offered to let me stay with him. But really I need to find out where Dave is going to live. He might want to stay in our house.'

'I doubt it. And usually, isn't it the man who moves out?'

'I suppose it is, but I'm the guilty party, so maybe I should move.'

'I would imagine Dave will want what's best for the children. And wouldn't that be for them to stay in familiar surroundings?'

'I think you're right,' Robyn agreed. 'So maybe *you* could move into Gerald's?'

'I've never even met the man!' said Jay.

'But we could soon change that – anyway, he's lovely.'

'That may be,' said Jay, draining his coffee. 'But how do you know he'd want a total stranger living in his house?'

'I don't to be honest. But I think he wants to help me. Why don't you come and meet him next week?'

'Fine!' he said cheerfully. 'Arrange it and I'll be there. By the way love, what do you want to do for your birthday? It's also next week isn't it?'

Robyn laughed. 'Do you know I'd forgotten all about it? Actually, I'm going to Brussels with Gerald the day after. Maybe you could come over and we could celebrate there.'

'Good idea! It's a place I've never been … do you realise you'll be a whole four years older than me next week?'

'Only for a month,' she smiled. 'And anyway, I've always fancied a toy boy.'

After they'd finished breakfast and were heading upstairs, Jay whispered,

'Seriously Robyn, it will work out, I'll make sure of it. We can take it as slowly as you like. I'm in no rush.'

She squeezed his arm. 'Thank you, sweetie. Have I told you lately that I love you?'

'Now who's speaking in clichés?' Jay replied. They both laughed. 'I love you too.'

It was lunchtime before they finally vacated the room after making love again, and the maid was chomping at the bit to get the room cleaned. As Robyn zipped up her holdall, she said,

'Dave offered to come and pick me up – but I think I'll get a train.'

'No, I'm going to drive you.' Jay insisted, taking her bag.

'Are you sure? It's in completely the opposite direction?'

'The car will have to get used to it,' he grinned. 'It's going to be making that journey a few times from now on.'

Jay dropped Robyn outside her house mid-afternoon. The lounge curtains were still drawn and there were no obvious signs of life.

'You get off and I'll ring you later once I've talked to Dave,' Robyn kissed him. As she prepared to get out of the car he said,

'Don't forget, I'll come over whenever you want. I'm actually looking forward to meeting the children.'

'You won't say that when you see Molly, she can be a right little madam,' warned Robyn.

'Hmm. I wonder who she gets that from.'

She tapped his shoulder playfully. 'Enough of the cheek. Go on, go home.' She shut the car door and blew him a kiss as he moved away.

The house was quiet as she let herself in through the front door. She opened the curtains to let the last bit of light in for the day. She assumed Dave must be out, so got the fright of her life as he strolled into the kitchen in his boxer shorts just as she was putting the kettle on.

'What on earth happened to your face?' Robyn asked as she saw the large black bruise above his left eye.

'I had an argument with Alex's fist. Two fights in two days. It's really not like me.'

'Your eye is worse than Jay's nose,' she said sympathetically. 'What did you do to Alex? It was an accident, I take it.'

'Not really. He didn't take too kindly to Sue having her mouth wrapped round my cock.'

Robyn spilt the water out of the kettle. 'I'm not surprised. It might be a silly question, but why let her put your cock in her mouth in the first place?'

'I was drunk and didn't realise what was going on?'

Robyn started to laugh, 'I've heard some things in my time but having your cock sucked by accident, that's a new one on me.'

'Honestly, I didn't realise until Alex walked in.'

'Why was she in your bed? I take it you were in bed.'

'She helped me upstairs and undressed me. I think I did make a pass, but it's all hazy.'

'Poor Alex. Is he okay?'

'He's a bloody nutcase, both of them are. He hit Sue across the face, and I intervened and it all went pear shape from then on.'

'I don't believe it! I thought they had problems, but I didn't think it was that bad.'

'But you haven't heard the best. Earlier on I shagged a young girl outside *Rogue*.'

'How young?' Robyn said alarmed, hoping he hadn't done anything too stupid.

'Nineteen. Why do you care?'

'Of course I care! But what do you want me to do? I haven't exactly got my own virtue intact.' Upset, she turned to switch the kettle on.

'Robyn what happened to us?' he said, his face white with distress.

'I don't know, love. Maybe we took each other for granted for far too long. Why don't you get dressed and I'll make us a drink. We need to talk about the future.'

'Great, just what I need with a raging hangover,' Dave said as he walked upstairs.

'I'll take your coffee into the lounge.'

'So, what's happening?' Dave asked as he took a seat at the opposite end of the room.

'I … I think we should try some time apart.'

'I thought we'd already decided that yesterday.'

'Well yes.'

'So … was the great lover all you remembered?'

'Dave, please.'

'I need to know.'

'Yes, then, he was, and I do want to try a relationship with him.'

'So that's it, seven years of marriage just gone! Aren't you in the least bit sorry?'

'Of course I am. But we tried, Dave.'

'Did we? I know I did but you wouldn't stop thinking about him. What has he got a ten inch cock or something?'

'If you're going to start I'm not having this discussion.'

'Why not? It was your idea … You just want me to make it so easy for you.' Dave glared at Robyn.

'No, it's not that. I thought we could talk like two rational adults.'

'What! About where you're going to fuck your new man?'

'If you're not going to calm down I'll go and see a solicitor.'

'Divorce already? That didn't take long.'

'I don't want a divorce … well, not yet.' Robyn sighed.

'So do I take it you want me to move out?'

'That's what we need to discuss.'

'What about the children? … I'll take them,' Dave offered.

'No, you bloody well won't! With your working arrangements.'

'But I want to see them.'

'Of course you can see them, Dave. Whenever you want.'

Dave scratched his head and drank the remains of his cold coffee.

'I'll go pack and stay at my mother's until I can find somewhere.'

'Are you sure?'

'No, I'm not sure, but what choice do I have?'

First thing Monday morning Dave visited the local letting agency. The only thing that was available at such short notice was a one-bedroom, first-floor flat above retail premises on the same street as his office. It was unfurnished, so he hired a removal van to take some bedroom furniture from the spare room, and he was going to purchase the rest. One bedroom wasn't ideal, but it was agreed he'd spend the weekends at the house while Robyn stayed with Jay in Leeds. His single life had started.

Today was Robyn's birthday – which was usually a big cause for family celebrations. Dave always chose a great birthday cake, with the children helping to blow out the candles over a special tea prepared by the two children and their daddy. This year would be very different and Robyn had chosen today to let Jay meet the children for the first time. It really would be a baptism by fire for poor Jay – lunch with Gerald at his house and then tea with Molly and Jake at *McDonalds*. Robyn hoped the "Happy Meals" would live up to their name, keeping Molly's temper tantrums in check. As she awaited Jay's arrival at Gerald's, Robyn was pacing up and down her office. She wanted so much for Gerald to approve of him – she valued his opinion, and he appeared to be such a good judge of character.

'Will you please sit down, Robyn. He'll be here when he's here, and you pacing up and down won't make it any sooner,' Gerald said impatiently.

'Sorry! I'm nervous. I want you to like him,' Robyn said, biting her thumb nail.

'If he's as nice as you say, then I'm sure I will. Have you finished packing my cases?'

'I've just got a few toiletries to put in. It won't take me long.'

Gerald was flying from Brussels to Paris to stay with a niece who'd invited him at the last minute, so at least

Robyn didn't have to worry about what he would do for Christmas.

Mrs. Bennett bustled into the office, 'A car's just pulled up. It might be him.'

'Thanks,' said Robyn at once. 'I'll go and see.'

She rushed to the door, opening it before Jay had time to knock. 'Hello darling! Come in.' She gave Jay a long kiss as Gerald steered his wheelchair into the hall.

'Put him down, you don't know where he's been,' Gerald joked and looked from Robyn to Jay.

'Robyn – I'm assuming this is Jay.'

'Yes, of course, sorry Gerald … Jay, this is Gerald Banfleet.'

'Pleased to meet you, sir.' Jay wasn't the slightest bit embarrassed as he shook Gerald's hand.

'Please call me Gerald. Everyone else seems to, since madam here came to work for me.'

'She has that effect on people.'

'Hey you two!' protested Robyn, 'No ganging up on me. Mrs. Bennett's made a beautiful lunch; let's go into the dining room so she can serve it for us.'

Robyn needn't have worried – the two men seemed to hit it off from the onset.

'Jay, tell me about your book,' Gerald said. 'Robyn tells me you've finished it.'

'I have finally. It's with the publishers and will be launched in spring of next year. You know its title I assume?'

'Yes, catchy. What kind of reader are you aiming at? General? Academic? Or both?'

'Anyone who has firsthand experience of infidelity. There's information in it for people who've cheated and those who find themselves the victim of adultery. I've used a lot of case studies so hopefully others will relate to the true stories.'

'Are you doing a book tour?' Gerald asked, sipping his red wine.

'Yes, I think so. The publishers want me to and, depending on how successful it is, they've got a few television interviews lined up.'

'Good for you. Have you anymore in the pipeline?'

'A few ideas I'm working on. I've thoroughly enjoyed writing and actually prefer it now to seeing clients. I think I've found my niche. A new project "*How to have an Amicable Divorce*" is something I'm considering. What do you think?'

Before Gerald could reply, Robyn interjected,

'You've never mentioned that to me.'

'Well, it's still up in the air at the moment,' Jay said. 'I was going to tell you. I've been playing around with the idea and writing a synopsis to present to the publishers.'

'It's a sad indictment of our society when books that sell are about people's misfortunes.' Gerald sighed.

'I agree, but while it happens, it's useful to have some pointers,' replied Jay.

'I suppose,' agreed Gerald, draining his wine. 'By the way, are you two going to move in together after Christmas?'

'Gerald! That's private,' Robyn answered.

'When you know as much about me as you do, I don't see anything as private.'

'I think it will depend how this afternoon goes,' Jay answered for both of them.

'Oh yes, you're meeting the devil's spawn,' Gerald joked.

'That's no way to speak about my children,' said Robyn laughing.

'I take it you've met them?' Jay asked.

'Yes, a few times. They're beautiful. The girl's a bit wilful, probably the red hair, but she'll never be bullied. Jake's a little angel. Don't be surprised if Molly speaks her mind though. The first thing she said to me was, "Why are your legs a funny shape?"'

'I know, the little monster! I could've killed her.'

'She was only saying what others think, you can't blame her for that.'

As soon as lunch was over, Robyn showed Jay round the house concentrating on the office where she worked.

'Da...da. The hub of operations. This is where it all happens,' she said pointing at her desk.

'You love it here, don't you?'

'I do. And I feel really lucky ... all those years in a job I hated. Who'd have thought caring for a grumpy old man would be my ideal employment.'

'I think you're more than his carer. He relies on you totally, I can tell.'

'I guess,' she said modestly.

'Have you brought everything for our Belgium trip?' Robyn asked excitedly.

'I have, it's in the car.'

'Gerald said I can leave early today seeing as I've got one hundred percent responsibility for him for the next three days. Do you want to come back to the house until it's time to collect the children?'

'Okay,' he smiled, 'but let me go and thank Gerald and Mrs. Bennett for a wonderful lunch first, and then I'm all yours.'

Gerald showed them to the front door, 'I'll see you bright and early at seven,' he said to Robyn. 'And I'll see you some time over the next few days in Brussels,' he said to Jay.

From the window he watched the car pull away and then steered his wheelchair back into the lounge.

'What a lovely man,' said Mrs. Bennett.

'He is. But whether he's the one for Robyn I'm not too sure.'

'Why ever not?' said Mrs Bennett, taken aback. 'They seem very much in love.'

'It's just one of my feelings. He's a free spirit and she isn't, despite trying her best. I think he'll wear her down eventually. She likes an ordered life and he doesn't, but I hope they prove me wrong.'

'So do I. I love a happy ending.' Mrs Bennett went back to the kitchen leaving her employer pondering on when exactly he'd become such a cynic.

As Jay followed Robyn back to the house, her next-door neighbour was just collecting a weekly shop from her car boot.

Robyn shouted across the drive, 'Hello, Mrs. Timothy, how are you?'

There was no response and Robyn assumed the woman hadn't heard her, 'Mrs. Timothy, how are you? Haven't seen you for a while.'

At this Mrs. Timothy looked straight through Robyn, scowled at Jay and turned away, muttering and shaking her head all the way to her front door. She disappeared inside and slammed it shut.

Robyn stood there in shock. Her family had lived next door to the Timothy's for over four years and they'd never been anything other than polite, sharing Christmas cards and putting each other's bins out at holiday times. Last year Robyn and Molly had even fed their cat, Puss, for two weeks.

And now Robyn apparently warranted the cold shoulder treatment. She opened her own front door, upset and shaking, 'Did you see that?'

'Take no notice of the old bag!' said Jay, putting his arm round her. 'It says far more about her lack of tolerance than anything you've done.'

'Is this what we're going to face from now on?'

'I doubt it. But it's nothing to do with anyone else. You just have to ignore it.'

'Easier said than done.'

She felt so uncomfortable that as Jay went to kiss her, she pushed him away.

'People might be watching.' With key in hand, Robyn looked around to see whether any curtains were twitching. As Robyn looked out of her lounge window, she caught sight of the old busy body chatting with another of the neighbours. *About me no doubt.*

'I think I'll have to move,' Robyn said, as Jay gently pulled her from the window and sat her down on the sofa.

'You're going to move the whole family after one small incident?'

'It's alright for you …you don't have to live here.'

'Well, I might one day, but I'll learn to ignore any spite. Anyhow, people would get used to us eventually,' Jay said.

Robyn was still unnerved when the time came to collect the children. Jay merely strolled to the car but Robyn almost sprinted, jumping into the driving seat and quickly backing out of the drive. She parked the car a few streets away from the school.

'Wait here, I'll collect Molly, and then we'll go for Jake.'

'Are you ashamed to be seen with me or something? The other Mums might be impressed that you've secured such a stunningly good looking toy boy,' Jay joked.

'Stop making fun of me, it's just taking a while to adjust that's all.'

As she got out of the car, her friend Debra was walking past.

'Hello, Robyn!' She bent down to look inside. 'Are you going to introduce me to your friend?' she said, giving Robyn a knowing look. Jay got out of the car.

'Debra, meet Jay and likewise,' Robyn said reluctantly.

'Hello, Debra, please to meet you.' He held out his hand.

'The pleasure's all mine,' she said, squeezing his. She turned to Robyn, 'Where do you get all the good looking men from? You've swapped one hunk for another.'

'Debra, please! You're embarrassing Jay.'

'I don't think its Jay, who's embarrassed,' Debra commented, after observing Robyn's scarlet cheeks.

Jay smiled, '"Hunk" is fine with me!'

'Are you going to walk with us to school?' Debra asked Jay.

'No, he's staying in the car,' Robyn said firmly.

'Why have you parked so far away? … I know you're ashamed to be seen with him.' Debra laughed, adding to Robyn's irritation.

'That's exactly what I said.' Jay nodded in agreement.

'Don't be ridiculous! … I'm not ashamed. I just don't want to flaunt my personal life all over the school playground.'

'It's too late for that,' said Debra. 'Everyone's talking about it. As we speak, some single mums are working out how long to leave it before offering to cook for the poor deserted husband.'

'You're joking!' Robyn groaned.

'I'm deadly serious. Dave has always been popular with the mums, and now he's collecting the children from school every other day, he's built up quite a fan club.'

'In that case I'm definitely coming with you, Robyn! I'll wait outside the school but the women need to see you with your new hunk.'

He laughed, but Robyn looked on the verge of tears. It was all getting too much for her. Debra realised the joke had gone too far and said swiftly,

'Lighten up Rob, these things happen. Go in with your head held high, they're only jealous. Come on, we'll all walk together.'

'But Molly hasn't even met Jay yet.'

'Then it will be easier in a crowd, it won't be as big a deal,' Debra said walking ahead. 'She can walk back here with Taylor.'

'Okay, I suppose.'

'I'll pretend Jay's with me if you like! I love a bit of gossip,' Debra sniggered.

'You just like stirring up trouble,' Robyn finally smiled.

'That's more like it, come on we'll be late.' Debra carried on walking rapidly down the street, followed by an amused Jay and ambivalent Robyn.

Jay stayed at the school gates as agreed, though he might as well have exhibited a notice saying,

'Robyn's new man, please stare!' However, he'd rather them all stare at him than give Robyn a hard time.

Molly came skipping out the school gate hand in hand with Taylor. They looked like two peas in a pod, both with striking red hair.

'They could be twins,' Jay commented to Debra.

'Everyone says that, in fact someone asked me if my husband had slept with Robyn Fisher! I didn't make the connection until I saw them together. And we've all been good friends ever since.'

Molly took one look at Jay, stuck her nose up in the air and waltzed past him.

'That's what she thinks of me,' Jay laughed as Robyn seized her daughter's hand and said,

'Molly don't be rude. Say hello to my friend Jay.'

'You're not as good looking as my Dad,' Molly said, looking down her nose as she spoke. Robyn took hold of her daughters' arm and turned her round. 'I'll not tell you again. Remember your manners.'

'Leave it, Robyn, she's okay,' Jay whispered.

'No, it's not okay. I haven't brought her up to be so rude!'

'Michael Biggs says you're sleeping with my Mummy,' proclaimed Molly loudly. 'Are you?'

Robyn was aghast. *How on earth does she know about such things?*

Jay remained impassive however and said lightly,

'Sometimes I have a sleep over at Mummy's. Do you ever have a sleep over at Taylor's?'

Molly nodded, her red curls bouncing. 'Yes, we get to stay up until nine o'clock and we eat sweets in bed, even though we're not supposed to.'

'Then that's like me and Mummy, but we stay up a bit longer 'cause we're older,' Jay explained, which seemed to pacify Molly entirely.

Debra gave Jay the thumbs up and Robyn breathed a sigh of relief. She hadn't expected Jay to be so good with children. Reaching the car, Debra and Taylor said goodbye and carried on up the road.

'Did you bring my Leapster?' Molly asked, settling herself on the back seat.

'Yes, in my handbag beside you,' said Robyn, starting the engine.

'Can I play with it?'

'You can for now, but not in McDonalds. We're all going to talk to one another instead.'

'Borrring,' said Molly as she reached into Robyn's bag to get out her game.

'Remind me again why I had children?' Robyn said quietly.

'She's only showing off,' Jay pointed out. 'It's perfectly natural.'

'How do you know what's perfectly natural? You haven't even got kids!'

'Because my first job in the hospital after graduation was in the Child Psychology Unit. I had to deal with all manner of dysfunctional children. Trust me Molly is positively angelic compared to some of the unfortunates I had to deal with.'

One child down, one to go, thought Robyn as she drove off to pick up her son.

Jake was the total opposite of his sister, a real delight. He was polite and even held Jay's hand as they crossed the car park. Robyn was so proud of her little boy.

'Right then, who's for a McDonalds?' Jay said to the children.

'Me! Me!'

Robyn sat and watched Jay interact with her children and knew she'd nothing to worry about. He would never replace their father, but he could be a good friend and a welcome ally. Maybe things would work out after all.

Chapter 28

January, the following year

Sarah gave birth to Barney Cartwright at five fifteen am on Monday 2nd January, four days late. Robyn had her hand pulverized through the uncomplicated, yet painful, birth, and Sarah was quite happy for Chris and Denizon to see the baby once he'd been cleaned up and was lying in her arms.

Chris was named as the father on the birth certificate, which made him immensely proud. A boy only needs one Godmother but Sarah made an exception and named Robyn and Denizon as Godmothers and Jay as Barney's Godfather, instead of Dave.

It was Parent's Evening at the school tonight, and Robyn and Dave were going together while Jay looked after the children. To avoid any testosterone battles, she usually had any discussion with Dave outside in the drive. But on this occasion, she was having an extended conversation with her mother, who was telling Robyn all about her new man – a retired businessman of fifty eight who was teaching Doreen to play golf.

Dave hooted his horn, but Robyn didn't come out. They were in danger of being late so he opened the front door and shouted, 'Robyn, are you ready?'

'She's just on the phone,' Jay shouted back. 'Come in and wait.'

'I don't have to be invited into my own bloody house, thank you very much.'

Jay was taken aback, 'Sorry, mate. I didn't mean anything by it.'

'I'm certainly not your mate … shagging my wife and looking after my children doesn't make us best friends.' Dave looked at Jay helping his two children into their nightclothes, a job he always used to do.

Always sensitive, Jake started to cry. Robyn heard the commotion, 'I'm going to have to hang up mum. I think

I'm about to witness world war three.' She went into the lounge.

'Hello, Dave. Sorry to keep you waiting. What's all this about?'

Dave snorted. 'Your boyfriend just invited me into my own house, that's all. The last time I checked the mortgage is in *my* name! Is that still the case?' He glared at her.

'You know damn well it is.' Robyn snapped. 'What's got into you, Dave? This isn't like you.' Robyn was as bewildered as Jay by Dave's spontaneous outburst.

'I just don't like being a guest in my own house.' He scowled at Jay this time.

'I'm sorry, but I never meant it like that.'

'Leave it now, Jay,' said Robyn picking up her coat. 'Come on Dave, we'll talk in the car.'

'Be good for Uncle Jay both of you,' she said to her subdued children. 'Mummy and Daddy won't be long.'

Sliding into the front passenger seat of Dave's Mercedes, she said sharply,

'Now, what was that *really* all about?'

By this time Dave had calmed down and said very quietly, 'Neither of you appreciate how hard it is watching another man do all the things I used to do with my children. He sees them six days a week as opposed to my four and he gets to put them to bed.'

'I *do* appreciate it. Obviously it's far from ideal from your viewpoint, but taking it out on Jay won't solve anything. He's only ever been pleasant to you.'

'As I've been to him.' He paused. 'Well, apart from the bloody nose.' Dave inwardly smiled as he remembered the satisfying punch.

'But we have to make the best of the awkward situation we're all in.' Robyn squeezed his hand as he changed gear.

'It just got to me today and I'm sorry.' Something *had* happened that day to make Dave edgy, but he didn't want to talk to Robyn about it yet, as nothing was finalised.

'It's my fault,' she said. 'I should've come to meet you outside and then none of this would have happened.'

'Let's forget about it.' He gave a half smile. 'Apologise to Jay for me. I know he didn't mean anything by it.'

Nothing more was said until they got to the school. Dave found the last parking space in the car park.

'I hope Molly's been okay at school. Miss Dodds did say she'd keep an eye on her after I told her me and you had split up.'

'Don't worry. I'm sure she's been fine. She's a tough cookie.'

While they were waiting to see Molly's form teacher, Robyn and Dave looked at their daughter's work in a large A3 folder. There was some beautiful handwriting, some quite complicated sums and a dozen or so paintings, one in particular caught Robyn's eye.

'Look at this, Dave.' Robyn held up a family portrait. Robyn was in the foreground with bright red hair, Jake was holding on to her hand and Molly was to one side in the middle of two men, holding hands with both.

'Oh dear!' Dave cringed. 'Let's see what Miss Dodds has to say about this.'

'Mr. and Mrs. Fisher, would you like to come over?' Robyn and Dave joined the young teacher at her desk.

'Did you look at Molly's work?' she said. 'She's doing very well. Her reading age is well above average, as is her maths. This is what we've been doing this term.' Miss Dodds laid out Molly's most recent work. 'I'm very pleased with her progress.' Robyn and Dave looked at each other and smiled.

'I've just got the one concern. We had an incident in the playground today,' Miss Dodds said. 'I nearly rang, but as I was seeing you tonight I thought I'd leave it until now.'

The smile left Robyn's face immediately, 'What is it?'

'Molly hit a boy today who was teasing her about having two daddies.'

'Oh no! How awful. Did she hurt him?'

'No, it wasn't very hard. Molly had to sit outside the Headmistresses office for the rest of playtime. But we talked about it, and she knows what she did was wrong.'

'We've just seen the picture she drew,' Dave said awkwardly. 'Are you sure she's okay?'

'Apart from this one incident, she seems to be taking it in her stride. Is everything working out for you as a family?'

'I thought it was. But obviously not,' Robyn admitted.

'From my limited experience, children cope well as long as they're kept in the loop and everything's out in the open.'

'We thought we'd been open, but maybe we haven't tried hard enough,' Robyn said looking across at Dave.

'If anything happens again I'll keep you informed,' Miss Dodds said.

'We'd appreciate that, thank you.'

The conversation reverted back to a discussion about Molly's musical ability and her talent for PE. The allotted time was soon over and Miss Dodds shook hands with them both.

As they walked back to the car, Robyn said, 'I didn't think Molly would ever hit another child. How can we make it better for the children?'

'I don't know, but we have to try.' Dave paused. 'I've got a suggestion. You could always throw him out and have me back.'

Robyn assumed it was a joke, but by the look on Dave's face she wasn't too sure. They were both silent all the way home.

It was teatime two days later before she found the right time to talk to Molly. Jay was playing upstairs with Jake, and Robyn shouted Molly to come into the kitchen,

'Molly, do you want to help Mummy make some buns?'

'Can we have green icing and sprinkles?' Molly shouted as she pulled out the kitchen chair to kneel on.

'As long as you only use two drops,' Robyn laughed, remembering the emerald green icing of last time.

'Can I beat the eggs?' Molly already had the whisk in her hand.

As Robyn started weighing out all the ingredients she asked Molly, 'Are you happy with Mummy and Jay living here, darling?'

'Yes, he's cool.' Suddenly she looked sad. 'But I miss Daddy.'

'I know you do, sweetheart. We all do.'

'So why can't he come and live here too? He could share my room,' Molly said excitedly.

Robyn smiled inwardly, 'I don't think Daddy would like that, somehow. Even though Mummy and Daddy are still friends, we don't want to live together anymore.'

'Michael Biggs has two Daddies, but he hates one of his. I don't hate anybody, but I love Daddy more.'

'And so you should. He'll always be your Daddy. Jay is just a good friend. You will tell me if you get upset with anything won't you?' Robyn tenderly squeezed her daughter's arm.

Molly pulled away and changing the subject, said, 'Get off, Mummy, I'm trying to beat the eggs. Can we have butterfly buns that Grandma makes?'

Robyn knew to let the subject drop. Children coped in very different ways to adults, thank God!

Robyn couldn't believe January was almost at an end. It didn't seem two minutes since she and Jay had seen the New Year in at Debra and Geoff's house. It was the first party they'd been to as a couple, and it had gone as well as could be expected. All her friends made Jay feel very welcome, although almost everyone asked about Dave and expressed sadness about the break-up. In order to avoid another scene, Robyn ensured she saw Dave outside when he visited – she wasn't risking Jay and Dave being in the same room again. On the whole, things were going well and Robyn had started to be optimistic about the future.

Just then the phone rang. She was due to go away with Gerald to Switzerland for a couple of nights and expected the early morning call to be him confirming the dates so she could book the flights. But it was Dave on the line.

'Hi Robyn, er… are you working today?'

'No, I'm off today and tomorrow. Are you alright? You sound a bit strange.'

He evaded the question, 'Would you be free to meet me for lunch today?'

'I've got a facial this morning, but I could come after that. What's this all about? Can't you tell me over the phone? I'm intrigued.'

There was a little pause, then he said, 'No, it's better if we meet. How about the Fox and Grapes?'

'That's fine,' said Robyn. 'About half past twelve okay? I should be able to make it by then.'

'Perfect! Thanks, I'll see you there.' He said nothing more and rang off, leaving Robyn feeling very unsettled.

If she was honest with herself, though it was totally unreasonable given her own situation, she was dreading the day when Dave started dating seriously and wondered if his secrecy had something to do with that. She quite liked the idea of both men being in her life, and she knew how she'd hate Dave to get re-married. Although, as yet, divorce had never really been a serious topic of conversation.

Robyn didn't usually dress up when she went for a facial, but today was different – she wanted to keep Dave on his toes. She carefully teamed a short navy skirt with a teal sweater, the one that he'd bought her from *French Connection*. High-heeled black boots complimented the outfit.

Since living with Jay, she'd worn the ring and bracelet he'd given her on a daily basis – but not when she was seeing Dave. His engagement ring came out of her jewellery box and onto her wedding finger. She scraped back her long hair into a bun and grabbed her ankle length black coat. Make-up would wait until after the facial. Fingers crossed, he wasn't going to tell her he had a girlfriend.

At lunchtime, watching an immaculately groomed Robyn walk into the pub, Dave didn't remember her making this much effort when they were together. She looked absolutely stunning, her skin almost glowing she looked so well. It didn't add up. One day she'd be casually, even a little scruffily dressed, with minimum make-up, cool and offhand with him. Then, as now, she made every effort to look fantastic.

Just when he thought he might be getting over her, she would pull something else out of the bag and keep him dangling. It was certainly confusing. Was she doing it to impress him? Or was her new life making her so happy that her beauty shone even more? Whatever it was, he knew he still loved her deeply – which made what he was about to reveal even harder.

They'd been apart for eight weeks now and excepting the drunken incident outside the bar with Stacey, Dave hadn't looked at another woman. He'd blotted the Sue and Alex incident out of his consciousness, even though Alex had rung up the following week to apologise for their behaviour. One or two of the mums at school had made it plain they were available, but he just couldn't summon up the enthusiasm to make the effort – no-one matched up to the beautiful woman walking towards him.

Robyn quickly found where he was sitting and bent over and kissed his cheek. He smelt his favourite fragrance, the one he bought her every Christmas. She usually only wore it on special occasions, so why today?

'Sorry, I'm a bit late, my facial appointment ran over.' She took off her coat and sat down.

'No problem,' Dave smiled, 'I've only been here a few minutes. What can I get you to drink?'

'A sparkling mineral water please.'

'Do you know what you'd like to eat?'

'What are you having?' She smiled at Dave as he stood up.

'I was just going to have a chicken Caesar salad, but have a look at the menu.'

She shook her head, still smiling. 'There's no need. I'll have the same as you, thanks.'

At the crowded bar, Dave ordered the food and drink and when he came back to the table, Robyn had moved her chair closer to his.

'They're bringing it over, might be a while though, it's getting busy so-'

Robyn interrupted him eagerly, 'Dave! Don't keep me in suspense. What's this all about?' 'Well,' he began slowly. 'I've had an offer from someone who wants to buy the company.'

Robyn suddenly relaxed, 'That's great news ... isn't it?' But looking at Dave's face she wasn't so sure.

'Yes, it's a really good offer,' he continued, his face still serious. 'And they want me to stay on as a consultant working with all my old clients.' His voice was muted, however, and Robyn was starting to feel apprehensive.

'I sense a but...' she said, 'what do-'

'They have an office in London,' he cut in. 'but the main part of the operation is in New Zealand.'

'New Zealand!' Robyn was stunned for a moment, 'Surely you could work from London or at least somewhere in the UK?'

He frowned and said glumly, 'That's just it. The CEO wants me to train his staff in all the latest software – and he's based in Auckland. If I want this deal to go through and, to be honest Robyn, I can't really turn it down. Then I'll have to go to New Zealand. No choice.'

'How long would you be gone? A month, six weeks?' Robyn felt her stomach churn. Since the split, no more than two days had elapsed without her seeing Dave or speaking to him on the phone.

'Probably about a year or so, I'm afraid, depending on how quickly the staff pick up the new programmes.' He looked directly at Robyn, who had gone very pale.

'But what about the children?' she asked. 'They've had so much disruption already, and they'll miss you so much.'

'Why do you think I wanted to meet? I'm so torn. On the one hand, it's a perfect opportunity for me to semi-retire and pursue different avenues, but on the other, I'd miss Molly and Jake, besides missing out on everything they're doing.'

Their food and drink had arrived by this time, but neither of them felt like eating.

'What about me?' Robyn's hand trembled as she picked up her sparkling water, wishing she'd asked for something stronger. She knew she had no right to ask Dave that question, but she couldn't help herself.

'Of course I'd miss you Robyn – but you have Jay now.'

Robyn bent her head over the chicken Caesar salad. What other answer could she have expected?

'When do you have to let them know?'

'The end of this week. They made the offer a few weeks ago, but I hadn't really considered it as a serious option until recently. They've been bombarding me with calls and e-mails. If I say no, I might never get another opportunity like this again.'

'Then it sounds as if you've made your decision … But why didn't you discuss it with me earlier?'

'I wanted to, but I didn't know what to say.'

'You could've thought of something!' Robyn rested her chin in her hands.

'Cheer up, Robyn. It might not be so bad. We can Skype all the time. Plus a year will fly by… you'll see and if I didn't think you and Jay could cope, I definitely wouldn't go, no matter what.'

Robyn was quiet. Her blissful, contented state of the past few weeks vanished in an instant with Dave's thunderbolt. Was she only happy because Dave was still in her life? She knew he still fancied her; she made sure of it by dressing like she had today, but with Dave gone she'd be left with a void – a void only he could fill. He'd been a part of her life since she was twenty one, and she couldn't imagine life without him.

'Say something, Rob,' Dave urged.

'I don't know what to say.' To her consternation, she felt tears pricking her eyes. 'If I ask you to stay it would be for purely selfish reasons – and I know that's not fair, so I won't.'

He put his arm round her shoulder and hugged her gently.

'Look, Rob. I have to start making a new life for myself. I've got to face facts. You're never coming back to me. I can see how happy you are.'

I'm only happy 'cause you're still here. But you don't know that because I haven't told you.

She cleared her throat and sipped some water.

'So, it looks like it's settled then, when are you going to tell the children?'

'This weekend. I'll show them how Skype works so they know they can see me. Try to pretend you're pleased for me, Rob. I feel really bad leaving things like this with you.'

'It's just a shock that's all … When do you actually go?'

'Sometime in the next month, as soon as things can be finalised.'

Shit! So soon.

'Will you work in London when you come back?' Robyn asked.

That's if you decide to come back at all!

'We'll see. Anyway, I don't intend to stay with the company forever. I have a few plans in the pipeline.'

'You've never mentioned anything to me.'

'I've had an awful lot of time to think these past few weeks, and I know you think things have been okay between us recently but watching you and Jay together never gets any easier. I need to spread my wings.'

'I know, I'm sorry. I'm just being selfish.'

Robyn picked at her salad but couldn't summon up much enthusiasm to enjoy it as Dave carried on talking about his new adventure. She could see how excited he was. Who wouldn't be, with such an amazing opportunity? Last year both of them would've been making plans for a new future together.

They parted after Dave's lunch hour was up. He hugged her again and kissed her cheek. 'Thanks for being so understanding. It's been so much easier than I anticipated.'

'My pleasure,' said Robyn through gritted teeth. 'I'll see you on Friday, when you come to stay with the children.'

'You will,' he said and waved goodbye as he crossed to his car.

Robyn had to talk to someone. Usually it would be Denizon or her mother, but she needed to hear the unbiased truth and there was only one person who'd be brutally honest with her and that was Gerald.

Tears were streaming down her face as she drove far too fast to his house. Abandoning, rather than parking her car, a foot from the kerb and after fumbling with the door key, she dashed inside.

'Gerald,' she shouted urgently.

'In here, Robyn,' he called from the lounge, and she rushed to him, almost panting for breath.

'Whatever is the matter, girl?' he asked. 'For Heaven's sake, sit down and calm yourself.'

'It's Dave,' she sobbed out hysterically. 'He's going to New Zealand to work.'

'Is that all?' said Gerald. 'Thank goodness. I thought someone had died.'

Robyn stopped crying and looked at him incredulously. 'What do you mean "is that all"? It's terrible.'

'Why? There's obviously a good reason he's going, isn't there?'

'Yes – his company's being bought out and they want him to train their staff in Auckland.'

'That's great news for him, Robyn. You should be happy for him.'

'But what about me?'

He looked at her sternly. 'What did you expect? Dave to stay around forever waiting on your whims? I'm glad he's going. It'll give him the chance of a decent life in a lovely country.'

Robyn felt crushed. 'How did I know you'd take his side?'

'I'm not taking anyone's side. I'm just giving you my honest opinion. I could say, "poor Robyn isn't it awful? You won't have two men at your beckon call." But it wouldn't be me and you know it.'

Robyn looked down at her feet, 'You're right as usual. But it's such a shock, Gerald. When he had sex with that girl outside the pub it didn't bother me at all. I knew he did it to get back at me. But this is different. This is a whole new life for him and I'm not going to be a part of it.'

'As my old Gran would say, "you can't have your cake and eat it." This way the choice is out of your hands.'

'But what if he meets a nice New Zealand girl and decides to stay?'

'Then you'll be pleased for him and wish him well.'

'But I can't,' said Robyn.

Gerald steered his chair to directly face Robyn's and gave her a steely look she'd never seen before.

'Up to now, I've been very patient with you,' he began as Robyn looked puzzled.

'Yes, this is me being patient,' he continued. 'But you're acting like a spoiled brat. You don't want Dave, but neither do you want anyone else to have him. You have some serious growing up to do and soon, Robyn. Because Dave is going to go to New Zealand with or without your blessing and I'm sure you'd rather part the best of friends.'

'Is that it?' Robyn was still shaking from Gerald's tirade.

'No!' He said. 'Listen. I've never met Dave. I just hear you talk about him, but I have met Jay and as much as I admire and like him as a person I don't think he's the right one for you. That's my opinion based on my knowledge of you both. If you have any doubt in your mind about letting Dave go for ever, now is the time to speak up, because when he gets to New Zealand, he'll start to forget about you, I promise.'

Robyn was stunned. 'You've never told me this before. About Jay I mean. Why?'

'That's because it's had nothing to do with me until now. It's obvious you're still uncertain who you really want from your reaction over Dave. I'm just telling you what I think, as you asked.'

She nodded. 'It's true. I do value your opinion. That's why I came and now I'm here, you're shouting at me.' Her voice trembled.

'But Robyn – you value everyone's opinion but your own. You can't decide between brown or white bread without asking advice first. It has to stop. I've seen you blossom these past few weeks, but I don't believe it's because of Jay like you seem to think. I believe it's because you're happy with your life. You really like working for me, though God knows why! You have both men eating out of your hands; you had a fabulous Christmas and virtually a second home in Spain. You're mother of two wonderful children and godmother to beautiful Barney… I could go on, but as I see it, all your life you've been expecting others to make you happy. You can do it yourself, you know. Millions do.'

Robyn just stared at Gerald. 'Gosh! Am I so transparent?'

'I've told you before, I've so little to do with my body, my mind works overtime and I observe.'

'What do you think I should do then?'

He sighed, 'Stop asking me stupid questions and make your own decisions.'

'What if I make the wrong one?' she asked hesitantly.

'Then you live with the consequences. When you had Dave you wanted Jay, and now you've got Jay you sound as if you want Dave. Can't you see how absurd that is?'

She shrugged her shoulders, her voice hardly above a whisper, 'When you put it like that, yes I suppose so.'

'Look at yourself, Robyn. You're a beautiful, intelligent woman who has everything going for her. You remind me so much of my Camille. She had every reason in the world to be ecstatically happy, but she couldn't let herself go and enjoy her life because self-doubt always got the better of her. It destroyed her in the end. I'd hate to see the same thing happen to you.'

Robyn was silent for a while, moved beyond words by Gerald's concern for her. Then standing up, she said firmly,

'I've got some thinking to do, haven't I?'

'You certainly have,' he agreed. 'When is Dave going?'

'He didn't say exactly, but I gather sooner rather than later. I'd better go and start sorting out my priorities.' She put her hand on Gerald's shoulder then picked up her car keys from the table. 'Thank you for listening.'

'Just a minute,' he said. 'Do you remember when you first told me about your affair I gave you some advice?'

Robyn shook her head.

'I suggested you take some time out on your own. Perhaps Dave going is a blessing. You'll be able to get used to doing things for yourself.'

'I'm not great on my own,' she confessed.

'Then you'd better learn,' said Gerald, bringing her out of her reverie. 'Because one day you will be alone. Even if you're married for fifty years there will be a time, and the sooner you get used to enjoying your own company the better. Trust me on that one.'

'Yes sir!' Robyn saluted him, smiling.

'That's better,' he smiled back. 'I knew I'd get you to call me "sir" sooner or later.'

And this time they both laughed.

Robyn was getting a little practice at being on her own as Jay was away for two nights doing something with his book. By the time he arrived home on Tuesday night, Robyn had just finished putting the children to bed. She hadn't spoken to him directly since Monday morning. They'd shared a few texts over the past two days, but that was all and she was distinctly put out.

'Hi love, I'm back,' he shouted from the hallway.

'So I hear,' she said, rather coldly.

'What's wrong?' He put his head round the door.

'You can't be that interested, otherwise you'd have rung me.'

He came into the lounge and sat down. 'I told you it was going to be a hectic time, It's been meeting after meeting … You could've rung me if you needed to chat,'

'I did ring, a few times actually, but your phone was always switched off.'

'I turned it off during the day and must have forgotten to switch it back on last night.'

'Too busy enjoying yourself, I assume?'

'Yes and no. It was work – but you'll never guess what, there's interest in the books from across the pond. A publisher in America wants to promote the first one, and is asking me to do a book tour. My new agent is arranging it all.'

Panic swept over Robyn. Not only was she losing one man from her life, she was losing two. The universe sure had a funny sense of humour.

'Um, didn't you think to mention this possibility before?' she added as he poured them both some wine.

'I'm telling you now,' said Jay, rather impatiently.

'I didn't even know you were looking for an agent,' Robyn commented, gulping her wine.

'Most new writers need a good agent to negotiate the best deals and arrange tours etc. I met Lindy yesterday and she's more than happy to take me on.'

'A woman?'

'Yes, Lindy from Matlock and Graves. They're a big agency with offices in London and America. They specialise in non-fiction. She was very impressed with me.'

I bet she was!

'So when is this tour thing likely to be then?'

'Probably March by the time it happens,' Jay drained his wine and poured another glass. 'You could come.'

Robyn shook her head. 'No, thanks. Anyway I don't see how I could come to America with you – what about the children?'

'Couldn't your mother or Dave have them for a few weeks?' he said casually.

'A few *weeks,*' exclaimed Robyn. 'I'm not leaving my children for a few weeks to swan round America with you.'

'Sorry, it was only a suggestion.'

'Anyway Dave won't be here! He'll be in New Zealand by then. He told me yesterday he's going for up to a year.'

'Ah, so that's why you're mad at me.'

'No! I'm mad because we're supposed to be in a relationship and you don't even tell me what's happening in your life until everything's arranged.'

'Now hang on a minute … do you expect me to stop my conversation with a prospective agent to ring my partner and ask if it's okay to accept her generous offer. Is that what you're saying?'

'No that's silly!' said Robyn at once. 'But I am used to being part of a team who discuss plans for the future.'

'Oh really,' he added sarcastically. 'I think you mean you like to be in *control* of a team who discuss plans for the future. I was really excited about coming back and telling you my news, I thought you'd be pleased.'

'I am. Really I am, I just-.'

'Is all this because Dave is leaving and you can't handle it or something?'

'I don't know. I'm sorry.'

Robyn realised she was acting unreasonably, but she didn't seem to be able to stop herself. Her ordered life was falling apart about around her ears and she was in danger of going into free fall any minute. Seeing her face, Jay took hold of her hand.

'Look, love. It's a big opportunity for me. Try not to put a damper on it. It won't affect how I feel about you. How could it? At least I won't be away as long as Dave, and you'll have your job and the children to keep you occupied.'

Robyn gave a small smile. 'That's true, I suppose. I'm just a bit jealous, everyone seems to be having adventures but me.'

'But you're going away with Gerald again soon,' he pointed out. 'Isn't it Switzerland next?'

'You know it is, but that's work, and anyway, I doubt I'll be able to go with Dave away. In fact, I'll probably have to give up my job.'

'Now you're being silly!' he said. 'There's no way on earth Gerald is going to get rid of you. He'll do anything to make sure you stay.'

'I hope so. But who knows?'

By this time, Jay really couldn't be bothered arguing. Robyn was in danger of spoiling his good mood and he said quickly,

'Why don't I run you a nice bath? And I'll give you a back rub. That usually makes you feel better and then maybe you'll fancy an early night.' He winked. 'Good news always makes me horny.'

But Robyn wasn't pacified. Things must be bad, she thought, when Jay's wink did nothing for her.

Chapter 29

February

Denizon had always wanted to arrange a surprise party and with Dave leaving it was the perfect opportunity. She'd suggested it to Robyn, who was more than happy for someone else to make an effort, because all she could do was mope about and couldn't raise a smile for anyone. Even Gerald couldn't rouse her out of the depression that had taken hold.

Denizon called round to see Robyn on her way to the party venue, 'Do you want to come and blow up some balloons?'

'Not really. I can't be bothered to go out.'

'Come on Rob! You can't be like this tonight. You've got to get Dave to his party later. He's not going to want to go anywhere with you looking like that. What have you told him, by the way?' Denizon asked.

But Robyn couldn't share her friend's excitement and said listlessly, 'I've said I've booked a table at the *Thai Palace* with his mum and Malcolm. They know not to say anything.'

'Good choice, you have to pass the Golf club to get there. What are you wearing?'

'I'm going to change into my cream satin dress there, I can't go out for Thai Green curry in a long dress, Dave would be suspicious. I'm going to suggest he dresses up for the meal, but I've got his dinner suit in the boot if he insists on going out in his jeans.'

'Does Jay mind not being invited?' asked Denizon. 'I just thought it would be awkward.'

'No, he appreciates its Dave's night. He's staying in Leeds and coming back over once Dave has gone on Monday.' She sighed.

'That's nice of him.'

'He might as well. I'm not exactly great company right now. I think he's fed up of not having sex.'

'That'll all change next week, surely.'

'I don't know.' Robyn shrugged her shoulders. 'Maybe.'

'Are you not looking forward to tonight at all?' Denizon asked in frustration.

'I'm trying so hard, Den, but I can't imagine him not being here whenever I need him.'

'Didn't you think something like this would happen eventually?'

'Him flying to the other side of the world, do you mean? No, I did not.'

'But he has to make his own life.'

'I know that,' said Robyn, not sounding very convinced. 'But I hadn't ruled out the possibility that we might get back together one day.'

'What!' Denizon exclaimed. 'That's news to me. I wish you'd make up your mind. I thought you were passionately in love with Jay.'

Robyn fidgeted with her finger, twisting the rings round. 'Well, I suppose so. But he's not really husband material, you know, Den. He's too self-centred. I don't mean that in a bad way, but he always thinks of his own needs first. I did know that about him and he does try, but it doesn't come naturally. I especially notice it with the kids. He's always suggesting we let them stay with a Grandparent or Dave so we can do things on our own. Family isn't his priority. I know he adores me and I love that, but I don't know what will happen in the long term.'

'I wish you'd make up your mind! … When does he go to America?'

Robyn frowned and nibbled at her thumb nail. 'Don't remind me, the first week in March.'

'How long for?'

'Only for four weeks initially, but he might be going back later if his tour goes well.'

Denizon smiled. 'That's not so bad. Four weeks will fly by. You can come to our house. Barney loves Jake.' She stood up. 'Come on, Rob. Can't I persuade you about blowing up some balloons? I can't do them all by myself.'

'You're a pest,' said Robyn. 'Okay – but I can't come for long. I said I'd help Dave finish packing,' she added her voice trailing off.

'But isn't he at work?'

'Only until two o'clock. It's his last day today.'

'Doesn't he think it strange that nobody has organised a leaving do or anything?'

'He hasn't mentioned it. Anyway, from what he said last week I think a few of them at the office were taking him out for a drink this lunchtime.'

'That's something, then,' said Denizon. 'Just as long as he knows people care about him. Now, you're clear about the plan tonight, aren't you? You text just as you are leaving the house and again as you pull up in the car park.'

'Yes, Denizon … Believe me, it's etched on my brain.'

Dave felt touched that Robyn had given up her Friday night with Jay to arrange a farewell dinner for the two of them, plus his Mum and Malcolm. He still loved spending time with her and had hoped since breaking the news of his imminent departure they might do more things together as a family. But, sadly, that hadn't happened – in fact he'd seen even less of her than usual. It was as if she was avoiding him.

When he arrived back at the house at three o'clock he expected Robyn to be at home as she said she'd help him do some last minute packing, but the house was deserted

Dave slowly walked from room to room, soaking up the atmosphere and recalling events that had taken place there – some good, some not so good. He remembered Molly cutting her head on the side of the kitchen table and the blood staining the new vinyl floor. He smiled as he trod on the beautiful wool rug in the lounge where, more than likely, Jake had been conceived. Dave plonked himself on the settee and let out a deep sigh as he remembered the nights cuddling up with Robyn, sharing a glass of wine and their day.

How had it all gone so terribly wrong? They'd been so happy and look at them now. It made him wonder how any couple survived married life.

This wasn't getting his packing done! He stood up and went to retrieve his case from the loft.

Robyn dashed through the front door a few minutes later. 'Dave?'

'Up here.'

'Sorry I'm late, where are you?' she shouted.

'I'm in our – sorry, your bedroom getting the last few things from my wardrobe,' he called back, opening the door. He was surprised, not to say a bit choked, to see so many of Jay's clothes hanging where once his own had been.

'Where are my summer shirts?' he asked Robyn as she came upstairs.

'Oh sorry, Dave. They're in the spare room. I didn't think you'd be needing them just yet.'

Dave wanted to ask whether she'd replaced everything about him so easily, but didn't want to get into a fight today of all days, especially when she'd arranged a special night for them.

'Um…. what do you want me to do? I could pack your toiletries?' Robyn offered. 'I don't think you've ever packed your own toilet bag before.' She laughed nervously.

'If you like, but I could manage. I've been doing quite a lot of things for myself recently.'

'I know, I'm sorry.'

Looking at Robyn's guilty expression, Dave suddenly felt overwhelmed, almost tearful. But he'd never been one to cry. Even when he held his children for the first time, although his throat had ached with emotion, he couldn't shed a tear. It was the same now – but his voice faltered as he said,

'I – I don't think I can go, Rob.'

Robyn desperately wanted to hug him tight, but summoning all her courage said lightly,

'Of course you can! It'll fly by, just you watch. You'll be so busy at work that you won't have time to think about us poor souls freezing to death in England.'

Dave swallowed hard and walked out of the bedroom to avoid looking at Robyn.

'Wait a sec! Molly wants you to take this with you, but she asked me to put it in your case because she'd cry giving it to you herself.'

Dave stood at the door to see Robyn holding up their daughter's favourite stuffed toy, a one-eared giraffe called Freddie.

'How will she sleep without him?' said Dave, taking Freddie and holding the little plush toy lovingly to his chest. Freddie had been Molly's bedfellow since her first birthday when Granddad Peter had given him as a special present.

Though trembling inside, Robyn said firmly, 'She's says she'll cope. And I think there may already be a replacement waiting in the wings. Swap giraffe for racoon!'

'That's so sweet of Molly – please put Freddie in between my socks. Oh, before I forget Rob, I've seen a solicitor, so if you want a divorce while I'm gone he's instructed to act on my behalf.'

Robyn sat down on the bed so suddenly she nearly sent Dave's case flying.

'Why on earth did you do that? What do you take me for?'

'But you and Jay might want to get married if I'm gone for a year.'

'I wouldn't dream of asking for a divorce while you were out of the country!' she said at once. 'I might be many things, but I don't think I'm totally heartless.'

'Well, the offer's there if you change your mind. Er – I'm just going to nip back to the office, I think I've left some important papers on my desk.' Dave knew he couldn't carry on this conversation without making a total fool of himself and muttered,

'I'll be back to get changed later and Rob, thanks for thinking about me for tonight. It means a lot, this meal.'

302 | Lindsay Harper

He'd done it – he'd had the divorce conversation without breaking down. Just the airport to go!

For the first time in their relationship Robyn was ready before Dave, but only because she needed to get changed again at the party.

'Come on Dave, we're going to be late,' she shouted up the stairs

'But it's only half past six,' he protested. 'I thought the table was booked for seven.'

'It is, but I forgot to mention I need to call at the golf club,' she said quickly. 'Mum left her mobile in the changing rooms and they're keeping it behind reception.'

'Okay,' Dave said, appearing on the landing. 'I'm ready now. I'm a bit disappointed the children didn't come home before going to your mum's though. I need to get my full quota in with them before I go away.'

Looking up at his serious face, Robyn felt a pang. She was finding it so difficult not to let anything slip. The children were already at the party waiting to jump out and surprise him.

'Yes, I know. Sorry, it would've been too much of a rush. You look nice,' she added as Dave walked down the stairs wearing his expensive black trousers and a cream striped shirt. He was such a good-looking man. Why hadn't she seen it every day of their married life?

'Do you think I need a tie?' he asked, not certain how formal he should play it.

'Not unless you want to put one on,' she smiled.

'You're looking nice as well, by the way,' he said.

'Thank you. It's the understated look.' Robyn was wearing a plain black dress with large earrings and necklace.

'Do you want me to drive there, if you're driving back?' he offered.

'No, it's your night, Dave. It's special. Let me spoil you. The car doors open. Get in and I'll lock up.' As he went down the path she sent Denizon a quick text, "Setting off now".

The golf club was on the way to the restaurant and she'd primed him already for the slight detour. She hoped he wouldn't spot Chris and Denizon's distinctive yellow VW Beetle Cabriolet at the far end of the car park. The room that Denizon had hired was round the side of the building with its own separate entrance. Robyn had somehow to get him inside and she hadn't quite worked out what to say.

But a couple of lamp posts in darkness gave her the perfect excuse.

'Do you mind coming with me,' she pointed. 'Those lights are out, and with the size of these heels I might fall.'

'Of course no problem,' he said at once, 'I'll lead the way if you tell me where.'

While she was getting out of the car Robyn hit "send" with the final pre-prepared text to Denizon, then grabbed Dave's arm in the gloom as they walked slowly round the side of the club.

'You'd think they'd have some light on down here, it's dangerous,' he remarked, as Robyn went slightly ahead of him, opened a door and stood to one side.

Curious, Dave peered into the total darkness of the room, then stepped forward. Suddenly lights blazed and there was a mighty roar as everyone shouted, 'SURPRISE!' and dozens of party poppers exploded.

Dave stood dazzled for a second, staring at the crowd of friends, family and colleagues who had come to wish him well. A big banner hanging above the table of food read,

'*GOOD LUCK DAVE* – Have a tinnie on us!'

'How did you arrange all this?' he asked Robyn, overwhelmed for the second time today.

'It's nothing to do with me!' she said, now wishing it had been. 'It was all Denizon's idea and her hard work. My job was to help blow up the balloons and bring you here.'

Dave squeezed her hand and, looking round, saw Denizon smiling from the other side of the room. He waved and beckoned.

'Come here you!' he said fondly and held out his arms.

'I hope you like the surprise,' she said, kissing his cheek.

'I love it, thank you so much.'

Dave didn't know who to talk to first. There must be over fifty people, all here to see him. His Mum and Malcolm waved, and he was amazed to see Robyn's father Peter and partner Marjorie, who had flown all the way from Spain, sitting on the same table with Robyn's mother, Doreen and her new man, Frank.

'Daddy, Daddy!' he heard from the back of the room. Chris had kept the children quiet in the corridor until the lights went on as Molly couldn't be trusted to be silent for one second. Molly and Jake both ran to Dave and flung themselves into their father's open arms.

He kissed and hugged them both repeatedly. 'You're here, you're here!'

'We'll see you again in a minute, Daddy,' said Molly at last. 'We're half way through a game with Uncle Chris.' Holding Jake's hand, she dragged him off behind her.

While Dave was saying hello to everyone, Robyn sneaked away to get ready. She slipped out of her plain black dress and wearing only the tiniest of white thongs, slithered into her cross cut satin long dress with a halter neck. It moulded to her figure perfectly. She exchanged the black high heels for cream and fastened a gold chain around her neck. The gold and diamond bracelet that Jay had bought would've looked perfect with her outfit but she couldn't wear it without Dave noticing. The finishing touches to her hair and makeup complete, she went to join the others.

Dave turned around as she walked towards him and her beauty took his breath away. How had he let the most stunning woman he had ever seen slip away from him?

'Wow! You look amazing,' he said to Robyn.

Giving her a brief hug, he couldn't help noticing the lack of underwear beneath her dress and desire surged through him. Robyn touched his arm.

'There's someone here I'd especially like you to meet. Follow me.' Like a puppy dog he obeyed, all the while staring at her perfectly formed pert behind. Robyn stopped near the big double doors at the side of the room, by a man in a wheelchair who was watching the proceedings with interest. She turned to Dave.

'Dave, I'd like to introduce you to my boss Gerald Banfleet, the man I moan about constantly. Gerald, this is my husband.'

She smiled at Gerald who had been brought to the party by Mrs. Bennett and a taxi. He noticed the total admiration on Dave's face as he shook Dave's hand.

'We meet at last, Mr. Banfleet. Robyn has told me so much about you. Thank you so much for taking the time to come and wish me well. I'm absolutely stunned to see all these people.'

'It's because you're so popular,' Robyn squeezed his arm affectionately. As Mrs. Bennett came round from behind Gerald's wheelchair smiling, Robyn said at once,

'And this is Mrs. Bennett, his housekeeper,'

'Don't forget general dogsbody,' Mrs. Bennett said chuckling.

'She's actually a saint,' Gerald said. 'Just like your wife.'

'I do know she loves her job and it seems to suit her.'

'So – you go on Monday, I hear? Are you looking forward to it?' Gerald asked.

'Yes and no, it's a marvellous opportunity but I'm going to miss everyone so much,' Dave said, his voice faltering as he tried to hold himself together.

Immediately Gerald said, 'Then you go and socialise with all your friends you're not going to see for a while, I'll catch up with you later.' Swinging his chair round, he asked Mrs. Bennett for a glass of water.

As Dave and Robyn made their way back through the throng, Dave saw Alex and Sue waving.

'What on earth are they doing here?' he whispered to Robyn.

'They're your oldest friends. I know you all had a bit of a hiccough but it's sorted now. They've made up and couldn't be happier. You actually did them a favour. It wasn't until Sue saw how jealous Alex was that she realised how much she loved him. Apparently she'd had the fling last year to make Alex notice her, but when it didn't work she resigned herself to eventually splitting up. Come on. Let's go and talk to them.'

Robyn never left Dave's side for the first hour or so. Where he went, she followed. They talked to parents, friends and Robyn met some of Dave's work colleagues she'd never talked to before. Denizon signalled Robyn from across the room.

'I'm going to start preparing the warm food … do you want to help?'

Robyn looked at Dave, who grinned mischievously. 'You get off and have a good time with the hot pies, I'll be fine. I'm going to talk to Debra and one of her friends who have been making a play for me. I might get lucky!'

Denizon walked into the kitchen with Robyn closely following, craning her neck to see who Dave was talking to.

'It's going well, don't you think?' Denizon said, as she lit the large ovens.

'It's great. You've done a fabulous job. What do you want me to do?'

'Just pass me the racks of food from over there.' Denizon pointed to trays of sausage rolls, pizzas and mini tartlets. 'You and Dave seem very friendly tonight, by the way. What is going on with you?'

'Who knows?' Robyn shrugged her shoulders.

'I've just seen you look daggers at Debra's friend. Don't tell me you're jealous!'

'I've never met anyone as fickle as me!' Robyn moaned. 'I'm getting pissed off with it! The phrase, "the grass is always greener" could definitely have been written with me in mind.' She slumped into a chair. 'When I'm with Dave I want Jay and when I'm with Jay I want Dave and soon I'll have neither.'

'To be honest Rob, that might be the best thing to happen. You having some time on your own to decide what you *really* want.'

Robyn sighed. 'Gerald says the same.'

'Well, maybe you'll eventually listen to one of us.' Denizon finished putting the trays of food in the oven and set the timer. 'We've just time for another drink before its all ready.'

Gerald tapped Mrs. Bennett on the hand, 'Please will you go and ask Dave if he can spare me five minutes outside.' Gerald steered his wheelchair to the door. He was feeling a bit claustrophobic. Over the past few years he'd grown unused to being in such a large crowd of people.

It was a cool, clear February night and the dark sky was ablaze with light from a full moon and millions of stars. His breath formed in the cold air. The chill hit his body and started to permeate through to his delicate bones. He moved the blanket up to cover his arms.

Dave suddenly appeared, panting a little, 'Are you okay, Mr. Banfleet? Mrs. Bennett said you wanted to see me. Do you want me to find Robyn for you?'

'No,' said Gerald firmly. 'It's you I want to see, if you can spare a couple of minutes.'

'Of course! And it's lovely to be outside for some fresh air. I'll miss this cold weather. It's thirty degrees in Auckland at the moment.'

Gerald cleared his throat. 'Forgive me, Dave – I know this question is a tad impertinent, and I don't know if Robyn mentioned I'm a plain speaking man …er … but do you still love your wife?'

Dave was taken aback by such a personal question from a virtual stranger but said almost at once, 'I do. I've never stopped loving her and can't imagine my life without loving her.'

'I can tell she loves you,' Gerald said, his voice adamant.

Dave hesitated. 'I know she's *fond* of me, but its Jay she loves.'

'Jay loves who Jay loves,' said Gerald dismissively, 'and when he loves them, he loves totally. But believe me, in his life he'll probably love upwards of ten Robyn's –and for her that's a recipe for disaster. I'm not disputing he loves her wholeheartedly for now, but in another ten years it would be a whole new ball game.'

Dave was confused for a moment. 'What are you trying to say?'

'In my own clumsy way, I'm saying *don't give up on her*. You only have to see you two tonight to know you were meant to be together. Forgive the cliché, but love is what's left when the lust has gone, and I think Robyn is starting to realise that. She fell in lust with Jay, just like she probably did with you at the beginning, but you know as well as me, it isn't lust that makes lasting relationships. Its companionship and total trust in each other.' Gerald's voice grew thin in the night air, but he continued, saying,

'I've seen her with Jay and she's wary of him. He's a loose cannon, and she's finding it hard to cope.'

'Maybe,' said Dave. 'But I don't want to be second best.'

Gerald shook his head at this. 'I don't think you are. She's got herself into a mess. She wanted to experience life with Jay just to see what she was missing, but now she has, I don't think it's what she thought it would be – or indeed what she actually wants.'

'But I'm going to the other side of the world on Monday. It's a bit late for reconciliation now.'

'It's never too late,' insisted Gerald. Just look up there at all those stars, our time is infinite, a few months in New Zealand is not going to change that.'

'Robyn said you were deep.' Dave laughed wistfully.

'I bet she said I was a lot more than that! I'm sorry if I'm telling you something you don't want to hear.'

'No, I appreciate your honesty,' said Dave, nevertheless feeling a bit shell-shocked 'I just don't know what to do with it.'

'Nothing, just bear in mind what I've told you and leave the rest to fate.'

'I've never really believed in fate before. Not like that, anyway.'

'Well, now is a good time to start! I'm getting a little chilly. Will you help me back inside?'

Dave helped Gerald guide the wheelchair through the narrow door and back into the party. Robyn had been pacing up and down with a drink in her hand, wondering what was going on. She saw Dave settle Gerald back beside Mrs. Bennett and go and talk to Chris and Denizon who were serving out the food. Robyn marched over to Gerald.

'What have you been saying to my husband?' she asked.

'Nothing much,' he replied casually. 'He took me outside for a breath of fresh air, that's all.' Robyn was certain there was more to it than that, but knew better than to push her stubborn employer. She forced a smile.

'Come on, the food's ready! I'll get some for you both,' she offered.

'Thank you,' Mrs. Bennett said, 'but nothing too fattening please.'

'That would be lovely, added Gerald, 'and I don't mind being fattened. Lead on.'

It was midnight before the last of the guests bade their final farewells to Dave leaving Robyn, Denizon and Chris to tidy up. Doreen had already taken Molly and Jake back to her house earlier in the evening as they were falling asleep on their feet.

'Let's just clean up the bulk of it and come back to tomorrow,' suggested Denizon. 'I did ask if we could do that and no-one is going to be using the room until Monday.'

'A good idea,' agreed Chris. Denizon handed him the remaining food, 'Take this to the car will you? I'll follow with these boxes.'

'I think everyone seemed to have a good time,' Robyn said to Dave who was almost falling asleep propped up in the chair. 'Wake up love! It's time to go home.' She tried to rouse him.

'Can't I stay here? I can't be bothered to move.'

'No, I think it would be too much of a shock to the cleaners,' she giggled.

'Help me up then,' he said, holding out his arms.

She tried pulling him up by his hands, but he was too heavy. She then attempted to lift him from under his arms but he still wouldn't move. He pulled her onto his lap.

'I'd marry you all over again you know, Rob. I've never wanted anyone else since we met and you're more beautiful now than you were then.'

'Get on with you! You've had far too much to drink,' Robyn laughed.

'I know and that's why I'm telling you. I didn't tell you enough when I was sober and I'm sorry. I do hope you'll be very happy with Jay if you stay together – but don't ever forget about me will you?' He buried his face in her neck.

'How could I ever forget about you?' she gulped. 'I've loved you for too long.'

'Can I kiss you?' Dave didn't wait for an answer, but bent her face to his. It had been a long time since he'd kissed her with such passion. She was breathless when he finally moved his mouth from hers.

'I'm sorry, but I needed something to remember you by.'

Robyn got up from his knee and turned her back so he wouldn't see the tears streaming down her cheeks.

'Let's find Denizon, she's giving us a lift home.' Robyn grabbed the coats and walked to the door.

Chapter 30

Robyn got up early Saturday morning, while Dave was still in bed in the spare room and drove over to Leeds to spend the weekend with Jay. After the kiss last night and Dave's outpouring of emotion, it was just too upsetting to be around him. In his flat she made every effort to be normal, but Jay knew what was bothering her. On Sunday, irritated by her lukewarm responses he said,

'Why don't you go back home and spend a few hours with him? He's leaving tomorrow and you're not going to see him for a year or so.'

'But I'm not going to see you soon either!'

'I'm going for four weeks; it's not exactly the same.'

'I don't think it's a good idea to go and see Dave,' she said. 'I'm with you now. I have to get on with my life. Dave needs to forget about me and meet somebody else.' Robyn didn't sound very convincing but Jay merely said,

'Well, if you're sure. So what do you want to do today?' He picked up the extra thick copy of *The Sunday Times*.

Sensing his indifferent mood, Robyn stroked his inner thigh, 'We could go back to bed?'

'I thought you said we couldn't spend all our time in bed?'

Robyn was beginning to realise that making love was what they did best and they struggled to find things to occupy the rest of their time. When they had the children it was different, because there were always activities to drive them to and playing to be done, but having so much time to herself was alien to Robyn and she couldn't relax in the same way as Jay. He could read a paper from cover to cover and then start on a book. Robyn would read a chapter and then be ready to move onto the next thing.

'I think I could do with a dog,' she said. 'Having a reason to walk everyday would be good for me.'

'Not in my flat you don't!' he said at once. 'All that moulting hair and wet dog smells, no way.'

'I didn't know you weren't a fan of dogs.'

'I like other people's, but dogs are so tying when you have one yourself. I couldn't be bothered to get up at some un-godly hour in the pouring rain to go for a walk.'

'You wouldn't need to, I would,' said Robyn.

'If anything, I'm more of a cat person myself,' he said. 'I like the fact that they're more independent.'

'I don't like cats; they're too aloof for me. I like the affection a dog gives.'

'Have you had a dog before then?' Jay asked idly, sorting out the Sunday supplements from the newspaper.

'Not since I've been married. We said we'd get one once the children were old enough to appreciate it. Molly always puts a puppy on her list to Santa. Mum and Dad had a mongrel when we were younger.'

'Sorry, I wouldn't want a dog. You could perhaps get a rabbit for the children?' he said, opening one of the glossy magazines.

It wasn't a big deal about the dog, but somehow Robyn felt cheated. She'd thought a dog would be part of their family life together, envisioning them taking "Fluffy" or something similar on long walks and to the seaside. Another illusion shattered…

'I think I'll go for a walk anyway, do you want to come?' she asked hopefully.

'No, it's a bit cold. You go and I'll do some work on my book.'

'Shall we go and look round the DIY shops later? We could choose some wallpaper for the lounge.'

'What for? Do you think it *needs* decorating?' Jay looked around.

'Well – magnolia on all the walls is a bit boring, don't you think?'

He sighed. 'Does it really matter? I don't like decorating. I usually pay someone when it gets desperate. My father never had the time or the inclination to teach me any DIY. He always got workmen in.'

'I could do it! I'm quite a dab hand,' Robyn boasted. 'My Dad was the opposite, he did everything himself and made sure he taught all three of us to look after our own houses. It saves a fortune.'

'Anyway, I don't even have an eye for colour.' Jay was tiring of this conversation and wanted to return to *The Sunday Times*.

'No, but I do. I think browns and black would look sophisticated in this room.'

'Whatever! If you want to have a go, then I won't stop you.'

That wasn't exactly the response Robyn was looking for. Dave had loved wandering round DIY stores with her, choosing the next project to work on. At length she said,

'I might go for a run instead of a walk.'

He looked up from his reading material, 'Good idea, you're bottom was a lot firmer when you were running all the time.'

Robyn was mortified. She didn't think Jay meant to be insulting, but she knew Dave would never have dreamed about commenting on her figure like that.

Quickly she got changed and set off round the park. If she'd stayed any longer in the flat there would've been an almighty row. Maybe she ought to go home, as she was probably more touchy than usual. It would be better when Dave was gone, she was sure of it.

Monday morning arrived far too soon for the Fisher household. Dave was due to leave the house at ten o'clock. His flight to Heathrow was scheduled at midday and then onwards to Los Angeles for the first stopover. Robyn had told Gerald she'd be in late, because even though Dave didn't want a big fuss, she couldn't go to work and let him set off all alone.

Molly wasn't really in a fit state to go to school, she'd been crying almost non-stop and her eyes could barely open they were so red and swollen.

'I don't want to go to school,' Molly sobbed.

'You have to, sweetheart. Say goodbye to Daddy now. He promises to Skype you later.'

Dave whispered to Robyn, 'Are you sure they have to go?'

'I think it's best to keep to the same routine, don't you?'

'I suppose.'

'I don't want you to go.' Molly said, hanging like a limpet onto Dave's leg.

'I know and Daddy wouldn't go unless he had to.' Dave squeezed her hand.

'Mummy, make him stay … please.'

I wish I could, but it's too late for that now.

'I can't do that, sweetheart. Lots of people need him at work.'

'But … I need him.' Molly threw herself onto the floor. Dave bent down and stroked her hair.

'Come and give Daddy a kiss, Jakey.' Robyn picked up her little boy and he clung to her neck.

'Let's just get them to school.' Dave couldn't bear this anymore.

Robyn strapped her two distraught children into the car and pulled out of the drive. Molly was still crying as they reached the school gates.

'Will you take them in?' Dave asked Robyn – he couldn't let his children see the tears that, at last, he was able to shed. He'd composed himself by the time Robyn climbed back behind the wheel and was glad he had when he looked at his wife's pale face.

Robyn had never felt as anxious. All those months on anti-depressants were nothing compared to how she was feeling at this moment and it threatened to swamp her. She was scared and sad and desperate. Although she saw traces of tears in Dave's eyes, she daren't cry herself in case the floodgates opened and she could never stop.

Back at the house Dave dashed upstairs leaving Robyn in the lounge. She heard a thump, thump as Dave brought his cases downstairs.

'I've ordered the taxi and it's on its way,' he said as he came to join her.

'So soon?' Robyn looked at her watch. 'But it's not even ten o'clock. I could make us a drink.'

'I need to leave, Rob. This is killing me, and if I don't set off now, I won't be able to go at all.' Robyn tried to compose herself. She knew she needed to stay strong for the both of them so she touched his cheek gently.

'Remember I love you, Dave, and I'm so sorry about everything. I've brought all this on you, and I feel awful you're having to leave your family because of me.'

He caught her hand in his. 'I love you too and I *am* coming back. You watch – it'll be the best thing to happen to us one way or another.'

The hoot of a horn sounded outside, but they stood still in the tightest of embraces until the taxi driver hooted again.

Reluctantly they parted and Dave said softly,

'I'll ring you later and we'll see each other on the web cam as soon as possible. Look after our babies for me.'

'I will!' Robyn gave a shaky smile. 'I might even increase their story-time to two per night like you do.'

'I was always such a soft touch.' He smiled ruefully, thinking about all the bedtime stories he would miss.

Neither of them cried as Dave picked up his two large suitcases and walked out of the front door and Robyn's life.

'Are you going on holiday mate?' The taxi driver asked as Dave climbed into the back, after they'd struggled to fit the cases in the boot.

'No, I'm going to work in New Zealand for a year.'

'She's waving at you,' the taxi driver said, seeing Robyn at the window. 'Wow! You're leaving *her* behind? Are you mad?'

In more ways than one, thought Dave sadly. 'Yes, I'm insane,' he said in a clipped voice. 'Now just drive me to the airport before I change my mind.'

'Whatever you say, mate.' The taxi driver pulled away. Dave couldn't look back. The pain in his heart was too much to bear.

Robyn felt numb. The man she'd shared her life with for thirteen years had left her and quite probably was never coming back. It was all her fault. She sat on the settee and stared into space. Even thinking was too much of an effort. One hour passed and then two and it wasn't until her phone rang that she moved an inch from her original position. It was Gerald,

'I'm just checking to make sure you're alright,' he said.

'Not really. I've let Dave go, and I think I've just made the biggest mistake of my life.'

'Well, it's done now. No point dwelling on it. Why don't you come to work and I'll keep you busy?'

'Right. I'll just tidy myself up, and I'll be there shortly.'

'That's the spirit.'

No sooner had she finished talking to Gerald than Jay rang.

'Has he gone?' he asked.

'Yes, he went about half past nine.' Robyn sounded lifeless.

'How are you? Do you want me to come over?'

'I'm going to work now but you can come over for tea, if you want.'

'I'll be there for five, then. Are you sure you're okay? You sound shocking.'

'I'll be fine. I'll see you later.' Even talking to Jay was too much effort.

Robyn made herself look presentable and went to work. Gerald had a long list of things to keep her busy, but looking at her tear-stained face he thought better of it.

'Would a cup of tea help?' he offered.

'A bottle of vodka would be better. Oops! Sorry that was in really bad taste,' she apologized, remembering too late about Camille's drinking problem.

'Don't worry about it. But I think tea would be better.'

'I thought you had lots of work for me to do.'

'That can wait.' He moved his chair towards her. 'Come and give me a hug.'

Robyn bent down and for the first time since working for him, she gave Gerald a hug.

'It will work out for the best, Robyn. I know it doesn't feel like it now, but you have a chance to see if what you and Jay have is real.'

'But he's going away soon as well. Why is everyone leaving me?'

'Because they have their own lives to follow, and I'm afraid you can't control everybody. Just let go and see what happens. Take a leaf out of Jay's book. Primarily he thinks of himself and it pays off for him. Just look at what's happened with his book! Concentrate on being yourself, your own person.'

'But it doesn't come naturally to me.'

'That's because you've spent too long interfering in everyone else's lives.'

'Ouch! That was a bit cutting.'

'The truth often is. Try this next time someone says something that you don't like – just smile and keep your mouth shut.'

'But…' Robyn began to protest.

'You could start now!' Gerald smiled.

Jay had no idea how he was going to tell Robyn his tour had been brought forward. She'd sounded so strange and distracted on the phone earlier. He knew she was terribly upset and this news would only make it worse, particularly as Lindy had arranged an extra two weeks in New York visiting radio and television stations plus appearances in large department stores. It was a real coup for her agency and brilliant for Jay's writing career.

He wished profoundly he could rewind the last couple of months because although he'd genuinely thought she was what he wanted, he regretted rushing into such an intense relationship with her. Robyn was the kind of person who needed time to adjust to new situations and he now realized she found his spontaneity too much to deal with.

Jay liked to go with the flow of life, accepting any new opportunities that came his way and embracing them with open arms, just like he'd done with his new book. He didn't want to have to feel guilty about going away – neither did he feel a need to share every part of his life. Unlike Robyn, who couldn't go to the toilet without telling him first.

He loved her, of that there was no doubt, but maybe he shouldn't have pushed her into living together so soon. But that was him all over. He'd always been the same – wanting something and having to have it immediately. Sometimes it paid off, but other times, like now, it put him in situations he found increasingly untenable. If only they could have kept their affair going in secret, they may have tired of each other naturally. But no, the lust won out, and he had to have her, even offering marriage when she was divorced. He felt appalled. Whatever had he been thinking?

"Jumping out of the frying pan into the fire" was a hackneyed phrase his father liked to use about him. Jay always vehemently denied it but maybe there was some truth in it after all. Just look at where he was now! He'd ended up with two children in his life when he wanted none.

This latest thing about decorating was just one example of the pressure he found stifling. She wanted to refurbish his flat and change all the rooms around. There was nothing wrong with it as it was and her insistence was beginning to rile him. He thought back to their first conversation when he told Robyn he only stayed with a partner while they made him happy and moved on when they didn't. Yet here he was embroiled in something that was in danger of ruining his peace of mind, and getting out of control.

He knew something had to give and thought about prospects in his new-found career. Lindy understood him. She wasn't at all demanding, the opposite if anything. She wanted whatever was best for her career – and his. That included him being a free spirit, making his own life decisions. She'd offered herself to him on a plate, but so far he'd refused. He'd decided he wasn't going to make the same mistake of cheating on anyone again. If or when the relationship with Robyn came to an end, he'd move on and hopefully Robyn would see that was best for them both and agree…

Jay waited until the children were in bed before telling Robyn his news over a glass of wine.

'But it was supposed to be March! And now you're telling me you go next *week*,' she said as her voice raised a full decibel. Jay got up from the sofa.

'I'm sorry, but it's New York. I can't turn it down.' Jay having correctly anticipated what her reaction would be braced himself for further recrimination.

However, remembering what Gerald had said to her this afternoon about letting people's lives unfold without her input, Robyn took a sharp intake of breath and was silent for a moment. Then she said quietly, 'I know you can't. I'm just being selfish. I'll miss you that's all.' She stood up and put her arms around his shoulders.

Jay was absolutely taken aback, but grateful to be spared a scene.

'I'll ring you as often as I can,' he assured her.

'Don't worry. I know you'll be busy. It's your big break Jay, you enjoy it.'

Gerald, you'd be proud of me! Now I've just got to mean it!

'Thanks for that Robyn, it means a lot.'

'I'm sorry if I've been a bit demanding recently,' she said kissing him. 'Now Dave has gone I can give our relationship the time it deserves. I hope I haven't left it too late.'

'I knew you were going through a lot, and I've tried to understand, but you don't always make it easy.'

'Gerald gave me a good talking to this afternoon and for once I'm going to listen.'

'Sounds good to me' he laughed and added, 'You look tired out though. Why don't you have an early night? I'll be up later.' He winked but Robyn had already left the room.

Chapter 31

March

Dave had been gone four weeks now and Jay for two. Instead of things getting easier, Robyn was finding life one long tribulation. Motherhood had always come naturally to her before, but now Molly was having one long temper tantrum after another; she was at a loss. Jake was a problem too; wetting the bed and having frequent night terrors. She felt totally alone – everyone around her seemed to be so busy with their own lives. Just when she could have done with the support, there was no-one there. The wonderful job suddenly felt like a chore and even Gerald's sarcasm, which usually made her laugh, sent her spiralling into a chasm of depression. So far she'd resisted the anti-depressants, but as each day passed, the thought of them became more appealing. It was either the tablets or the red wine.

Denizon was worried. Robyn was at the lowest ebb she'd ever known her friend to be. She'd seen Robyn depressed before, of course. They'd known each other since the age of five, but this present situation was more than that. It was almost like she'd lost the will to live, dragging herself through endless days. She did feel some of the responsibility lay on her own shoulders because ever since having Barney in her life everyone, apart from Chris, had taken a back seat.

Barney's mother, Sarah, had found a new man and it appeared he was "the one". He was divorced with a four year old son and Denizon assumed that having the two children would be an ideal ready-made family for Sarah, but the opposite was true. She was dropping Barney off to them more than ever. The excuses came thick and fast – she just needed to shop and Barney made everything so hard work or they were taking little Tyler swimming and a baby would only get in the way.

Not that Denizon minded, she loved having Barney, but the rest of her life was suffering, including her friendship with Robyn, who needed her more than ever. When she remembered she would ask Robyn and the children for tea but Robyn always declined, saying it was too much trouble. The two weeks Robyn had with only Jay in her life were at least tolerable for her friend, but since both men were now off the scene, Robyn's life had fallen apart.

Denizon was determined to try and make it better. First of all, she tried phoning, but again had to leave a message since Robyn never seemed to answer her calls anymore. It went straight to voicemail.

'Hi Rob; ring me when you've got a minute.' It was as though Robyn screened her calls only speaking to who she wanted, when she wanted.

When Robyn didn't respond, Denizon decided it was time to take action – she got in her car and went in search of her best friend. There was no-one at Robyn's house and she made Gerald's her next stop. Robyn's car wasn't parked outside, but she knocked on the door anyway. Perhaps Gerald could shed some light on where his assistant had disappeared to.

Mrs. Bennett let Denizon in and Gerald appeared in the hallway.

'I'm so sorry to disturb you, Mr. Banfleet. I don't know if you remember me from Dave's leaving party, I'm Robyn's friend, Denizon. I was wondering if you've seen her. She's not answering her phone, she doesn't appear to be at home and I'm worried.'

'You and me both,' said Gerald, looking serious. 'She booked the day off, and when I asked where she was going, she evaded the question. I'm usually able to talk to her about anything, lift her mood, but not this time.'

'She won't talk to me either. I can't think where she could be. I've rung my husband to see if he's heard anything and she's not at her mothers.'

'Maybe she's gone for some counselling,' suggested Gerald. 'I know it helped her last time and she was nothing like as bad as this.'

'Do you think I should ring the doctor's surgery?'

'No, I think that's taking it a bit too far. She may just want to be on her own. The time to really worry is if she doesn't come back tonight,' Denizon looked panic stricken, and hastily he added, 'but I'm sure she'll be fine. When I do see her I've got a plan.'

'What is it?' Denizon asked.

'I can't tell you, it's a secret,' Gerald said, tapping the side of his nose. 'All I will say is that it stands a good chance of getting the old Robyn back. I want everyone to know I'm doing it for purely selfish reasons, I need my reliable assistant. Her work is suffering and, as a consequence, so is my business.'

'Get on with you,' said Mrs. Bennett, 'you worship the ground that girl walks on, you're miserable watching her so unhappy.'

'Ssh! You'll be making me out to be soft and that's not good for my reputation.' Gerald said, half laughing.

'If she does contact you will you tell her to ring me? Here's my number.' Denizon handed Mrs. Bennett a card. 'I need to know she's safe. The only other thing I can do is try and catch her when she picks up her children.'

'We will, I promise.' Mrs. Bennett squeezed Denizon's hand.

In the meantime, Robyn was safe and sound in Leeds. Having gone primarily to see Julie, she also wanted to re-visit some of the places she'd been with Jay. Maybe recalling happy memories might help put some feeling back in her life. She popped into the restaurant of the Theroux for a quick coffee but just sitting down in the same seats brought tears to her eyes.

Maybe a walk along the river might help. She stopped at the place where Jay kissed her for the first time, closing her eyes and trying to feel his lips on hers. There was a bench close by and she sat down, resting her chin in her hands. Thoughts kept bombarding her brain. First, Jay would appear in her mind only to be replaced by Dave a second later.

This isn't working! Maybe Julie will cheer me up.

Julie was already sitting at a table in the *Cafe Rouge* when Robyn walked in and did a double take when she saw her friend's new look. It was a few months since they'd seen each other, the only contact since had been through Facebook and e-mail. Julie looked radiant – her hair was in a short pixie style with vibrant flashes of copper sprinkled throughout. When she stood up to give Robyn a kiss, the biggest difference was apparent – Julie was pregnant.

'When did that happen?' Robyn asked, pointing at the bulge.

'I'm five months. I was going to message you, but I wanted to tell you face to face. I'm also engaged.' Julie proudly held out her left hand to show Robyn a beautiful sapphire surrounded by diamonds.

'It's beautiful and congratulations,' said Robyn giving her another hug. 'But you can't have a celebration though, because if you remember, I've already been to your engagement party.' They both laughed.

'We're not. We're saving it for the wedding which you *are* invited to.' Julie reached in her bag and pulled out an invitation addressed to Robyn Fisher plus one. 'I didn't write a name on it because I didn't know who you were actually with for sure. You have to admit your life can be chaotic!'

'Tell me about it! What do you think it's like living it?'

'From your last e-mail I got the feeling you're having a hard time. I'm so glad you suggested we meet up.'

'I don't want to talk about me; I'm just a miserable cow. I want to know about baby and Steve and the wedding.'

Julie spent the next fifteen minutes, until the food arrived, bringing Robyn up to date with all her news. She was having a girl, the wedding was in May and both houses were up for sale.

'So the love nest is being sold?' Robyn thought back to all the times she and Jay had made love in Steve's spare bedroom.

'Yes, Cheryl told me that some of the neighbours thought Steve was running a brothel.'

'Oops! Sorry about that,' Robyn said, buttering a roll.

'It doesn't matter. We're leaving Garforth anyway and buying a new house. It's gorgeous. It's got four bedrooms and two en suites, and I love it.'

'That sounds great. New baby, new house.' Robyn paused, envy surging through her. 'I've been thinking of selling my house ... It's too big for me, and I don't know if Dave or even Jay will come back. I'd be better in a smaller semi.'

'But I thought you and Jay were a couple,' said Julie surprised. 'You gave me the impression you were more or less living together. What happened?'

'He's gone to America on a book tour with his agent Lindy, who has the 'hots' for him. He says he's coming back, but I'm not sure I want him to.'

'I can't believe it, you were so in love.'

'I know – but that was when we were playing at being a couple, the reality was completely different.' Robyn heard herself admit the truth for the first time.

'For a start, he's never wanted children and found himself lumbered with two. Don't get me wrong, he's great with them and he's godfather to my nephew Barney, but he's a better uncle than dad. His ex-partner, Maria, had his baby girl in Italy and he didn't even look at the photograph she sent him; that's how interested he is in children, even his own daughter.'

'So do you intend to finish with him when he comes back?'

'I don't know,' replied Robyn, pushing away the remains of her lunch. 'Perhaps I'll just see what happens. I get the feeling he's not terribly happy either, and I'm no good with decisions.'

Two cappuccinos later, they were finally up to date with all their news as Robyn described how painful it had been when Dave left.

'To be honest, Robyn, it sounds like you regret letting him go,' said Julie bluntly. 'I wish I'd have met him. I'd have known straight away who was best for you.'

'Oh, I've heard plenty of opinions about that over the last year. But I still don't know what I want. Maybe I never will. Perhaps, I'm just destined to live a sad and lonely life.'

'You can't be serious, Robyn. I'll get out my violin in a minute! You've got so much going for you, and men aren't always necessary! I lived for years on my own.'

'And you were miserable, you told me.'

'Some of the time, possibly. But things are different now. Sometimes you have to let things go so you can attract new things to take their place. Look at me. Life really does have a way of working itself out. You just have to let it.' She touched Robyn's hand affectionately.

'Don't worry! I'm just feeling pathetically sorry for myself. But I've felt better talking to you, than I've felt since Dave and Jay left.'

'Then we should do this more often.'

'I'd like that. You're a good friend, Julie.' Robyn reached over and squeezed her friend's hand. 'I'm so glad we met.'

'Me too!' she chuckled. 'Do you realise It's nearly a year ago since I lusted after Max Hammond at the seminar? Have you seen he's got another book out?'

'What's *this* one about?' Robyn asked, sounding sceptical.

'Don't be like that. Without that seminar, I wouldn't be where I am today,' said Julie, patting her bulge.

'Sorry,' said Robyn at once, trying to smile. 'I really am bitter and twisted.'

'It's called "Keeping Your Relationship Alive." You ought to get it, Robyn. It could help, you never know.'

'I'll ask him to send me a copy. The problem is – I don't know which relationship I want to keep alive.'

'Robyn, you're shocking!'

They both laughed as Robyn looked at her watch.

'I'd better be getting back to collect the children. I don't like being late now because I don't know where I'd be without my child-minder. Pauline's been a godsend… So – if I don't see you before, I'll see you at your wedding.'

'Looking forward to both already.'

As Robyn was driving home she thought about her life.

I really will make more of an effort. Denizon and Gerald have been so patient with me and all I've done is throw the kindness back in their faces. From here on in, I'm going to stop being a miserable cow. Julie says I don't need a man to make me happy, so this is me going it alone! What's the saying? Tomorrow is the first day of the rest of your life. Something like that! So watch out, I'm coming!

The new improved Robyn arrived at work before nine o'clock the following morning, raring to go. She found her desk was strewn with papers and, puzzled, she picked up at least five brown A4 files with a different name on each.

'What on earth are all these files?' she said, turning to Gerald as she heard him come into the room.

'Potentially one of them is your temporary replacement.'

'Why do I need a temporary replacement? Robyn asked beginning to panic, just as she'd resolved to pull herself together. *Has my work been slipping that much?*

'Because you're taking an extended holiday,' he told her decisively.

'Where to?' Robyn was baffled. *Is this his way of easing me out gently?*

Gerald steered himself to his desk and picked something up. He swung his chair round.

'Look here! In my poor gnarled hands I have two envelopes. Listen carefully, in my right hand.' Gerald tried hard to lift his hand so Robyn could see the envelope. 'I have an open ended ticket to Auckland, New Zealand.' He held up the other hand. 'In my left hand is an open ended ticket to New York.'

Robyn was dumbfounded. 'Why would you do that?'

'Because I can't watch you die a slow death from doubt and indecision in front of my eyes. I'm supposed to be the one to depart this earth next, not you. All you have to do is choose one envelope.'

'But those tickets must've cost you a fortune!' Robyn felt so choked, she could hardly continue.

'I...I can't let you do that for me.'

'You can't stop me!' he said gleefully. 'And let me worry about the cost. I've got plenty of money and very little opportunity to spend it.'

Robyn pondered this for a few seconds, 'Let's just say I go for this wild scheme of yours,' she said at last. 'What happens to the tickets I don't choose?'

'Mrs. Bennett will have a well deserved extended vacation. Without her, I wouldn't be here to make this gesture; I'd have self destructed years ago. Her poor long suffering husband has been totally supportive when I've needed her at all hours, and I'd like to show my deep appreciation by giving them a holiday they'll never forget.'

'They're very different locations, though,' Robyn declared.

'True – but I know her, and she will love either.'

Robyn looked at her future, dangling from Gerald's distorted fingers in small white envelopes.

'You are the kindest, most annoying man I've ever had the privilege to know.' She bent down and kissed his cheek.

'Never mind that!' he protested with mock severity. 'Make a decision girl! Where's it to be? We haven't got all day and I want my coffee.'

Tears smarting her eyes, Robyn snatched the envelope out of Gerald's right hand saying, 'I only hope Mrs. Bennett, has plenty of warm clothes! Because I've heard New York is exceptionally cold in the spring.'

Just one more week to go, then Robyn and the children would be joining Dave in the newly-rented beach-side apartment in Auckland. He'd since shown her pictures and it looked idyllic – the perfect place to start a new life together.

She smiled every time she recalled the conversation with Dave on Skype the day after she'd been given the tickets.

'Say hello to Daddy,' Robyn said to the children, as Dave slowly came into view on Robyn's laptop. Jake couldn't quite get the hang of the concept and kept looking behind the computer every time Dave spoke.

'He's there,' she said to her son as she pointed to the screen. 'It looks like Daddy's only next door, when he's actually at the other side of the world.' Robyn had bought a large globe and showed Molly every day where her Daddy was staying.

'Hello, my angels,' Dave said, as he caught sight of his children sitting on the settee. 'What have you been doing today?'

Robyn had made Molly promise not to blurt out about the tickets until she'd had a word with Dave first. She let them catch up on all the news and Dave read them a story. He'd taken his own copy of the "Twits" and read a chapter out loud when time permitted.

Robyn looked at Molly and winked, 'You go and play like we agreed, so I can have a word with Daddy.' For once, Molly did exactly as she was told. Holding Jake's hand, she led him into the playroom.

'Impressive, Rob! You've got them well trained. I think that's the first time she's not answered back. What's your secret?' Dave asked.

'Oh you know, I'm just a genius,' she said modestly.

Robyn looked at her husband sitting on the balcony of his harbour apartment sipping a cold can of lager. He looked gorgeous. His tan was darkening daily, and the designer stubble and long hair really suited him. He'd never looked so relaxed. This lifestyle obviously suited him, she thought as she realised in a couple of weeks she'd be there sitting on the balcony with him. That's if, he was excited by her news.

'Dave, I've got something to ask you?' Robyn said tentatively. Dave's relaxed expression changed to one of worry.

'What is it?' he asked, nervously.

Robyn smiled, 'Why do you always assume the worst?'

'Because isn't it today that Jay's coming home?'

Robyn was surprised he'd remembered because she hadn't told him recently.

'Yes, but it's nothing to do with him. What would you say if I said I wanted to visit you?' She paused, waiting for his reaction.

Dave looked surprised, 'You want to come all this way for a holiday. I thought you might go to Majorca or somewhere.' He saw the look of disappointment on Robyn's face and immediately added,

'Are you serious? You'd come all this way to see me.'

She couldn't contain herself any longer. Robyn held up the tickets.

'It's already booked.' She waved them in front of the screen.

'I'm slightly confused,' Dave admitted. 'You've bought tickets already, but Jay isn't even back yet.'

'Will you shut up about Jay! I don't want to be with him. I want you. I made the biggest mistake in the world, letting you go from my life and I want to change it … if you'll have me.'

Dave sat silently bemused.

'Say something Dave! Are you pleased?'

'Er, yes. I'm just a little shocked. You've never given me any indication this is what you were thinking.'

'I know. It's easy to pretend when you only see me on a seventeen inch screen from across the other side of the world, but I'm miserable without you.' Robyn had hoped for a different reaction from Dave and was starting to wonder if her plan was going to backfire.

'When have you booked the holiday?' Dave asked, thinking practically. 'Not to put a damper on things, but I only rent a studio apartment. It's not big enough for all four of us.'

'It's not a holiday. Gerald bought us an open ended ticket and I thought we'd come for three months, if that's alright by you?'

'What about school for Molly?' Dave still wasn't showing any emotion.

'I've spoke to the education authority and we can home-school her until we come back. Is that all you've got to say?'

Slowly, the realisation started to show in Dave's face and he smiled, 'The sly old devil! Gerald said I'd to leave it all to fate. But, I didn't think he saw *himself* as fate.'

Robyn looked puzzled.

'Never mind, I'll explain later.' Dave's face became serious, 'Are you sure this time? We've already been down this path, and it was hard enough then. I swear I couldn't go through it all again.'

'I promise you, Dave, it's what I want. I've had plenty of time to think since you've both been gone, and it's you I love – totally! I want our marriage to work. I wasn't ready before, but I am now.' She added, hopefully, 'that's if you still want me.'

'Oh Robyn, of course I want you! I've never stopped.' And so it went on, the two of them swearing undying love for each other until Molly popped her head round the door and said, 'Can we come in yet?'

'Of course you can, sweetheart, Daddy said yes.'

Despite the giddy excitement, Robyn awoke with an overwhelming feeling of trepidation hanging over her. She opened one eye and looked at the clock. She'd been dreading today so much and, despite her best effort at stopping time, it was finally here. In twelve hours Jay was back from New York and she couldn't believe she hadn't told him about her plans.

Whatever was I thinking? Why couldn't I just tell him?

She knew what she wanted to say – writing down different conversations and practising them in front of a mirror and there had been plenty of opportunity during the phone calls. He was following a whirlwind schedule which meant they didn't speak very often, but that was just an excuse. Every time she had the opportunity to tell him she bottled out, convincing herself that it would be better said face-to-face. She couldn't imagine what his reaction was going to be. He was so distraught when she finished with him last time. This would be even worse.

Jay had arranged to come straight round to Robyn's house tonight from the airport. Molly and Jake were spending the night at Denizon's to give the two of them some time to talk. Luckily, she had a busy day ahead. Robyn's temporary replacement, a young girl called Fiona, was coming in to work today to learn about the job. At least it would help take her mind off things.

But, sadly, it didn't.

'If I were you, Robyn I'd take the rest of the day off.' Gerald said exasperated. 'How on earth is the poor girl going to learn anything when you haven't a clue what you're doing yourself?'

'Sorry, Gerald, and I'm sorry Fiona.'

'It's okay. I know what tonight means to you. Seriously, you go home and Fiona can learn from Mrs. Bennett today.'

'Thanks, Gerald … I promise I'll be better tomorrow.'

Just as long as I can get tonight over with.

It took a lot to make the usually calm Jay anxious, but he felt physically sick as he drove at top speed to Robyn's house, after dropping Lindy off at his flat in Leeds. The time in New York had been good for his thought process and he now knew for certain what he wanted, and it wasn't Robyn. Lindy was perfect for him. She was an attractive, career-minded woman who wanted the same things as he wanted from life and that didn't include children.

For the first few nights, after dinner and drinks in the bar, they'd shared a hug and goodnight kiss. Jay finally succumbed to her not so subtle, advances after a week of being in the adjacent hotel room. The love-making was unbelievable, probably due to her younger years and flexibility from hours of yoga. And since then they'd been inseparable. Together all day for work and in bed together every night. It felt perfect, but how was he going to explain that to Robyn? She would be totally heartbroken.

Jay arrived at Robyn's well before the time he'd indicated in his text. He sat in the driveway summoning up the courage to go inside. This was going to be the hardest conversation ever because he *had* really loved Robyn and the news would leave her devastated. The lounge curtain moved and he caught a glimpse of her looking out of the window. She waved. This was it, now or never! He got out of the car, returning the wave.

Robyn remained standing by the lounge window as Jay walked into the room.

'Hello, you,' Jay said, unsure of what to say.

'Hello, Jay. Did you have a good flight? You're earlier than you said.'

'Yes, thanks. Sorry, is it inconvenient?' He remained standing by the door.

'No, no, come in. The children are with Denizon and Chris.'

'Robyn...er'

'Jay. I've....' they both said simultaneously.

'Sorry, you first,' said Robyn, hoping to delay the inevitable. 'Can I pour you a glass of wine, or I've got your favourite, Lochaber?'

'A small Scotch would be great, thanks,' he said, taking a seat in the leather armchair.

Robyn poured two drinks and handed Jay a not-so-small measure. She couldn't help but notice Jay fidgeting in his seat and biting his thumb nail – always a tell-tale sign. Plus, guilt was written all over his face.

'How's Lindy?' Robyn said, thinking she'd give Jay an opportunity to tell his story first.

At the mention of her name, Jay's face broke into a large grin. This was the confirmation Robyn needed.

'She's great, thanks. The book tour went really well, and the American office is really pleased with her work. In fact, they've asked if she wants to relocate to the New York office permanently.'

'And are you going with her?' she asked coldly. Despite Robyn's own decision to leave, she couldn't help but feel rejected at being replaced so easily.

Jay was taken aback. 'Er…Yes. What made you ask that?' he said averting his eyes.

'Oh, nothing really,' she snapped. 'It could be your cool demeanour, the nail biting, the awkward look on your face. Need I go on?'

'Honest, Rob, I really didn't mean for it to happen. But we just clicked.'

'You mean like we did?'

Jay looked down at his feet.

'I'm really sorry, but Lindy and I have been together for three weeks now.' Jay paused, waiting for the inevitable fireworks.

Robyn started laughing and Jay stared not knowing what to think.

'And here I was, losing sleep thinking of how to tell you I'm going to New Zealand to be with Dave.'

'You're kidding!' It was Jay's turn to laugh, but with relief. 'When did you decide that?'

'It was Gerald actually. He gave me the choice of two destinations, New York to see you or New Zealand to see Dave.' Since Jay's revelation, she wasn't going to spare his feelings. 'And I chose Dave. I'm bloody glad I did after your bombshell.'

'Well, I don't know what to say.' Jay took a large gulp from his glass.

'To be honest, Jay, I'm not surprised. Before you went it wasn't right between us, was it?'

Jay shook his head in agreement as Robyn continued, 'I knew I'd made a mistake when I was completely devastated at Dave leaving. If I'd have been over him it wouldn't have affected me like it did. I knew you weren't happy with my over demanding ways. Dave knew that about me and accepted it, but with you it never sat comfortably. We're two completely different personalities.'

'I did love you, you know?' Jay looked at Robyn.

'I know, and I loved you,' Robyn said earnestly. 'I'm not sorry for our time together. You've taught me a lot, and I've learned a lot about myself.'

'What happens next?' Jay asked.

'Well, I've already taken the liberty of packing your things. There's a case waiting for you upstairs.'

'What about Molly, Jake and little Barney? I'd like to stay in touch.'

'Whatever you want, but isn't it going to be hard from New York?'

'It is. But an adopted uncle in the "Big Apple" is really cool,' he said, enthusiastically.

'Let's not get carried away just yet!' From Jay's previous record, Robyn knew he would've moved on a few more times before any of the children were old enough to visit him.

'Should I say goodbye to them?'

'Let me do it for you. They're both so excited at going to see Dave they can't think about anything else.'

'It sounds like it's all worked out for the best?'

'I guess so,' Robyn agreed.

'Well, I'll just get my stuff then … So is this it?'

'I think so. When are you going to America?'

'As soon as Lindy can sort everything out. How about you?'

'We leave next week.'

Jay walked across to where Robyn was standing and clumsily gave her a hug. 'Goodbye then, Robyn.'

She kissed his cheek, 'Goodbye, Jay. I wish you well and hope one day you'll find real happiness.'

'I think I have this time,' Jay said with conviction.

Robyn just smiled. Where had she heard words like that before?

How to Have an Amicable
Divorce.

Coming May 2014

Chapter 1

May

Denizon smiled as she saw whose name was flashing up on caller display.

'Hello love, how's it going? Are you still having a wonderful time?'

'Yes brilliant, thanks,' answered Robyn, her best friend and sister-in-law, speaking from the other side of the world in New Zealand.

'You'll be home soon, won't you? I can't believe you've been there eight weeks already.'

'Neither can I,' Robyn paused. 'In fact, that's the main reason I'm ringing. I've decided to stay.'

'What forever?' Denizon panicked.

'No, not forever, silly. Just for four more weeks. Gerald has been invited to spend time at his niece's new villa on the Cap D'Azur so I thought I'd take advantage of the extra time off and spend it with my wonderful husband.'

'I take it, it's still going well?'

'I can't believe how well. It's like being in a new relationship but better. We've fallen in love all over again.'

'I'm really pleased for you, Rob.'

'The training is also going better than anticipated and hopefully, Dave will be finished in about six weeks, so he'll be coming back to England then. He'll have to be located in London for another few months but at least we can spend weekends together … How's my darling brother?'

Denizon sighed. 'Chris is fine. He's been promoted to Crew Manager.'

'That's great, isn't it?' Robyn asked on listening to her friends sigh.

'Yes,' Denizon said tentatively. 'But he's been away on two residential courses so far and he's got another one coming up.'

'Let me guess, you're bored.'

'I suppose a bit, my best friend is at the other side of the world and my husband is never here.'

'You've got Barney.'

'I know, but he's not great with the conversation.'

'Cheer up, love. You sound like I did a few weeks ago … Are you doing much with your art at the moment?'

'Funny you should mention that. I received a phone call yesterday from the University. The Art Department are looking for tutors to teach a summer school and wondered if I'd be interested.'

'Well then, that's something to do,' Robyn said enthusiastically. 'Are you going to apply?'

'I think so, but I've never taught before. There's a training course in a couple of weeks that I could go on to teach me to teach. It would mean I couldn't have Barney for a couple of weeks.'

'Well, I'm sure Sarah could cope for two weeks. She leaves him with you enough. It's only fair you have some time to do what you want and I think it'd be good for you.'

'You're probably right. I'll ring them back and tell them I'll do the training course. If I enjoy it, who knows it might lead to something else.'

'I think that's great news. You'd be a good teacher.'

'Thanks, love… Hadn't you better be going? This'll be costing you a fortune.'

'I suppose so. I'll message you next week to arrange a time when we can all get together to Skype.'

'Oh! Before I forget, Jay and Max were on Breakfast television this morning talking about Jay's book,' Denizon added.

'I thought he was in America.'

'He was, but he's back to do a short book tour round London.'

'Was he good? I assume Max was.'

'He was actually, a natural in front of the camera.'

'It figures! What were they talking about?'

'About affairs in general and why people have them. Max was defending monogamy and Jay was giving his contrary opinion, sharing his views on being with a partner as long as they make you happy. It was interesting, especially seeing as I know him personally.'

'Did he mention his partner?' Robyn asked, with an edge to her voice.

'Only that's he's with someone who he's compatible with.'

'For now,' Robyn said scathingly.

'You sound bitter! You're not are you?'

'No, not really. I made my choice as well and I'm so happy I chose Dave. It's just that I know his book was written when we were together and I helped him with a lot of it. I just don't get any credit.'

'Don't start all that again,' Denizon reprimanded. 'You've got a perfect life now, don't even think about Jay.'

'Ay, Ay captain. On that note I'm going now and we'll speak next week. Love you, Den.'

'Love you too, Rob. Take care.' She placed the phone back in its cradle and smiled. Her friend would never change.

If she was honest the thought of teaching scared her. Being an artist was a very solitary profession and her own paintings were personal to her. She wouldn't know how to bring out the best in her students or even if they'd appreciate what she had to say. But Robyn was right – it would be good for her – because not only was she bored, she was lonely.

Without Robyn on the other end of the phone or just round the corner she had nobody. Both her parents had been dead years and she was their only offspring. Robyn was the closest thing to a sister she'd ever known and totally relied on her for everything. She'd never been one for making friends easily and had got so used to her own company all day that sometimes she found it difficult to start conversations, which she knew frustrated her husband, Chris who was the most gregarious person she had ever met.

She often thought it was why Chris had been tempted to seek out the company of other women throughout their married life and probably why she'd made allowances for that particular trait. Chris loved going out and socialising whereas she preferred a good book or a black and white film. Robyn had loaned her Dr. Max Hammond's book, "Effective Communication" and it made her realise that the two of them didn't have a lot to talk about. She had become infatuated with him at age sixteen and hadn't really looked at another man until she finally snared him six years ago.

Chris loved her, she knew that, but she just wasn't stimulating enough for him and he wasn't intellectual enough for her. He was ruled by his body and she was ruled by her brain. Since her dice with death last year their relationship had been the best it'd ever been. It was the first time since they'd got together she could honestly say she trusted him. But it had been to the detriment of his personality. He no longer went out as much, offering to spend every evening with her. She could see the life slowly seeping out of him, as he tried his best to be something he wasn't.

The recent promotion at work seemed to perk him up slightly and even though she missed his company, she knew it was best for his sanity. *Maybe tutoring would be the incentive I need to make new friends – and going out to work at a real job could, potentially, make me more interesting.* It was with that thought she picked up the phone to ring the university and booked herself on the short teacher-training course

Chapter 2

End of July

Denizon opened the big double doors and tentatively popped her head around. It was graveyard quiet – the University seemed spooky with no students milling around. Her high heels made a resounding click as she walked along the deserted corridor to the Art Department faculty office. She knocked on the door.

'Come in, come in!' Denizon opened the door and was greeted by a tall, slim man – his longish wavy hair slightly greying at the temples. She smiled inwardly as she noticed his suit, which would have looked much more at home in the 1970's.

'Is it Mrs Denizon Cartwright?' The man asked smiling.

'Yes, but please just call me Denizon. I always feel so old when I'm called Mrs. Cartwright.'

'Hello, Denizon, I'm Professor Damien Johnson and likewise, please call me Damien. I'll be showing you round today.' He held out his hand.

'Pleased to meet you, Damien.' Denizon smiled as he shook her hand firmly.

Denizon didn't know what to expect from the induction day but had hoped there would be plenty of people around so she could blend in easily.

'Is it just us?' she asked looking around.

'For the moment, yes. The other two tutors are a married couple who are coming up from Mid-Glamorgan and have been a bit delayed.'

'Oh, is it Greg and Sian?' Denizon perked up at the news.

'Yes, do you know them?'

'They were on the same training course as me. They're both lovely.'

'I haven't met them yet. I was at a conference in America all the time you were on your teacher-training course. Hence, it's the first time we've met … can I get you a drink?'

'If you have tea?'

'I'm sure that can be arranged, although I can't swear to its provenance, we all drink coffee here, it keeps us awake.'

'I have my own tea-bag if it helps?'

'My, you are well prepared. Follow me to the most important room in the department, the kitchen.'

'Isn't it quiet without the students?' Denizon said following the professor further into the building.

'Just how I like it. I'd get so much more work done if it was like this all the time, but sadly, I wouldn't get paid.'

Denizon didn't know whether to laugh at his attempt at a joke – but didn't as he looked deadly serious.

'How many are enrolled on my course?'

'I'll have to check, but from memory about twenty five.'

Denizon swallowed audibly. 'That many? I was hoping for about ten.'

'Don't worry you'll be fine. 'Watercolours' is always the most popular course. Trust me, it's a piece of cake – everyone is so enthusiastic. All you have to do is put a few items on a desk and get them to paint. Add a few excursions and you're sorted.'

'You make it sound so easy.'

'Summer schools are easy. At least all your students make an effort which is more than can be said for mine … have you got that tea bag?'

'Sorry, yes.' Denizon fished out the limp bag from a side pocket in her handbag.

'Our secretary bought biscuits before she went on annual leave,' Damien said as he reached into the cupboard. 'Can I interest you in a Vienna whirl?' Denizon politely took one.

'Let's go through to the room that'll be your home for the next four weeks.'

Damien spent the next half an hour showing Denizon where everything was kept in the large art studio. Just then the phone rang.

'Excuse me. I'll just have to get that.'

He left Denizon standing at the front of the room, by what would be her desk. She sighed. *Maybe this isn't such a good idea after all. What if I can't do it? I could be a laughing stock. Why did I let Robyn talk me into it?'*

'That was Greg on the phone.' Damien said as he walked back into the room. 'There's been an accident on the M62 and they're in standing traffic. Who knows how long they'll be … Can I buy you lunch?'

'Er …'

'Oh, no nothing like that …' he added as he saw the shocked looked on Denizon's face. 'It comes out of the departmental budget. We should all be having lunch but as the others aren't here yet, we don't want to go hungry.'

Denizon breathed a sigh of relief. 'In that case, that'd be lovely?'

'Let's get out of here. The refectory is open but it's not great. I know a lovely pub, not too far … would that be okay? We can take my car.'

'Er … yes. If you're sure?'

Damien held open the door to the red open top MG sports car and Denizon slid in.

'Have you got anything to tie back that lovely hair? It gets pretty windy with the roof down.'

Denizon fished in her bag and pulled out an old scrunchy. She quickly scraped her long blonde hair back in a pony-tail as Damien screeched out of the car park.

Chris Cartwright, newly appointed Crew Manager at Hull North Fire Station closed the door to his office.

'Jen, you can't talk to me like that here. You know what the lad's are like.'

'Oh Chris, lighten up – no-one heard.'

'That's not the point. Anyway, I'm now your superior officer, you have to treat me with respect.' Chris smiled at his beautiful colleague, her long ebony hair shimmering in the glint of the sun.

'In that case you should punish me.'

'Yes, I should. You can stay behind after your shift. I'll find some extra duties for you.' Chris smirked.

'Don't tease me, Chris! It's been ages since we spent any time together.' She walked across the room and stood in front of him.

'I know, Jen but this new job … and you know how it is with Denizon.'

'But we have so much fun together,' she said stroking the few hairs sticking out of the top of his uniform shirt.

'But what about Craig? You've just got engaged!'

'Oh, him. You know why I'm with him and it's not for his stunning good looks and rippling muscles. He's not a patch on you.' She reached up and kissed him.

'Jen, what are you doing? Not here. Anyone can see in.'

'In that case, come here.' She led him by the hand into the large office store cupboard.

'Kiss me!' she said as she started to open her blouse, exposing her firm double G breasts. 'You haven't seen them since they've been done, have you?'

'No … wow! They're magnificent.'

Chris reached out and exposed one nipple, fingering it gently.

'God, Jen, you're such a tease.'

'I said kiss me.' Jen reached up and thrust her tongue into his waiting mouth.

'What if the bell goes off?' Chris said as he drew breath.

'Then we'll stop, but I want you now.' She reached down and unzipped him.

Chris's bulging erection forced its way out of his trousers.

'That's more like it!' she said admiring his length.

Chris slammed the door closed with his foot and grabbed hold of his willing colleague. It was only a matter of seconds before he was thrusting himself deep inside her.

'Oh, Jen! How can I be strong when you do this to me?' Chris said collapsing down the wall, his legs giving way.

'I don't want you to be strong. I want you to be mine. I know we'll never be together but this makes my life bearable. Don't stop wanting me.' Jen sat down beside him, resting her head on his shoulder.

'How can I ever stop wanting you? You're gorgeous … how much did they cost?'

'A few thousand I think. Craig wanted me to have them done. Do you like them?'

'I do, but there was nothing wrong with them before,' Chris said, groping one of her large breasts.

'Do you know you're the only reason I come to work? Craig wants me to pack it in and spend all my time doing hot yoga and personal training so I can have the body he dreams of.'

'So, why don't you?'

'Because I'd be bored out of my mind and I wouldn't see you.'

'But, Jen, I can't keep seeing you. I promised Denizon I'd stop messing about.'

'Like that's going to happen with your willpower. I didn't have to exactly force you.'

'That's true … but it has to stop. I've got my new job now which I don't want to lose.'

'But I won't put any pressure on you, I promise. Just let's get together occasionally, like today. There's no harm done.'

'I suppose not – just don't go telling anyone. They all think I'm squeaky clean now.'

'I'm sure! The day Chris Cartwright stops looking at other women is the day the world will end. Trust me on that one!'

'Cheeky! Come here, it's time for your punishment.'

Denizon got out of the car at the Altisadora. 'I thought you said it wasn't far. We're nearly at the coast.'

'Sorry. It's such a nice day I got carried away. I intended to go to the Horse and Jockey down the road from the university… have you been here before?'

'Yes, my husband brought me for a meal for our first wedding anniversary.'

'How long have you been married?' Damien asked locking his car door.

Denizon paused. *Gosh! He's rather forward. Is this what all bosses are like? It's such a long time since I worked for anyone I've forgotten.*

'Sorry, I'm just being nosy.'

'It's okay, coming up to four years that's all.'

'Let's go and find a seat in the garden. It seems such a shame to be inside on a day like today.'

Damien led them to a quiet table at the furthest end of the beer garden.

'What can I get you to drink?'

'Just a lime and soda, no ice, thanks,' replied Denizon.

'Are you sure I can't tempt you to anything stronger? It's a lovely day for a glass of cool, clear Pinot Grigio. I'm having one.'

'Go on then, I'll have a small one.'

'You look at the menu while I get us a drink. Choose the most expensive thing, it's not often I get to use the expense account.'

They both ordered sirloin with a salad and as Damien came back from the bar he moved his chair closer to Denizon's.

'So tell me all about my new watercolour tutor. Normally, I would have been on the interview panel but as I mentioned I wasn't in the country.'

'What is there to tell? I'm an artist, partly commercial. I do calendars and work for large companies and I paint for fun. I sell my work and have a couple of exhibitions a year. I suppose, I earn a decent living.'

'So why do you want to tutor?'

Denizon paused. *Should I tell him the truth? That I'm a boring housewife and want to do something that will make me more interesting ... no possibly not!*

'Because I'd like to give something back to the art world.'

Damien laughed. 'You're joking right?'

'Er ... I'm not sure what you mean.'

'Being an artist is the hardest job in the world. Just when you think you couldn't get any lower you get another kick in the teeth. You want to give something back, spare me!' Damien took a long drink of wine. 'Sorry ... I don't know where that came from.'

'I'm not normally perceptive when it comes to people –
I spend too much time alone but I do get the impression
you're not very happy with your job.'

'I don't think you need to be perceptive. I'm going
through a bad phase, just ignore me.' Damien sighed and
rubbed his eyes. 'My budget has been nearly halved and I
have to put on summer school courses that bring in more
money than my foundation degree students. It's hard that's
all … I don't know why I'm telling you this. I wanted us to
come out and enjoy this beautiful day.'

'Don't worry its fine.'

'No, I am sorry. Let's talk about something else … so;
what books do you like to read?'

'How do you know I like reading?'

'I can just tell. You seem very much like me and I love
reading.'

Denizon glanced at her watch and saw it was nearly
three o'clock.

'My word, is that the time. I should be getting back.
We've been sitting here for two hours.'

'Really? But hasn't it been fun?' he added.

Denizon smiled. 'It has actually. It's lovely spending
time with someone with the same interests as me.'

'Doesn't your husband share your passion for reading?'

'You must be joking! The last book Chris read was for
GCSE English – unless you count the Fire Service Manual.'

'Your husband's a fireman?'

'His actual title is Crew Manager. He's just been
promoted. Honestly, that's one of the real reasons I took
this job. He spends so long at work I wanted to get out and
meet some new people … are you married?'

'I was – I've been separated for years.' Damien paused. 'I've just had a thought. I belong to a group called the Bohemian players. Have you heard of them?'

Denizon shook her head.

'We get together once a month and talk about art, literature and theatre. It's not everyone's thing but I think you'd enjoy it. This month's meeting is tomorrow night. Would you be interested in coming along?'

Denizon didn't even need to think about it. 'Sounds great! Where's it at?'

'We meet at each other's houses. If you like I could pick you up.'

She reached into her handbag for her diary. *Is Chris on a late? … Yes he is, great.*

'That would be fine. What time do you want me to be ready?'

'It starts at 7.30, so is 7 okay?'

'I'll be waiting.'

Change of mind! This job was a very good idea.

About the Author:

Lindsay lives in Yorkshire, England with wonderful husband, Paul. She has two grown up children, three young grandchildren, and four springer spaniels! She gave up working full time in 2010 to write and has self-published three metaphysical romances to sell at Mind, Body and Spirit fairs. After having fantastic reviews she decided to embark on her passion - contemporary women's fiction and now wants to reach a wider audience – hence 5 Prince. When she's not writing, she's a homeopath, a dog walker and a DIY enthusiast. For fun she loves Ashtanga yoga, Ascension meditation and the sea - and one day would love to live by it.

Lightning Source UK Ltd.
Milton Keynes UK
UKOW02f1806300814

237792UK00001B/29/P